ANOTHER STUPID LOVE SONG

ANOTHER STUPID LOVE SONG

MIRANDA MACLEOD
EM STEVENS

CHAPTER ONE

"Top off?" asked the man standing beside the sporty gunmetal gray Mercedes.

"Excuse me?" Max shot him a withering glare from behind her dark sunglasses. She'd had her share of lewd propositions shouted at her from audience members over the years, but this guy—Carl, the name tag on his black polo shirt read—was taking it to a whole new level. What did he think, she was going to strip for him right here in the rental car parking lot?

"Would you like the top off your car?" he clarified in a lazy drawl that reminded Max of a phonograph on too slow a speed. She wondered if there was a switch she could flip to make him go faster. Two decades spent up north had ruined her for southern living. "It's a convertible, ma'am."

"Oh. Yes, please." Feeling foolish, and clearly more

worn out from travel than she'd realized, Max tugged on her simple white T-shirt, discreetly pulling it away from her sweat-drenched back. She'd worn a stylish jacket over it when boarding the plane, but she'd nixed it the moment she stepped onto the sweltering jetway in Raleigh. "I forgot how hot it gets here."

"This is mild," Carl informed her with the good-natured laugh of a man who was accustomed to living a short drive from Hell's front gates.

It'd been snowing when she'd woken up that morning in her apartment in New York City, that kind of surprise mid-April flurry with wind so fierce a person could lose hope winter would ever end. Meanwhile, the bare hint of a breeze would've been welcome right now, but no such luck. The air was as still and thick as a bowl of chili you could stand a fork in. The more she thought about it, the more Max was inclined to wonder if her earlier reluctance to strip off all her clothes for Carl's amusement had been a bit hasty.

"Where are you traveling from today, Ms...?"

Uh...

This was the second time Max's brain had short-circuited in as many seconds, but this time she had a good reason. She almost never gave strangers her real name. Whenever possible, her assistant booked everything under an alias as a precaution. Fake name, fake backstory. You couldn't be too careful when you were a woman in the public eye, especially one known for dressing sexily and dancing provocatively on stage. But unlike most trips, this time Max would be responsible for getting herself around, which meant she'd have to hand over her real driver's license to this guy. It wasn't like she could use one of her go-to aliases.

"It's Max. Maxine Gardner. I just flew in from La Guardia."

She handed him the packet she'd picked up from the rental counter in the airport and waited for the inevitable reaction the revelation of her name was bound to provoke. As the seconds dragged on and nothing happened, a terrible thought struck her like a fist to the abs she had to work extra hard to keep rock solid these days. Maybe this guy, who looked barely old enough to shave, was too young to know who she was. Or care. Just when she was briefly considering praying for a meteorite to strike her down where she stood, she caught the telltale hitch of breath.

Call off that meteorite. Maxie's still got it.

"Oh, wow. I thought it might be you." Carl squinted at the plain baseball cap that concealed Max's signature shock of blonde hair. "You were on *The Late Show* last week, right? I've been listening to the Matchstick Girls nonstop every day since. You were amazing."

"Thanks, man." For once, Max's smile at being recognized was genuine. Learning she'd finally slipped into irrelevance while standing on the rooftop of an off-airport parking structure in North Carolina, of all places, would've sucked. "It meant a lot to get to do that. You know, for Grace."

The name of her recently deceased bandmate sliced like a newly sharpened knife, quickly and deeply, so it took a moment for the pain to register through the shock. This wasn't a dream. Grace Weathers was really dead. Which made the reason Max had come to town that much more despicable. Not that she planned to share that with the guy whose sole job was to hand her the car keys so she could be on her way.

"Do you think I could get a selfie?" He transformed from borderline grown-up to extremely awkward teen as his face flushed a deep shade of red.

Exhausted to near the point of collapse, Max wanted nothing more than to drive the few miles to her hotel, peel off her sweat-stained clothes, and take a luxurious hot shower in the suite she'd booked at the best spa resort in town. But some small part of her couldn't forget all those years ago, before she'd made it big, how it had felt to be the one asking for an autograph after a show, only to be jeered at by an overinflated asshole who'd forgotten what it was like on a fan's side of the scene.

Autographs. Now that was old-school.

"Sure thing, Carl." Ignoring her aching back and overripe pits, Max leaned in and plastered on her best punk-rock smile as the kid snapped a few shots. She hoped she didn't look as shitty as she felt. The tabloids would love an excuse to speculate on her nonexistent drug addiction again. Or link her romantically to yet another random guy she wasn't dating. Not that Max hadn't encouraged those types of stories a time or two over the years to keep people from sniffing out whatever woman she *had* been dating.

I don't give a shit what your sexuality is, a record label executive had once told her, *as long as it doesn't make headlines.* In the 1990s, keeping quiet had been about self-preservation. Now it was an ugly habit, one Max lacked the energy–or maybe courage–to break.

After the selfie was done, Max was finally allowed to climb into the driver's seat of her rental. She scanned the dashboard with the same trepidation as if she'd been given control over a commercial airliner. So many gauges and buttons. As she started the ignition, it would not have come as a surprise to hear the roar of jet engines. Instead, it purred like a kitten in a sunny window.

Because it's a Mercedes Benz, you moron. Max took a deep breath. *Calm the fuck down.*

She might not have been behind the wheel much lately, but she'd been a licensed driver for twenty-five years. Driving hadn't changed *that* much, even if this car did start with a push button instead of a key. All Max needed was to pair her phone with the car's Bluetooth, which ended up being easier than expected. After that, she punched the hotel address into her navigation app.

ETA: eleven minutes.

Slowly, Max put the car in reverse. When she'd backed out of the parking space without hitting anything, her confidence doubled. She shifted into drive, and the tires squealed the whole way down the ramp to the exit.

Gawd, she hated driving.

One of the perks of Max's rock star life was never having to get behind the wheel. People assumed it was so she could party harder, and that was one time her so-called drug problem rumors were fine by her. Because the truth was way more embarrassing. With each passing year, changes in technology made a little less sense to her. New vehicles were more computer than car, and sometimes Max wasn't even sure how to find a decent radio station. As if to prove her point, the car's high-end surround sound speakers began to blare "Constant Burning," the final Matchstick Girls' hit that had made everything go up in flames, ironically.

With acid in the back of her throat, Max shut off the radio. She'd endure a hundred years of silence before she'd willingly listen to that song all the way through. Of course, given the craziness of her life, sometimes the prospect of blocking out all the noise around her seemed kind of nice.

As it was, she'd barely made it outside of the parking structure before her phone rang. It didn't require a glance at the screen to know it was her manager. There was no one else for it to be.

"Skip. How do you survive when I'm unavailable?"

On the main road now, Max hunched closer to the wheel, examining the green road signs and trying to figure out which lane she needed to be in for the interstate. She tried putting on her turn signal but initiated the windshield wipers.

Fuck.

"I've been on pins and needles the whole time," Skip assured her with that ingratiating tone he used when he wanted something from her. In other words, every time they spoke. "Okay, now that we got the chitchat out of the way, did you remember to bring the photo albums of you and the girls from the old days like I told you to?"

"You practically packed them for me." Max rolled her aching shoulders. Those albums had weighed a ton in her carry-on bag. "I don't know why you think this will work. Considering Cindy Weathers has always been a woman of her word, I fully expect her to claw my face off when I see her tomorrow. Besides, the Matchstick Girls are yesterday's news."

Except they weren't. Even that young man at the rental car agency had confirmed it. Nostalgia was a strange animal. In the past several weeks, people had been discovering the late 1990s all-girl band, and it was because of Grace.

"You girls are having a revival now that Grace is dead." At least Skip managed to sound neutral about the news, rather than gleeful. But Max had worked with him since she was fourteen and knew that his mind never stopped thinking about how to make a profit.

Coldhearted bastard.

Max wanted to tell Skip exactly where he could go, but her throat was too tight for the words to escape. For some reason, her memory flashed to high school, when all the kids used to spell out the word *hell* upside down on their calculators, thinking they were oh so clever.

Go to 7734, Skip.

Apparently, coming back to where she'd grown up was bringing out the teenager in her. That wasn't good news. Fourteen-year-old Max had been a hot mess.

Forty-two-year-old Max was at least better at hiding it.

"Turn left at the next exit," the GPS on her phone said while Skip was telling her something that sounded important.

"Hold on, Skip. I need to turn off the GPS. I can't listen to two nags at the same time." She wished she'd told Carl to keep the top closed so she could run the air-conditioning. Even at full speed with the wind on her face, Max might as well have been in a sauna. One with bugs the size of flying wombats. How could she have forgotten about those? Add it to the list of reasons she avoided this place like the plague.

"You really need to sell this, Max," Skip droned on, barely pausing for breath despite her plea. "Get Cindy onboard for a reunion tour this summer. Large venues, merchandise out the ass. The Hawthorne Bunnies had to cancel because their lead singer is in court mandated rehab. There will never be another chance at something this huge. We can nab all their spots, but only if we secure this now. Everything's reserved, and the promoter is ready to go public and start selling tickets like *yesterday*, but Cindy won't return their calls. You're the only one who can get her to see reason."

"Explain to me again why you think that's true," Max snapped, her long day finally fraying her very last nerve. "Cindy and I haven't talked in over twenty years. Anyway, you said it back then. I'm a solo act. Have been for years. My last tour, I was filling stadiums all on my own. Now, you're insisting I organize a reunion tour for a group whose last big hit was in 1999, for Christ's sake."

"*Your* last big solo hit was eight years ago, Maxine." Skip had that asshole edge in his tone now, which Max actually preferred. He always was a straight shooter when it got rough. "Your last two records sank more spectacularly than the Titanic."

"Low blow, Skip." Well, *that* wasn't the kind of straight shooting she liked. Max stuck her tongue out at the phone. *Peak adult, right there.*

"Telling you like it is."

"I'm the one who told you on both of those albums I wasn't feeling the music and wanted to try something fresh. The last thing the world needs is another stupid love song." Max glanced over her shoulder to ease into the other lane. The whole driving thing was coming back to her, getting a little easier with each mile. Surely, recording hits and filling stadiums could come back to her just as easily, given the chance.

"Love songs sell, and so does nostalgia. Your audience is too old for fresh. I don't know how else to get this across, so I'm just going to say it." His voice was tight, as if he knew what he was about to say would do nothing to improve her already piss-poor mood but didn't care. "Grace's death might be the best thing that's happened to your career in I don't know how long."

"She was a friend," Max growled, gripping the steering wheel and imagining it was her manager's neck. "I wouldn't be here if it weren't for her."

Grace had been a senior in high school when Max was but a lowly freshman. They'd had choir together in second period and were only a few weeks into the school year when Grace had invited Max to join her and her sister's newly formed garage band. Soon, they'd started playing gigs at local dive bars. A year later, they had a record contract. Skip liked to take credit, but Max knew she owed everything to Grace. The Matchstick Girls had lifted Max out of a hellish home life before the worst of the damage could be done and put her on the road to fame and fortune.

Now, Grace was gone way before her time.

"You didn't hire me to hold your hand and pass you the tissues," Skip said. "You wouldn't be here if it weren't for me, either, remember? I've been your manager since day one. I'm telling you how to keep that success because I know how people work."

"Well, they're a mystery to me. I still don't get why Cindy said yes to meeting up tomorrow. We were barely speaking by the last tour. I skipped her wedding."

And Grace's funeral, too. Although that hadn't been Max's fault. She'd fully intended to go until the paparazzi came out of the woodwork, trailing her everywhere she went. The thought of bringing that kind of chaos with her to something as private as a funeral made Max change her mind and stay home.

"Cindy's almost fifty," Skip pointed out, "and she got hit in the gut with the worst kind of reminder of her own mortality. She'll want to feel young again, and with Grace gone, you're the only person on the planet who knows what those glory days were like. Share some of your fond memories of her dead sister, and you're golden."

"Can you please *stop* saying that?" If Max heard the word *dead* again, she might go on a rampage. She knew that was the wrong word, but the heat was melting her brain. "Show a little bit of goddamn respect, will ya?"

"I'm trying to cut through your stubbornness, Maxie." Skip softened his tone. "You're still very much alive, and I don't want to have to start booking you to play at state fairs where you'll be sharing the stage with trained bears and clog-dancing grannies. You should go out on a high."

"I have no intention of going out at all. Besides, I sincerely doubt my career is at such a dire juncture." Even as she said it, Max feared she was wrong. Maybe it *was* that bad. To be fair, Skip had saved her ass a time or two before, and she knew he'd want to keep doing it. If she made money, he made money.

"I need you to listen to me. You have one shot—*one* —to avoid becoming a sorry has-been. Do you want to continue living in your fancy New York apartment?" He didn't wait for an answer, because he already knew it. "Then you need to do what I say. Get Cindy to agree to the reunion tour, because I'm running out of ways to keep you viable."

A passing vehicle honked at Max as her car drifted too far to the right. That was when she realized she was no longer on the interstate her hotel was supposed to be off of, but on a smaller highway that wasn't right at all but felt vaguely familiar nonetheless. The stoplight up ahead was turning red, and Max quickly applied her foot to the brake.

"Where the fuck am I?" The dark screen on the GPS she'd turned off was zero help. "As much as I'm enjoying your pep talk, Skip, I gotta go, or I'll never make it to the hotel."

"Don't forget—"

As Max ended the call, the light flicked from red to green, and she mumbled, "Come on, come on, come on," under her breath as the cars in front of her rolled into motion at a snail's pace. Her foot punched the gas, only to have to slam the brakes hard, the light already flipping from green to the world's shortest yellow, her tires screeching, and Max lurching against the seat, initiating a spasm in her lower back.

Flipping fantastic.

"What godforsaken town have I ended up in?" Max yelled, taking advantage of being stopped to grab the phone and fire up the navigation again. The answer on the screen astonished her. *"This* is Holly Springs?"

Perhaps it was no wonder Max had ended up here, her subconscious taking over navigating while she'd been distracted by Skip. She'd made the drive home from playing late night gigs in Raleigh a million times in her youth. She could do it blindfolded, which might've been preferable.

Seeing her surroundings was the disorienting part.

The year she was born, the population of her hometown had been under a thousand. When she'd left at eighteen and never looked back, it had still been well under ten. But now? The genteel suburban sprawl surrounding her was completely unrecognizable. The town had quadrupled in size, or maybe more.

Head spinning like she'd been plunked down in an episode of *The Twilight Zone,* Max struggled to gain her bearings. The main road into town was still there, but everything else had changed.

No, not quite everything.

Up ahead was a three-story brick building. It had been built as a drugstore in the nineteenth century, the type of place that used to have a soda fountain serving chocolate malts. It housed some other business now, but the building itself was reassuringly unchanged.

Acting purely from muscle memory, Max hung a left and then a quick right at the end of the street where a white house had been standing for about as long as the old brick drugstore. Other old houses lined the street as she continued to drive. Would the one she was looking for but didn't want to see be there, too?

Why am I doing this?

With each passing block, a déjà vu tingling worked through her body. It was all so familiar, but it wasn't quite right. She pulled the car to the curb, putting it in park.

Max stared, a sea of emotions roiling beneath her surface calm.

On the left was a modest house. She remembered it well. Mr. Knight had lived there and would sometimes let her come in after school when Max's father wasn't home. Or when he was passed out drunk and didn't hear her knocking.

Her memory offered flashes of the rundown house with its rickety porch. She could see her old man sitting there in his grease-stained wife beater, a grizzled five o'clock shadow over sunken cheeks, baseball cap pulled low, the trembling hand clutching the ever-present beer can.

What her eyes saw when she turned her head couldn't have been more different. A modern apartment complex, freshly painted and beautifully landscaped. It was the type of place that offered stainless steel appliances and granite countertops, where young professionals prepared homemade dinners from meal kits after coming home from the office.

Did any of them have a clue how it used to be?

"It's gone," Max whispered as if fearing by speaking too loudly, the unhappy home of her childhood would shimmer back into existence. But it remained a thing of the past, just like him.

Max felt her world was a little safer for it.

She stared for a long time before putting the hotel's address back into the GPS. As Max pulled out onto the beltline again, she began to wonder if this much had changed in her absence, could Cindy have undergone a transformation, too? If so, Maxine might actually have a chance at bringing her old bandmate on board.

Hope, dangerous and fickle, ignited deep inside as she drove.

CHAPTER TWO

"I shouldn't have agreed to this." Grabbing a handful of disinfecting wipes from their carton, Jade scrubbed the kitchen counter with all her might, her brown curls flying in every direction as the headband she'd put on earlier failed to contain them. It was at least the third pass she'd made, and if she kept at it with the same intensity much longer, she was likely to wear a hole right through the speckled quartz.

But Jade couldn't stop herself. She had exactly two means of stress relief in her arsenal: playing the drums and cleaning. With an hour to go before her mother's former bandmate—the woman Jade had come to think of as her mother's arch nemesis—arrived for lunch, sanitizing her space seemed the better option.

"Are you kidding me?" Lottie leaned into her camera so her face blew up to scary proportions and fixed Jade with a look of such incredulity, it was impossible not to laugh. "When the world's hottest rock star asks to come over for lunch, one *never* says no. That kind of stuff doesn't even happen here in LA."

Jade rolled her eyes over her best friend's predictable response. "Please. Maxine Gardner isn't even in the top ten—no, make that top twenty—of hottest rock stars."

"Oh, yeah?" Lottie smirked, one bright pink circle appearing on each of her freckled cheeks. "Who would you put at number one?"

"Easy. Dolly Parton." Jade gave the countertop a final swipe before tossing the cleaning rags in the trash.

"She's not a rock star," Lottie argued.

"The Rock and Roll Hall of Fame disagrees. You dare disparage Dolly?" Jade wagged her finger. "Sacrilege."

"Okay, okay." Lottie relented, waving her hands in the air. They blurred on the screen. "But hottest? Come on. You wouldn't sleep with Dolly Parton. She's... *old.*"

"Not much older than Maxine Gardner," Jade teased, biting back a grin at the fury on her friend's face. "And I'm not sure I'd kick Dolly out of bed."

"You better not let your aunt hear you say that, because Maxine's a hell of a lot younger than Cindy,"

Lottie spluttered, clearly overcome by this uncouth assessment of her idol. "She's a veritable queer icon."

"She's never admitted to being queer. Ever. She's still being linked to men in the media all the damn time." Jade crossed her arms in triumph. "Rumors and innuendo are *so* last century. Dolly Parton is a queer icon."

"You're telling me *this* woman isn't hot?" Lottie pulled out her phone, holding it so Jade could see the photo of the rocker on her lock screen, clad in leather and with her blonde pompadour tinged with daring blue streaks.

Jade shrugged, averting her eyes as discreetly as she could manage. She did this partially because she hated the woman in the photo for what had happened between her and Jade's mom and aunt so many years ago. Also because Max was objectively attractive, which was annoying beyond words.

As if sensing Jade's weakness, Lottie pushed the phone closer to the camera, rendering the image a blur of pixels. It didn't matter. Jade knew exactly what Maxine Gardner looked like. "Admit you'd rather have *her* in your bed than Dolly Parton, or I swear I'll report you to the authorities to have your lesbian card revoked."

Jade let out a snort. "I admit nothing."

"You have a vendetta against that poor, gorgeous woman." Lottie pulled the phone image away and gave it one last, lustful look. With a pang, Jade missed her bestie. The move to LA. had been good for Lottie, who wanted to pursue a music career there, but it had been challenging to keep up the friendship with weekly Zoom meetings.

Still, she wasn't about to let her friend off the hook. "Of course, I do, and she's hardly poor. She's a rich, unfeeling rock princess whose songs about love keep falling flat because the bitch doesn't have a heart. Not only did she stab my aunt in the back, but she hurt my mom, Lottie. My *mom*." Jade turned her head away, not wanting to let on how close she was to tears. "Mom and Aunt Cindy started the Matchstick Girls. They invited Max to join when she was just a kid, a total nobody from the wrong side of the tracks. They were supposed to be equals, but Max hogged the spotlight and became a star because of their hard work."

"Because she's hot!" Lottie tossed her hands into the air like the reason should be obvious, but this time Jade was more melancholy than amused.

"So was my mom." Jade shut her eyes but not before a tear could escape, one that had nothing to do with the breakup of a girl band that had happened when Jade was in kindergarten. It had been two months since her mother had succumbed to the hepatitis-C that had ravaged her body, unseen, for years. Sometimes the grief still overwhelmed Jade.

She detected the shift in her friend over thousands of miles, their connection still that strong. Lottie had calmed down and was nodding. "Your mom was the best. She supported and loved me for who I was before anyone else, and that made her the most beautiful woman in the world to me. In a totally non-sexy kinda way, because the first rule of friendships is never lust after your BFF's mom."

Jade made a sound that was half cackle and half sob. "It's a good rule. Can we extend it to anyone your BFF's mom was ever in a band with?"

"If you're talking about Cindy, the answer is yes." Lottie pulled a face that let Jade know exactly what her friend thought regarding sex with her aunt. "You're not fooling me. I've known you since we were in preschool, and I remember how you used to cry when your mom was away on tour. You wanted her home with you, not off in the spotlight. Like it or not, Max did you a solid by going solo."

"That might be true, but it doesn't mean I have to condone how she did it." Even as she said it, Jade knew a small part of her did owe Max for the fact she'd had her mom around as much as she had growing up. Hell, the way her mom used to party when she was on the road, she might not have even made it to forty-six if she'd kept up that life-style. Every year she'd been home had been a blessing.

It didn't mean Jade had to admit it, or that she owed the selfish rocker a goddamn thing. "You know she didn't even come to Mom's funeral. Who does that but then two months later requests a private lunch meet-up? Why Aunt Cindy agreed is beyond me. And in *my* house."

"Neutral territory?" Lottie suggested. She was sipping at iced coffee, and Jade decided not to mention the oat milk latte mustache gracing her friend's upper lip. Not yet, at least.

"Maybe." Actually, it was because Aunt Cindy was having her kitchen remodeled, but Jade liked the sound of Lottie's theory more. It made them sound like generals negotiating a truce. "If you think I'm the one who despises Maxine Gardner, that's only because you haven't asked my aunt how she feels. Did you know on their last album, Cindy and my mom—their vocals were completely rearranged without their permission in the final mix to minimize them and make Max stand out?"

Lottie frowned at this challenge to her encyclopedic knowledge of all things Matchstick Girls. "I know it sounded a little different from their other songs, but are you sure it was done with malicious intent? None of the rumors on the fan forums have ever gone that far."

"Yep. It's one hundred percent fact, unlike your wishful thinking that your fantasy crush likes kissing girls as much as you do."

"But, why?" It was obvious Lottie didn't like what she was hearing but still wanted to hear every word. Jade was all too happy to throw Max under the bus.

"The Matchstick Girls had become the Maxine

Gardner show by then. Have you seen the video for Constant Burning?" Jade shook her head at her friend's lascivious grin. "Of course, you have. You know it's all closeups of Max's stupid pouty face. That's *it*. It had the band's name on it, but the video proved Max saw herself as a solo act. Mom was devastated at the betrayal, and the band broke up right after. I'll never forgive the woman for that."

"Again, your mom came home to raise you because of it." Lottie's tone was gentle, making her reasonable words all the more grating. "That was what you wanted more than anything. You wished for it when you blew out the candles at your fifth birthday party, remember?"

Yeah, Jade remembered. She could still picture the kids around her grandma's kitchen table. The glow of the candles. Lottie—still several years away from transitioning—in that dapper suit and bow tie her mom had insisted she wear. And Jade's mom off on a tour bus somewhere, doing goodness knew what. Of course, little Jade had made that wish.

"I didn't want my mom to get hurt!" Jade's lower lip trembled. Selfishly, she'd wanted, just once, for her mom to choose her over the music.

"I know, I know." Lottie tucked her hands into her armpits. She was probably feeling the same urge to hug that Jade had, the distance between them stinging. "That was so long ago. Things change. People change."

People might change but not a spoiled diva who

wanted everything for herself and would ruin anyone who got in her way. *That* didn't change.

Not wanting to argue, and considering Lottie's opinion was too lust-soaked to ever be swayed, Jade shrugged and looked at the fridge behind her. "I should put out the vegetable platter."

"We can keep talking if you need to."

Jade shook her head, suddenly feeling raw and craving solitude. "I'm okay. I know you have a class to teach." Lottie's piano skills were in high demand in LA, with many big-listing names hiring her to tutor their children.

Lips pursed, Lottie appeared ready to argue. Prepared, Jade didn't give her the chance.

"Maxine Gardner probably has a houseful of servants," Jade commented, for no real reason other than feeling that a person who employed a houseful of servants was certainly worthy of scorn. If there was one thing Jade was in the mood to do, it was some good old scorn-heaping.

"Trying to poke the bear so I'll exit the call in a huff and you can avoid those big feels?"

"You don't know me," Jade grumbled. "I'm just... super nervous about this."

"You shouldn't be. You're lucky." Lottie's eyes grew large, and Jade could have sworn she saw hearts floating in them. "Serving canapés to Maxine Gardner would be the highlight of my entire existence."

"You're such a goof. You've been an amazing friend.

Before and after Mom—" Jade's throat closed. "I appreciate you offering to listen."

Lottie didn't seem convinced by Jade's bravado, but she gave in without pressing the issue. "Okay. You text me, though. If you need me to drop everything and hop back on Zoom, I will. And if you feel bold enough to get something signed for me…"

"You're such a shameless fangirl," Jade informed her with a smirk.

"Not going to deny that. Maxine Gardner is at the top of my spank bank, and you will not make me feel guilty about it."

"Ew." Jade shut her eyes. "Definitely time to go."

The call ended at the same moment the front door opened. Jade feared Max had arrived early, but presumably she would've knocked. Unlike Aunt Cindy, who blew into the house with the intensity of a hurricane, displaying a military-level precision that made it hard to believe she'd once been in a rock band. Or that she'd ever been anything but a middle-aged suburban woman with big hair who was wearing elastic waistband jeans and a shirt with bedazzled flowers on it. Her aunt rocked the southern lady look like nobody's business.

Carrying bags loaded with food, Cindy breezed in and immediately began issuing orders. "Hey there, Kitten. Grab some plates and silverware, will you? We'll set up in the dining room, I think. Also, some wine glasses. I'm going to need a glass like, five minutes ago."

"Already done, Aunt Cindy." Jade chuckled as her aunt stopped in her tracks, appearing to take in the details of her environment for the first time. Jade plucked one of the glasses from the table and poured it halfway full with chilled white wine, handing it to her aunt without commentary.

Once the glass was in her hand, Cindy seemed to release all her nerves in a rush. "I shouldn't have said yes to this."

"To lunch with your sworn enemy?" Jade couldn't contain her *I told you so* look.

"I don't know what got into me." Cindy moaned as she sank into a dining room chair and took what under any other circumstances would be called a slug of her wine. "Max has this way of getting what she wants. You don't understand, Kitten. She's so *persuasive.*"

As if Jade didn't know something about persuasive women. Being raised by her mother and her aunt, not to mention a grandmother who had been every bit as formidable as either of them, if not more so, Jade had rarely known a moment's peace when her own desires came into conflict with any of theirs.

As if to drive home this thought, Cindy bounded from her chair, nearly sloshing the wine out of her glass. "Guess who I ran into today."

"I have no idea," Jade replied, though given her aunt's exuberance, she could only hope *ran into* was a figure of speech. They already had enough medical bills on their plate from her mother's final days without having to add a stranger's ER visit to the stack.

"Peggy James. She said Frank Kowalski's retiring at the end of the season, and you know what that means."

Jade's brain buzzed as she tried to fill as much missing information as she could into the number of blanks Cindy had left for her. "Peggy James from the symphony?"

"Exactly." Cindy nodded before adding, "Frank's been the principal percussionist since—"

"1974," Jade finished. Frank Kowalski and his nearly fifty-year drumming gig had been legendary in the Weathers' household, mentioned every time Jade dared bring up her desire to play anything but classical music for a living. "I guess that means a full-time opening for a new principal percussionist is coming soon?"

"Like your mother always wanted for you." A grin spread across Cindy's face, the skin wrinkling at the edges of her eyes. "A steady income, retirement plan, the works. It's like a sign. I saw a butterfly in the back-yard this morning as I was heading out. I thought it might've been your mama, and this was her way of looking out for you."

Sure. Because everyone's dead mother came back as a flying insect to convince an old man to retire from a job he'd held for half a century so her daughter could send in an application. That totally checked out. Not that Jade would scoff at Cindy's beliefs. If she needed her sister to be a butterfly sometimes in order to get to the other side of this shit mountain of grief, Jade wouldn't take that away from her.

Wrinkling her nose, Jade asked, "Did Peggy even mention me in all this?"

"That's the best part!" This time, a few drops of wine did spill over the top of Cindy's glass. She licked them off and kept speaking, undeterred. "She didn't just mention you. She said you've got it in the bag. They won't even open auditions if you're willing to sign a contract. Which, of course, I told her you were."

Naturally.

A permanent contract with the premier symphony in the area. Jade knew plenty of musicians who'd kill for that kind of position and security. That certainly had been Jade's mother's dream for her. But was it what Jade wanted? Fifty years on stage, banging a kettle drum and clanging a triangle. That was a hell of a long time.

For the first time, Jade wondered if Max's visit might have a silver lining to it. The woman was a force of nature, as Cindy had said. Jade could use a bit of that *I do what I want* mojo. There was a long list of things Jade had done to make her mom happy. Cindy, too, by proxy. It was easier, in many ways, to let someone else dictate her choices, especially when she wasn't sure *what* she wanted.

But if she didn't figure it out soon and fight for it, her future would be set in stone around her.

Cindy sighed and sipped her wine. "Anyway, we'll get that sorted out after lunch. Oh, God. What do you think Max wants, coming here after all these years?"

"Probably to talk about Mom. Maybe she'll apologize."

One of Cindy's eyebrows skyrocketed. "For breaking up the band or skipping Grace's funeral? I'm still pissed about that." This was followed by a large swallow of wine, finishing off the glass.

"Maybe she's come here to get the band back together," Jade joked.

"Wouldn't that be a riot?" Cindy made a half-hearted laugh.

Digging her toes into the rug, Jade considered. It was an outlandish idea, but it spoke to something that had been rattling around in Jade's chest ever since her mom had died. Playing music, the kind that came from the heart and not from classical music scores that had been done a hundred times over, held an appeal she couldn't seem to shake. She'd even scribbled down some song lyrics on those late nights when sleep was hard to come by.

Jade had grown up in a house of music. Her mother may have abandoned recording and touring, but she'd never stopped playing. In the basement sat two sets of drums and a variety of other instruments. The room had been remodeled with sound absorbing panels to keep the neighbors happy.

It was a room of joyous memories, she and her mother playing together for hours on end. Jade missed the abandon of simply jamming with someone else. Cindy used to join in, too. It had felt like their own little band sometimes. The realization she might never do it again hit Jade with the force of a large ocean wave, pulling her under and leaving her breathless as she scrambled for the safety of the surface. Tentatively she asked, "Do you think she would be up to playing music with us? Downstairs, I mean."

"Max? I don't know," Cindy said doubtfully. "Will there be a crowd of people around to tell her how great she is?"

"Wow. Harsh." Jade laughed at her aunt's snarky comeback. Like hell this woman couldn't hold her own against her former friend. "Why *did* you agree to have her over? You seem particularly combative about it now."

"I'm not! I mean, maybe I am, but..." Cindy's shoulders slumped, and Jade could see the sadness in her eyes. "She's the only one who remembers what it was like when we were all young and had our whole lives ahead of us. I don't know. Maybe it's weak of me to be willing to forgive her now just because I'm sad, but—"

"I don't think it's weak. If anything, it's brave." Jade paused at the sound of a car on the quiet road, idling as it reached the house. The engine shut off, and both of them stiffened, locking eyes. "Is that her?"

Cindy went to the nearest window, peering out through the blinds. "Fancy Mercedes convertible? Sure seems like her."

"Remember this was your idea," Jade said before walking to the foyer, tensing for the inevitable knocking or ringing of the bell.

This was it. Maxine Gardner, sexy rock singer, betrayer of all those Jade held dear, would be on the front stoop in a matter of seconds. "It'll be fine."

"No one should trust my judgment," Cindy grumbled.

Noted, Jade thought, her body barely containing her jangled nerves as she stared at the front door.

CHAPTER THREE

The house in Holly Springs where Grace had lived wasn't at all what Max had expected to find. Beyond the shock of driving through cookie-cutter neighborhood after cookie-cutter neighborhood that hadn't existed during her childhood, the whole place was so *suburban*.

How the hell had the fiercely punk rock Grace Weathers ended up with a three-car garage, a perfectly manicured green lawn, and solar lights lining the path to the front door? She'd even had one of those goddamn seasonal wreaths that gets swapped out every four months. However, the spring wreath hanging there now had seen better days, and the more Max squinted, the more she suspected it had been hanging there since last Easter.

Was that when Grace had fallen ill?

Not knowing made her feel like the shittiest friend in the world.

Max swung her legs out of the car and got as far as standing before she hesitated. She smoothed down the tunic tank top she wore under a black moto-cut blazer, wrinkling her nose at how sweaty her palms were. All she had to do was walk up to the front door and press the doorbell. Then she could fulfill her duty as a useful cog in the gears of Skip and the concert promotion execs' grand plans. Knowing that was what she'd become felt even less punk rock than Grace's house.

She made it up to the door and reached out, her finger shaking. How was it possible she could stand on a stage in front of thousands of screaming fans without freezing, but apparently, entering a run-of-the-mill house was her Kryptonite?

Perhaps it was because she'd never experienced this side of life, growing up in a nice neighborhood where hopscotch was chalked on the driveways and kids' bikes littered the front lawns. She wondered if Grace had spent time out here with her kid, watering the grass or something while her daughter ran through the spray. It was impossible to picture.

Unable to press the doorbell, Max took a step back. There still time to turn around and leave. She could tell Skip that Cindy had nixed the tour plans or let him do his own dirty work.

Come on, she urged herself. *Turn around now, and beat a hasty retreat.*

Then get ready for a big career on the state fair circuit, Max could almost hear Skip say.

Fuck.

Max's heart beat a three-chord punch on repeat in her ribs as she pressed the pineapple-shaped doorbell and waited for Cindy to answer. She braced for an awkward reunion, half afraid her former bandmate—Max wasn't even sure she could still call Cindy a friend after all the water under the bridge—would turn her away on sight.

Max squared her shoulders. It would be fine. She could handle whatever Cindy threw at her. Though hopefully it wouldn't be something particularly sharp or anything really solid, like that amber-colored glass ashtray her dad had hurled at her once when he'd suspected she'd been making out with a boy behind the house. That monstrosity had left a mark. If he'd known the truth, that it was a girl she'd been back there with, Max might not have lived to fight another day.

Regardless, throwing things was bad and to be avoided.

The door swung open ever so slowly, and when the woman on the other side was revealed, Max had to blink several times to take in what she was seeing.

That was *not* Cindy.

The young woman had a thin torso, showcased in a crop top and high-waisted jeans. Pert breasts and strong shoulders came next. Light brown skin, cheeks dusted with freckles. Her nose and mouth were familiar, but the mass of dark curls pulled up to showcase an undercut were not. Her youthful face looked like a smudge of a memory, a blurred photograph of someone Max had once known.

Something backfired in Max's brain as she understood who she was looking at. The tells weren't just in the nose and freckles but in the way her lush bottom lip was caught in her teeth—Grace's nervous tic, passed down to her daughter.

This was the kid. Jade, wasn't it?

An unexpected souvenir from prom night, Jade had been born the year after Grace had graduated high school, right before the band had landed their first big record contract.

Max did some mental math, her heart nearly stopping when she realized it had been twenty-seven years. No wonder there were no tricycles on the lawn. But it was one thing to know it had been twenty-seven years and another thing to see a blaring sign of her own age waiting just inside the house.

"Unacceptable," Maxine blurted without thinking.

"Excuse me!" Jade's face burned scarlet. Gray eyes looked down as if trying to search out what about her Maxine had deemed unacceptable. It was a most uncomfortable time to realize the girl—*woman*, rather—had been blessed with quite a bit more height than Max's five-foot-four frame.

Max's cheeks went up in flames. "I wasn't prepared to see Grace—er, I mean you. It is you, right?"

"That depends on who you think I am?" Her tone was wrapped in barbed wire beneath a veneer of cordiality.

This did not bode well, making it clear how monumental Max's task would be. If Grace's daughter was battle ready right out of the gate, it could only be because her mother's stories had made her so. Surely, Cindy would be even more formidable and thoroughly pissed. Max wasn't stupid enough to think she didn't have a reason to be.

I should never have agreed to this lunch.

"You must be Jade," Max answered, mostly because anything clever escaped her. "I thought Cindy would answer the door. I'm sorry. I should..." *What? Run?*

"She's here. Cindy, I mean. If she's the only one you want to talk to, I can leave." Jade sounded all too willing to do just that, like she'd be relieved to be dismissed.

"I wouldn't dream of kicking you out of your mom's —er, your house." *I am making a complete mess of this.* "Fuck. I'm sorry. Let me start over. Hi. I'm Max." Her blood was rushing hot, and it wasn't just from embarrassment. Though every part of her knew it was wrong, Max couldn't stop staring at the beauty in front of her, twisting into knots and not knowing what to say or do.

Though Jade's eyes still burned with what had to

be anger, there was a pink blush creeping up, making the freckles stand out in stark relief. It gave Max hope that she hadn't completely bombed the lunch before it had begun.

"Oh my God, it's really you!" Coming out of nowhere, Cindy hip-checked Jade and tossed her arms around Max's shoulders. "Why aren't you letting her in, Kitten?"

Kitten? The wholesome nickname coming from an older relative morphed into something completely unsuitable for public consumption the moment Max's imagination got a hold of it.

She was surely going to hell.

"Are you taller, or am I shorter?" Cindy babbled, clearly unaware of Max's inappropriate thoughts toward the woman's niece. Max would already be dead if Cindy knew.

Shoving all imagining of Jade from her mind, Max sank into the embrace. It felt painfully familiar, even after all the time that had passed. "I don't know. It's been way too long."

"It has." There was a hitch in Cindy's words.

All the anxiety surrounding her mission came crashing back in, but Max managed to keep it cool. "I'm having a difficult time wrapping my head around the fact that Grace's kid isn't a kid anymore."

Thankfully, Cindy smirked and rolled her eyes. "Don't I know it? She's like this constant reminder that time isn't on my side. At least she's cool as hell

38

and fun to be around, so I can't stay mad at her for long."

Max hadn't picked up any cool or fun vibes, only red-hot anger that had yet to be explained. "I'm so sorry about Grace. I still can't believe..." She couldn't get the rest out.

"Yeah." Cindy bobbed her head, turning around and flicking a tear off her cheek before her steely mask slid into place. Max recognized it as her old game face before stepping onto the stage. "I'm starving. Could we move this inside and eat?"

Max's relief bubbled up. Any excuse to move away from haunting the front stoop was a good one as she tried not to sneak glances at Jade. Stepping inside, Max kept trying to picture Grace in this house but couldn't. Not the black-leather wearing rock chick who had partied harder than any of them.

The house was cozy, with hallways leading everywhere instead of the open concept multi-purpose rooms that seemed so popular in new architecture. The prints on the walls were artsy, with not a band poster in sight, nor were there any instruments to be seen. Not even a piano. Had Grace given up music completely? It was a terrible thought. That woman had played drums like no one Max had encountered before or since.

In every room, the furniture matched and came in shades of beige and gray, with a few accent pillows to add color. It looked like the home of someone who held an office in the PTA, drove a minivan, and enjoyed cooking healthy dinners for her family. Whomever her friend had become once the band broke up, Max hadn't a clue.

"It's a nice home," Max said. It felt robotic, though, because all Max could think was how grateful she was that this hadn't been her life, too.

Cindy threw a look over her shoulder. "A big difference from your place in New York, I imagine?" There was a teasing lilt to the question, and Maxine gathered Cindy was reading her mind.

"It is a bit different, yes," Max admitted. "Do you live nearby?"

"Yep, but my kitchen is being renovated, so..." Cindy finished the statement with a shrug, leading Max to wonder if this was the truth or if Cindy had chosen Grace's house for their meeting for a different reason.

Or for the shock value of watching Max work out who Grace had become. A middle-aged mom. Squinting, Max tried to conjure up the image of Grace's heavily tattooed body pushing a vacuum over the rug or fluffing decorative pillows, humming to herself.

No fucking way.

All the time they were passing through rooms, Cindy pointing them out as they went, Max could feel Jade trailing a few steps. The hot intensity of resentment, or whatever the emotion was that Max couldn't quite place, emanated off the young woman the whole way. Was the anger about the cruelty of losing her mother at such a young age? Or was it directed squarely at Max?

Both, perhaps.

Maybe the woman had been raised to be conservative and hated the rock and roll lifestyle Max represented. That couldn't be the case, though. Her cool hair and funky clothing suggested Jade hadn't rebelled against her mother's past by becoming a pearl-clutching young Republican.

Max couldn't give this any more thought because as soon as they moved to the dining room, a wall of smells hit her, a delightful blast from her youth. "Oh, wow. Did you get takeout from Curry Palace?"

Cindy laughed. "Yeah. I remember how much you loved it. I figured if we were going to drive down nostalgia road, we may as well go all in."

"Hell yes." Max inhaled deeply, her salivary glands working overtime as memories flashed through her mind. "How many times did we stop in there on the way back from a gig? I think it was the only place aside from fast food that was open late back in the day."

Max moved around the table, unsure of what to do. It was strange. Surreal, really, being in a home that belonged to someone she'd adored but at the same time made her feel like she was on an alien planet. How bizarre it was to be in the room with a person she'd known since the days when pimples had dotted her jawline.

And there stood Jade, looking like the ghost of her mother.

"Heads-up, the vindaloo is level eleven spicy." Cindy pointed to one of the containers as her eyes wandered from Max to Jade and back again. The uncertainty in them was endearing, and secretly, Max felt relieved to discover she wasn't the only one feeling out of sorts by this reunion. "It might even be a twelve."

Max raised an eyebrow, fairly certain she knew where this was heading. "I thought they only went to ten."

"Not if you say ten is for wusses, and you want it authentically spicy for an old friend who always had to have it spicier than anyone else could handle." Cindy shrugged, but her eyes were glittering with mischief. Oh yeah. She was definitely going there, and Max was ready for it. "I thought we could have a little competition, for old time's sake."

Was that all it was? Or was Cindy aware of Max's true reason for coming here and wanted to make her jump through hoops to see if she was still worthy? An understanding shimmered between them, or so it seemed to Max. Either play the game like they used to do, or go home empty-handed. Far be it from Max to turn her back on a dare.

Max's mouth spread slowly into a grin. "Bring it."

"What's going on?" Jade broke in, sounding much too serious for someone her age. "Aunt Cindy, you don't eat spicy food."

Without dignifying Jade's comment with a response, Cindy gestured that they should all sit down. There was a shift in her body, reminding Max how so long ago this woman had been the ringleader, the instigator, the source of a million terrible—and terribly funny—ideas. Maybe the old Cindy hadn't disappeared after all. "Here's how we play. I'm going to fill our plates with rice. Then we'll start with the mildest curry, all of us taking a bite. We move up in spice level, spoonful by spoonful. The last person to need water wins."

"Why are you doing this?" It was evident Jade didn't see the appeal. "You'll make yourself sick."

"It's our thing, and I'll be fine." Cindy's curt response showed she wouldn't be cowed by her overly cautious niece. She dished out rice followed by a large glob of *saag*, before handing the plate to Max and then fixing her own. "Jade? You in?"

Jade crossed her arms. "I'll make my own plate. I prefer to taste my food, not compete with it." Jade did as she'd said she would, steering clear of the contents of the spiciest containers.

As if noticing this, Cindy gave an exaggerated roll of her eyes. "I guess it's just the two of us."

Max picked up her fork, ready to run whatever gauntlet was required to get Cindy to say yes to the reunion tour. "Shall we?"

The two of them took a bite. Max sighed as her taste buds sparked a hundred lovely memories. The creamy spinach dish was as good as she remembered but not remotely hot.

"Next round." Cindy dolloped what looked like butter chicken onto both plates.

Max let out a satisfied moan after sampling it, but again, the heat factor was well on the wimpy side. "I thought you said you got hot. I think you've gone soft."

"Me? I'm worried about you. It's going to get worse. So much worse." Cindy's laugh could only be described as sinister.

This was a test for sure, and if Max wanted to convince her old friend to give up her cozy suburban life this summer for a crowded tour bus and grueling schedule, one thing was certain. No matter how hot the food got, Max could not back down.

The contents of the fourth container caused Max's nose to run. The heat factor was definitely increasing. Max cleared her throat involuntarily, sucking in some air to cool the flames that had erupted on the tip of her tongue.

"Ready to toss in the towel?" Cindy mocked.

"Never." Max ran her hand through her hair, her jaw hardening in determination.

"This is stupid." Jade turned to her aunt. "What about your acid reflux? I'm pretty sure your doctor wouldn't approve of whatever the hell this pissing contest is supposed to accomplish."

"Oh, hush." Cindy dished out the next round.

After this bite, sweat collected along Max's upper lip, and the only saving grace was the fact Cindy occasionally fanned her own skin with her shirt. If Max was suffering, she wasn't alone.

Time to get into her head, Max thought. She clapped her hands together with way more enthusiasm than her belly was feeling as she eyed the containers eagerly. "What's next? Level seven?"

"You didn't even have to count on your fingers." Cindy teased. She licked her lips as if to show she shared Max's excitement and then dished out two bite-sized scoops of tikka masala.

The sting of it was immediate, followed by the slow burn down Max's throat. *Must not give up.* Max allowed herself the tiniest glimpse of the water glass, but that was all. It had become increasingly clear with each bite that her entire future depended on outlasting Cindy at what Jade had rightly recognized as a juvenile game. But Max was eight years Cindy's junior, and defeat wasn't in her vocabulary.

"Your water is right there, Cindy," Max taunted as Cindy took a bite, her face flushing. "I'm sure the heartburn is kicking in. Duck out now. You made it much farther than I thought you would."

"I know what you're doing." Cindy shoved her water closer to Max. "You always talked a big game, but we know deep down walking the walk is another story."

"Oh, yeah?" Sure, Max's esophagus was on fire, but

she had a stomach of steel. After all the years she'd spent touring, well beyond when Cindy had retreated to a world of sensible and well-balanced meals, it was a given she would come out of this contest victorious. Wasn't it?

Max's T-shirt was sticking to the slick of her armpits, and her mouth continued to tingle. She had to admit the heat was getting uncomfortable. Jade looked her way, and instead of the concern she'd shown her aunt, her lips were pressed into a shit-eating smirk. There was no doubt the woman wanted to see her fail. Why did Grace's daughter despise Max so?

"Dish out eight," Max barked, all the more determined to win, as if that would earn her Jade's respect as well as Cindy's.

Level eight was dished, chewed, and swallowed. It hurt like hell. For her part, Cindy had the look of a woman who was about to pass out. Max hoped she would, just to make the pain end.

"Give up?" Finally deciding to join in the fun of shit-talking, Jade had become Max's tormenter, dragging a finger around the lip of a water glass in a lazy, teasing way.

"N-nope." Only Max's voice was turning into a croak, and it was a good thing she didn't have any upcoming performances that week, or Skip would be furious. "Nine time, baby."

Nine was *brutal*. Gut-busting, fire-breathing, moan-inducing brutal. There wasn't really flavor anymore. It was more akin to taking a bite of molten lava and hoping it wouldn't kill her. Max yearned for water or possibly the sweet relief of death.

Jade looked almost concerned. It was hard to tell. Max's eyes were too watery to see clearly.

"Here comes the last dish. This one goes to eleven." Cindy laughed at the old *Spinal Tap* movie reference, but there was a wariness about her. Perhaps she was feeling guilty, too, as she should for coming up with this abominable idea. Had they really thought this was *fun* once upon a time? At least Cindy had the decency to reduce the spoonful she plopped on the plates.

"Over the lips, past the gums, look out stomach, here it comes." Max scooped up the off-the-charts vindaloo onto her fork. Taking a deep breath, she put it in her mouth.

And promptly spewed it out all over the table, practically lunging for her water.

CHAPTER FOUR

The moment Max started coughing, any enjoyment Jade may have found in the woman's suffering evaporated. Her instinct to help, honed from months of constant caring for her ill mother, kicked into overdrive. She jolted from her chair, dashing into the kitchen while calling out, "I'll get some milk!"

When Jade returned, Max had tears streaming down her crimson cheeks. Profanity also flowed freely, a deep, guttural cursing of Cindy, of the food, of the water doing nothing, of God herself for inventing peppers in the first place.

"Here, drink this." Jade pushed the glass of white liquid at her guest before turning to her aunt. "Go get your heartburn pills. Don't argue."

Given her reddening cheeks, Jade's aunt was feeling the burn herself, for sure. Cindy didn't put up a fight, jumping up and going in search of her purse where the pills were kept. But Max, despite the pain she was clearly undergoing, hesitated long enough to eye the milk with distaste.

"Water?" she croaked.

Jade shook her head. "Dairy products are much more effective at canceling out the heat."

As Jade stared at Max's watery eyes, red-laced sclera making the blue almost sapphire, it was impossible to deny how stunning the woman was. Lottie had been right in a way that formed a rock in Jade's belly. When it came to the world's hottest rock star, Maxine Gardner was definitely in the running. But she'd also come here on a mission. Jade was sure of it. The pieces of the puzzle weren't quite adding up. Otherwise, why would the woman have gone along with Cindy's stupid game? Max wanted something.

After guzzling down the milk, Max managed to mumble a thank you, or so Jade believed, given how garbled the words were. The woman's tongue was probably swollen to twice its regular size. Fortunately, the fire-engine red of her face was beginning to shift to a less imposing pink, although it had a ways to go before it made it back to a neutral peach.

"Beat by an older and much wiser woman," Cindy crowed, coming back to the dining room with two pills cradled in her palm. She popped them into her mouth, chasing them down with milk.

Jade pointed a finger at her aunt. "Not sure wise

can be applied to either of you. You were both acting like you don't have the good sense God gave a flea."

"I can't believe I didn't record that," Cindy continued, ignoring Jade completely. "It would've been internet fucking gold. After all these years, Maxine Gardner can't take the heat."

"You wouldn't be so cruel." With the milk gone, Max took a long chug from her water glass.

"No. Cruelty was never *my* specialty." Cindy's tone made it clear she did not believe the same could be said of Max. "But I'm an old fuddy-duddy, someone who still believes friends should show up to things like weddings and funerals without fail, so what do I know?"

Jade almost gasped, surprised at the sudden, vicious jab. Her aunt wasn't pulling punches.

"You're right." Max slumped a little in her chair, and Jade was surprised that of all the possibilities, this was the thing that drained the fight out of her. "There were reasons in both cases, of course, but no excuse."

Was that an apology? The actual words *I'm sorry* hadn't been said, but based on what Jade had gleaned of Max's personality, she figured it was about as close as the woman could get without breaking something. She wondered whether the sentiment was sincere, or if it was because the rocker was still in a world of hurt from the vindaloo and looking for any form of absolution she could get, however fleeting.

"Do you remember that time in Chicago—no, it

was Philly, naturally, when we were pelted with milk cartons while on stage?" Cindy, who was mopping her brow with a fresh napkin, didn't outright offer forgiveness, but the way she was changing the subject so quickly made Jade think it was implied or at least that a tentative peace had been established.

This was a good thing. If her aunt had been this brutal with lunch, Jade hated to think how much pain she could have inflicted with dessert. Max seemed to realize her narrow escape too, her whole frame losing some of its nervous tautness as she chuckled at the shared memory.

"How could I forget that? Those single serving size cartons stung." Max tapped a spot next to her eye, which Jade realized was a small scar. "Got this to always remember it by."

"That's right." Cindy clasped a hand to her mouth. "They threw a frozen milk at you. You had to get two stitches. I completely forgot about that."

"Are you saying people in the audience threw things at you?" Jade couldn't disguise her shock. She'd heard some horror stories from her mom and aunt over the years about their time on the road but never anything so violent.

"That was in the early days, when the guys wanted to show us girls we didn't belong on the stage." There was an edge to Max's tone that suggested this only the tip of the iceberg.

"That first tour wasn't for wimps. That's for sure."

Cindy turned her attention back to Max. "It feels like another lifetime."

When her aunt spoke of the old days with the band, it was usually with bitterness tinged with relief at how her life had turned out since leaving the music industry behind. This was the first time Jade detected a wistfulness in Cindy's tone that suggested her true feelings were more nuanced than she let on.

"I can't get over it, looking around this house." Max's eyes scanned the walls, and she let out a small sigh. "There's zero evidence of our past, not a hint of what a legend Grace was. Did she really walk away from it all and never look back? I can't imagine music not being a part of her life."

"You only think that because you haven't seen the basement," Jade blurted. Aside from joking with her aunt earlier about Max wanting to jam with them, she hadn't actually intended to mention the music room at all. But she'd been surprisingly touched by how sad Max had sounded, and it struck her as wrong that someone who had clearly loved and admired her mother at one time should believe Grace Weathers would ever give up on music. "Come on. I'll show you."

Jade hopped out of her chair, suddenly eager to show off what had been her mom's favorite spot in the house. For good reason. The music room was fucking incredible. Even a star like Max would have to think so, and deep down, Jade knew part of her was hoping to impress this woman who couldn't quite hide her disdain for what Jade knew was a milquetoast suburban house. She'd argued with her mom a million times about it, but Grace had always been so conscious of wanting to fit in with the other parents, for Jade's sake. Guilt, maybe, for those first five years when she'd barely been around.

The basement, though—that was the embodiment of who Grace truly had been. It was the one place where Jade could still feel her presence. The first week after her mom's death, Jade had retreated to the music room on many a sleepless night, curling up on the sofa and finding some small amount of peace.

Jade led the way down the carpeted stairs, flipping on the lights and taking a step back to allow Max the full effect. The little gasp the woman made when she entered the room did not disappoint.

The instruments, the records, the soundproofing, were all top-notch. There were two drum kits and a variety of acoustic and electric stringed instruments. An extensive vinyl collection was arranged in cubbies by color, creating a rainbow that just about begged a person to pull out an album and listen. All of it was badass, and Jade knew it.

She was pretty sure Max knew it, too. For some reason, this made her beyond pleased.

"Oh, wow." Max walked up to one of the framed Matchstick Girls tour posters with the same level of reverence as she might've displayed toward a sacred religious icon. "Look at how young we were."

"Babies," Cindy agreed, joining Max and Jade in the room. "Hence why the Philly assholes threw milk cartons at us instead of beer cans. They thought they were being clever."

"Do you ever miss it?" Max asked, still taking in the space. "The good parts, that is. It did get better after that first year."

There was a pregnant pause long enough for Jade to wonder where her aunt's *no* was. "Yeah, sometimes I do." It seemed Cindy was doing her best not to sound forlorn, but it was evident from her slumped shoulders that the memories were hitting her hard, along with perhaps more than a little regret. "We had some great times."

Hand stroking the neck of a Fender, Max looked up, eyes bright. "Let's play something!" She became animated, like the proverbial kid in a candy store, as she turned toward the instruments set up in the center of the room.

"A record?" Cindy asked, eyeing the instruments with a wariness that made it clear she knew what Max was hinting at.

"Come on," Max cajoled. "You know what I'm saying. One song, for old time's sake."

Cindy shook her head. "We'd need a drummer."

Jade scrunched her nose at her aunt, who knew perfectly well what a bullshit excuse it was. "I can do it." Jade might have mixed feelings about Maxine's presence, but she wasn't going to miss a chance to play her mother's songs with her mother's band this one time. Some opportunities were too rare to miss, no matter the circumstances.

Cindy shot Jade a half-baked look of betrayal.

"You drum?" The entirety of Maxine's focus was on Jade. It was a heavy, heated thing. Jade didn't know what to do with a look like that, except slide her eyes quickly away in search of safety. Or a fire extinguisher.

Maxine Gardner is a veritable queer icon. Lottie's voice echoed in Jade's head like a warning bell. No wonder. If she could get Jade's body to react so forcefully with nothing but a look, Jade could only imagine what else the woman could do. But it was ridiculous to speculate about such a thing. Not only did Jade dislike Max for the disloyalty she'd shown her bandmates in breaking up the Matchstick Girls, but because if Max was into women, she was also so deep in the closet she had to be halfway to Narnia by now. Jade was from a different generation, one that didn't play those kinds of games, and she had no patience for people who denied who they were.

"If you thought Grace was good," Cindy replied, casting a pointed look in Jade's direction that somehow conveyed both pride and warning at the same time, "just you wait."

The corners of Max's mouth quirked. "Do you know any of our songs? Think you can keep up?"

"It's not exactly Mahler's Sixth Symphony, now is it?" Jade experienced a rush of wine-inspired prickles in her cheeks as she realized how elitist that had sounded.

"A particularly percussion-heavy piece," Cindy added when the blank look on Max's face made it clear she had no idea what Jade was referencing. "Jade's going to be joining the North Carolina Symphony as the principal percussionist next season."

"Really?" Max looked suitably impressed, but instead of feeling proud, Jade was surprised by what could only be described as dread at Cindy's premature announcement.

"I'm… It's possible." What was it Jade had been thinking earlier about not having patience for people who couldn't own who they were?

Talk about the pot criticizing the kettle.

Jade was cool with people knowing she was gay but terrified of telling her aunt how she really felt about joining the symphony. It sounded even more dreadfully dull than it had a few hours ago when she'd first been informed of it. Yet, Jade couldn't gather the courage to tell Cindy no. It felt wrong to hurt her aunt like that so soon after Grace had passed. Besides, what else would Jade even do?

"It's the job of a lifetime," Cindy effused, clearly unaware of the sinking effect her words were having on her niece's stomach. "For a musician, this level of security doesn't fall into your lap every day. The man who's retiring has been in the position for five decades."

"Five decades," Max repeated, sounding like her mouth was full of marbles. "That's... impressive."

Jade agreed. It *was* impressive, in the same way watching a tsunami wipe out a village was technically impressive, along with being horrifying and awful. Desperate to get the dueling images out of her mind of a killer tsunami and herself in her seventies pounding on a kettle drum, Jade sat down behind her mom's favorite drum set. "Which song should we start with?"

Cindy approached the keyboard with caution, her fingers hovering above the keys for a moment before she plunked them down, committing to the task at hand. "How about 'Dreaming'?"

"That's one of my faves." Max chose a guitar from a hook on the wall, hoisting the strap over her head before plugging the instrument into a nearby amp. She flew through tuning it up. "You remember the words?"

Jade held her breath, expecting Cindy to make a snarky comeback, like "Why do you need us to sing when you'll cut us out anyway?" But her aunt refrained, instead giving Max a pleasant, almost enthusiastic nod. It might've been the first time Cindy had ever passed up an opportunity to rehash that particular grievance, and to Max's face, this time, too. Although maybe that explained it. Cindy talked a good game, but when it came down to it, she was all bark and no bite.

Jade could relate.

As soon as they began to play, it was like they'd been doing it all their lives. It made sense that Max and Cindy would play well together, considering their history. But for Jade, it was another matter. She should've felt awkward. This wasn't her usual kind of music, and she'd never played with Max before. Yet she felt liberated, like she was soaring above the clouds. Jade had no explanation for it, except whenever she played on her mom's set, she felt as if her mom sat on her shoulder, whispering encouragement. Maybe it was exactly what she needed after the sorrow and loss of the last few months.

When the song came to an end, Jade was out of breath. Cindy and Max appeared to be in similar states. They all shared the flush of elation at what they'd managed to create.

"Damnnnn!" Max dragged out the word when she'd finally collected herself enough to speak. "Cindy wasn't lying. You *are* good. Are you sure you've never considered joining a rock band? Because I have some connections."

Jade nearly laughed, assuming it was a cheesy line Max used on everyone, until it struck her the woman was totally serious. She tried to say something in response, but her throat was too dry to speak.

Play in a rock band, for real? A feeling like hope fluttered in Jade's chest. That sounded so...

"Grace didn't want that life for Jade. Never." Cindy

sliced the air with her hand, effectively throwing cold water over Jade's head.

No, her mom hadn't wanted it. But did Jade feel the same? With her mom no longer with her, questions like that were creeping into Jade's head with alarmingly increased frequency these days. Everything had changed with her mother's death, and Jade was only beginning to understand all that entailed.

"The symphony sounds steady and all, but a drummer—" Max clutched her shirt over her heart. "A drummer with this kind of talent shouldn't sit out of sight, waiting to hit a triangle with a little stick. She should be—" Max acted out hitting drums with great enthusiasm and a complete lack of finesse.

"You look like a Muppet." The words were out of Jade's mouth before she could consider how Max's rock star ego might react to criticism. Luckily for her, Max laughed.

"Animal! Animal!" Max chanted, doing a fantastic impression of the famous furry character.

"You're a nut," Jade said, but what she wanted was to ask how Max had managed to put into words the exact thoughts that had been running a hundred miles an hour through her own head.

How did the woman whom Jade had been certain would be a nemesis suddenly seem her most likely ally? Could this meeting be the key to changing the trajectory of her future?

Max shot Jade a look. Jade didn't know how to

translate it, but she wanted to learn. A link seemed to snap in place between them in that moment, for better or worse, tying them together. "Let's play another song."

Cindy offered up a different song title, another selection from the Matchstick Girls' first album. They melted into the music, playing their hearts out until the final chords, which lingered in the air above them before dissipating like an early-morning fog.

"Duuuuude!" Max let out an appreciative whistle. "It's like the band never broke up."

Overcome with emotion and the sense of her mom's nearness, Jade flicked away a tear.

"Okay, okay, hear me out." Max paused a beat, her cheeks flushed with excitement. She was speaking to Cindy, but her eyes kept darting to Jade. "What if we did a tribute tour to honor Grace?"

Everything about the suggestion came across as perfectly natural and genuine, a spontaneous reaction to an emotional moment. Even so, Jade found herself instantly on high alert. It was too perfect. All her earlier mistrust of Maxine Gardner, conniving backstabber extraordinaire, came flooding back. One did not simply switch from eating vindaloo to discussing van life. The woman was up to something.

"Grace would have hated the idea." Cindy's mouth was a tight slash, but Jade knew her aunt well enough to hear the weakness behind the words. Cindy was tempted.

"Definitely," Max offered. "But Skip had this crazy idea about it, and I was like 'no way man, they'll never say yes.' But then..." She fluttered her hands around as if to say *look at us!* "It felt good to play her music. All our greatest hits came from Grace. Plus, you could make money to put into your music school, and I imagine you'd get a big boost in enrollment after a tour like this."

Cindy's eyes had a murderous hue, but she didn't speak. Jade recalled what her aunt had said about how persuasive Max could be. It appeared she was witnessing a firsthand demonstration. Worse, she found herself being reeled in as well.

"We'd need a drummer." Max stared pointedly at Jade.

Finally, Cindy found her voice. "No way. Don't even think it. Grace busted her ass to position Jade for a job that doesn't involve all the shit we endured. Remember that scar next to your eye?"

Jade crossed her arms, annoyance loosening her tongue. "Seems like I should get a say in my own life."

"Oh, lighten up," Cindy soothed. "Skip always paraded grandiose ideas around. It isn't really going to happen. Tours take a ton of time and investment. It's not something you can up and do on a whim."

"Now, hold on." Max had her hand on her hip. "Like I said, he came to me because—"

"I can't believe you're still letting him manage you." Cindy made it sound like a diss as she folded her arms over her chest. "I'm not sure I could believe anything that man promises. Besides, Grace's dying wish was for me to protect her only daughter. I'm pretty sure this would not be on the list of approved activities."

Jade's head was spinning, but one thing was certain. While she didn't know how to talk to her aunt about her reluctance to start a career in the symphony, she didn't want every other aspect of her life decided by the woman, either. "I'm not a child anymore," Jade argued, her determination to take part in this tour increasing by the second. "I'm twenty-seven years old."

"I know, Kitten. But—"

"I'm going to text him for information," Max interrupted, her thumbs flying with a speed that would impress any millennial, clearly wanting to derail Cindy's train of thought. Despite suspecting it was a selfish move on Max's part, Jade was grateful. The last thing she wanted was a full-blown argument with her aunt. "Let's play another song."

"I don't need information," Cindy declared. "I won't change my mind. Besides, I wouldn't be able to leave Rick by himself for so long."

Everything about her aunt's demeanor shouted this was not true, and Jade was fairly sure Max could sense it, reading her former bandmate like an open book.

"Hey, how is Rick, anyway?" There was a calculating glint in Max's eyes. "Man, he was the best sound engineer I ever met. He still working in the biz?"

"On and off." Cindy pressed her lips together, and Jade knew she was thinking about how quickly Uncle Rick would jump at this chance. The highlight of his life these days was when an out-of-town gospel act performed at the big Baptist church and needed a sound guy. Jade could almost see him sitting up and begging like a puppy for Cindy to say yes and take him along.

Max jumped, reaching into her pocket and pulling out her phone, despite the fact Jade hadn't heard it ring or even vibrate. A grin spread across Max's face as she scanned the screen. "Skip was serious. He says he can pull something together for the summer if we're all in. So, what do you say, Cindy?"

Jade's aunt drew in a breath, holding it until she looked like she would burst. An opportunity they'd never considered suddenly flopped into their laps. "I... I need to sleep on it. And talk to Rick." Jade's heart leaped at the news, but her excitement was short-lived as Cindy looked pointedly in her direction and added, "Don't hold your breath, Kitten."

CHAPTER FIVE

Back at Jade's house the next morning, Max sat at the edge of the sofa, eyes glued to Cindy like a runner waiting for a starting pistol. She'd been on edge the entire night. She was certain she'd convinced Cindy to say yes... mostly. Skip would have been quick to tell her "mostly" didn't pay royalties, which is why she'd been ducking his calls and messages. She needed to be on her A-game to work any and all needed magic that morning on the chance Cindy said no.

"Damnit, Max. Fine, we'll do it." Cindy crossed her arms, but for as much as she seemed to want everyone to think she was put out by the announcement, her expression held way too much excitement. "I'll have you know Rick is who you should thank."

Max's breath left in a whoosh. She'd said yes! Before she could so much as pump a fist in the air, though, she found a finger in her face. "There are rules," Cindy said with firm authority.

"Lay them on me," Max settled comfortably into the cushioned back of the couch. Jade was perched in a chair like a bird, arms wrapped around her knees and gray eyes bright.

No wonder Grace had been able to tolerate the rest of the house looking so boring. This basement was fucking *incredible*. Max felt a tug as it occurred to her that even though she could afford something similar, she never stayed at her home long enough to warrant this kind of space. If she had a room like this, and people to share it with, maybe it would be harder to leave.

Cindy shot Max a *look*. That was one part of the good ol' days Max had not been looking forward to. Cindy had been four years older than Grace and eight years older than Max, and had taken it upon herself from day one to be a mother hen. Apparently, some things didn't fade with time, as she seemed to have stepped squarely into that role with Jade, too.

"One." Cindy held up a finger as she began enumerating her stipulations. "There will be no partying on the tour bus. At all. No late-night drinking sessions, no drugs. It didn't do us any good in our teens, and it would be fucking disastrous now. I'm married and haven't stayed up past eleven in basically a decade, so I'll be struggling with the schedule enough as it is."

Max wasn't actually a large partier anymore, but she bristled at being told what to do. A quick glance at Jade suggested she felt the same. Still, Max was going to have to compromise if she wanted this to work out. "No problem. Although it's tour *buses*, plural. We'll have at least two, possibly three."

"Three?" Cindy's eyes grew huge, and Max wanted to laugh. Things had changed a lot since the early days of piling into a station wagon with Cindy's parents and pulling all their gear in a trailer hitched to the back.

"Two is the minimum," Max confirmed, knowing she sounded cocky, but she'd worked her ass off for all of this time for a rock star lifestyle, and part of her wanted Cindy to witness what she'd walked away from, even if Max suspected the executives would trim costs wherever possible, and two was in all likelihood the maximum. The Hawthorne Bunnies had three stars who made demands. It wasn't like Jade had the same power. "This is the big time now. Did you have any other rules?"

"Uh…" Cindy still seemed so flustered Max wasn't sure she would continue, but after a few slow blinks, she managed to gather her wits. "Second, no sex with groupies, roadies, or anyone on the buses."

That knocked the wind from her sails. No sex? On *tour*?

"May I ask why?" It was Jade who huffed at this, which caught Max off guard, though it shouldn't have.

Obviously, Jade was old enough to have sex if she wanted to, and well beyond the point of having her aunt tell her what to do where that was concerned.

Maybe the issue was that up until now, Max had been doing a stellar job keeping Jade and sex in two very separate boxes. Now the boxes had been opened and their contents mixed as they spilled across the floor. It was like Max had been forbidden from thinking about a pink elephant. As if on cue, her brain was flooded with images that set fire to her cheeks—and other places, too, but for a very different reason.

"Because I don't want to listen to it," Cindy shot back. "Those buses aren't as large as you think, and I'm too old to bleach the sound from my brain, okay?"

"Max said there might be three buses. There are three of us—"

"Oh no," Cindy said with a chuckle that bordered on evil. "I'm not letting my eyes off you, Kitten."

Max was shocked at the interaction. After all, Grace's daughter was a full-grown adult. Fifteen years Max's junior, sure, but old enough to make her own choices. Also gorgeous and cool enough that she had to have experience. Jade radiated silent fury. Her eyes drifted, ever so briefly, to Max. Did the woman sense what Max was thinking about right now? Hopefully not, or she might kick Max out of her house on the spot.

Cindy held up a third finger, and Max tensed as she

realized they weren't in the clear yet. "Finally, Jade, I want you to promise to take the symphony job."

"I'm done making promises about my future when I don't exactly know what I want," Jade said in the steeliest of tones.

Interesting. She'd given in, mostly, when it came to parties and sex. Max wondered why this was the line in the sand as far as Jade was concerned, especially when Cindy had made it sound like a dream job. Whose dream, though? Max thought she was beginning to understand, but Cindy's scrunched face said she wasn't taking Jade's words onboard.

"When does their season start?" Max jumped in to ask, hoping she could smooth a path before a battle could potentially derail the tour.

"September," Cindy replied. "Rehearsals begin right after Labor Day."

Perfect. Skip had already told Max the tour dates would run from the end of June to the end of August, so there was no conflict. "What if I promise we'll have Jade back in plenty of time to take the job if she wants it?"

Flipping her attention to Max, Cindy let out an anguished sigh but gave a slight nod. "If that's the best I can get."

"It is," Jade was quick to assure her as she shot Max a grateful glance.

Cindy raised an eyebrow, staring down Max. "In case you need me to put this in plain English, my main condition for participating in this tour is that Jade will effectively be encased in Bubble Wrap at all times. All of the less than wholesome experiences we had on the road will *not* be happening to her."

"You've got a deal." Max full-heartedly endorsed this sentiment, knowing it was the least she could do for Grace, even if Cindy was probably overstepping her duties as an aunt. Make that definitely overstepping. But Max didn't need to be a mediator. She needed this tour to go off without a hitch.

"In that case, have Skip send me the details as soon as he draws them up." Cindy wore an expression of shock, like she couldn't quite believe what she was saying. Frankly, neither could Max. As hard as she'd been willing to try, she'd never expected to win her bandmate over.

I might save my career after all.

Jade shifted her focus to Cindy, casually asking, "Do you need to tell the school? You'll need teacher coverage, and the students ought to know."

Cindy slapped her hands to her cheeks. "Oh gosh, yes. There's not a lot of time to get things ready for our absence."

"You should probably call from upstairs," Jade told her. "Cell phone reception is crap down here."

The moment Cindy went upstairs, Jade whipped around on Max, her eyes burning with intensity. "What are you *really* up to?"

"What?" Max was taken aback by this unexpected

turn of events. All of Jade's ire had been directed at her aunt—or so Max had assumed. Now, she was pinned by Jade's accusatory stare and wondered how much in the hot seat she was. "I thought it would be nice to pay tribute to—"

"Oh, no you don't." Jade snapped her fingers, shutting Max down. "Are you expecting me to believe that one text with Skip resulted in three tour buses? You said it was his idea, not his plan."

"W-what?" Max stuttered as she realized Jade was onto her this whole time. What could she say to dig herself out of this hole?

"This tour was already a done deal, wasn't it? That's why you came here to see us. It had nothing to do with paying your respects and everything to do with getting Cindy to sign on."

"I-I—" Max's heart raced like a trapped animal. Without Jade, Max was certain Cindy would bail, and the career Maxine was desperate to salvage would go right down the toilet.

"Don't try to deny it." Jade stared her down until Max shut her mouth and stopped struggling.

"The tour was already set up," Max ventured. Before Jade could fully "aha!" her, she continued. "But for another band, at least a year in the making. They had to cancel at the last minute when their lead singer went to court-ordered rehab after a very public incident, and with the sudden renewed interest in the Matchstick Girls, my manager and the concert promoter saw an opportunity to salvage some of the money they stood to lose on deposits by booking us into the slot."

The truth, or at least this part of it, seemed the wisest move. It earned her an unexpectedly warm smile from Jade. "To be honest, I am thrilled for this opportunity. I've felt like I was going crazy inside this house these past weeks, and I'm desperate for an escape. I won't tell Cindy what you did, on one condition."

"Okay." Max swallowed hard, terrified to find out what Jade was going to demand from her. Whatever it was, she'd have to pay up. Skip had made it clear she didn't have a choice.

"All that Bubble Wrap crap my aunt was insisting on? You're going to make sure that doesn't happen. I want to know what my mom's life was like, what was so thrilling about it that she chose it instead of me until I was five years old."

Max's mind felt as if it were breaking at this bit of information. Was that really what Jade thought about Grace?

"Jade, it was never—" Max began, but Jade held up a hand.

"I made my peace with her. It's not about that. But she treated that time in her life like she was a former CIA operative, never talking about it despite how many times I asked her to tell me." Jade's voice wobbled. "I've watched documentaries on VH1 and the like, but come on. That's not the full picture. This seems like it'll bring me closer to her."

Damn. How could Max say no to that? "Just to make sure I understand you correctly, you keep your aunt on board, and I agree to let you have the real rock star experience?"

"That's pretty much it. So, Maxine Gardner, do *we* have a deal?" Jade stressed the *we* in the question, her eyes twinkling with the almost certain victory that was at hand.

None of this was going to plan. Max had enough sense to know that being in the middle of two head-strong women was dangerous and would ultimately end in disaster. But, Skip's warning about the imminent demise of Max's career if this tour didn't happen trumped all common sense. "Yes, I think we do."

Before they could say anything else, Cindy bounded down the stairs, looking ten years younger. "The staff is on it and crazy excited." Her cheeks pinked. "I think I scored major cool points."

Max and Jade exchanged glances that felt like a handshake.

"We'll need to begin rehearsing ASAP." Max scooted a little closer to the edge of the couch, putting space between her and Jade. It felt like they'd been caught in the basement with their shirts off instead of conspiring to have fun on tour. "When can you two come to New York to get started?"

"New York?" Cindy burst into laughter.

"What?" Max wasn't sure she wanted to know the answer.

"It's two to one, Maxie. Besides, I have a business to run. There's no way I can go to New York. You'll have to come here." Cindy stated it as a done deal.

"Impossible," Max declared. "Where will we rehearse?"

Jade very unhelpfully waved to the music room that surrounded them. "How about right here?"

"But—"

Cindy cut off Max with a loud *uh-uh*. "It's settled. If you need a place to crash, you can stay here."

"What?" Jade's jaw dropped, and Max would've been lying to say she didn't get some enjoyment out of watching the woman squirm after being so completely called out. "First, you invite her to my house for lunch, and now, you expect me to let her live here?"

Max couldn't tell if Jade was perplexed, angry, or a combination of the two. But as much fun as it was to see Jade in full panic mode, Max didn't want to take a chance that Cindy's preposterous suggestion would stick. "My couch surfing days are long since over. I'll book a hotel." And make Skip pay for it. He owed Max for pulling off this miracle.

ONCE SHE WAS in her hotel room, Maxine kicked off her shoes and socks and hung her blazer. She'd skipped a bra and stripped out of her tight jeans. After too much food and drink consumed during this visit, the waistband had moved into the uncomfortably tight zone. In a T-shirt and boy shorts, she flopped onto the bed and tore open the bottle of antacids she'd picked up in the lobby, shoving a few of the chalky discs into her mouth. She chewed and swallowed before dialing.

"Max, my dream queen," Skip said in lieu of "hello."

She didn't feel like a dream queen. Getting used to the family dynamics between Cindy and Jade had left her wrung out. "You've called and texted nonstop for hours. What can I do for you, Skip?"

"Get excited, baby! Ticket sales are set to announce tomorrow."

"What?" Max sat up on the bed, groaning as her tortured stomach rebelled. "Why didn't you tell me it was that soon?" Her stomach lurched at how close to disaster she'd been.

"Because I knew you'd come through." He paused, making her squirm. "You're good at convincing. It's what kept you afloat for the past decade."

Max knew without him having to say it that Skip was referring to her two failed albums, although it was hardly fair that she had to shoulder all the blame. But that didn't matter anymore. This tour was sure to put her on the map again. The next album she recorded would be on her terms. Her label just didn't know it yet.

Time to change the subject.

"Guess what," Max teased. "I have extra good news. So good, you hardly deserve it."

"You're killing me," Skip said, unable to hide his eagerness. "What else?"

"I've got our drummer."

"What, for the tour? Already? Who?"

"Jade Weathers."

"Who the hell is—wait. Weathers? You can't mean Grace's kid. She's like, ten."

"Twenty-seven, old man. I can report firsthand that girl can slay on the drums. She already knows the songs, too."

"Fuck me, that's good. Is she hot? Please tell me she's hot."

"Ew! Don't be a creep," Max shot back. Skip was pushing late fifties.

"Not like that, Max, give me some credit. If she's hot *and* a great drummer *and* Grace's kid, she's going to be perfect for photos, interviews, press circuit shit. The same way you were for the Matchstick Girls."

Oh, right. As much as Max hated the double standard, she knew how much looks could play a part in successful marketing. It wasn't lost on her that the double standard was part of what the Matchstick Girls had railed against so hard when they'd gotten started. Yet her own career had continued for this long with thanks in part to a team of stylists, makeup artists, pilates instructors, and more. How Max looked, particularly now that she was forty-two, mattered. It mattered to the tour promoters, her record label, Skip, *and* her fans.

As much as she hated herself for it, it mattered to her, too.

She got it, even if, for just a moment, she wished Skip was in her room so she could punch him in the dick. "Yeah, she's hot."

Mega hot. Make you think inappropriate thoughts hot.

"I feel like I'm dreaming. This is perfect. *Perfect.*"

She imagined he was salivating over this. "I'm glad you think so because there's been a slight change in plans."

"Oh?" Skip sounded worried.

"We won't be coming back to New York to rehearse. Cindy's insisting on doing all that down here."

"Is that all?" Given it wasn't life or death and didn't inconvenience him in any way, it was clear Skip couldn't give a rat's ass at how much it disrupted Max's life.

"Yeah. That means I'm going to need a place to stay while we get this all nailed down."

"Fine." He responded so quickly she knew they'd hit the point in the conversation where he wasn't listening to her anymore, anyway.

"On your dime, Skip."

"I'll have my people take care of it," he promised. Max made a mental note to see to it they followed through, and not some crappy motel, either. "The first show is at the end of June. Before the buses roll out, we'll need the three of you to do some promotional travel, too. We need to crank up the publicity like, yesterday. I'll fly out there next week to see how it's going."

"No way," Max argued. She could still feel how tenuous Cindy's acceptance had been. "Not that soon. I doubt Cindy will be pleased to see you, and we'll need at least four to five weeks of practice before we're ready for an audience, anyway."

"Whatever you say," Skip assured her, which hopefully meant he had heard what she said and agreed to it. "You did good, Maxie."

"Thanks." She *felt* good. Well, except for her stomach, which was still angry at her over the spicy food contest. "Talk to you soon."

They hung up, and she turned on the TV but didn't pay attention to what was on. Her mind replayed the day. It flashed over the things that had startled her, like the house that looked like it could be on HGTV with its décor, and Cindy's ability to be the same person Max had been in a band with and yet look so different. Max was older, too, but still the same jeans and T-shirts woman she'd always been. Cindy was wearing Chicos and Tommy Bahamas instead of miniskirts and Doc Martens. What Skip would say when he got a look at Cindy was anyone's guess, but that wasn't Max's concern.

What she kept drifting back to was Jade. *She'd* been a surprise. Obviously, Max had seen her now and then when she was a kid. But encountering her as a fully formed *adult* was bizarre.

A very well-formed human, at that. Which could be a problem.

No one in the band had ever known about Max's attraction to women, a conscious choice on her part not to share. If they'd suspected, they'd never said. It had been easier that way, considering the homophobia in the music industry back then. Hell, it had been the 1990s. Homophobia had been *everywhere*. Max had never worried what Grace or Cindy would think about her if they'd known. It had simply been safer not to tell them. Once you tell a secret, it rarely stayed one for long.

At forty-two, with the way the world had changed, it wasn't a skeleton that still needed to be hidden in the back of the closet. Not really, anyway. Still, Max had hesitated, preferring to keep her private life exactly that.

Her own fucking business.

Maybe Cindy's ridiculous rule about no sex on the road wasn't such a bad thing after all. Because one thing was for certain. Jade Weathers was one hundred percent off-limits.

CHAPTER SIX

J ade glanced at her watch, noting that both Cindy and Max weren't expected for an hour. There was nothing else for her to do aside from wait. What she wanted to do was nap.

Jade had been up two hours before her normal rising time to clean the house and get some last-minute groceries at the store. Apparently, emergency cinnamon rolls were a thing. She'd tried on seven different outfits, for God knew what reason. She'd become obsessed with wanting to convey she could rock with the best of them but also that she possessed an astute music business sense—or something like that. Considering she couldn't assemble the right words for what she wanted, it was little surprise Jade had ended up in jeans and a T-shirt. She'd chosen a Matchstick Girls concert shirt, circa 1998, needing her mom close to her in whatever way she could find. It was buttery soft with age and wear.

Jade waited in the music room. She'd left a key under the mat for Max to let herself in when she arrived, along with a note that said to come downstairs. Jade needed something to occupy her mind, to keep it from racing full tilt down the various crazy paths it had been taking since this sudden turn of life events. Jade, in a rock band? It was impossible to believe.

Yet it was true. And scary.

Strumming the guitar helped at first. Music usually provided distraction. Unfortunately, she was comfortable enough with the instrument that her mind still managed to wander.

Her life had suddenly surpassed "dream come true" and now danced along the river of the surreal. If the tour worked out, Jade would have her get out of jail card, and by that, she meant not playing for the symphony until the best years of her life had passed her by.

It wasn't that she hated the idea of working at the symphony. She loved classical as much as she did rock, pop, R&B... But they expected dedication and time. At twenty-seven, she wasn't sure she was prepared to dedicate so much of herself to a dream that had belonged to her mom.

Part of Jade wondered if she was currently on cloud nine because she'd been desperate for something good to come along. How long had she spent watching her mother's decline and preparing for her death? Then death finally happened, and a huge hole was left, a canyon in the middle of her existence.

No mother, no direction, no sense of how to move forward in her life.

Max had shown up at her doorstep with a perfectly-timed nudge back into the world of the living. It was possible Jade was grasping at every straw, hoping for an escape from the void.

"Hey!" the husky singer's voice called out from upstairs.

"Down here!" Jade suppressed a shiver of anticipation, but of what? The rehearsal? The tour?

Seeing Maxine Gardner, world's sexiest rock star, again?

Jade gritted her teeth, attributing that final thought to Lottie, in whose voice it had been said in her head. She wondered how many minutes it would be before her best friend found an excuse to call so she could introduce herself via video chat to her idol. It would be a miracle if the super-fan made it a full hour. Jade wished she'd been able to place a wager on it with someone. She'd have cleaned up so much her winnings would've made the tour money pale in comparison.

Oh, right. The tour.

Now that this tour thing was real, she needed to stay levelheaded. If she couldn't, she feared she'd ruin the entirety of the experience by doing something embarrassing, like tripping over her drum kit and gashing her forehead open.

Stay cool, Jade.

She picked up her favorite acoustic guitar, playing again, because her mind worked best when engaged with music.

Footsteps descended, and her fingers slipped, flubbing the chord progression.

Max stepped through the low-ceilinged basement door, grasping a carrier filled with coffees. Her gaze landed on Jade, sprawled on the couch with the guitar in her lap, sharp and assessing. "I see Grace's legacy extends past drums."

"Um, yeah. We worked our way through most of the basics. Drums, guitar, bass, ukulele, banjo, though I'm not proficient on the latter. Piano, which I love, but I have zero interest in playing for anything more than fun."

"Jesus, you're more talented than I am. Also, more talented than at least sixty percent of the musicians I know." Max's nose crinkled. "Please tell me you have a horrible singing voice."

"Atrocious." A lie. She sang soprano and had studied with an instructor enough to keep pitch and have smooth transitions. She might never be a superstar, but being able to stay in key went a long way.

"Thank God." Max set the coffees down on a side table. Today, she was wearing an oversized black T-shirt with the neck cut out so it slunk down to show off the ink Max had on her collarbone and one slim shoulder, as well as an occasional shadowed hint of breasts. Tight jeans in a dark wash, black boots, and a black leather wristband completed the look.

The entire ensemble left Jade searching for some-place else to look, feeling an odd sensation, which she blamed Lottie for. Her bestie had brought to Jade's attention that Max was actually attractive. Not simply the devil Jade had imagined, given the trash talk she'd heard about her for so many years from her mom and aunt.

"Where's Cindy?"

"Not here yet."

"It's not like her to be late."

"You're an hour early."

"I am?" Max looked at her phone and made a face. "I came straight from the airport, but... I can go to my rental if you need more time to—" She finished the statement with a helpless shrug.

"Don't worry about it." Jade's pulse was as light and fast as a hummingbird's wings. She was dying to start rehearsals, if only to calm herself down. She motioned to the coffees because the best thing for anxiety was definitely a jolt of caffeine, said no one ever. "Is one of those for me?"

"No," Max said without a hint of a smile. She leveled her eyes onto Jade's. "It's my big secret, my addiction to coffee. I've been to treatment programs and everything, but at this point, I fear it's too set to ever break."

"I didn't—"

"I'm just pulling your leg," Max said in a deadpan tone. "Take your pick. They're all the same."

Jade let out a nervous titter, and it wasn't like she was the type to act that way. She didn't know what it was about Max that made her feel like a giddy teenager, but it was annoying as hell. She was in the company of a woman who'd had an established music career since Jade was in diapers.

Jade chose a cup from the carrier. "Thanks. I have some here, but it's a generic roast. Nothing to be excited about."

Max sat on a nearby chair, her large cup cradled between both hands. "Don't let me stop you from playing. There's nothing I like better than listening to good music."

Flustered, Jade shook her head. "I was just passing the time. It's really nothing special—" She made to put the guitar to the side, but Max protested.

"No, don't stop. Play something for me. Whatever it was you were working on before I came down. What was it?"

Heat prickled at Jade's cheeks. "Songs: Ohia. You know, Jason Molina?"

"Fuck yeah, I know it."

Jade still hesitated. She was decent on guitar. It was as familiar as her drum kit. If it had been anyone else asking her to play, she would've launched right in. Music was like food—best when shared.

But sharing it was also intimate, and Jade was a bit worried she'd throw up. Or completely botch the song and *then* throw up.

On the other hand, if she didn't play, she'd have to talk. Somehow that felt even more intimidating. Now that Max wasn't the monster Jade had imagined, relating to plain ol' Max, a woman with real thoughts and feelings, seemed a hell of a lot harder than Jade had expected.

At times like these, music was always the easiest answer.

C sharp to E, B, and return to C sharp. Her fingers picked at the individual notes within the chords. The beginning was soothing, a slow lull into the intro lyrics.

She missed a note when Max began to sing. Molina sang in a tenor range that was like listening to a neighbor belt out at church. Though the lyrics weren't in any hymnal, that was for certain. Max's gravel-laced range was mezzo-soprano and lent itself well to the song, turning the lyrics into something husky and full of longing.

Once she recovered from the surprise, Jade sank into the song. She watched Max's foot tap, setting out the beat. Not that Jade needed it, but it helped her sync with Max's pacing.

The end of the song was rapidly approaching, and

Jade was so lost to the music she began to sing, alternating with Max and adjusting her own soprano voice to meet the lower pitch.

Finally, the last notes were plucked. She lightly set her fingers on the strings, cutting off their remaining vibrations.

"Damn it," Max exclaimed.

"What?" Jade blinked herself out of her musical haze, uncertain what had gone wrong.

"You said you were a terrible singer," Max complained but with a broad smile that said she was joking. Jade thought there was even something akin to admiration in the older woman's features. "You're really good at harmonizing."

Jade shrugged, sheepish, her eyes on Max's fingers as they rested on the guitar strings. "Confession time... I took voice lessons."

Max sighed. "Of course, you did. I was lucky as hell at fifteen to get away with five chords. I didn't branch out until I was eighteen, and even then, I stuck to the six strings. I can play bass if I have to, but it will never be my first choice."

They were talking about music, but somehow, the conversation was tipping into an intimacy Jade wasn't prepared for. Max wasn't exactly the enemy, but Jade knew enough not to trust her entirely. Being on friendly terms with her was one thing. They were bandmates now. But becoming real friends was a danger. How much would it have hurt her mom to see? She didn't want to answer that.

Jade gripped the guitar to hide her trembling hands and to stick to what she knew best. "The songs y'all were playing back then didn't need serious chord progressions. That was the whole point. Male bands were playing absolute bare-bones punk at the time, yet the expectations for girl groups was full-range, frilly songs. You were leveling the playing field."

Delight twinkled in Max's eyes. "I wouldn't say we were leveling the playing field. In my cocky youth, I wanted to burn it down."

"There was that time you threatened to throw a Molotov cocktail into the pit because men were jeering." Jade smiled as she remembered one of the few stories her mother had shared.

Max's laugh came in a rush, a waterfall of mirth Jade wanted to bathe in. "One, it was an airplane bottle. It wouldn't have done much damage. Two, did your mom tell you that?"

This was the tricky bit. This particular story had been shared with her, but Grace had kept most of the wild ones well-guarded. She'd relent if Jade pestered, parsing out just enough of her past to whet an appetite rather than satisfy. Most of Jade's knowledge came from the internet and had occasionally been verified by Lottie, the Matchstick Girl's super fan. Right now, Jade wanted every drop of information she could get.

"Mom didn't share much. She didn't want to focus on that part of her life."

Something dark flitted over Max's face. "I suppose I understand that desire. It wasn't particularly glamorous. But we weren't all VH1 *Behind the Music* unhinged, you know. Hell, we only really toured a handful of years before the band broke up." There was bitterness there, hovering behind the words.

Odd, considering Max had been the reason for the band's demise. It wasn't like her career was hurting, either. Could it be that she harbored regrets?

Eager to change the subject, Jade said, "I'll text Cindy to let her know you're here."

"Oh, don't bother her, considering I rudely showed up early."

"I suppose we could go upstairs and watch TV," Jade suggested, feeling like an idiot for her lack of hosting skills. Staying in the music room and getting to know the real Max seemed more dangerous.

Max appeared to consider the idea. "Are you a fan of *The Floor is Lava*?"

"You *watch* that?"

"Heck yeah, I do! I love it when they replay people's faces as they eat it and slowly slide into that nasty red liquid."

Jade shook her head. "I don't know how that makes me feel. Like maybe you lost a cool point or two."

Max's hand flew to her chest, over her heart. "Ouch! You're ruthless. Grace was that way, too."

"That we can agree on. Mom wasn't one for padding the edges."

There was a moment, stiff as a starched shirt with memory. The older woman shook her head, sending her blonde hair into spikes.

"TV's out. Let's play instead. May I?" Max gestured to the other instruments waiting in the basement. Jade licked her lips before nodding. Somehow, each new thing with Max shook her. Like she'd never be able to accept this was really happening. She was enjoying herself. Max wasn't the evil harpy she'd expected.

Max chose another acoustic guitar, a Martin D-42. Its sound was so sumptuous that simply being tuned seemed to resonate through the air. "Shit, this is gorgeous," Max muttered, stroking the curved shape in appreciation.

They sat close enough their knees kept brushing, and Jade had to twist toward the woman to keep from knocking her with the neck. The space between them crackled with possibilities, but what did that mean?

It *had* to be all in Jade's head. They were two music nerds geeking out over cool equipment.

Max strummed the opening chords of one of the Matchstick Girl's hits, "Sand in My Hands." Immediately, Jade knew how to fall in, riffing on the baseline as a rhythm guitar. Her foot instinctually began to tap so that her knee and thigh pressed and rubbed against Max's.

The music saved her from making a complete,

gawking mess of herself. It was comfort, a foundation she could always trust to keep her from toppling over. She didn't know what in the hell was going on in her head, but she knew music.

The other woman nodded in appreciation, her gaze locked on Jade's as they found ease in the song. When Max began to sing, Jade was ready for it. She shut her eyes and fell into the husky voice, the press of steel strings into calloused fingertips, and the sounds that made her whole.

It was different from playing with her mother, or Cindy, or occasionally Cindy's students. There was a trust in the air that allowed her to relax into the song instead of eyeing the other person to make sure they stayed in time.

At the chorus, she sang, weaving her voice in with Max's, the crispness of her high notes straddling Max's raspy lower ones. They sounded so fucking good together. Better than singing to the music streaming in her car.

The final chorus finished, and Jade carefully pared down the rhythm guitar so that the last notes were plucked by Max, the resonance of the guitar filling her like sultry smoke.

Jade opened her eyes to discover Max's body leaning toward hers. Blue eyes smoldered in such a way that Jade's breath hitched. Her mouth parted. The flow of the song had made her heady, and a woozy heat hummed in every corner of her body. Max's resonance seemed to remain there, and Jade found herself hungry for more. Of what, she couldn't say.

"Wow," Max managed before blinking several times and leaning back a bit too fast.

"Yeah," Jade added, unsure what exactly Max was wowing. Her own body was in a deep state of *wow*, culminating in a throb between her legs, and that simply was never going to happen. Not with the woman her mother had gone to the grave without fully being able to forgive for the heartbreak she'd caused. It would be wrong on too many levels to count.

CHAPTER SEVEN

"Okay," Max managed to say, mopping her brow with a bandana as the final chord of the song died away. "I think that's enough for today."

"Enough for this *week*," Cindy corrected, looking dead on her feet. "It's Friday night and Memorial Day weekend. I want my three days off."

"Are you sure we don't need to run that last one again?" Jade, coated in sweat, with wild eyes and wilder hair, looked just as eager to play as she'd been three hours before.

Like she'd been for every day of practice so far, for almost five weeks straight.

Warmth flared in Max's core, feeling that connection with a fellow musician. One who seemed to know her every thought before she did. It would be a lie for

Max to say that making music with Jade was better than sex.

But it wasn't that far off, either.

Max tamped down the part of her that wanted to respond to Jade's enthusiasm with a raucous *hell yeah, let's go again!* Max was used to grueling rehearsal times and needing to be able to stand and play her best for hours on end. The past week had been a lot, even for her, but Cindy was flagging, and Max knew she needed to respect that. Too many bands let stress tear them apart. She was in a band again, and if one bandmate was struggling, it meant they all took a break.

"Honestly, we've gotten through way more than I thought we would," Max said as much for her own benefit as the others. "We've made it through the live arrangements of all fifteen songs that will make up our seventy-five-minute set, plus a song for the encore. We sound fabulous."

"You're being generous." Cindy guzzled water from a bottle, wincing in pain. "I didn't think I'd forgotten as much as I had."

"Are you kidding me? I'm shocked we're grooving this well together." Max wasn't lying, although she would have if it'd been necessary. She had strict orders from Skip to keep Cindy happy at all costs. Her continued participation was the lynchpin of the entire tour. If she walked, Jade would, too, and everything would collapse. *No pressure or anything.*

Cindy, always the hypercritical one, didn't look

convinced. "The music isn't coming back to me as seamlessly as I'd hoped."

"We have a bit more time to practice before we head into rehearsals and promo," Max said gently. Her buzz from playing was still burning inside her, but she'd forgotten how effectively Cindy could operate as a fire extinguisher. "Would you feel better if we ran through the last song again before we break for the night?"

Jade perked up, her sticks still in motion, though silently striking air. "Totally. I can practice whenever."

Cindy shot Jade a wry smile. "Not all of us have your youthful endurance."

An impulse had Max saying, "Hold on there. I'm still fine," as if it was critical she not be lumped in with *non*-youths. It wasn't a lie. Max was tired, sure, because she was human. But this was her job. She could press on.

"Yeah, yeah," Cindy muttered, glaring. "Sure."

"Don't act like an old lady." Jade gently chided her aunt. "I know you better than most. You're loving this."

"What I'm loving is the weekend," Cindy countered. "I'll need all of the days off to recover. No extra anything."

"Sure," Jade agreed. "Why don't we finish the session playing your favorite song? End on a high."

"Which one would that be?" Cindy asked, almost as if it was a test for her niece.

"The hit you wrote, naturally," Jade said with a smug smile.

"Oh, that one." Cindy tried to sound bored, but there was an extra pep in the way her fingers tickled the keyboard. "I guess we can do that one if you really want to."

Max began strumming her guitar, glad to see Cindy had perked up. Despite it having been years since Max had played this particular selection, it sounded great. Even picky Cindy seemed pleased. As the song ended, the sound of clapping came from the stairs.

Max whirled in the direction of the noise, adrenaline shooting through her. It took a moment for her brain to register who the guy with the artfully scraggly hair and salt-and-pepper beard actually was. "Skip?"

Cindy's nose wrinkled like she'd caught a whiff of something foul. "Oh. It's you."

Ignoring her, the manager raised a hand in greeting. "Sorry to barge in on you, ladies."

"How *did* you get in?" Jade asked, her eyes bugging out. Max could hardly blame her, considering she'd never met the man before, and he was currently standing inside her house.

"I tried ringing and knocking, but I don't think you could hear me from down here. Luckily, the door was unlocked."

Jade whipped her head toward Cindy, who had been the last to arrive. Cindy responded with an *oops* expression.

"Now that we've determined how you got in, maybe you could tell us why you're here. A week early." Max fought to keep an even tone despite her irritation that he would drop in like this, unannounced, when he'd promised her space to pull the band together before his visit.

"Hey, I was too excited to stay away any longer and had to see how it's going."

Max nodded. "I see." She saw through him. He was there to check on his investment.

"I'm glad I did. This tour will be killer if that's how well you guys play together. Where are my manners?" He turned toward Jade, a look of fake modesty settling over his usually shark-like features. "I'm Skip Boswell, Max's manager. Yours too now, I guess." His eyes raked over Jade, making Max want to rip his head off, even though there was nothing objectively inappropriate in his manner. "Wow. You're the spitting image of your mother. Max didn't exaggerate one bit."

"Uh, thank you. Can I get you something to drink or anything?" Jade looked every bit as uncomfortable with Skip's visit as Max felt, but she was handling it with more decorum than Max would've been able to muster at the same age. Or even now.

"You ladies sound amazing. I love your vibe together. One hundred and ten percent better than I thought you'd be at this point. Although, frankly, Cindy, I wasn't expecting you to look so… *suburban*." The word itself wasn't insulting, but his tone more than made up for that. Max was ready to escort him out, even if she'd had a similar reaction to Cindy's appearance when she'd first seen her.

"I see you haven't changed much." Cindy crossed her arms over her chest, planting her feet for a battle. At least, Max was confident Cindy could hold her own.

"Relax. It's nothing we can't handle. We just need you to look like that girl again." He jerked his chin to the poster behind them, an original Matchstick Girls concert poster from 1997. It showcased a Cindy that was forty pounds slimmer and wearing a miniskirt. "That's all."

"That's all?" Daggers shot from Cindy's eyes. "If you want me to look like that again, I hope you have a time machine."

"I've got something even better." He plastered on a chewing gum commercial smile. "Have you ever heard of a Luxury Wellness Resort?"

"I don't think so." It was worth noting how Cindy's entire demeanor shifted at the words *luxury* and *resort*.

"All the top stars go to them," Skip explained. "Two weeks, total immersion in fitness, nutrition, and stress relief. How do you think Cate Blanchett got in shape for her most recent movie?"

"Cate Blanchett?" Cindy was seeing stars, for sure, of the Hollywood variety.

"There's a place in Malibu. Very exclusive. I'm

booking you in there until rehearsals begin in LA, starting tomorrow."

"That's more than two weeks." Cindy's jaw dropped, and Jade couldn't blame her. Talk about being sideswiped. "What about practice? I still have a life and a business to run. I can't leave early when I'll already be away for so long."

"At the resort, you'll have your own personal chef, facials, a trainer, daily massages—"

"Daily?" Cindy's expression flickered, and Max could see her teetering on the edge of giving in.

Skip nodded. "Twenty-four seven of absolute pampering, and they'll give you exercises and a meal plan and everything. You'll come out looking like a super model."

"That sounds… lovely."

Max wanted badly to remind her about the three-day weekend she'd been griping about. But being pampered apparently beat out barbecuing.

"You deserve it. As for practice, that's the other reason I stopped by. Max and Jade, there's been a change of plans. Practice is done. You two are heading to Austin in the morning for an in-studio interview and jam session. My marketing consultant tells me Matchstick songs are the hottest thing with Gen Zers right now, and I was able to book you on the college radio station at UT. It'll be great publicity. I'll text you the details. Okay, I gotta scram. Cindy, my assistant will be in touch with the deets on the spa, but I'm sure we can get you in by tomorrow. Just need to pull some strings. Bye, ladies."

Max was pretty sure Skip hadn't paused even once to take a breath while imparting any of that news, and he sure as hell hadn't wanted to stick around long enough for a reaction. Although, frankly, she wasn't sure how to react. Cindy was being sent to a fancy boot camp? She and Jade were being shipped off to Austin with less than twenty-four hours' notice? Skip was, she knew, an expert in asking forgiveness, because he didn't give a shit about permission.

After the coast was clear, Max and Cindy exchanged a look that said yes, they'd experienced this before.

"What the hell just happened?" Jade asked, looking ashen.

"Same old Skip. He waltzes into town, blows things up, and then skedaddles without getting his hands dirty," Cindy muttered, tugging at her jeans in a self-conscious way Max couldn't recall seeing before. "Who'll play the keyboard if you two get to LA before this fat camp Skip's sending me to is over?"

"That's not what it is at all, Cindy," Max rushed to reassure her, wishing Skip would pop back in so she could kick him in the nuts. "Skip's an ass."

"But the songs," Cindy pressed. "Jade hasn't played some of the later ones. She's going to need all the practice she can get."

"Lottie could do it," Jade suggested, not looking overly convinced. "She's a big fan and knows every song. In fact, she nearly hopped on a plane to come out here and meet you when she found out about all this."

"Sounds perfect," Max said, wondering who Lottie was and what Jade's hesitation was.

Jade bit her lip. "I'm not sure. She thinks you're really hot and might make it weird with her excitement."

"Me?" Max didn't know how to begin processing this information or if she even wanted to. A woman, a young one at that if she was the same age as Jade, found Max attractive? There were way too many landmines.

Cindy snorted. "It's sure as hell not me Lottie has a crush on. But I can vouch for her musical skills. If she's willing to help, go for it."

"More than likely, you'll be in LA in time." Because Skip was determined but also cheap.

"Anyway, I'd better be off so I can get ready for this luxury whatever it was Skip called it."

"This is an interesting turn." Max scratched the back of her neck, uneasy. "I'd better get back to my place and pack for Austin."

"I'll see you in the morning," Jade said as Max headed up the stairs.

A trip alone with Jade? An interesting turn indeed.

THE HUM of the airplane was a drone that Max couldn't quite tune out. She'd never been able to sleep on planes, anyway, even if they were red-eyes. Most of her European and Asian appearances now had scheduled room for jet lag because she couldn't push through forty-eight hours of minimal sleep and still perform well anymore.

Jade, on the other hand, apparently had no issue sleeping on planes. The young woman had barely managed to stumble from the cab to the plane for their early flight. At one point, the TSA had asked Jade a question about her drumsticks, and Jade had mumbled that she needed them to stir her coffee.

Now, brown curls pulled in a high bun were nestled on Max's shoulder. Soft snores competed with the hum and buzz of flight and quiet conversations all around. Full, pink lips had fallen apart in sleep, a sensual and innocent image that Max was struggling not to study too closely.

Thank God Cindy had been shipped off to *how to become cool again* camp, which is what Max had started calling it every time Cindy started using the *F* word. Stupid Skip and his unattainable beauty standards.

Max could imagine exactly how pinched Cindy's

face would be at the sight of Jade's head tucked into Max's shoulder nook. It wasn't like Max could be blamed, and technically, Cindy had said Jade should be protected at all costs. Wasn't it better for Jade to be curled up with Max instead of some stranger who might take advantage of the situation? Max wouldn't ever cross that line.

She did wonder, though, how Jade looked so peaceful. A shoulder couldn't be *that* comfortable, particularly hers, since Max was aware of the sharp boniness of her frame. Part genetics and part lifestyle, Max was not Hollywood slim but the kind of muscled cut of Sheryl Crow. Her abs were the product of belting out songs on stage for years, not crunches. The only places she put on weight were her hips and ass, and fortunately, dancing on stage and cutting down on junk food had helped her to continue to shimmy into her skinny jeans.

Skip had gotten Max into Pilates, and he threatened hiring a personal trainer. There was nothing more punk rock than a woman in yoga pants struggling to maintain the figure of her youth. Yeah, right.

She was still able to keep up appearances with only the smallest of compromises. And three-hundred-dollar face creams.

Jade murmured in her sleep, a sweet and indecipherable tangle of sounds. Without thinking, Max reached and tucked some errant curls from Jade's bun behind her ear. A thrill accompanied the touch, followed by a swallow of guilt that scalded like too-hot coffee.

Sighing, she peered out the window. They were cruising above the clouds. While the promoters hadn't paid for first class tickets, they had at least paid for a direct flight to Austin, skipping the madness of a changeover in Atlanta.

At one point, the Atlanta airport had felt like a second home. That's when Max had doubled down, asking to go back to tour buses as much as possible over flying.

The seat belt light dinged on, and the pilot began his monotone info dump of how much longer the flight would be, the weather, the...

Max tuned it out.

Instead, she opened her phone and grimaced as she paid an exorbitant amount for some Wi-Fi, needing the distraction of the internet. It was embarrassing and vain, but she had a google alert set up for her name. A new article popped up.

She scrolled through, skimming. There were the normal references to the Matchstick Girls, catching up new readers on their history, which, Max wanted to gripe, felt deeply hyperbolized. Sometimes she struggled to remember that 1994 was nearly thirty years ago.

That time was still so rich in her mind. The colors, the clothes, the music... It all came back in vivid detail when she thought about it.

Jade shifted in her sleep, turning into Max, a hand flopping onto Max's stomach. Her middle tightened on instinct at the touch, her skin flaring alive with nerves. She was officially the world's most uncomfortable teddy bear, all bony shoulders and stiff, upright position created by too-small airplane seats.

All of Max's attention was on that hand, the press of it searing through her T-shirt.

Jade had chosen to wear ripped jeans and an oversized plaid shirt tied off at the waist to showcase an hourglass figure. Honestly, Jade's clothing choices would have made her just as at home in the nineties as they did now.

Only, Max supposed, it was now considered retro. The way bellbottoms had been for her generation. Like when she'd rolled into a restaurant back then and they'd be playing the Bee Gees, making Max's parents cringe. Now those same restaurants probably played TLC or No Doubt in that same retro nod.

Fuck. That was a depressing connection.

Max pressed her head firmly back into the headrest of her seat, eyes squeezed shut. Recently the reminders of how much time had passed kept slamming into her like ocean waves on a windy day.

How the hell am I forty-two?

She didn't *feel* forty-something. Her thirties hadn't felt any different from her twenties, which had only differed from her teens in that she could legally purchase alcohol and rent hotel rooms without a guardian. It had been a steady life of making music and playing shows. The time had passed, sure, but she felt the same as she always had.

There was a spot of turbulence, the kind of gut-flopping drop that made every passenger panic for a moment. Max had experienced enough of them to *not* lose her cool, except this time was different. The drop had shifted Jade's hand from her stomach to a mere inch above the apex of Max's thighs.

She couldn't deny the immediate squeeze between her legs, the rush of liquid heat. Max's cheeks burned. She should wake Jade. God, she should wake her.

If she did, though, the awkwardness would be bear-sized and just as bristled. If she waited, perhaps the hand would move back to relative safety of its own accord.

Exhaling, she went back to the article, praying for a distraction. It didn't work out as planned, as the author quickly shifted focus to Jade, speculating that excitement about Grace Weathers' daughter was the reason for the uptick in ticket sales. Max's brow furrowed. Surely, she'd be a draw, too. She was, after all, the original lead singer. Her name came first on the fucking Wikipedia page. Max was the one who'd since made over ten solo albums.

Jade was Grace's daughter. The end. Was she truly the biggest reason people would come to see the show?

That's my ego talking.

Max reached her free hand up to scrub her face. She'd been as shocked to see Jade all grown-up and eager to join the band as the person who'd written the article seemed to be. That was a *good* thing. Jade's relationship to Grace, her talent... it was what was going to sell tickets, not just to older fans who'd be there for the original group but maybe newer ones as well.

That kind of exposure could be great for Max. A new audience would certainly elate Skip and make securing a new record deal after the tour easier, forestalling the threat of the state fair circuit for a few years, at least. Hopefully, by then, Max's nest egg would allow her to retire and not become that artist who appeared at a Taste of Durham, where attendees tried to place the singer while eating a fried Snickers on a stick.

So long as Max could keep some of the spotlight on her.

"What're you reading?"

Max startled at the sleep-addled question. Particularly as Jade hadn't moved from her position, curled into a Max-pillow.

"The buzz surrounding the upcoming tour. It's a good report." She waited for Jade's response, some acute reaction to their closeness and the hand resting in such a personal place.

"Mmmkay." Jade burrowed in deeper, and Max shook her head, unable to understand how someone could sleep so soundly. Had Jade been awake enough to realize how close they were? Close enough to smell each other's shampoos and share body heat?

The hand did snake back up, moving in an agonizingly sensitive arc along Max's body before being tucked under Jade's chin. *Jesus.*

There was another announcement from the pilot. Time to power down the Wi-Fi and electronics. Max didn't need to be told twice. She shut off her phone and tried to relax, preparing for the stomach-lifting sensation of the plane's descent.

Her public persona was built firmly on a foundation of "I don't give a shit." Which meant she couldn't let herself get caught up in silly jealousy. It had been *one* article. Her reputation also relied heavily on her sexuality remaining vague. Jade's current position was making Max feel anything but subtle.

There was a hefty bump of turbulence and a *lurch* as the plane dropped a smidge. Jade didn't rouse in the least.

Max gripped the armrest on the side that wasn't being overtaken by Jade's sleeping form. Honestly, she should have woken her up. Most likely Jade would be mortified and apologetic for hours once she realized she'd spent the entire flight clinging to Max.

But it had been... nice, in an oh-so-wrong way.

Jade's shampoo had some generic floral scent that gravitated toward "fresh" or "waterfall" or something. Her warmth helped chase away the stale air chill of the plane. It was comforting, and hadn't Max started this endeavor wanting the closeness of a band again? Lone-liness was the bane of celebrity.

This was the sort of thing Grace or Cindy would've done all those years ago. It meant nothing then, and it didn't mean anything now.

The plane was descending, the noise of the wind outside cranking up a notch. The tables secured to the backs of seats rattled, and some of the passengers around her had paled.

Just before the plane touched down, Jade jolted up, the back of her hand swiping away some drool. Horri-fied eyes turned to Max, and sure enough, she knew Jade would be apologizing.

"Stop right there," Max said, voice huskier than she'd intended. There was a chill along the side where Jade had snuggled, and she missed the warmth. "You needed the rest. It's smart to learn how to get it where you can. I would have woken you up if it bothered me, and if you say you're sorry even once, I won't take you to my favorite barbecue joint."

Jade's mouth opened, shut, opened again, and then pulled into a hesitant smile. "Yeah, okay."

Soon enough, they settled in amongst the mob around the carousel that was groaning as it puked out suitcases onto a conveyor belt. Right when sweat started to trickle down Max's back, their guitar cases slumped out and onto the belt, sneaking around until she and Jade could grab them. Max pointed to a driver who was waiting for them with a sign, their names scrawled in Sharpie.

There was no time to breathe. He'd take them straight from the airport to the radio station.

The show was, in its own way, already on the road.

CHAPTER EIGHT

P ublicity. Just the word made Jade feel as if she'd been dropped into a tank full of tarantulas. With Cindy at boot camp, now Jade had to do half of the talking in the interview.

Her stomach roiled and threatened to revolt.

Max leaned over and stage-whispered, "You look ready to bolt. Or puke."

The wet heat of her breath sent a shiver trickling down Jade's spine. "I'm going to blow this and also possibly chunks."

They were sitting in the studio, waiting to be interviewed on air. It was a college radio station in Texas, something Max had assured Jade would be a great introduction to what was to come.

"You really won't. Skip approves questions ahead of time. What we practiced is what they'll ask. You'll be fine. Just be yourself."

"Yeah, that's what I'm worried about."

Max rolled her eyes dramatically, but it seemed to contain support, mollifying Jade somewhat. Until another thought struck like a gong to the side of the head, blurring her vision. "What if they go off script?"

"Then I'll handle it." Max was all smooth confidence, and Jade forced herself to remember Max had been doing things like this for longer than Jade's first step as a baby. Max would have Jade's back, and if she didn't, then it'd be the proof Jade needed about whether or not to trust Max, because Jade's mind swung back and forth more than a swing on an elementary playground during lunch recess.

Jade's leg bounced up and down. She wished she had a pair of sticks in her hands, even if she didn't have drums to play. The smooth wood and familiar grip would soothe her; she was certain. *Next time.*

There were going to be many next times, assuming she didn't screw this one up. The tour would begin at the end of June, but given how this interview opportunity sprung up out of nowhere, Jade assumed Skip would do it again and again and again. Jade didn't know much about tours, but she'd been told a battery of press to create hype and publicity was a necessary evil, especially in today's world, where fans wanted access to their favorite singers all the time thanks to the rise of social media, which Jade enjoyed until right about now.

"I don't know how you do this all the time," Jade

complained, trying to still her leg. Her fingers picked up the pace, drumming against her knee instead. "We haven't started, and I'm already exhausted."

"Now you really sound like Grace." Max said it gently, not like an attack. "She'd start the tours already beat."

"Okay, maybe exhausted isn't the right word. Torn? I'm excited about the rest of it, just not the *talk to people* part. Thinking about it is what makes me want to nap for hours."

"I mean I'm pretty sure the people part was what she hated most. I'm confident once you get a feel for it, though, you'll do great. Grace never got a feel for it. Or if she did, that feeling was straight animosity. Fortunately, her growling at interviewers often added to our mystique."

"She didn't!"

Max chuckled. "Oh, definitely. Like a feral animal. Actually, I always looked forward to her snarling. Maybe you can do that if they catch you off guard."

The story did the trick. Jade was too busy trying to imagine her mom's gnashing teeth directed at some poor schmuck to think about what she was about to do. It wasn't hard to picture. Grace often had a lip curled whenever the PTA contacted her for bake sales and field trips.

When one of the producers came and waved them in, Jade was still laughing inside, her anxiety unspooling.

Max had somehow known the perfect way to get Jade out of her own head.

The recording room was smaller than she'd expected and *hot*. The sticky feel of unmoving air and the smell of sweat and coffee assaulted her. In a corner, there was a guitar set up and ready. Beside it was a bongo drum, a tambourine, and a kazoo.

What the fuck had she gotten herself into?

Max pointed to a swivel chair in front of a microphone. Jade sank into it. Max sat next to her, confident and in her element. While the radio hosts, whose names Jade had already forgotten, welcomed them, Max took a set of headphones and slid them over Jade's ears.

Fingertips brushed through strands of hair and the casualness of the movement stole Jade's breath.

Max fit her own headset on and gave Jade a quick *you got this* wink. Heat began to smolder in Jade's stomach, having nothing to do with nerves or ambient air temperature. Not for the first time, and it should be the last. Jade had too much riding on this tour to give in to whatever the fuck she sometimes experienced around the hot rock star.

Dammit, Lottie!

The headsets made everything sharper. The two men—both college students—spoke. "This is going to be great," one said. It was a bit loud but crisp in Jade's ears.

"Try the microphone." The other pointed.

She leaned forward, lips almost pressing the soft black foam bulb. "Like this?"

The three people around her winced. Max pointed to the distance between her mouth and the mic. It was an easy foot at least. "You don't need to lean in. They're set to pick us up from here."

"Oh." Jade blushed. "Sorry."

The men smiled and gave her a thumbs-up. "We're going live in a minute. Are you ready?"

Jade sighed. "No."

"Try not to sigh," one offered. "Or move your chair too much. The mics will pick up a lot. Our sound engineer can work out some of it, but the less extra noise we make, the better."

Jesus. She was going to screw this up. Suddenly afraid to move, speak, or even breathe wrong, Jade held herself tightly enough her shoulders pinched. Someone outside the booth began a countdown in her headphones. Her heart raced just ahead of the "Five... four... three..."

There was a hand gesture, and the radio jockeys launched in. "Good morning, folks. You've tuned into..."

Blood whooshed in Jade's ears, and it took Max's foot nudging hers under the table to keep her tethered to the moment. Max left her leg there, a warm heat pressing into Jade's calf. The pressure let Jade know she wasn't alone. She had someone with her who'd keep her on track.

Leaning into the touch, she let herself open to the moment. That is, until the questions veered from the professional to the personal.

"So, Max, you were last seen spending time with Kirk Evans of Negative Ghostwriter. There was lots of speculation that the two of you got close on that tour. Will he be joining you on this one?"

Jade vaguely recalled Lottie mentioning that news, certain it was pure speculation. Now that she'd spent time with Max, she wasn't sure who was right—Lottie or the tabloids. Her leg burned where it was pressed against Max's, and she discovered she was holding her breath as she waited for Max's answer.

"I've never talked about my private life, and I'm not going to start now," Max teased, managing to sound flirty and suggestive without saying much at all. "Kirk's a phenomenal musician. Full stop."

The two jockeys didn't look surprised or disappointed. Jade was, though. Why would Max be so ambiguous? Especially now?

"What about you, Jade? Got a special fella cheering you on?"

Her nose scrunched. "No 'fellas' ever and currently no lady, either. I'm here to play music."

Once more the hosts of the show rolled with the lack of information. "Makes sense," one said before nodding to the instruments. "Speaking of music, would you mind playing a bit?"

"Sure," Max said before waiting for the engineer

to signal through the window that it was safe to move. She quickly handed Jade the percussion pieces before sliding the acoustic guitar's strap over her neck. One strum showed it was already in tune.

She looked to Jade, and a spike of something like anticipation pierced Jade's chest. Jade's hands moved on instinct, counting them off. The music fell into place, wrapping them up in a bubble so perfect it blocked all other distractions out. It was just Maxine, Jade, and the music in a booth that was suddenly feeling like a sauna.

Maxine's cheeks were flushed and Jade's pulse a staccato beat by the time the final note faded.

"Wow!" One of the jockeys said, leaning back in his chair. "That was awesome."

"The two of you sound like you've been playing together for years!" added the other. "Really well done!"

Jade and Max moved away from the instruments and back to their seats, pulling the headphones on again. "Thanks," Max said in her smokiest voice. "Jade is Grace's protege. I suppose in a way we *have* been playing together for years."

This time Jade wasn't stiff when the attention was on her. Max's calf moved back into place, nestled close. It was no longer needed, but Jade welcomed the pressure and support.

"How old were you when you began to learn

drums?" the man with darker hair, peeking from under a baseball hat, asked.

"Three," Jade answered confidently. "My mom gave me lots of rhythm toys before that, but three was when she put sticks in my hand. She turned it into a call and response game, where she'd play something on a table, or a chair, or whatever, and I had to copy her. It was great."

She'd worried, perhaps, that talking about Grace publicly would feel like a betrayal. Her mom valued privacy. But this didn't feel like airing her mother's laundry. It felt more like... celebrating the bond she'd had with her mother, keeping her memory alive. Besides, her mom had shaped Jade, for better or worse.

"That's incredible," the other said, not missing a beat. They reminded Jade a bit of Max and herself. The way they seemed to intuit how to fill the space, to keep the conversation moving. That's what playing with Max was like. "The news of your mother's passing really hit us hard at the station."

It wasn't a question, and Jade had been prepared for this. It was impossible to do a tribute tour without talking about who was being honored.

"That's nice to hear," she said without flinching. "I grew up with my mother's music, not just because she was my teacher, but because I found her album collection and fell in love with her eclectic taste. She loved everything from classical to world music and instilled that passion in me. I think you can see that in the Matchstick Girls. They pushed the envelope of what it meant to be women *and* musicians. It's a privilege to be able to tour in place of my mom, my hero."

That was what Skip had instructed. Mention a story about her mom and then pivot the discussion back to the tour. Remind people it was a once-in-a-lifetime opportunity to hear them play.

"The ticket sales caught everyone by surprise," the other jockey, his shirt a painfully bright orange, said. "Twenty-eight shows in eight weeks. It all came together so quickly. I heard LA and New York are already sold out. Though there's been some controversy about the price of the tickets. After all, when the band started, you were playing shows for five dollars a ticket. Now, some of the seats in LA were going for hundreds. What's the reasoning behind it?"

Skip had told Max and Jade the news earlier, but it still made her dizzy to hear it. LA had sold out in six hours. New York in fourteen. The other cities were still selling, but the tickets were going fast.

Jade also heard what the jockeys were saying. "As someone in their twenties, I totally get where you're coming from. Most of the shows I go to are in small clubs and are, like, twenty dollars tops. And the Matchstick Girls weren't large venue famous in the nineties. But I feel like you're suggesting this is selling out. Is that right?"

They blushed and looked at each other. "Maybe a bit."

Max tapped her with her foot under the table before leaning forward enough that Jade knew she'd take over. "I think it was fair for us to weigh our options. We could stay true to something we were trying to accomplish in the early nineties, which was to get our message out and fight against a patriarchal music scene. That meant accepting shitty pay at small venues because we were women, right?

"But now a few things are different. Our name and legacy are so much larger now than they were then. So the question is, do we accept getting paid shit again to 'not sell out' or do we demand to be paid what we're worth as women, as musicians, and as a band that helped influence the scene and open doors for other female-led bands?"

"Yeah, that's fair," one of the boys conceded, hands held in supplication for them, despite knowing the audience listening wouldn't see it. "I mean, my mom bought tickets for us for the New York show, insisting I needed it for my 'musical education.'" He let out a laugh. "She's going to die when she finds out I interviewed you two."

Jade wondered if it would bother Max to hear that his *mother* was the one excited about the tour. Just in case, she said, "You're lucky as hell. Max is a damned rock goddess, and we all need to soak up this experience while it lasts."

Smooth. Confident. Her pulse was steady and her answers heartfelt. She'd been so scared of saying something dumb or mispronouncing a word. But once in the seat, with the steadfast figure of Max by her side, it had come easily. Like Max had promised.

Reaching under the table, Jade took Max's hand and gave it a squeeze. Being on the show, feeling the praise from the DJs and the buzz from making music, Jade's confidence was skyrocketing.

Max squeezed her hand back.

After the engineer signaled the microphones were off, everyone stripped from their headsets and stood. Jade's shirt was damp, and she was eager to get out of the small room and breathe some fresh air. Before that could happen, the dark-haired host stopped them.

"Great interview. Thanks so much." Instead of his confident radio persona, this sounded a bit closer to gushing. Jade's chest swelled.

"What're y'all up to now?" the other asked.

Maxine said, "Going to eat," at the same time Jade asked, "What do you suggest?"

The weight of Maxine's surprised gaze felt heavy, and Jade resisted the urge to look at her feet.

"Well"—he reached up to take off his baseball cap and ruffle the hair underneath—"there aren't any good shows tonight, but I hear there's a DJ at Summit. It's going to be pretty sweet if you like that sort of thing."

As it happened, Jade loved dancing. The show

suddenly sounded like the perfect opportunity to get out and experience a new city.

Despite being taller, Jade had to walk quickly to keep up with Max's clipped strides. "Can we go?"

Max stopped when they were out of earshot. "Absolutely not. Cindy would *murder* me if I took you out late on the first night of what will be a very long couple of months."

At first, Jade started to flag, a history of resigning herself in the face of strong personalities having molded her. But this was her tour every bit as much as it was Max's and Cindy's. "I seem to recall we made a deal, and Cindy's getting to have her fun, so why shouldn't I?"

Max's lips pursed as if she wanted to clarify that Cindy's spa wasn't exactly "fun," so Jade pressed harder. "Please? I love dancing, and I've never been to Austin!"

The air froze, static, and she was certain she was about to hear a firm no.

"Maybe. Could I eat before making major decisions?"

Ha! A maybe was two steps away from a yes. Nodding, Jade flashed Max her most winning smile. It almost looked as if Max were blushing, but then the woman shoved open the door and stepped into the harsh city sunlight.

Steps and heart light, Jade was all too happy to follow.

CHAPTER NINE

Stepping outside, Max shielded her eyes from the blazing sun. This was the problem with anywhere in the South. It might not even be June yet, but it felt like summer already. She shrugged out of her blazer. Stomach growling, she'd take the sun's heat if it meant escaping the pressure to break one of Cindy's rules already.

Perhaps trying to butter her up, Jade patted her stomach. "Food please. I'm starving."

Max had to admit her body's demand for food was taking charge. It would also be easier to let Jade down when they weren't at risk of being low blood sugar hangry.

The ride Skip had hired for the day was waiting for them. Before the chauffeur could open the door, Jade was there, holding it open. Max's eyes narrowed. *I see what you're doing.* She slid into the air-conditioned back, sagging into the leather seats.

Once inside as well, Jade handed her a bottle of water. Yeah, the woman was coming on hard and strong, which were two traits Max found unbelievably sexy. But this was Jade, who was gorgeous and talented. She didn't need to be exhibiting more qualities Max desired. Not when Cindy had... how had she described it? Wrapped her in Bubble Wrap?

Max asked the driver to take them to Black's BBQ on Guadalupe. Food would distract her. *And bring me to my fucking senses.*

A woman gaped for all of a moment when Max and Jade walked in. Recognition blazed over her features, but she stayed professional, and Max made a mental note to offer an autograph before they left.

The hostess led them to a table near a window, as far removed from the crowded dining area as possible. It was a small table, the space underneath was tight enough their knees brushed each time they shifted. A gurgle in her stomach was the only thing more on her mind than the close proximity to Jade.

"I'm so hungry I could cry. I should've brought a snack on the plane." Jade's gaze devoured the menu.

"Would you have stayed awake for a snack?"

Pink blossomed on Jade's cheeks. "Probably not."

"Okay, this is my favorite spot in town. Do you trust me to order for you?" Max's fingers were drumming on her knee. Why was she so nervous? It was much-needed food after a long morning. It wasn't as if they were on a date. She was probably anxious over letting Jade down about going dancing. They were getting along so well.

"Sure, so long as we're not doing another spice-off. I enjoy tasting my food, not surviving the experience."

That wouldn't be difficult to avoid; Max wasn't sure her stomach had ever fully recovered from the level eleven fiasco.

A server came, and Max ordered for them. Shortly after, large plates arrived heaped with brisket, sausage, beans, slaw, and hush puppies teetering on it all.

She waited in anticipation and laughed in delight when Jade tried the brisket. The woman had pulled a face that wasn't entirely complimentary.

"It's definitely different from pork and vinegar," she said politely.

"Ah, yes. Welcome to the ongoing debate of who has the best barbecue. It's a battle with intense opinions and deep-seated resentments. For me, I prefer this and Memphis, but I will concede that there's a place in my heart for your pork and vinegar tastes as well."

Jade shot her a look that suggested Max was deeply wrong in not putting NC first, but she didn't pick up the debate. They ate, and it was amazing, so good in fact that conversation essentially stopped while they tucked in. That is, until Jade snuck in a quick, "I bet there's time to nap at the hotel before going out tonight."

Uh-oh.

Max leaned back, bracing her hands on her thighs. "About that. We really can't."

"We really, really can. I bet you could line up VIP entrances and everything. You're Maxine fucking Gardner."

Was Jade slathering it on thick as butter? Absolutely. Was it working? All too well. Max shifted uncomfortably in her chair. "That's all true, but it'll run late, and I'm beat. Surely, some sleep and HBO is just as much fun?"

Jade's face fell, and Max resisted a strong impulse to take her comment back and do anything to earn a winning smile again. Knowing she was at the root of the disappointment was painful. Max found wearing the "adult" pants in this particular situation uncomfortable.

They were Cindy's pants, so to speak, and they did not fit well at all.

"I can't believe you're going to side with Cindy on this," Jade said, her eyes flashing dangerously. "Should I remind you I'm twenty-seven? I don't actually need you to take me out. I can do it on my own. I'm not afraid of my aunt."

Oh, that clever girl. "I'm not afraid of her." Not entirely true, but Max had a badass reputation to uphold. "You're right. You could go by yourself."

She was also right about being twenty-seven. Grace had gotten pregnant her final year of high school. Her daughter wasn't that far from thirty, had a promising and reputable career waiting for her after this, and had asked to go dancing. Not snort coke off a stripper's butt cheek.

Jade looked to be gearing up to accept the challenge, but Max waved her off, changing her mind. "You win. But could we go to the hotel first? Can I at least be responsible enough to get the details before we hit the town?"

To her delight, Jade flashed another one of those smiles that made Max's tummy do flips. "Yes, totally. Hotel. Details. *Fun.*"

Max sighed dramatically, but inside there was a flicker of excitement. She hadn't been dancing since Kristy, a fling who loved clubs and being seen with a celebrity a bit more than Max had been comfortable with. That had been, God, almost a decade ago.

They paid, and Max signed a napkin for the hostess. And the waitress. And several other waitstaff, cooks, and customers, along with taking a dozen or so selfies with fans. Jade found herself being pulled into the photos as well, and Max tried not to laugh at the wide-eyed, *deer in headlights* pictures of Jade.

Leaving the restaurant took almost twenty minutes. By the time she was in the car, Max was wiped and desperate for clean sheets and a shower.

She was also in desperate need of a private moment to prepare herself for taking Jade out.

Rock star Maxine was totally on board with it. But Cindy was speaking with her again. Hell, she was willing to tour again, and Max's career was completely in the woman's well-manicured suburban hands. There was no doubt that if Cindy knew about the club, Max would be toast.

Maybe I can pretend to get food poisoning and get out of it.

She and Jade finally made it to the front desk of the hotel. Max pushed her sunglasses up to hold back her damp, frizzy hair. "We have reservations. Maxine Gardner and Jade Weathers."

The receptionist scanned her computer and asked for IDs, a requirement that had made it increasingly difficult over the years to utilize an assumed name. The strap of Max's duffel bag was digging painfully into her shoulder. But things checked out, and the receptionist slid over a small envelope containing two keys, a single room number on top.

Max paused.

The receptionist smiled, though it threatened to droop in confusion. "Is something wrong?" she asked hesitantly.

"Isn't there another room?"

Now the poor woman's brow furrowed, and she looked at the screen again. "No, I'm sorry. The reservation is for one room, two full beds. Is there a problem?"

There was. Max had asked her assistant to request two rooms. She'd been assured everything was taken care of. She wasn't sure where the communication had broken down, but whoever was at fault was going to have an unpleasant call from her in the near future. That wouldn't fix the problem at the moment, though.

"There must have been a miscommunication," Max managed to grind out. She reached into her bag to pull out her wallet. "I'll take another room and pay for it here." *And save the receipt because they sure as hell are reimbursing me for their screwup.*

Jade stepped closer, perhaps to offer her support, but Max got a whiff of that fresh-scented shampoo and was reminded of another reason why sharing a room was off the table.

The woman behind the desk looked nervous. "I'm sorry, but we don't have any more available rooms. There's a dentist's conference this weekend, and we're fully booked."

Max could feel her blood pressure rise. Things were happening so quickly she felt like she was losing her grip on the situation.

"It's not a big deal," Jade offered, placing her hand on Max's shoulder. Ironically, the thrill Max felt from that touch added yet another layer to her panic.

Steeling herself, she made sure to smile at both Jade and the hotel clerk. "It is, but it isn't your fault. We'll be fine in the single room."

"I'm sorry about the miscommunication," the

woman said, and there was no missing the relief in her voice at not having to deal with the situation herself. "Here are some complimentary drink vouchers for the hotel bar as a thank you for your understanding."

Max could use those drinks. Unfortunately, she was too busy panicking, not over losing some privacy, but over spending even more time with a woman who made her pulse race. Max needed to be on her best behavior. Jade was strictly hands-off.

At least there are two beds.

She couldn't, *wouldn't,* break all of Cindy's rules.

CHAPTER TEN

M ax had stiffened at the counter of the hotel. That stiffness had increased in intensity for the duration of the elevator ride up to the thirteenth floor. By the time Jade watched the woman swipe the key card at the door, she worried Max's shoulder muscles would snap like an overstretched rubber band.

Had Jade pushed too hard about going out? Guilt stirred in her chest. It hadn't felt like a huge ask, to explore city night life during this surreal experience. Max's tightrope-like cinched body suggested otherwise.

The rocker's mercurial attitude was setting off red flags in Jade's mind. This was something she needed to remember. Her mom's life had been devastated by this woman. Jade had been a child, just starting school, but she remembered all the mornings Grace had stayed in bed with the window curtains drawn, weighed down by the band's breakup.

The room door swung open, and Jade sucked in a breath as they entered. The room was *nice*. Lottie would describe it as "swanky as fuck." There were two full-sized beds covered in pillowy white duvets. The walls were painted in a neutral soft blue, rather than the textured and antiquated wallpapers Jade associated with hotels. The carpet was clean, and the bathroom to her right was spacious and had an enormous tub in addition to the shower.

She couldn't believe the concert promoters had planned on *two* of these rooms to begin with.

Max stalked to the bed closest to the windows and tossed her bag on the end, essentially claiming it. The best bed, naturally, farthest from the bathroom and right next to the windows with the view.

Jade's mouth tightened. Things had been going so well, too. "Guess I'll take this one," Jade muttered, putting her duffel next to the other bed. *But as soon as you go to the restroom, I'm stealing the TV remote.* Max was probably used to people bending over backward for her. Well, if she thought Jade was going to be a complete pushover, she'd be surprised to learn how much of Grace's attitude Jade had inherited.

"I'm hitting the shower," Max announced in a tight voice. Jade watched as the woman opened her suitcase and quickly removed the things she'd need for the shower. There was an efficiency to the packing that spoke of years of practice. Jade's only times in hotels had been weekend trips with her mom to Asheville or the Outer Banks.

"Cool."

The awkwardness hung in the room even after Max shut the bathroom door behind her. Jade sighed. In a burst of defiance, she slumped onto Max's bed, only to moan as she sank into the mattress. Her belly was full of good food, and the day's early flight hit her hard. She wouldn't be moving anytime soon. Maybe she could fall asleep now and dream through whatever was making Max upset.

The sound of the shower came through the walls. Instead of lulling Jade deeper into relaxation, she found her body revving with the sudden knowledge that Max was naked mere feet from her. Lottie would be freaking out if she knew. Jade could almost imagine the too-detailed fan-fiction spilling from her friend's mouth in graphic detail.

Not that Lottie was the only one who could get lost in fantasy. Jade shook her head, attempting to dislodge the flashed imaginings of smooth skin and taut muscles, of water streaming through blonde hair and between pert breasts. *Lottie would never let me hear the end of this.* Yet the heat building between Jade's legs surely rivaled the temperature of the shower Max was currently enjoying.

For a moment, Jade considered quickly relieving the growing tightness. Max would never have to know.

Hell, she *couldn't* know. That would kick off the tour on the wrong foot for sure. Besides, queer icon or not, Max had yet to do or say anything to confirm she might be interested in women. The morning's interview had confirmed nothing.

No, Jade didn't need to be venturing down that path. Max was hot. Like, smoking hot. But she was probably flirty with everyone to get what she wanted. Her ability to make Jade forget how hurt Grace and Cindy had been was something to be wary of. And Jade was experiencing firsthand how the woman's personality turned on a dime.

There will be no hand in the pants for Maxine Gardner, Jade decided. An affirmation that did little to alleviate the throb there. Cindy's "no sex" rule couldn't have come at a worse time, when Jade realized it had been too long since she'd been intimate with anyone. That was probably why she was so hot and bothered by a woman she'd sworn to dislike.

Groaning, Jade managed to roll onto her stomach, pressing her face into the covers. She was too old for school-girl crushes like this. She needed to focus on the tour and decide what she wanted from life after. Whether it was committing to the symphony or figuring out a way to convince Cindy that Jade wanted something other than the career that had been laid out for her by the meddling women in the family.

She was so lost in those thoughts that she missed

the shower shutting off. Instead, it was Max's embarrassed voice calling from the bathroom. "Hey, Jade?"

"Yeah?"

"I forgot to bring my change of clothes. Would you grab some things from my bag?"

Stunned, Jade didn't move. Max had been so precise in her preparation for the shower. How on earth did she forget the most essential items?

Heat prickled up Jade's neck as she scooted from the bed and went to the bag, unsure of what she was supposed to bring. Carefully, she rifled through neatly folded items until she found jeans, a *Def Leppard* T-shirt, and...

The heat burned up to her cheeks like wildfire. Lacy thongs. Sleek, black boy shorts. Scraps of flimsy fabric Jade could only pretend to know did something on the body. Someone on eBay would probably pay big bucks for a pair of Maxine Gardner's panties.

Unsure, she grabbed the pair at the top, thinking that at least it was one of the normal looking ones. Surely that would work, right? Holding her bundle, Jade went to the door and gave a timid knock.

When it opened she dropped her gaze to her feet but not quickly enough. Max was wrapped in a microscopic towel, her hair still dripping. The woman's chest and shoulders were covered in tattoos, the ink creating a map of art that begged to be examined. The hint of cleavage and short hem of the towel had left little to the imagination. Jade had a great imagination and was currently cursing herself for it.

She felt Max's stare and thrust out the clothing.

"Thanks." Max took the clothing, but rather than close the door again, she simply stood there. Could she see inside Jade's mind? Was she, at that very moment, laughing at the way Jade's skin tingled with a hunger she'd not planned for? Or was she still angry at Jade for wanting something so basic as the freedom to be an adult?

"Wow." The wry tone caught Jade off guard, and she looked up before she could stop herself, only to find the seemingly "normal" pair she'd grabbed was a pair of fire engine red, scarcely-there string panties. They were currently dangling from Max's outstretched finger.

"You said to get you clothing," she replied, her humiliation striking a match under her skin, sending flames scorching over every inch of her. Where was the air conditioner? She needed to crank it on because she was about to combust from embarrassment. Though dying might be preferable. In an effort to at least appear nonplussed, Jade added, "so I got what you packed."

"Would *you* wear these under denim?"

Absolutely not. Jade wasn't even sure how or when they were supposed to be worn at all. While she appreciated sexy lingerie, she personally had no desire to try anything other than good, old-fashioned cotton on herself. "Not that I looked, but it didn't seem like you had many, uh, basic options."

The energy between them crackled, and Jade fought to think of lemon juice in open cuts. Or her neighbor, who liked to mow his yard with no shirt, his pelt of back hair on display. She clawed desperately at the memory of how stiff and unhappy Max had seemed before, back straight as a crowbar and eyes like steel.

None of it worked. The only thing she was aware of was the woman in a too-small towel in front of her, smelling of expensive shampoo, holding out panties Jade would love to see her in. Then take them back off... with her teeth.

Max laughed, a soft laugh you'd expect from someone who was on the cusp of giving up. But what was she struggling with? It couldn't be the same kind of flame-blooded desire Jade was suffering from. Right?

"Sorry I shut down a bit there," the woman said with a shrug, the sparrow tattoo on that shoulder lifting as though about to take flight. "I'm reconciling with sharing a room with somebody. I haven't shared in a very long time and forgot to bring my clothes."

"Oh." Jade licked her lips, unsure of how to respond. She needed Max to be dressed like, yesterday. Maybe in a nun's habit or one of those snug onesie pajamas that turned a person into a cuddly potato sack. Hoping to regain a bit of dignity, she asked, "Is that why you seemed so unhappy in the elevator?"

"What are you talking about?"

"When we found out there was only one room, you seemed upset and tense all the way into the room. I've been worrying I did something wrong or made you mad, and you didn't want to be around me."

Jade froze as Max took a step closer. The woman hugged her clothes to her chest, anchoring the teeny towel in place. Those hotel towels weren't meant to be worn for anything longer than thirty seconds, and by the amount of upper thigh now exposed, time was up. Max's free hand landed on Jade's shoulder, and Jade swallowed hard.

"You were perfect today. If all the people I've traveled with were as fun and smart and talented as you, I might've been more willing to share my space."

Jade's mouth was an absolute desert. "Oh. Cool. Um, I'll let you get dressed."

Max's hand dropped, and Jade could feel the warmth of it after, like it had seared her skin. Max tipped her head to the side and smiled in a way that made Jade's knees turn to jelly. "Sure." Her lips pursed. "Though now that I'm looking at these fancy pants"—Max gave the red scrap masquerading as panties a whirl—"I'm thinking we get ready to go out and have some fun. That was the deal, right?"

That had been... a real conversation. Max had been honest, and Jade had responded in kind. It'd been easy. A far cry from the way Jade's inability to once tell Grace, and now Cindy, that perhaps a life in a stiff suit

140

at the back of an orchestra didn't hold the same appeal it had when she'd been ten. She wasn't sure what that meant and opted for distraction.

"Yeah, that sounds good. But you should, uh, probably get dressed first."

BOTH OF THEM were dressed to kill. Max had traded the jeans and tee for a dress short enough Jade was worried a gentle breeze would show off the red panties. As for Jade, she'd opted for high-waisted skinny jeans and an oversized, sequined black tank top, her blue sports bra flashing peeks here and there. Her curls were piled up and her undercut on display, though that had as much to do with the Austin heat as attempting to look stylish.

"What if it's sold out?" Jade asked as they stood in the hotel lobby.

Max's eyebrow arched. "Do you think that matters? Oh, babe, I'm going to show you what I'm capable of." With a twinkle in her eye, Max had her phone out and was texting away.

Thumbs hooked in pockets, Jade waited with a nervous knot in her belly.

Not too long after, a stretch limo pulled up to the front of the hotel. Jade looked around, curious about what high-rolling dentist from the convention was traveling in such luxury. Max grabbed her hand and tugged. "There's our ride."

A *limo*.

The chauffeur was waiting with the door open for them. Max ducked in first, and Jade's heart threatened to detonate at the red flash she'd known was coming. She hoped the low lights of the back would hide her crimson cheeks.

"I've never been in a limo," she admitted as she looked around for a non-existent seat belt.

"Tonight will be a night of many firsts, I expect," Max said in a throaty way that yanked Jade's focus from her quest for safety. The woman was holding out a bottle of Dom Perignon. "Let's do this."

The expensive champagne in the limousine had only been an appetizer. Jade felt pulled along, caught in Max's fabulous riptide, as they ate at an upscale restaurant. It was the kind she'd only seen on TV, with tiny plates of food that looked like art that arrived in multiple courses. After that, Max had the chauffeur take them to Summit, where sure enough, they skipped the line completely and were escorted to a private VIP entrance.

I'd only been teasing. Now it was clear Max had taken her challenge seriously.

In a private balcony in the club, Jade felt tipsy with more than just the champagne and drinks from dinner. Each new experience with Max made her feel as if she were in a movie. There was going out and having fun, and then there was partying with a rock star.

She clutched the railing of their balcony and looked down at the writhing bodies on the dance floor below. The bass throbbed through the club, the DJ having an expert sense of timing. His transitions were smoother than silk.

Max moved to stand next to her, close enough their arms and shoulders brushed. Jade swallowed.

"What do you think?" Max asked, leaning in and speaking loudly to be heard over the music.

"This is incredible."

It wasn't a lie. More impressive than the fancy things, though, had been Max's ability to keep the conversation going. The woman was a wealth of music history and surprisingly well-read. She attributed it to long hours on the road. Whatever the reason, the conversation never lulled.

"Let's dance!" Max took Jade's hand and led her down to the main floor. They waded in through the writhing bodies, and while there were a few curious glances toward Max, it felt to Jade like it was just the two of them.

Max began to sway her hips and shoulders in an easy, confident way. The beat made its way into Jade's body, commanding and primal, and she responded by falling into it, moving to the rhythm.

There was, as Jade's camp counselors had liked to say, "room for Jesus" between the two of them. Yet the air fizzed with the buzz and energy of the crowd, and Jade couldn't keep her eyes off the hypnotic side to side of Max's hips.

They danced through several transitions, the set moving fluidly until the tempo slowed. The distance between Max and Jade closed. Sweat dripped between Jade's breasts, and feeling bold, she rested her hands lightly on Max's waist, moving with the other woman's body. She was supposed to be dancing, right?

It had to be the champagne. In fact, Jade should get some water. Some very cold water. Maybe dumped all over her head so she could shake free of the increasing desire taking hold of her. She wasn't sure anymore if they were just dancing.

She was saved, not by an ice shower but by the clock. Maxine snuck a look at her phone and yelped loudly enough the dancers around them startled. "It's three!" she mouthed, eyes wide.

3:00 a.m.? How—when—had that happened?

With her rock star power, it took Max no time at all to close their tab and get an escort to the waiting limo. By the time they'd pulled up to the hotel, Max was drooping on Jade's shoulder. She kept a hand on Jade's shoulder as they stumbled to the elevator.

Every nerve in Jade's body was on alert. Each touch of Max's seemed to promise… something. But that, she told herself, was wishful thinking. It was late, and they'd been dancing hard. Too many drinks playing tricks in her head.

Max stumbled into the room and immediately disappeared into the bathroom. Jade fumbled with her clothes, changing into pajamas and chiding herself for letting her mind go rampant. Minutes later, Max reappeared in a T-shirt and sleep shorts. "G'night," she managed before falling onto the bed.

Jade sighed, unsure of what exactly she wanted. She brushed her teeth and washed her face and, finally, convinced herself that sleep was the answer to all her worries. Worried about an attraction to a possibly straight bandmate? Get some sleep. Unsure if she's flirting or just really nice? You probably need some sleep. On the edge of wanting to make reckless choices?

God, I need to sleep.

She got into bed, the ceiling only spinning the slightest bit. Her muscles ached, and her mouth was dry. Jade should have been out before her head hit the pillow. Only there was this one spring that seemed to punch up through the mattress and straight into her hip.

Grunting, she tried rolling to the other side of the bed. There were some loud squeaks and thumps until she tried to find a comfortable position. A comfortable position, though, was not to be found. Shift, squeak, get poked, move.

"What're you doing over there?" Max's muffled voice was full of accusation.

"Having a hard time getting comfy." Jade willed

herself to be still. What else was she going to do? Maybe if she forced herself to not move, she'd get used to the weird bumps in the mattress and sleep would come.

It didn't come. All that came were aches and pains, and soon she couldn't *not* move. The squeaking and shifting commenced once more.

Her situation was made worse by the buzzing in her bones, leftover from long hours and too many drinks and very loud music. She was lit up like a candle with no way to blow herself out. Her mind wandered to dancing with Max.

They moved together as well as they played together. There was a synchronicity between them. Jade couldn't help thinking about the other ways they'd match up. It was a bad train of thought to follow, as her mattress was still poking her, her body was taxed beyond coherency, and now she was hot, and it wasn't from the Texas heat.

Jade tried to buckle in for the longest night of her life.

CHAPTER ELEVEN

The bed creaked again. It was the fifth time in thirty-seven seconds. Not that Max was counting.

Okay. She totally was.

First, that whole shower thing had revved Max's mind with thoughts that should never have been in her head. Then there had been what, in any other world, would have been a fantastic date. Good food with a stunning woman and dancing that had made Max's body heat up like a bonfire. Now, the sound of Jade squirming on the bed next to Max's was treating her imagination to visions that could probably get her arrested in several states.

But Cindy had been clear about the rules. No sex on the buses, and keep Jade swathed in Bubble Wrap. While Cindy hadn't specified no sex with Jade ever, it didn't take a rocket scientist to know such a clause was implied.

On the flip side, Jade had also been clear. No Bubble Wrap. She hadn't seemed too keen about the no sex decree, either. She was also most definitely an adult, as evidenced by the way she'd held Max on the dance floor and moved with the kind of confidence that came with experience.

The mattress squeaked again.

Shit. Now all Max could picture was unwrapping Jade from a dress made of Bubble Wrap, like a delectable present from a box. That was *not* where she needed her thoughts right now. She'd give about anything for a useful distraction. Her skin tingled with unspent sexual energy, though, and it was fraying her patience.

"What's the problem?" Max snapped when Jade moved yet again, causing the bed to groan like it was possessed by a poltergeist.

"A spring's poking me," Jade whimpered after a moment of hesitation.

Max rolled her eyes in the darkness. What a princess. "Do you want to switch beds?"

"You think you can manage avoiding a spring in the middle of this tiny mattress?" Jade's tone made it a challenge, one Max could hardly back down from.

"Life on the road has taught me how to cope with everything," Max informed her with an abundance of bravado, clicking on the bedside lamp.

As if the light had been a starting pistol, Jade popped out of the bed. "Go for it!"

Max grabbed her pillow and took it along, pretty much out of spite. She wasn't attached to the thing. It wasn't even a very good pillow. But it was hers, damn it. She slid into the bed. "See it's as sim—mother fucker, that hurts." The mattress may as well have been filled with sharp sticks.

Jade snuggled under the covers of the other bed. The comfortable, non-pokey one. "I'm sorry. What does the word *sim* mean? Are you talking about the game?" The woman stretched out with a contented sigh. "This is so much better."

Max glared in Jade's direction, cursing her. "I think it's more than one spring." She wiggled, desperate to find that perfect spot where nothing poked. The bed protested loudly but did not yield.

"I tried telling you." There was no doubt Jade was smiling. Max could hear it.

"You didn't say it was a bed of nails," Max growled. She missed her mattress.

Jade rolled onto her side. "I thought you said you can sleep anywhere, like a true rock star."

"I don't remember saying that last part."

"Your tone implied it."

Max moved one leg and yelped as something metallic bit into the flesh. "Does that mean I don't get my bed back?"

"That depends." The way Jade drew out her response made it clear she would drive a hard bargain.

"On?" Max's muscles tensed even more than they already were from her contortionist pose. Jade had a way of getting Maxine to ignore common sense.

"If I get to stay in it. I won't sleep in that one." Jade added, "Of course, there's always the floor."

Damn her. She was enjoying this. Worse, Max found the idea of sharing the tight space with Jade far too enticing, and not just because she got her cozy mattress back.

"I can't make you sleep on the floor," Max said, playing dumb to get a rise out of her.

"I was talking about you. I have a bed, and I don't want to vacate it."

Max mustered some faux outrage, which was hard considering what she wanted to do was laugh. "That's *my* bed!"

"Didn't my mom and aunt teach you about no take backs?"

Unable to stop it any longer, laughter bubbled out of Max. "I can hear them saying it now."

"It was their thing. Being sisters and all." There was a hint of sadness in Jade's tone that plucked at Max's heart. Sometimes, she forgot how much Jade had been through, how strong the young woman was. They were similar in that respect. Survivors.

Max eyed the carpet, not wanting to get overly

familiar with it. Enduring was one thing. Unnecessary suffering was another.

"What's the matter, Rock Star?" Jade teased, recovering smoothly from her earlier melancholy. "You going to take the rest of the night to decide what to do?"

"There's hardly any night left. We have to get up in five hours to make our flights, and sleep would be nice." Max let out a defeated sigh.

"Come on." Jade lifted the covers, scooting over toward the window side.

Max hesitated. "What would Cindy think?" It felt daring to ask it out loud, like tempting fate with a red cape.

"Why are you worried about what she'd think?"

"I respect her. I wouldn't want her to get the wrong idea." *Because I have many wrong ideas playing in my head, each more appealing than the last.*

Jade started to speak but stopped. Too late, Max feared she might've taken it wrong, like Max had been implying it was Jade's behavior that concerned her, when it was the opposite that was true. But Jade wouldn't know that, at least not if Max had done as good a job as she thought with covering her tracks over the years. Despite the occasional rumor, no one had ever publicly outed Max.

Max swallowed, banishing every lustful thought she'd ever entertained to the darkest recesses of her mind. "There really isn't a better choice, is there?"

"I'm sure we can act like grown-ups." Jade's stilted tone did not ease Max's mind on having not offended the woman. "At least, I know I can."

Max gnashed her teeth, but the dig was deserved, considering she'd basically made it sound like Jade wouldn't be able to keep her hands to herself.

As her back started to ache from the uncomfortable position she was in, a resigned Max climbed into the not nearly large enough bed beside Jade. She turned off the light and settled in as best she could, hanging onto the edge for dear life.

"Relax. This isn't the first time I've shared a bed with a woman. Oh, although I guess it could be the first time for you."

"What does that mean?" The pit of Max's stomach went cold, a response conditioned by a lifetime of waiting for the accusations—and sometimes heavy objects—to fly.

"Nothing," Jade assured her, although it hadn't sounded like nothing. "You're probably used to sleeping with men, right?"

"I thought the goal was sleep," Max said curtly. Was Jade fishing, or had she guessed that Max was a lot of things but straight wasn't one of them? It wasn't like Max put much effort into keeping up the charade these days, other than taking the occasional male friend as a plus one to music industry events. People assumed what they wanted to about Max's private life, which was no more her concern than it was any of their damn business. Besides, she was in her forties now, practically invisible.

"I've heard so much chatter about you. It's hard to know what to believe." The woman was almost as adept at keeping things vague as Max was.

"Yeah, yeah," Max said sarcastically. "Your generation has been burping out their every thought online since birth. Some of us aren't used to being so open." Or, in this case, out. Once more, Max tried to imagine not being so secretive, but the idea brought cold dread out from deep within. It was too much to examine, not even to ease the mind of the woman next to her. "Privacy is a privilege."

"Is *that* what you call it?"

"What?" Max's skin was on the verge of crawling off her bones.

"Never mind. We should sleep." Jade's tone was brusque, or else Max was reading her own feelings into it.

"Fine," Max growled, her eyes wide open, staring at the bed that'd gotten her into this predicament. She'd made it a rule to never talk about her private life with people outside of her bubble, and Jade was well outside of that bubble.

Yes, they were going on tour together, but that didn't automatically make them besties, now did it? Max didn't have to explain herself. She wasn't the sharing type, so that made her wonder who exactly was in her secret sphere. Max's mind sputtered and came up empty.

"It's different for some people," Max heard herself blurt out seconds after vowing not to say another word. "My generation—things were complicated."

"Oh?"

"Say you were a kid with an abusive father, growing up on the wrong side of the tracks. Hypothetically," Max added without much conviction. *Real subtle, Max.*

"Naturally."

"Maybe a lot of people in your community were hostile toward gays. Family included." Max drew in a breath, struggling to recover from what had to be the understatement of the year. That cold knot of dread grew to glacial proportions in her gut. "But maybe you find yourself getting away from the alcoholic father and all the haters and are given the chance to build a new life—but it's made absolutely clear that public image is everything, no matter what happens behind closed doors. That's what my generation dealt with."

Max tensed, awaiting a response. It was as close to a full confession about her sexuality as she was likely to come where Jade was concerned. Max wasn't even sure why she'd said as much as she had.

One second passed and then another. There wasn't a sound coming from behind her. Had Jade fallen asleep? Probably for the best.

"That sounds—" Jade's words were almost as quiet as the sigh that escaped her at the end of them. "I'm sorry, but things changed, even for your generation. Look at Melissa Etheridge."

"She had a lot of power."

"Okay," Jade countered. "What about Melissa Ferrick?"

"Who's that?" Max knew exactly who it was, and that this question was a trap. Melissa Ferrick's song "Drive" had become a lesbian anthem. Admitting she knew it—which of course, she did, and she had even met the woman in person once after a show—would be as good as confirming everything else.

Would that be so bad?

Rumors were fine. They added to her bad girl image. She made waves in the LGBTQ+ community by being openly supportive and affirming. Confirmation about herself, on the other hand, could sink her chance at a comeback. Nothing was worth that risk.

"You really don't know who Melissa Ferrick is?"

Max should've been annoyed, but instead, she found herself on the verge of laughing again. Something about Jade brought that out in her like no one Max could remember. The woman was persistent. She'd give her that much. "Should I?"

"Hmph." The noise sounded like it had been grunted into a pillow. "Not if you really were speaking hypothetically, I guess."

"How else would I have been speaking?" Guilt niggled Max's insides, having little appetite for keeping up her old, tired lies. She was so practiced in dodging she did it without thinking. But what choice did she have?

Jade settled into quiet breathing, and for a moment, Max assumed she'd drifted off to sleep. Her own eyes felt like sandpaper. But then Jade asked, "Was that part about your dad hypothetical?"

"My father—" Max's throat tightened, forcing her to cough before continuing. "The less said about that drunk bastard, the better."

"I'm sorry." The soft brush of Jade's hand against her shoulder brought tears to Max's eyes, making her grateful for the darkness that kept them hidden. "What about your mom?"

"Left when I was a kid."

"I don't even know who my dad is. Not sure my mom knew. But maybe it's better that way. I guess we're both alone."

Max focused all her awareness on that one spot on her shoulder where Jade's hand continued to rest. The connection between them was palpable, a stretched elastic band awaiting the inevitable snap that would draw them together. If the circumstances had been different, she would have turned over in bed and pulled Jade close, consequences be damned. But no matter how tempting it was, Max couldn't let that happen. She shifted closer to the edge of the bed, and Jade's fingers slipped away.

There was a yawn, followed by soft breathing, as Jade presumably drifted off to sleep. For Max it wasn't so easy. Her thoughts were racing, her body humming like a too-tight guitar string on the verge of breaking. How would she survive two months in the close confines of life on the road with Jade if she couldn't get through a single night of sharing a bed?

Humming filled Max's ears, and it took her longer than it should have to realize the sound was coming from her own throat. What was the song?

Max's heart skipped as it came to her. Melissa Ferrick's "Drive."

She sucked in her breath, the song coming to an abrupt end.

A chuckle came from the other side of the bed, the other occupant not quite as asleep as Max had assumed.

"I was starting to wonder..." Jade's words trailed off into the darkness.

THE BLARING of a phone alarm sent Max bolting upright in bed.

"Shit. It's nine-thirty." Jade sat up beside her, hair going all directions like a shocked owl. "My alarm was supposed to go off at eight. I'm going to be late for my flight."

Jade tumbled off the edge of the bed, already a flurry of motion as she tossed loose items into her bag.

"Put some clothes on. I'll order a car." Sleep still clouding her head, Max pulled up the ride share app on her phone. "They'll be here in seven minutes. Can you make it?"

"Yep." Jade was already in the bathroom, a foamy toothbrush in her mouth, obscuring her words. "Can you?"

"I'm a true rock star, remember? I can do anything." Max grabbed a shirt and jeans as she rushed through the morning routine, not beating Jade but doing a halfway decent job.

The two of them were running down the hallway of the hotel as Max received the notification their driver had arrived and would only wait five minutes.

The elevator took three.

Outside, Max practically threw her body in front of the Honda Accord as it started to pull away from the curb.

"Nicely done." Jade's eyes sparkled with an admiration that warmed Max's heart more than was appropriate. The only response Max could risk under the circumstances was a shrug.

True rock star, she reminded herself as she clambered into the back seat. *Aloof and in control.* Her near confession in bed, in the dark, had been a moment of vulnerability she couldn't afford. Like she'd said, it had been made clear to her early on that her image was everything. Reputations required diligence and caution to uphold.

Jade rested her head against the car window, giving in to the siren call of sleep. Max resisted the urge to smooth her adorably tangled hair. She'd gotten used to Jade being there, making good conversation and even better music. This was just the beginning of the comeback tour, and already the woman had made it feel less like a job and more like fun. When was the last time Max had truly enjoyed being on tour?

At the airport, Jade's terminal was on the opposite side, so she gave Max a hug so quick it didn't have time to register before dashing toward security. Duffel slung over shoulder, Max watched her disappear before turning to head toward her own terminal.

Max stood at a computer, punching in the details for her New York flight. Her apartment was waiting for her. Her assistant would have the fridge stocked with fresh food, and housekeeping would have cleaned, placing Egyptian cotton sheets on her bed. It was a king-sized mattress with no poking springs and plenty of room for sharing. There wouldn't be any sharing, though, because Max lived alone.

As she waited for boarding, Max paid to upgrade to first class. Space should be a luxury, right? Not pressed up to her neighbor, close enough to smell their shampoo?

But the coffee the flight attendant brought her didn't warm up Max. The roominess didn't provide comfort. Max had spent most of her adult career flying solo—literally and figuratively. Now, as the plane took off, one question pounded away like drums in her mind.

Who was going to sleep on her shoulder during this flight?

CHAPTER TWELVE

J ade blinked rapidly as her eyes struggled to transition from the bright LA sunshine outside to the dimly lit interior of the Mexican restaurant where she and Lottie had arranged to meet. She heard her friend's excited squeal coming from the direction of the crowd even before she saw her.

"I can't believe you're finally here!" Lottie launched herself off the barstool, wrapping her arms around Jade. "In another week, you're going to be famous. I can say I knew you when."

"I wouldn't go that far," Jade cautioned, the brightly painted tiles on the walls causing her head to swim almost as much as the prospect of becoming a star.

Lottie took Jade by the shoulders. "You're going on tour with the Matchstick Girls. That's a huge fucking deal! I'd give my left tit for that opportunity, and you know how much I paid for them."

Jade's eyebrow shot up. "It's unfortunate we couldn't use you for rehearsals, since Cindy's leaving boot camp in time, but we could actually use you as a backup musician. If you really wanted to. I bet I could add in some piano accompaniment that I know you'd slay."

Her friend's face pinched in pain, and Jade waited as Lottie took three very deep breaths. That level of control wasn't something Lottie was known for, but Jade appreciated that she wasn't chasing her friend, whooping with joy, down an LA street.

To her surprise, Lottie said, "No, thank you."

"What?" Jade blinked her eyes a few times, waiting for the joke. When Lottie remained silent, hands lightly gripping Jade's shoulders, she asked, "Are you serious? You said you'd give your left tit. That's your favorite boob."

"I *know*," Lottie sighed. "Such a good breast." Jade watched in amused disbelief as Lottie reached down and gave ol' lefty a quick pat. "What I'm not prepared to give up are some of the opportunities in LA this summer. I'm house-sitting for that record exec, remember? I plan on leaving demos hidden all over his house. Plus, I have an opportunity at Disneyland and a gig on the kid's show—"

"The one with the giant purple costume? I thought you hated that gig."

"I did. But now it's kind of fun, and it's good money. I'm not going to find something like that again if I take an entire summer off."

Jade couldn't quite believe her ears, but she knew a decided Lottie. Still, she pressed one more time. "Are you sure?"

"One hundred percent. Although I'm going to need a large, frozen drink with an umbrella to nurse the pain of making an adult choice."

A fleeting thought of the symphony job flew through Jade's head, and she wondered, briefly, if she should also be making a painful adult choice. As her friend loosened her grip, Jade gave a nervous tug to one of her dangling earrings. She'd hoped visiting Lottie would prove a respite before the craziness of the tour fully took over, but Jade found she missed Max, who would have had advice on how to be comfortable with the prospect of fame. "I've never performed for more than a few dozen people, and next week, I'll be on a tour in front of thousands."

"You're a great musician, one of the best I know," Lottie assured her. "And from what you've told me, the practices have been going well."

"It's not the music that has me worried." Jade said, a knot forming in her belly. Her skin prickled, remembering the warmth of waking up next to Maxine. "That part's easy. It's eight weeks of forced captivity with my band members."

"Well, if it's your aunt Cindy you're talking

about…" Lottie began, but her voice trailed off, and her eyes widened. "Unless it's *not* Cindy you mean." It came out like a line for a soap opera, full of dramatic suspicion.

"What?" Jade tried to laugh off the idea while signaling furiously to the young woman behind the bar that she needed a drink.

The bartender paused in front of them, jacking up an eyebrow in lieu of actually asking to take their orders. Jade requested a margarita on the rocks, extra large.

"Another for me, and more chips and salsa, please," Lottie batted her lashes at the woman, earning a devilish smile in return. Jade simply shook her head at her best friend's talent. Lottie could charm the pants off a snake. "Okay. Now, tell me everything about the legendary Maxine Gardner and why you're nervous about being trapped with her."

"Why do you think this has anything to do with her?" Jade deflected, eyes darting to the colorful paper banners hanging from the ceiling.

"Because you have exactly two band members, darling. Process of elimination."

Jade was about to argue, but Lottie crossed her arms and fixed her with a *don't fuck with me* stare. Jade blew out a breath, the hairs on her forehead tickling. "Fine. Where do I start?"

"With the juicy stuff, naturally. I mean, you've been

hanging out with Maxine for over a month. I can't even put into words how jealous I am."

"I haven't even seen Max in two weeks." *But I've been thinking about her for every moment of that time.*

"Oh, it's Max, is it?" Lottie teased. "How very intimate."

"Nothing could be farther from the truth," Jade protested. "Even the night we spent together in the hotel room in Austin was perfectly professional."

By the way Lottie's face expanded in slow motion, understanding stretching each feature into a caricature of itself, Jade knew she'd made a mistake.

"Hold it right there, sister." Lottie poked a hard finger in Jade's sternum. "You spent the night in a hotel together? Start there."

The bartender set down the drinks, and Lottie immediately lifted the glass to her lips, licking the salt on the rim with extra vim for the bartender's benefit.

"You're so bad." Jade laughed, amazed by her best friend's propensity for flirting. It was clear from the bartender's pink cheeks that she was eating it up, too.

"If you think this is me being bad"—Lottie lifted her glass by its cactus-shaped stem—"I'm not sure I want to know about the hotel, after all. You probably went over accounting spreadsheets together. It'll ruin my fantasy."

"Does your fantasy include being in the same bed?" Jade teased mischievously. "A really small one?" She wasn't sure why she was sharing this. The time to divulge to her best friend would have been weeks ago. Jade's mind drifted toward Max's "hypothetical" situation, and margarita soured in her stomach.

"I knew you had it in you!" Lottie squealed as she slapped Jade's thigh then licked a fingertip and made a sizzling sound as she held it in the air. "Girl, you're on fire!"

Why had she said anything? Maybe it was because Jade didn't want to admit how acutely she'd been feeling Max's absence. "Okay, okay. Reel it in," Jade cautioned, desperate to backtrack. "Nothing happened."

"Why not?" Lottie pouted. "Do you still hate her?"

Jade paused for a moment, considering her answer. "I wouldn't say that. Max isn't anything like how I thought she would be."

"Which is a good thing, considering you thought she'd be a grade A bitch."

"Turns out she's actually human, which makes things weirdly complicated." The time spent with Max had managed to erase Grace's hurt from Jade's mind. It was becoming more difficult to reconcile the woman her mother had ranted about versus the fun, smart, and easygoing woman Jade was making music with.

"Complicated because you shared a bed with her?" Lottie frowned as she licked more salt from her glass, clearly disappointed there were no salacious details. "Oh, shit. You're trying to say she snores."

"That's not what I was hinting at, my shallow

friend." Jade rolled her eyes. "I meant she's vulnerable."

"Ugh," Lottie groaned. "That's not what I'm looking for in an idol. Didn't you get to have any fun?"

"Well, yes." Jade's cheeks grew warm as she thought back to the night in question. "I'd be lying if I said she hadn't shown me what that whole rock star life was really like. A big ass limo. Private rooms at a hot nightclub."

A curious thing happened as Jade gushed about the time spent in Austin. She was describing events that had been incredible, not because of their "rock star" quality but because she'd been experiencing them with Max.

"That sounds amazing," Lottie gushed, caught up in the more glamorous aspects of the story. "You've made me even more jealous. I've always been certain that, if given the opportunity, I'd be very good at being a celebrity."

"I'm sorry," Jade replied, having spent most of their friendship watching Lottie fight hard to be seen as she wanted. At least LA had been far kinder to her best friend than North Carolina had been. "I shouldn't brag."

Lottie blinked, looking perplexed. "And deny me the pleasure of living vicariously through you? You absolutely should brag and in far more detail than you have been."

"For one thing, I know you've had the biggest

crush on Max since forever. I would *never* betray you by going after her. That's, like, rule number one of the friend code of ethics."

"Are you serious?" To Jade's surprise, Lottie dissolved into a fit of laughter that lasted long enough several patrons of the restaurant turned to gawk. "Oh, honey. I know the difference between reality and fantasy. Celebrity crushes don't count as *actual* crushes. Besides, I've started dating someone. You know, in *real* life." Lottie casually pointed to the bartender, waggling her brows as she did.

Jade looked to the woman and then to Lottie, a grin spreading across her face. She was an idiot sometimes. "Really? I should've known the flirting was getting over-the-top, even for you. Is she another reason you're turning down touring with us?"

"I wondered if you would notice," Lottie said with a chuckle. "And yes, she is part of my reasoning as well. So anyway, now you know I've got nothing but goodwill where you and Maxine—no, sorry, I mean *Max*—are concerned. I want *all* the details."

A lock inside her slid open, and Jade discovered she wished there were details. "There's really nothing to tell. She's a killer musician and great at her job." Jade took a large swig of her margarita, savoring the tangy burn on her throat.

Instead of speaking, Lottie stared deeply into Jade's eyes. "You want to fuck her."

"What? No." The glass slipped from Jade's fingers

as she went to set it down, nearly sending the contents spraying everywhere.

"You do. Your eyes have never been able to lie to me." Lottie flashed a triumphant grin. "I can totally tell."

"That's really not—" Jade's tongue got tangled, like it wanted no part of this lie. Her core was approaching the surface temperature of Venus. Admitting any desire out loud would make it real and, worse, tempt fate. She scrabbled for an excuse. "Even if I did, I'm not going to. I promised Cindy."

"Cindy made you promise not to fuck Max?" Lottie looked aghast. "Wow. What kind of dirt must your aunt have on the woman to put a rule like that in place?"

"Nothing, as far as I know," Jade insisted. "Everyone thinks Max is straight."

"Except you, clearly."

Jade swallowed hard, not liking the certainty in her friend's tone. "Why do you say that?"

"Because if you didn't think she would be into fucking you, at least hypothetically, you would've led with that instead. *Cindy won't let me*," Lottie added, mimicking Jade in a high-pitched tone. "Puh-lease."

Jade's memory flitted back to the conversation between Max and her in the hotel. "Funny you should use the word hypothetical. That's what she said, too."

"Max told you she would hypothetically be into fucking you? That had to have been one hell of a conversation." Lottie gave an exaggerated wink, her mirth keeping the conversation from veering into dangerous waters.

"No," Jade said with a snort. "She hinted at a bunch of stuff in her past that made it seem like she was in the closet and that she'd stayed there for a reason. It had nothing to do with me."

"Pity." Lottie licked more salt from the rim, her girlfriend pretending to swoon while pouring a beer from a tap, making Lottie giggle. "Can I give you a piece of advice?"

"I've never been able to stop you before."

"True, so here goes nothing. My advice? Fuck Max."

"Like, tell her to go to hell?" Jade asked, pretty sure that wasn't what her friend had meant.

"Nah, honey. I mean, you know." Lottie proceeded to make a series of crude hand gestures that left little doubt in Jade's mind what she was trying to say. "Get it out of your system. Then focus on the tour, because that's the most important part of this adventure. You were meant to be a rock star. So be one, bitch!"

"Lottie, I love you. I really do." Jade took a final sip of her margarita, crunching on a piece of ice before adding, "But that is probably the worst piece of advice I've ever been given."

JADE'S HEART beat in her ears as she stood on the stage and stared out into the vast emptiness of the arena with its row upon row of seats. She'd been on stages more than a few times before while playing guest spots with the symphony, but nothing like this. This was the fucking Hollywood Bowl. Was there anywhere else like it in the world?

"What's the capacity of this place?" she asked, not because she had a burning need to know, but because Max had arrived on the stage, and Jade knew she needed to say something but was drawing a blank.

"About seventeen thousand," Max answered, not meeting Jade's gaze, leaving her to wonder if their fourteen days apart—not that Jade was counting or anything—had wrecked that unspoken connection that had begun to form between the two of them.

Before Jade could put this question to the test, Cindy bounded onto the stage, looking like a million bucks. Or, perhaps more accurately, looking like however much Skip had spent on that stay at the spa. Whatever it had cost, it was worth every penny. Gone were the mom jeans, replaced by skin tight leggings that showed off her still-shapely legs, paired with a brightly colored top in an attractive style that shaved ten years off the woman's appearance. In fact, every-thing about Cindy, from her skin to her hair, seemed to radiate a youthful glow.

Max met Jade's eye, and it was clear they both felt the same sense of surprise at the transformation. Maybe Jade's concern over losing the connection between them had been unfounded. They seemed as much on the same frequency now as they had been in Austin, a situation that came with its own set of challenges.

Just do it and get it out of your system. Lottie's advice echoed in Jade's head, but instead of sounding terrible, it was beginning to have an enticing ring to it. Jade shook her head, hoping to drive the thought right out of her brain.

"Excuse me, young lady," Max called out in a serious tone. "You can't be here right now. Only band members."

"I am in the band." Cindy rested a hand on her hip, trying to look stern but flushing with too much pride to pull it off. "Just who do you think I am?"

Playing into Max's joke, Jade dramatically counted everyone on her fingers, including the three backup musicians who were taking out their instruments in preparation for warming up. "The only person we're missing is Cindy Weathers. Have you seen her anywhere?"

"I *am* her, you goose." Cindy feigned annoyance, though it was easy to see she was on the edge of breaking into a grin. "But if you're not going to appreciate me, I can always leave."

"Don't you dare." Jade rushed her aunt, giving her a hug, holding on for dear life. "I'm already freaking out about the reality of this whole thing."

Her aunt held her tightly. "You're shaking like a leaf."

The only thing Jade could say was, "Seventeen thousand."

"Seventeen thousand leaves?" Cindy laughed.

"No. People." Jade's stomach clenched as the reality of it washed over her with terrifying force. "The show is sold out, meaning every single seat will be filled."

Cindy bobbed her head, her eyes panning the stage. "It's been a long time since I've been in this situation, but I want you to know it's fundamentally no different than when we're playing in the basement. Just a little louder."

"Yeah." Max picked up on Cindy's thread, an encouragement in her tone that sent an instant calm through Jade's nerves. "You totally got this. We may have the experience, but it's no secret you're the best musician out of all of us. Not only was your mom a rocker, but she instilled her love of music in you from day one. This is in your blood."

But seventeen *thousand*?

"If only I had your belief in me." Jade swallowed, wishing she could muster even a fraction of Max's natural confidence. It was impressive, not to mention sexy as hell.

Don't even think that word, Jade cautioned herself. Pairing sex and Max in the same sentence was a dangerous path. Lottie had gotten deeper into her head than she'd realized, and she silently cursed her beloved best friend.

"The best way to work through your jitters," Max told her, "is to rehearse the shit out of things. We have a week to nail this, so let's do it."

"Yeah..." Jade looked out again at the seemingly endless sea of seats that were destined to be filled with screaming fans. She'd never felt like such an imposter in her life. "Let's nail this."

The addition of backup musicians brought a richness to the band's sound that quickly took Jade's mind off her fears. Back in her basement, they'd sounded good but at the level of a talented garage band or a favorite group performing at a local dive bar. On stage, with all the wizardry that entailed, they sounded like legends, when the Matchstick Girls were at the pinnacle of their career.

Jade was in awe, but when they reached the fourth song in their set list, it became apparent there was a big problem. The sound coming from the backup guitarist as she tried to play along with a particularly challenging bit was akin to nothing Jade had ever heard before, though she imagined it might sound a little like murdering a kitten.

"Sorry!" The guitarist's face went up in flames as the song came to an abrupt stop.

"It's okay. It's a tricky piece," Max said in a diplomatic tone, though Jade sensed from her spot behind the drums that Max was one frayed nerve away from snapping.

Or maybe that was Jade projecting her own mood on the situation. It probably wasn't a fair comparison, but she'd been able to get the complicated chord and picking combination before she'd had a "teen" in her age.

You learned it from the source. Jade reached into her memories, the warmth of Grace's exacting instruction filling her heart even as her throat tightened.

Getting up, Jade made her way to the woman. "Hey. What's your name again?"

"Roxie," the woman replied.

"Roxie." Jade offered an encouraging smile. "Do you mind if I borrow your guitar to show you?"

The guitarist handed over the instrument with a look of such relief it was easy to believe she thought the thing cursed. Perhaps if Jade modeled it the way her mother had, Roxie would see the subtle tricks that made the transitions smooth.

"Okay, watch how I do this. Max, can you start at the top?" Jade played along with Max with an easy precision that was only in part due to practice. The more she and Max had rehearsed over the past weeks, the more Jade felt she could sense where the music would take them, so that what had started as a routine playthrough quickly turned into an improvisation that was almost sensuous in its passion and creativity.

Jade's body became the music, a buzzing hive of creative energy that seemed to spin around between her and Max, drawing them together.

When the song came to an end, Cindy let out a cheer. "Now, that's how it's played. Do it again!"

Suddenly aware of her surroundings, Jade felt herself flush. She felt raw and exposed, as if she'd been interrupted doing something much more intimate than playing guitar. Instead of doing as her aunt had requested, Jade handed the instrument back to the wide-eyed musician. "You try it now."

The guitarist played through the section of music with Max, more successfully this time but with nowhere near the finesse.

When the song was done, Max looked as though she were contemplating something particularly complex. "Roxie, do you happen to play drums?"

"Whoa!" Jade held a hand up as panic zinged through her. "Why are you asking her that?"

Max ran the tip of her tongue along her bottom lip, clearly searching for the right words to get Jade to take a step back from the ledge she'd suddenly perched herself on. "All I was thinking is the drum part on this particular song is nothing special, whereas the guitar—"

"Hell no," Jade heard herself say. Her palms were

beginning to sweat. "You want me to stand out here in the middle of this stage with nothing between me and seventeen thousand people but one little guitar?"

"Your mom used to love the spotlight, and you're just like her. The audience will eat you up," Cindy said, probably meaning it as encouragement. It had the opposite effect, sending Jade deeper into a tailspin.

"And spit me out!" Jade argued, dizziness overtaking her as she stared at all those empty seats.

"No, they won't." Max's volume was low, but there was a strength to her words that helped Jade find her footing, as if hearing Max's assurance made it true. Just like when they played, Max had a way of making everything around them disappear.

They had sounded amazing together, and that was even before the vocal harmonies, which the two of them had nailed in practice time and again. It wasn't a far stretch to imagine recreating that magic on stage.

Even so, Jade couldn't agree to do it. Not when the thought of being so exposed in front of such a tremendous crowd made her want to throw up.

"Let me work with Roxie," Jade pleaded, praying Max would see in her eyes how vital it was not to push her on this. "I'm sure I can get her to where we need to be."

There was a slight flicker of disappointment on Max's face. It tore at Jade's heart but faded almost instantly as Max gave a nod and even tacked on the tiniest hint of a reassuring smile. "Okay. Let's run through it again with Jade on drums and Roxie doing the guitar, and we'll make some time for them to practice more later."

As Jade made her way back to the relative safety of her seat behind the drums, she couldn't help but feel surprised at how much Max understood her.

And how that made her heart flutter.

CHAPTER THIRTEEN

M ax closed her eyes against the intensity of the setting sun as she absently strummed the acoustic guitar in her lap. She'd come to the hotel rooftop for some privacy before drinks with Jade and Cindy, at least as much as was possible now that she'd be living life on the road for the next two months. There was a bar a short distance behind her and plenty of seating scattered across the outdoor space, but it was a Monday night, and patrons were few and far between, too self-important and wrapped up in their own business to pay any attention to their surroundings. It was the perfect place to unwind and contemplate what lay ahead.

After the intensity of rehearsal week, the show was coming together like an amazing dream brought to life. As much as Max tried to pretend this was old hat to her, the truth was she'd never had an experience quite like this before.

Sure, she'd played the Hollywood Bowl a time or two, but always in a larger ensemble. Never as the headliner. As big as she'd made it in her solo career, everything about this tour was bigger and better. Even the tour buses, which they'd loaded up earlier in the day with all the luggage and equipment they'd be taking with them, had been more luxurious than anything Max had ridden in before.

After decades of busting her ass and never quite reaching the pinnacle, everything Max had ever dreamed of was being offered to her on a silver platter. All because one person had died, and another had gone to rehab, and a lot of people with money didn't want to lose their shirts. Life was as strange as it was unpredictable. But if this was truly her one last chance to stake a claim to the title of rock and roll legend— well, she was going to grab it with both hands and hold on for dear life. However she'd ended up here, it was her job to make it count.

Max's fingers picked out a melody on the guitar strings, lost in her thoughts until a shadow fell over her. Her eyes fluttered open, and her heart skipped a beat.

Dear God, I've gone to heaven.

Max's eyes widened as Jade approached, her gaze drifting up and down the young woman's body with an agonizing slowness she couldn't control. It took herculean effort for Max to mask the sudden surge of desire behind a casual grin.

"You look nice." Max set the guitar aside, rising from the cushioned rattan love seat so she could reach out to tug at one of the sleeves of Jade's dress shirt, which were rolled up to expose her muscular forearms. "What brought this on?"

Jade rubbed at her undercut and avoided Max's eyes, clearly embarrassed, even though it was equally evident from the crisp shirt, sleek trousers, and gleaming wingtip shoes that she'd dressed to impress. "I was out of clean clothes. I sent a load down to the front desk this morning, but it hasn't come back yet."

It was a plausible excuse. Even so, a part of Max hoped it was a lie. It was more than a little nice to imagine Jade getting all gussied up to impress *her*. Although if that had been the motivation, it was a thoroughly unnecessary gesture. It was becoming increasingly evident with each rising degree of Max's internal thermostat that Jade could wear pretty much anything and grab her attention.

Or nothing at all. That would *certainly* get her attention.

Normally, a thought like that would've sent Max running, but tonight she felt emboldened. The stars had aligned in her favor. She was a rock star on the verge of becoming a living legend, on an LA rooftop at sunset. The world was her fucking oyster, and it was about time she started living like it.

"I might have to have a talk with our wardrobe people," Max said with a purr in her voice and a wicked grin on her lips. "If this is what happens when your laundry's delayed, it would be a real shame for it not to happen more often."

Jade peeked up through downcast lashes, meeting Max's smoldering gaze. A current passed between them, an acknowledgement of sorts that yes, this was unabashed flirting, and if allowed to continue, there would be no stopping it. Max settled back into her seat, patting the cushion next to her in silent invitation. With a look that said Jade knew exactly what Max was up to, the woman took a seat beside her. Instead of looking at Max, Jade picked up a bar menu from the nearby cocktail table and studied it with deliberate intensity.

As Max reached for her guitar once more, her nerves were as taut as the steel strings that were plucked with each stolen glance at Jade. There was no sense in asking if continuing what she'd started was a good idea, because of course it wasn't. As attractive as the woman was, she was way too young for Max, besides being the daughter of one of Max's dearest friends. Not to mention the fact this whole tour was only happening because Max had sworn a solemn oath to Cindy to keep the girl safe from every possible danger at all times. Presumably, that included protecting Jade from Max's own baser instincts.

With Jade sitting so close, looking like she did, hell if Max knew how to pull that one off.

"Now that we've finished a week of rehearsals"—Max crossed her legs and leaned back, her guitar nestled comfortably in her lap like an extension of her body and a shield, though whether to protect herself or Jade was anyone's guess—"what do you think?"

"Surreal." Jade set the menu down but didn't signal for a server, reinforcing Max's suspicion that grabbing it had been a ploy. "After the first day, I think I worked out the jitters. This doesn't mean that tomorrow, when I hit the stage, I won't completely freeze."

"No way will that happen. You're a pro—"

"Seventeen *thousand* people."

"I should have lied about the seating capacity." Max leaned in, placing a finger on Jade's lips, unable to stop herself even as alarm bells sounded in her head. "If you start to feel like you're going to freeze when we're on stage, look at me."

"Like this?" Jade stared hard into Max's eyes. The effect was instant and overwhelming.

"Yeah." Max cleared her throat to avoid sounding like a chipmunk on helium. "That works."

"Drinks?" Fighting a wicked smile, Jade motioned toward a passing server. "Could I get that craft beer you have on tap?"

The server jotted down the order, shifting her attention toward Max.

"Iced tea for me." Whether ordered out of caution

or cowardice, Max wasn't sure. All she knew was there would be zero booze tonight. Her grip on the situation was slipping with each passing second. The last thing she needed was some liquid courage to kick her willpower to the curb. "Where's Cindy? I thought she'd be joining us."

Bringing up Jade's overly protective mother hen of an aunt was a smart move. Unlike getting involved with Jade, which would pretty much be the dumbest thing she could do. If Max was standing two feet from the mountain top of success, it was equally true she was one bad move away from playing pathetic lounges and the festival circuits for the rest of her life.

"Aunt Cindy and Uncle Rick are back in their room." Jade gave an exaggerated shudder. "Let's just say Uncle Rick is very much enjoying the results of his wife's spa makeover, and the walls of our adjoining rooms are shockingly thin for such a highly rated hotel."

"Oh God." Max clapped a hand over her mouth as her body shook from laughter.

"It's completely unfair," Jade declared through fits of giggles. "She's the one who came up with the no sex rule in the first place."

"Technically, she said no sex on the tour bus," Max pointed out, blood rushing to her cheeks as Jade lifted one eyebrow.

"An interesting detail I'd forgotten." Jade leaned forward slightly, and for a moment, it seemed she was going to say more, but the server arrived with their drinks. Jade held up her glass, giving it a slight lift. "Cheers."

Max downed half her iced tea in one go. Whose bright idea had it been to stay sober?

Jade sipped her beer, her eyes following the curve of Max's guitar. "I guess it's just us this evening. Unless you were intending to practice on your own and want me to leave."

"Oh, this?" Max gestured toward the guitar. "Nah. I was goofing off, trying to unwind."

"It's a well-known fact that playing guitar is the *second* best way to relax. But I guess we can't *all* be on our second honeymoons." Jade gave a teasing laugh.

"Good for them, though," Max said, meaning it. "I can't imagine what it would be like to be with the same person for so many years, but it's great if they can still manage to find that spark."

"Can't imagine, or never wanted to try?" As so often happened, Jade's seemingly innocent remark lodged deep beneath Max's skin.

Max started plucking a chord progression, needing to do something with her hands as Jade's question tugged at the hidden recesses of her mind, threatening to dig into a lot of thoughts she usually kept safely buried. When not answering became awkward under Jade's steady gaze, Max said, "It was never in the cards."

"Yes, yes. Back in *your* day…" Jade delivered the

line with an exaggerated frown and the voice of a grumpy old man. "I haven't forgotten your hypothetical explanation of all the theoretical roadblocks to your happiness."

"You joke, but it was true." Max fidgeted in her seat. It was the closest they'd come to revisiting that night they'd spent in Austin together. With all the conflicting emotions already coursing through her, this was about the last thing Max wanted to talk about. "Anyway, it's fine. I'm not the settling down in the suburbs type."

Jade surprised her with a knowing look, like she could see into Max's soul. "Doesn't necessarily mean a part of you didn't want the fairytale."

Max tipped her head back, and she focused on the sky, like the memories were painted in the pinks and oranges of a sunset LA.'s evening electric lights were determined to prolong. Had she ever wanted what Cindy and Grace had found? A home and a family? "Sometimes not getting what you want can be a blessing in disguise. You learn to channel it, turn the disappointment and frustration into art."

Jade looked thoughtful as she took another swallow of beer. "Your bravado was what made you famous. I've seen clips of you all performing at the height of things. Cindy and Mom were sneer-faced and surly as they played their instruments like they were weapons. When you were belting out lyrics, your body was a coil of anger."

"We were all pissed off for different reasons. Channeling that made it easier to hide the fear," Max admitted, wondering if she still had it in her to feel that anger now, or if the years had mellowed her. Without the anger, would the fear win? "The scene itself was like a war zone, though, and we were still children."

"What do you mean a war zone?"

"Okay, remember this was years ago, and it's not like this anymore, but beer bottles were hurled at our heads. Large men would push to the front of the stage and scream these awful things at us. Things they wanted to do to our bodies, how they wanted us to die, shit like that." Max frowned. "It scared me just as much as it fueled me. Fuck them for telling me there was no space for us. And fuck them for exerting that kind of bullshit effort to make girls feel small."

"Fuck them all." Jade downed the rest of her beer, slamming the empty glass onto the coffee table. "Including the ones who told you it was impossible to find a happily ever after if you wanted to keep your career. Hypothetically speaking."

Max couldn't help but laugh softly. "You're just like her."

"Who?"

"Your mom." Max had been avoiding mentioning Grace whenever possible because how awkward was that under the circumstances, with Max barely able to keep herself from imagining Jade naked from one minute to the next. Perhaps it was for the best. Like a bucket of ice poured over her head. "She'd give me that exact same look, along with the one that said *you got this*. She always had a way of making me believe anything."

"She really did." Jade flicked a tear away. It was subtle, but Max noticed, and her heart clenched, connected across the lonely childhoods they'd both endured. "I thought I'd feel closer to my mom on this tour. See what it was like for her. Maybe understand a bit more about why she left me behind."

It was the same reasoning Jade had voiced when she'd first agreed to tour. Max had let it slide, then, but couldn't any longer. Not when it was clearly a burr in Jade's heart.

"It wasn't like that." Max's tone was firm. Grace had many flaws, but she'd been nothing like Max's father. She'd cared in every way she knew how, no matter how poorly she'd shown it sometimes. "She had a kid she needed to support, and we were being promised heaps of money. Grace had only just managed her high school diploma. Music was what she knew."

"That's what she said, but to a kid, it felt less like music was what she knew and more like what she loved more than anything. That's neither here nor there. I was hoping to get into her head a little. But this tour is nothing like what y'all were doing, is it?"

"Nope. Not even a little. That last tour was for our third album. We had audiences in Europe and Asia by then. Interviews in rock magazines, our CDs in stores, openings for bigger bands, and there was still barely enough money for rent. We were getting dissed all the time."

"Here we are, kicking things off at the Hollywood Bowl." Jade closed her eyes, humming softly under her breath.

The melody caught Max's attention, a hook she couldn't help but bite. "What's that?"

"Oh, it's something I've been working on off and on. It's nothing."

"Can you hum it again?" Jade did, Max picking up the melody pretty quickly and reproducing it on her guitar. "Okay, now give me the words."

Jade laughed nervously. "I'm not ready for that."

"What do you mean?"

"Uh, you're a rock star. I can't just vomit out all the random crap that's been niggling at my brain—"

"Why not? I used to do it all the time when we were in the bus on tour. It's one of the best ways to reach the next level."

"I think *your* next level and *my* next level are very different planes," Jade said. "Or have you not noticed how all the people at the bar keep craning their necks to get a glimpse at you? In that totally LA way of wanting to stare at a celebrity while pretending it's no big deal, of course."

Max's eyes darted to the bar, where she observed at least four people doing exactly what Jade had described. LA was a funny place. They could break into a full concert, and everyone would be too cool to acknowledge it was happening. "I hate to break this to you, but I'm pretty sure they're staring at you. In twenty-four hours, you're performing live at the Hollywood Bowl. It doesn't get much more rock star than that."

"Yeah, but I'm just the replacement on the drums." Jade shrugged as if to show she didn't mind. "They'd all much rather see my mom."

"You're much more than a fill-in." Max set the guitar beside her leg and inched closer to Jade, placing her hand on the woman's arm. The night had finally fallen, the small bulbs strung above their heads lighting up like a starry ceiling. They reflected in Jade's dark eyes, twinkling, and Max felt herself falling in. On impulse, Max grabbed her guitar and handed it to Jade. "If you won't sing it, play it."

Wordlessly, Jade complied. Like magic, the music took them into that special space that only the two of them occupied. What would it be like if Jade was ever willing to step out from behind the drums and take center stage? The audience would be as enthralled as Max was, no doubt. Deep down, she knew the truth. While Max had greater name recognition and rampant nostalgia on her side, Jade was the future. She was the real star, and the rest of them would simply exist in her orbit if she ever allowed herself to shine as brightly as she was capable of doing.

Part of Max wanted so desperately to see that happen, and part of her was terrified of being eclipsed for good.

A handful of people clapped, doing their best to act cool, like private jam sessions on a rooftop were part of their everyday lives because they were special snowflakes.

"I'm dying to know the words." Max leaned closer, drawn toward Jade like gravity.

"Maybe soon." Jade glanced down, her thick lashes veiling her eyes.

"I'd like that," Max whispered. They were so close their mouths were nearly touching. Every inch of Max was on high alert, vibrating in anticipation.

As if reading her thoughts, Jade lifted her eyes and gave a saucy grin, boldness dancing in her gaze. "About this tour bus loophole you found—"

"There you are!" Cindy's familiar voice called out from a distance. "Why are you so far from the bar?"

Max snapped back like a turtle into her shell.

As Jade's head swiveled toward her aunt, her face turned cherry red.

"What are you two up to?" Cindy sat down next to Jade, tossing her arm over her niece's shoulders.

"Just a jam session. Totally innocent."

Stop babbling, Max!

"Innocent...?" Cindy's eyes probed Max's and then Jade's. "Am I missing something?"

"Of course not," Jade said soothingly, clearly more

skilled at playing it cool under pressure than Max was. "Other than I ordered a beer despite Max assuring me drinking wouldn't be on the Cindy-approved list. Where's Uncle Rick?"

"He'll be up soon," Cindy said. "Don't be ridiculous, Max. One beer isn't going to throw Jade into a spiral of debauchery."

Maxine almost choked on her tea, swallowing too hard and coughing.

Jade roughly patted her back, a thumping that Max was certain the woman was enjoying too much. "Actually, I was thinking of making it an early night," Jade said, smooth as anything. "What about you, Max? You thinking of heading to bed?"

Her brain short-circuiting under the pressure, Max shot to her feet. "Need another drink."

After that stellar performance, Max strode to the bar. Was Jade offering what Max thought she was offering? Flirtation was one thing, straddling the line that still remained in the safe zone. Following Jade downstairs would hurl her headfirst into danger with Cindy *right there*.

One of the men who'd been eyeing her and Jade earlier took the opportunity to sidle up to her. "You look familiar." There was a curious lilt to his comment that Max was all too familiar with.

"Is that right?" Max gave a casual glance to see if Cindy was watching, guilt and fear warring inside her. If Cindy caught on what had been brewing between her and Jade, Max was a dead woman. Confirming Cindy was, indeed, looking on, Max edged closer to the guy, placing a hand on his shoulder. She hated how easily this charade came to her. "Who do I look like?"

"Max somebody."

Max did her best not to roll her eyes. "This is your lucky night because I am Max Somebody."

"Can I buy you a drink?"

"I'm not sure you can afford me." That much Max knew was true, though she would continue to put on a show for another minute or two if it would cement her reputation with Cindy, and anyone else on the patio who may have construed the chemistry between her and Jade as exactly what it was.

The guy offered her a smug smile, the type that made her want to punch him in his bleach-white teeth on principal. "Try me."

"Iced tea, heavy on the ice." Max threw in a teasing smile, but only for Cindy's benefit.

Laughing, the man tilted his head back. Max leaned in closer, turning up the charm. Her mouth tasted like acid.

Out of the corner of her eyes, Max spied Jade jumping to her feet. The next moment, the woman was storming off while Cindy looked perplexed.

Shit. Max's stomach dropped as she realized she'd overplayed her hand. Max wanted to give chase and explain the whole thing to Jade but feared if she did, it'd out her to Cindy. She'd done her job too well.

Shame flooded Max, and she was transported to those early years, terrified Cindy and Grace would discover the truth about her.

At forty-two years old, would she ever be able to let go of all the pretense and fear and simply be?

CHAPTER FOURTEEN

T he roar of the crowd swelled to a fever pitch as Jade paced backstage, waiting for the opening band to take one final bow. It should've been nervous energy propelling her, but mostly, Jade was pissed.

The day had gone by in a blur after a sleepless night filled with more thoughts of Max than the woman deserved. Had she really been on the verge of inviting Max into her bed, only to have it turn into a catastrophe of epic proportion? Every thought of it made Jade want to turn stabby.

The only thing that had gotten Jade through the day with some semblance of her sanity intact was lunch with Lottie and the knowledge her best friend would be watching from the VIP section tonight. Despite her celebrity crush, Lottie had been perfectly appalled at Max's behavior and very much in Jade's outraged and hurt corner. That was what she needed right now. A best friend.

Fuck Max.

Or rather, don't fuck her. As far as Jade was concerned, aside from the obvious professional entanglement over the next two months due to being on tour and playing music together in twenty-eight cities, Maxine Gardner was as good as dead to her. Her mother was probably laughing her ass off in the afterlife, an *I told you so* being crooned in sing-song fashion.

The opening band was off the stage, high-fiving each other as they passed by on their way to the dressing rooms. The crew had gone out to dismantle their equipment and set up for the Matchstick Girls to take the stage. Cindy was in the prep area now. Max, too, although Jade was doing her best not to make eye contact or otherwise acknowledge her existence. The backup musicians were there, looking pumped up and ready to go.

Shit was getting real.

"It's almost time." Cindy waved for everyone to draw near. "Let's take a moment."

Oh, God. Was Cindy going to make everyone pray?

The backup musicians gathered closer, linking arms. Despite her best intentions, Jade furtively sought out Max, exchanging a tortured look that confirmed her fears, even as they both joined the circle.

Since when was Cindy religious? Maybe this was going to be a drum circle or something.

Cindy drew a breath. "Dear God—"

Nope. It was definitely a prayer. A lifetime of living in the South had wiggled its way into Cindy's bones.

"I'm surrounded by a talented group of women who've worked their buttocks off for this very night. For some, it's their first time performing. We ask for your love." Cindy squeezed Jade's arm, and Jade pondered whether the word buttocks was okay to use in a prayer, especially when Cindy had no problem throwing out four-letter words the rest of the time. "To all of you"—she looked around the circle—"kick some fucking ass because you're goddamn rockers. You got that? This is for Grace!"

Ah. That answered that.

Everyone let out a cheer, and Jade had to admit her throat was clogged with emotion as every hair stood up, and only partially from fear of being struck down by a lightning bolt for using that many swear words in a conversation with the supreme creator of the universe.

Before Jade could confront her aunt about her "encouragement," there was a commotion followed by assistants waving that the band was expected on stage.

"It's okay," Max whispered into Jade's ear. "Settle down, and try to relax."

Was Max for real with that bullshit?

Surely, it went without saying that telling someone

who's on the brink of performing live in front of the population of a medium sized town to *settle down* has the exact opposite effect. It was akin to telling an angry woman to "calm down" when she was rightfully pissed off. Also, where did she get off giving Jade advice after that stunt she'd pulled at the rooftop bar? You didn't get to almost kiss someone, chicken out, and then offer them life advice.

Jade wanted to say all of this and then some, but Max was walking ahead of her with what could only be described as a cocky saunter, the outstanding ass in skin-tight jeans taunting Jade with every hip sway. Something akin to hatred spilled into her veins, coursing through her. How dare Max seem so confident when she was a total wreck under her rock star cool veneer?

Before Jade grasped what was happening, she was fully on the stage, and they were being introduced to the crowd, who were manic with joy. Or perhaps they were all hoping to see the band fail like in the early days, so they could laugh their asses off while throwing milk cartons and bottles of beer.

Hell no. That's not going to happen.

The sound of the crowd was a force of nature. Yet Jade didn't find herself bowled over. The voices and shouts and cheers blended together into a single noise, a hum that lit her nerves up and bolstered her.

The Matchstick Girls were legendary, and Jade's mom was the reason all these people had turned out tonight. They might not care about Jade, but they loved Grace. If there was one thing Jade knew she could do, it was play her heart out and make her mom proud.

Pumping a fist into the air in salute to the crowd, all seventeen thousand of them, Jade took her position at the drums. She raised her drumsticks in the air, forming a cross with them because while she wasn't overly religious, or even superstitious, another prayer couldn't hurt. She waited for the nod from Max to start the first number on their fifteen song setlist, an oldie but a goodie that was sure to get the crowd on their feet.

This one's for you, Mom.

With the first crash of the drums, Jade's fear melted, and she tapped into something even more powerful: anger.

Anger over basically being abandoned for her first five years while her mom was on the road because fans like the ones they were playing for tonight had demanded it.

Anger that her mother had died so very young.

Anger toward Max for toying with Jade like she was a plaything instead of a human being with emotions. Jade might have been able to overlook Max's cowardliness for not being open about her sexuality, but to go from almost kissing Jade one minute to pouncing on a drunk guy at the bar? That had been one step too far.

A final crest of anger carried her through to the end

of the song, her hair flying wildly while sweat drenched her body. When it was done, the crowd was whipped up into a frenzy. The vibrations of their cries rattled.

"Hello, LA!" Max yelled into the mic.

The audience responded with a deafening roar. Pumped with adrenaline, Jade reveled in it instead of cowering as she might otherwise have done. Being on stage was like a drug, transforming her. Nothing felt real, or maybe it felt more than real. It was impossible to tell.

"We're the Matchstick Girls!" Max was saying, though Jade didn't know why. It wasn't like anyone there didn't know who they were. To hear the intensity of the fans, they might as well have been gods.

"On keyboard is our big boss, Cindy Weathers!" Cindy raised her hands before playing a few powerful chords, the crowd eating it up. "We've got Roxie joining us on the guitar tonight." The backup musician picked out a quick tune as the crowd cheered. "Let's not forget Grace's daughter, the beautiful and badass bitch on drums, Jade Weathers!"

Jade pelted the drums with a fury. Out in the invisible sea of humanity, feet stomped until the whole place seemed to shake.

"And I'm Maxine Gardner." With that, she counted down the next song, leading into one of the angrier Matchstick songs that Jade needed now more than ever to exorcize the demons inside her. Or if she couldn't rid herself of them, she was going to let them kick her playing into the highest gear ever.

As her sticks connected, the reverberations worked all the way through her. Never before had she felt so in sync with the music. She could hear the crowd. Feel the crowd. See them. But she didn't fear them. Not like she had leading up to this moment. They loved her, and much to her surprise, she loved them back. She loved them for helping her connect with everything important in her life, because right now, the only thing that really mattered was the music.

This was what she'd wanted all of her life, but hadn't realized how much until now. Music—that was what mattered and nothing else, damn the consequences.

Song after song, Jade was on fire. Time flew. How many songs had they played? Jade flipped through the setlist in her head, shocked to discover they were nearing the end, the final song she had refused to play alongside Max. Her heart sank as she caught sight of Roxie, turning green. Despite all her hard work over the past week, it was clear the woman wasn't showtime ready.

Jade fucking was.

Springing to her feet, she motioned for Roxie to hand over the guitar. Startled but with a look of immense relief, the woman struggled with the strap before handing the instrument to Jade, trading her for the drumsticks.

Sensing something was happening, Max swiveled her head, her jaw dropping slightly, as Jade slid the guitar into place. Jade responded by jumping into the song, her fingers nimble and powerful, hitting the first nearly impossible combination. Max's expression was unreadable even as she went with the change like it was no surprise.

Adrenaline pumping, Jade approached Max, fingers still flying along the strings, so she could sing into Max's mic. The first time Max had heard Jade sing, there'd been a playful jealousy because of how good Jade was. What Max hadn't known was Jade had been holding back.

Not anymore.

Jade reached so deep within herself she could barely stay on her feet. Max's eyebrows shot up her forehead. The crowd lost their minds.

Max edged closer, her competitive streak obvious to Jade even if the audience didn't have a clue. Their lips were practically on each other as they sang.

And sang.

It. Was. Glorious.

They didn't stop when the song ended but repeated half of it, not wanting the moment to end.

Holy shit. Jade had never experienced something so amazing.

By the time the music finally stopped, no one really noticed because the crowd was lit up. The stomping and shaking were at earthquake level.

Max, Jade, and Cindy linked hands and took a bow. Another. And another.

As they left the stage, no one wanted them to go, least of all Jade. It was like she'd discovered herself for the first time and couldn't let it go.

Cindy and Max met eyes, with Max holding up one finger. Cindy nodded.

Much to the crowd's relief, they piled back onto the stage to play the one song they'd held in reserve. The one that had torn the group apart.

"Constant Burning."

It was the Matchstick Girls' biggest hit, but the irony had always been that Cindy and Grace had been removed from the recording in post-production. If they were going to sing it tonight, on what was supposed to be a tribute tour for Jade's mother, no way was she going to let history repeat itself. She ushered Roxie back to the drums and joined Max at the mic.

Max opened her mouth like she was going to say something, maybe question what Jade was doing, but she changed her mind. The mics would pick up any sound, and whatever else Max might be, she was certainly a professional. She gave Jade a nod, pretending like this was all part of the plan.

Too bad the woman's acting skills had so thoroughly deserted her when Cindy had joined them at the bar. If she'd followed Jade's lead then, they could've spent a wild night together. A new burst of anger-laced adrenaline shot through Jade's body like rocket fuel.

They started to play.

Jade belted out the lyrics, reaching deep inside to a point she didn't know she had. The well of emotion within her expanded until she no longer knew limits. She was vaguely aware her performance was likely to blow Max out of the water, and she didn't care. Or maybe she was glad. Maybe this was revenge on Grace's behalf, served twenty years past due.

Or maybe it was Jade finally finding who she was meant to be. All of the above could be true.

As if understanding the momentousness of what was transpiring, Max switched gears, letting Jade take the solos, and only chiming in for the chorus.

Tears streamed down Jade's cheeks, and she was pretty sure there wasn't a dry eye in the house.

At the end, Jade held up her fist. "That was for my mom!"

The crowd went berserk, but at this point Jade was spent, wrung out like a washcloth. She left the stage in a daze, searching for Lottie in a sea of VIP well-wishers. She'd just spotted her best friend when Max pulled Jade aside.

"We need to talk."

Jade raised an eyebrow at Max's stiff demeanor. Was the woman going to reprimand Jade for the best performance of a lifetime? Jade wouldn't let her.

"Lottie's waiting."

The other woman's lips pressed tight. "After the meet and greet," Max insisted. She was giving off a strange vibe Jade couldn't identify, something powerful enough Jade couldn't say no.

"I'll meet you at the bus." With that, Jade raised her hand to get Lottie's attention and darted off, leaving Max behind.

TWO HOURS HAD PASSED, maybe three. Jade had lost count and had yet to come down from the high of performing for that massive crowd. She and Lottie had drunk champagne and danced before finally saying goodbye with long hugs.

Two tour buses waited in a secure location behind the venue. They were shiny black, the sides covered in purple swirls and loops. The windows were dark enough that seeing inside would be impossible. Jade thought they looked large enough to carry a football team and a marching band.

In reality, twenty-five people would call the buses home for the next eight weeks. Despite their luxuriousness, the quarters in each would be cramped with twelve bunks so small they were affectionately referred to as coffins. There were two bedrooms, one on each bus. Cindy and Rick had claimed one, Max the other.

Jade was young and could sleep anywhere, or so they'd told her, so she'd been assigned one of the bunks outside her aunt's room.

The driver of the bus was opening the underside storage and carefully packing the instruments in. After long and careful consideration, Jade had brought Grace's kit instead of her own. While she was less familiar with her mom's set, it felt like the only choice for a Matchstick Girls tour. Tonight had proven her correct.

Jade's kit was still in the basement, along with her mom's records, instruments, and memories. There was a pile of paperwork from the symphony on the dining room table, the details of the job offer made official in black and white. Jade had been ignoring it. That was what she'd be coming home to when all this was done. A house empty of people but filled with memories and a future that chafed. How could she choose a safe, boring life after this?

Suddenly overcome with exhaustion, Jade wanted nothing more than to climb into her bunk and go to sleep. One foot and then the other, to the stairs, and up them. The smell of cleaning supplies and upholstery hit her. She'd been warned that tour buses could get smelly, but right now they were fresh and clean. Full of potential.

There were two couches—couches, in a bus! They were upholstered in a beautiful sage green, the color soothing and inviting. There was a kitchenette as well, two mini fridges with glass fronts. Inside were rows and rows of soda, sparkling water, bottled water, smoothies, and snacks lined up and ready. Past the kitchenette was a thick velvet curtain pulled partway across the opening. Beyond, Jade could make out the rows of bunks, stacked three high.

Her aunt was slipping through the door to her bedroom when she caught sight of Jade and smiled. "Heading to bed, Kitten?"

Jade nodded. "I'm beat."

"That's because we slayed it out there tonight. You especially." Pride radiated from Cindy's face, along with a faint glow from all the champagne. "Is it everything you thought it would be?"

Was it? Jade wasn't even sure anymore. It felt more like a dream with each passing second, like it could all slip through her fingers before she had a chance to grasp it and hold it close.

"Twenty-seven more shows to go," she said with a laugh, because the last thing her aunt needed was for Jade to be morose on their very first night on tour.

Her aunt shut the bedroom door, and Jade made her way to her bunk, noting a few spaces were already occupied but by no means all. The drive tonight would be short, just three hours or so to San Diego, so the partying could go on a little longer for those who wanted it. Jade, however, would not be among them.

It was only as she pulled back her covers that Jade's memory was triggered.

Max.

Jade had promised to meet her at the bus so they could talk. What they had to talk about, Jade didn't know. Maybe Max wanted to lecture her for wiping the stage with Max's ass on those duets. As Jade turned back to the door, she couldn't help smile a little at the thought. If she could make one wish, it would be for Maxine Gardner to regret rejecting her for that asshole at the bar for the rest of her life.

Was that too much to ask?

The driver of Max's bus was in his seat, barely looking up from a book when Jade entered. More of the bunks were filled on this bus. Fewer partiers, apparently. All the way at the back, Max's bedroom door was slightly ajar.

Nerves jangling, Jade lifted her hand to tap anyway, not wanting to barge in. The door swung inward, and Jade's breath caught as Max filled the opening, her expression the very picture of rage.

"What the hell was that tonight?" Max demanded after shutting the door.

"A concert," was Jade's flippant reply, overcome with an urge to poke the grouchy bear with a stick. "I would think you'd know that by now."

"Don't be cute." Max folded her arms, every muscle tensed. "Did you and Roxie agree to the switch in advance?"

"It was more of a spur of the moment thing." Jade tilted her head to one side, folding her arms across her chest to mimic Max and prove she wouldn't be intimidated. The Matchstick Girls had started as a band of equals back in her mom's day, and by God, it was going to stay that way. No way would Jade let Max boss her around.

"It was a risk," Max pressed, her anger showing no sign of abating.

"It worked." Jade stood her ground. That part was no lie. The gamble had paid off beyond Jade's wildest hopes, and there was no way Max hadn't recognized the resulting magic.

"It did. Your instinct paid off. It was fucking brilliant. It still would've been nice to be let in on the plan in advance."

Somehow having Max admit Jade was right was less satisfying than it should've been. Jade was looking for a fight, her hurt over Maxine's rejection still jabbing without mercy at her heart. "Oh yes, because it's all about you. Everything is all about you, isn't it?"

Max placed a hand on her chest. "What'd I do? I think I did everything possible to pivot to your whim so the audience had no idea it wasn't planned. Were you having a hissy fit or something? Not getting enough time on the mic so everyone could be convinced you're the better singer?"

"I was talking about last night, you ass." The words lanced the wound, and Jade bit her lip, refusing to show weakness.

Max's face went ashen. Though she didn't reply,

there was little doubt she knew exactly what Jade was talking about and lacked the ability to deny it. The real kicker was even filled with hurt and anger, Jade still found Max irresistible. That realization made Jade go for the kill.

"How do you think that made me feel? One minute your lips are nearly on mine, and I'm inviting you to my room. The next, you're off banging some groupie or whatever it was you got up to with your batting eyelashes."

"I think that's carrying it a little far." Max's face twisted with a hundred emotions at once, none of which Jade understood.

Except one. Lust.

That one made Jade's blood boil, even as it stoked the flames she'd been doing everything in her power to extinguish since last night. "Hell no. You don't get to tell me—" The bus lurched forward, causing Jade to lose her balance. "Shit. Are we moving?"

There was another, stronger jolt, and Jade went tumbling forward. Max's arms reached out to break her fall. A second later, Jade was smashed against the bedroom door by the force of Max's body being thrown into hers as the bus gathered speed.

Then she was aware of nothing except the heat of Max's mouth covering hers.

CHAPTER FIFTEEN

Max didn't care about anything but Jade's fingers gripping her hair, lips locked with hers in desperate wanting. She breathed in the soapy clean scent that surrounded them, grateful they'd both had the foresight to wash the performance grime from their bodies before boarding the bus. Not that she'd ever considered this possibility while doing it, at least not as anything but a fantasy as the hot water had rinsed the suds from her skin.

The reality was so much more than Max had ever imagined, teasing the promise of everything she'd ever wanted. Her body burned at every touch.

What the hell are you doing? A small voice inside Max's head struggled to be heard, even as she fell deeper into Jade's embrace, her fingers twisting through the woman's mass of dark curls as they devoured one another with reckless abandon. *We shouldn't do this.*

Silencing the voice, Max pressed on. Logic faded against the pure, overwhelming heat of desire. It was Jade who finally broke away, resting her forehead against Max's, her breath coming in gasps.

"You're such an idiot," Jade said. Before Max could respond, Jade was kissing her again, pecking out a staccato rhythm with her lips all over Max's face. "I'm completely furious with you."

"Yeah." Max gulped for air, tilting her head back and sideways to allow better access to her throat and neck. "I can tell."

This would've been the perfect opportunity for Max to pull away, for sanity to be restored. Giving into temptation with Jade was a huge mistake. It only added complications. Max should put a stop to it immediately. Cindy would be beyond pissed at her. Apparently, Jade already was.

But there was no stopping the desire coursing through Max's body, fueled by the insatiable hunger of Jade's mouth. As wrong as it was, Jade's anger was hot as hell. Super fucking hot.

Stop, Max, the voice in her head tried again. *Stop it right now!*

Max did not stop.

Freeing one hand from a mess of curls, Max's fingers went to work on the buttons of Jade's shirt. The small white discs offered little resistance, and the shirt slid off, baring Jade's smooth, dusky skin. Rounded breasts were nestled in soft, navy blue lace. The anticipation of more spurred Max's every movement as she trailed her hands along Jade's narrow waist.

Tell her this is a bad idea.

Max's thoughts were fuzzy and jumbled, but her traitorous mouth managed to utter, "You're so fucking beautiful," right before diving for a taste of exposed flesh as Jade let out a gasping moan.

In other words, the exact opposite of stopping things before they went too far.

"You're overdressed," Jade replied, slipping her hands under the hem of Max's camisole, palms skimming along her ribs until Max lifted her arms and the camisole was pulled up and over.

Goose bumps prickled along her flesh as Jade stared at her greedily. Max reached behind to unhook her bra, letting it fall off. Stepping close, she wrapped her arms around Jade's shoulders and kissed her again, their fronts pressed tight. The small buds of Jade's nipples rubbed against her sensitive skin, and she gasped.

Needing more, Max maneuvered Jade to the bed, which was about the same size as the one they'd shared in Austin, yet took up the majority of the small space. They tumbled down together, mouths constantly seeking the other. Jade's tongue slipped into hers, and Max moaned, letting herself be rolled onto her back.

Jade tugged off Max's jeans, and the panties were quickly eighty-sixed, as well.

Jade, on top, gave Max a slow once-over while unbuttoning her own jeans, a look so gluttonous and sexy Max's body burned. The pressure building between her legs reached an intensity she honestly couldn't remember ever feeling before.

As Jade lowered her long, strong body on top of Max's she bit at her lower lip. A final warning issued in Max's brain. Like maybe she should slow this down? Or stop it entirely? But it was less a flare and more a tiny, ineffective flicker that fizzled out like a wet match.

Then Jade's mouth found her nipple, and Max sighed, arching into the wet warmth and drag of teeth, pulling her further into the abyss. Executive function and impulse control had never been Max's strongest skills. Sex and gratification, on the other hand, were things she was exceptionally good at.

Jade palmed Max's other breast, her mouth drawing it in deep. Maxine felt the tug travel from her breasts straight to the apex of her thighs. She took Jade's free hand and guided it to her slick heat. They moaned together as fingers sank into her, curling up as they slowly explored.

"Fuck," Max hissed, wanting to be louder but remembering that a thin door stood between their passion and a half-dozen or more sleeping crew members.

Jade released the nipple she'd been teasing and shifted up so that she could straddle Max. Her core was there, dark curls damp and glistening. Her pace increased, fingers thrusting with quiet strength. Max's legs fell open, and she could smell the sweet musk and the damp saltiness of sex starting to cling to their skin.

Head swimming with the pulsing, aching need her body felt, Max reached down and added her hand next to Jade's. As Jade fucked Max thoroughly with strong, able fingers, Max rubbed her clit with the flat, firm strokes she liked.

Panting, her hips rocked with need, her pleasure beginning to coil in. It collapsed in on itself, squeezing into a tight ball of sensation so intense it almost hurt.

Max moaned, her skin growing fevered with heat. The confusing anger emanating from Jade, along with the fear of being found out by someone who she couldn't ghost, was now making reaching climax a struggle.

"What do you need?" Jade demanded.

"Another finger. Fuck me hard," Max managed, her voice raspy and thick.

Jade shifted, twisting so she could do as asked. Max felt the stretch of the third finger and gasped, elated. The pace increased, the slick sound of Jade's attention battling with Max's muffled moans.

Then Jade added her other hand, her fingers

pressing down hard on Max's, moving with them at a rapid pace. The grinding pressure was what had been missing.

That small, condensed ball of sensation exploded out, a star going supernova, and Max jerked as she came.

Her body buzzed and hummed in the afterglow.

Jade looked pleased-as-punch, and that cocky grin was such a turn-on. Needing to even the playing field, Max rolled, taking Jade with her. They switched, Jade lying back, flush fanning across her cheeks. She appeared suddenly vulnerable, but also wanting, and Max was drawn to that, to the way Jade could flip back and forth between assertive and submissive.

Bracing up on her arms, she leaned in and kissed Jade. It was languid, all the frenetic energy they'd begun with spent. Now was the time for savoring. She licked and nipped. Jade's mouth tasted of honey. Their tongues danced, teasing and tasting.

She waited until Jade's hips were rolling, lifting from the mattress in a silent plea.

Taking her time, Max kissed the freckles that spread from cheeks to neck, licking along them. She started to move toward Jade's breasts when the woman put her hands on Max's shoulders.

"I love sucking on tits, but I'm not big on having mine touched." There was a hesitation there, a fear of rejection Max understood all too well.

"I only want to do what makes you feel good," Max assured her.

She moved down farther, dragging her tongue in tantalizing circles along Jade's taut waist and biting gently at her hips. Max gave Jade the chance to sink back into the act.

When Jade's legs fell open farther, Max was eager. She scooted down, moving between thighs, and inhaled. The scent was sweet and heady. Jade was soaked, and Max leaned in, dragging a tongue through the slickness.

Jade's groan punctuated the air, and Max grinned to herself while reaching up, quickly, to cover Jade's mouth. Lust-flooded eyes stared, and Max mouthed "thin door." Jade nodded and let her head fall back, leaving Max to continue the task she was aching for.

Falling into the taste, the smell, the heat, she licked and sucked until she needed to put a hand on Jade's stomach to hold her in place. Max took Jade's clit into her mouth and pulled, tongue moving in time, until the woman under her clenched tight with a muted cry.

"God," Jade said breathlessly, "that was incredible."

"Mmm." Max pressed a gentle kiss to damp curls before crawling up to drape herself next to Jade, an arm thrown across the woman's stomach and her leg draped over Jade's toned thighs.

She took in the rise and fall of Jade's chest, her breaths still occasionally twitching as she came down.

Max loved the curve of Jade's kiss-swollen lips and the way their bodies fit together so well in bed.

The loud hum of the bus hurtling toward San Diego helped drown out some of the niggling thoughts at the back of Max's mind that she had no interest in analyzing. After all, she was in bed with a beautiful woman. They'd had fantastic sex. Jade was as in sync with Max between the sheets as she was when they had instruments in their hands.

It had been a long time since she hadn't wanted to hop right out of bed after sex. Something about Jade had her hooked, and that deserved investigation.

Her eyelids were heavy. They should talk, probably. This situation was sticky and not just because they were still sweat-slicked and naked. But as her body began to filter the night's drinks and her mind tried to filter the night's activities, Max wanted nothing more than to sleep.

She wanted to enjoy this moment.

But there was no hiding the fact that Jade was on the wrong bus. If Cindy discovered that, all hell would break loose.

"Uh…" Max hesitated. "We need to get you onto the other bus."

"Got any ideas that don't involve Mission Impossible level stunts?" Jade offered a lazy, sex-drunk grin. "It's been a while since I did parkour."

"Oh, I would love to see that, but I have a better idea." Max reached for her phone and texted the driver to stop at the next twenty-four-hour gas station. "Hopefully, Cindy's already fast asleep, so when the buses pull in for my Cool Ranch Dorito fix, you can slip onto your bus."

"This really isn't how I pictured the tour starting off."

Max couldn't tell if Jade was happy, sad, angry, or all of the above.

CHAPTER SIXTEEN

A week into the tour, the sounds coming from Aunt Cindy and Uncle Rick's room remained as frequent as they were unbearable, like someone was watching a dirty movie on a loop. The musicians and crew who were riding on the bus along with them sat huddled in the front lounge, earphones on to preserve some shred of dignity. For Jade, it didn't help. Even if she couldn't hear them, knowing what was going on behind that door—and being aware that every single person on the bus knew it, too—was utterly mortifying.

When the buses pulled off the highway in the middle of nowhere between Denver and Dallas to refuel, Jade seized her chance for escape. She grabbed her backpack, stuffing it with the essentials to survive the remaining hours of the long trip.

Cindy came out of the back bedroom, her hair

mussed. She wore a red silk kimono robe with long black fringe, looking for all the world like a Victorian brothel owner. Or maybe that was what Jade couldn't help picturing under the circumstances. "Where're you headed, Kitten?"

"Change of scenery," Jade replied, keeping it brief. If her aunt tried to stall her, she wasn't sure she'd survive to the state line. "See ya on the flip side."

Before Cindy could lodge a complaint, Jade was off their bus and barreling toward Max's at full speed. It was only when she was more than halfway there that she remembered how action-packed the week had been. Between shows, travel, and setup, she and Max hadn't had a moment alone since... *that night*. With hours of driving ahead, they would have to discuss it. Which was worse, listening to her aunt and uncle going at it like horny teenagers or facing the music from her own reckless decisions?

Jade honestly wasn't sure.

But it was too late to turn back now. Jade was already standing in front of the open door. The driver gave her a knowing look. Clearly, he hadn't forgotten about the emergency snack stop on night one and was under no pretenses about the true reason for it. Jade climbed the stairs into the coach, cheeks aflame.

While one of the sound technicians made himself a sandwich at the kitchenette, and Roxie played a game of cards with another backup musician on the far sofa,

Max sat off to the side in a love seat, one leg draped over the arm, looking relaxed.

"You okay?" Max straightened as Jade approached, instantly scooting over to make room.

Jade sank into the seat beside Max and spoke low. "Do you remember the no sex on the tour bus rule?"

Max's face burst into flames, her eyes widening as they darted, panicked, at the others present.

"I didn't mean us," Jade whispered. It rankled how quickly Max was primed and ready to panic. Whether or not Jade agreed with Max's choice to remain closeted, she wasn't so cruel as to out her. "It's my aunt and uncle. They've been holed up in their room day and night like a couple of rabbits on Viagra, and my ears can't take it anymore."

The redness in Max's face shifted to green even as she was clearly trying not to laugh. She waved a hand around her. "*Mi casa es su casa.*"

Grateful for the easy welcome, Jade yawned, stretching her arms to ease the cramped muscles in her back. "It is weird how quickly these metal buckets start to feel like home."

"A home you can't sleep in, apparently," Max said as Jade yawned again. "Meanwhile, most of the crew's napping on this bus. You sure you don't want to join them? My room's at your disposal."

"I've never been one for day sleeping, unless I'm on airplanes. Or did you have something other than napping in mind?" Jade chuckled as Max's expression morphed into one of shock as she grabbed hold of the elephant in the room and paraded it out like the circus had come to town. "I'm kidding." Maybe not so much kidding as testing the waters, but Jade was unsure of where she and Max stood. She'd only come with an idea of where they *should* stand.

"About that, though…" Max's expression became even more uneasy than when they'd been talking about Cindy's sex life. The woman's body radiated unease. "Could we talk in my room?"

"Yeah, sure."

Maxine proceeded to make a show of grabbing her guitar and asking Jade to come "work out some lyrics" with her. Rolling her inner eyes, Jade wished she could tell Max she was only making it more obvious.

As soon as the door was shut, Max whirled and said, "I've been thinking—"

"That it was the heat of the moment, nothing to be embarrassed over, but definitely a one-time deal?" Jade interjected, determined to beat her to the punch and not come off like some lovesick groupie. No offense to her bestie, but it wasn't like Jade was Lottie. Max might not be the black cloak wearing villain she'd imagined, and yes, she was damn good in bed, but Jade was a realist. Even when that realism was wrapped up in disappointment. "I totally agree."

Max frowned. "You do?"

"Uh, yeah." Jade let a laugh escape at Max's obvious confusion over the turn of events. "God, you must be so used to women—excuse me, I mean *people* throwing themselves at you on the road, desperate to make you fall in love with them and whisk them away to some fairytale rock star romance."

I won't be one of them. Preemptive approach to minimize potential pain.

"I just… I didn't want you to, you know—"

"Get hurt?" Jade filled in. "Look, I may be younger than you, but I'm a grown woman. I know how the world works. And I'm not the clingy type."

"Are you sure you're okay with it all? You were pretty keyed up after the concert, and we never really talked about why." The genuine concern in Max's tone was as unexpected as it was unnerving. Jade would never have thought a rock legend would spare a second thought for whatever girl she'd fucked after a concert. Was it because she was worried it would affect Jade's performance on stage? It hadn't so far, so they were pretty much in the clear. Unless the unthinkable was true. Could it be that under all her punk rock bravado, Maxine Gardner actually had a tender heart?

"Max, trust me." Jade leaned forward, looking directly into Max's bright blue eyes. A shiver materialized out of nowhere, passing through her in a most unnerving way, but Jade didn't drop her gaze. "The other night was a lot of things. My first time in front of an audience of seventeen thousand people, for instance. A major emotional gut punch because of my mom. But what happened with us? It was like yoga."

"Yoga?" Max scoffed. "I don't know what the hell kind of yoga y'all have in North Carolina these days, but that was nothing like the classes I've done in New York."

Jade laughed so hard she snorted, ridiculously charmed by Max's brief relapse into the southern accent of her youth. So flippin' adorable. "I meant it was a way to relax and achieve balance after some stressful days."

"Okay," Max said with a thoughtful nod. "Yoga. I assume if things get stressful again, we'll need to avoid doing any more... *yoga*."

"Exactly. It would be way too risky. Not because I'd turn into a lovesick groupie," Jade assured her quickly, wanting to be sure they were completely on the same page. "But because I'm sure half the people on this bus are on Aunt Cindy's payroll, willing to report any infraction of her rules at the drop of a hat."

"I hadn't thought of that," Max admitted, some of her earlier discomfort slipping back into her features. It was obvious that despite the pains she'd taken to stay publicly in the closet over the years, she'd never had reason to question the loyalty of her bandmates and crew. Probably because unlike Jade, Max did not have a meddling aunt to contend with.

Jade shrugged. She was too used to her crazy family to let it weigh on her for long. Looking out the tinted bus windows, she sighed. "It's kinda nice not traveling at night, even if the scenery isn't much. Sand, sand, and more sand."

"The true rock star life no one tells you about." Max perked up visibly as the buses merged onto the next long stretch of highway. "Oh, I keep forgetting to give you something, but now that we have hours to fill." She hefted a shoulder, reaching into a bag on the floor of the bus. Max pulled out a small, wrapped box. She smiled as she held it out to Jade.

Heart in throat, Jade took the gift. She tugged at the paper until the tape gave, and it ripped. In her hands was a photo of Grace. Her mom on the drums, hair wild. The photographer had managed to freeze the moment perfectly, sweat drops suspended in air and sticks in the process of descending to the drum skins.

It was her mother's face, eyes shut and smile radiating bliss, that struck straight at Jade's heart. The sheer ecstasy conveyed in the photo was riveting.

"I found it in my apartment," Max said softly, "and I meant to give it to you the night before the tour started, but... uh, we both know I screwed *that* up. Here's to hoping better late than never. Also, I'm still kicking myself because I had to miss her funeral."

"Had to miss it?"

"When I arrived, there were too many paparazzi. I didn't want to take anything away from Grace."

"I didn't know."

It was sweet, and coming from Max made it even

sweeter. It made Jade wonder how much of what her mom had believed about Max and the band's final days had been real and how much had been fiction. Max truly seemed to care. But Jade couldn't go down that path, riddled as it was with anxiety boxed up tight against a day in the distant future when she couldn't avoid thinking about it anymore. Maybe Jade would be dead by then and wouldn't have to deal with it at all.

She sniffled, all at once aware of the tears threatening to pour from her eyes.

"Hey, I'm so sorry." Max's eyes darted around as if seeking out a magic wand to turn off the crying. "I didn't mean to upset you."

"You didn't. It's very sweet. Almost shocking coming from you." Jade tried to laugh, but it only caused more tears. "With the tour going non-stop, and the lack of sleep, I can't stop thinking how..." Jade swallowed, unable to finish the sentence.

"Go on," Max said softly and sweetly.

"I-I really like being on tour," Jade started with a stutter. "Which will make walking away from it so hard. You get to keep this life. According to the socials, your career is on the up. What do I have to look forward to? The symphony for the next fifty years?"

"Does that have to be your future?"

The sickening resentment had been growing for weeks, and Jade couldn't stop herself from vomiting the worst of it. "My mom did a shitty thing and basically made me promise on her deathbed that I wouldn't make the mistakes she made, that I would have a stable, reliable future. Now that she's gone, I guess Cindy has decided to pick up the torch on her behalf and run with it for all she's worth."

Max sat, stunned.

Jade wasn't quite finished. God, how had she not known just how angry she was? Where had all this emotion been? "I want to take that fucking torch and burn my stupid promise to the ground."

It felt good to say it out loud, but as she emptied some of the vitriol, guilt clung to her like a demon in a horror flick. Was this another stage of grief? Did she truly want to go back on her word, or was she acting out because the loss of her mom hurt so damned bad, and for the first time since Grace had gotten sick, Jade was experiencing something that passed for happiness?

"You *do* want to be like your mom?" Max's question ended on a seriously iffy lilt, like she was fencing for the answer and afraid of upsetting Jade more. "Because you're getting a pretty late start on a lot of her choices."

"Choices?" Jade snorted. That was being charitable. "You mean the stupid mistakes? Yeah. I've always wanted to be more like her. I've loved every fucking second of this so far. The more shows we do, the more it feels right."

"We should talk to Cindy."

We? Jade wanted to ask but instead went with, "How?"

Max tapped a fingernail on her front tooth. "I need to noodle that some. I know Grace wouldn't want you to be miserable for the rest of your life. Her parents weren't exactly tripping over themselves when Grace hit the road the first time, but they didn't stop her, either."

"I'll try to remember that detail, but it was a deathbed promise." A flash of a memory, her mother's face yellowed, her body frail, and those eyes so fierce they'd speared Jade straight through with their insistence.

Max nodded. "We have similar family problems, even if they are also entirely different."

Jade's head was filled with snot and shame, leaving her with little ability for riddles. "What does that mean?"

"I was a huge disappointment to my father. Like a chain wrapped around his throat. He didn't want me to do anything except wait around and be his punching bag. When I left, it was a huge relief, despite the fact I was still a child. Unlike you, I promised myself never to look back. It's come at a cost. There's always a cost to be someone's child. You're the peacemaker type. I'm the burn everything to the ground type. Yet, our issues revolve around our parents and their disappointment in our decisions."

"Disappointment. I should get that tattooed on my forehead."

"I recommend your backside or somewhere else not many will see." Max winked.

Jade snorted with laughter. "Are you saying my backside is disappointing?"

Max's cheeks flushed. "Definitely not. Do you know what helps me when I can't figure something out in my head?"

"What?"

"I write a song."

After hesitating for a moment, Jade reached into her bag and pulled out a notebook. She'd been thinking about sharing it since that night on the rooftop in LA, when Max had asked about the words to the song she was humming. Jade still didn't know whether she could trust the woman, but she felt compelled to take the risk. Times like this, it felt like Max was the only person she could be completely authentic with. She tossed the notebook onto Max's lap. "Been there. Done that."

Max cracked the notebook open, flipping through all the filled pages. "Is there more than one notebook?"

"Older stuff, mostly crap. This is the one I've been working on this past year." *The good stuff*, Jade left unsaid, for fear she would be wrong. Watching Maxine thumb through the pages was upping her anxiety.

"What kind of song do you want to write? Please don't say a stupid love song."

Max whistled and then smiled, making Max look so much like herself on the original posters. "Let's try writing about disappointing our parents. That's always a fun topic."

"Way ahead of you." Jade's confidence wavered, and she wanted to snatch the pages from Max's hands before the woman realized Jade had no future as a rock star. A fresh sheet of paper and a fresh start with Maxine were definitely called for.

As if sensing Jade's mood swing, Max said, "It's hard sharing something from your heart. But take it from me, as someone who's been stifled by a record company just penning songs that the corporate bigwigs think will sell will crush your soul even more than pursuing your dreams." Horror crashed into her eyes. "I'm sorry. I shouldn't have said that. I have no idea how hard it's been for you, being on the tour, knowing your promise."

"It's okay. I knew what you meant."

"Can I see the song?"

"Do you promise not to laugh?"

"I would never."

Jade took the notebook, flipping to the page and reluctantly handing it to Max. As she read it, Jade saw the lyrics behind her closed lids.

When I was three, my mom/ put drumsticks in my hand.

She taught me to play hard and fast / To let my feelings fly-

Until my wanting grew too big /And she encouraged me to hide.

"I can feel the hurt on the page. Like the words are popping with carbonation. They need to be let out, or they'll explode."

Jade sensed Max was thinking before *Jade* exploded.

"In three weeks, we'll be in New Orleans, and we'll have a few days of R & R before we're back on the road. I think I can—" Max shifted in her seat. "I'm going to call in a favor."

"Do you know some voodoo psychic medium who can talk my mom's ghost into freeing me from my promise?" That seemed almost within Max's rock star wheelhouse.

The woman hit her with a sexy, playful grin. "Well, New Orleans would be the place for that, but no, I have something else in mind."

"Which is?" Jade looked at Max with meaning.

Max tapped her fingertips to her lips. "I don't want to promise anything, but I think it might help."

"Okay."

"No, seriously." Max reached for Jade's hand. All of a sudden, Jade found herself wondering if her emphatic assertion that she could never fall for Max or have her heart broken like some foolish groupie had been a little premature.

CHAPTER SEVENTEEN

"**K**now what I'm thinking?" Max stepped off the sidewalk on Bourbon Street in New Orleans as a family of tourists barreled toward her, oblivious to anything but their bickering. Even almost getting mowed down wasn't enough to ruin her mood. After four solid weeks on the road, having a few days off at the halfway point of the tour was just what the doctor ordered.

Spending as much of that time exploring her favorite city with Jade was icing on the cake. Once they'd cleared the air about the night they'd spent together, Max's mind had been put at ease, even if her ego might've been a little bruised by how quickly Jade dismissed the idea of ever having feelings for her. But it had freed Max to enjoy the younger woman's company without any niggling fear of inappropriateness, and the result had been an easy friendship that had made the past few weeks a delight. It was like all the best of touring with the original Matchstick Girls, without the angsty drama that had come from being so young and full of rage.

"If you're about to suggest we go into the Hustler Club over there, I'm going to stop you right now." Jade took a sip from the straw stuck out of the drink she was holding, a potent concoction in a ubiquitous green plastic to-go cup that was appropriately—if somewhat ominously—shaped like a hand grenade.

"The Hustler Club?" Max blinked, uncertain how the conversation had gotten sidetracked, though if she had to guess, she was going to blame Jade's drink.

"While I see nothing wrong with women being expressive with their bodies, that place screams frat boys on spring break." Jade held out her massive plastic cup, which looked similar to something you'd give a kid at an amusement park, aside from the booze. "Do you know the best part of New Orleans? These beauties." She gave a little shake to emphasize.

"*That* was what I was trying to ask," Max interjected, chuckling at Jade's tipsy stream of consciousness rant, "at least until you brought up the strip club—"

"Did the thought of titties knock the words right out of your head?" Jade jabbed her elbow into Max's side. Luckily, she continued to keep her eyes forward, or she would have spied Max's cheeks catching fire at the mention of tits. "What's in these things again?"

Good question, Max thought. It sure was going straight to Jade's head, not that Max was complaining. It was pretty adorable to see the surprisingly responsible young woman so relaxed now that they'd been set free from their tightly regimented schedule for a few days.

"Let's see." Max squinted, trying to recall the menu description. "I think it was gin, vodka, rum, and melon liquor."

"That explains it." Jade giggled as she took another sip. "It's basically as deadly as it sounds. You sure you don't want one?"

Max shook her head. "The mint julep I had before was plenty. My goal is to stay sober enough to ensure you don't end up headfirst in the Mississippi."

As they continued along the street, jazz music drifted out of one of the bars. Since it was barely after four in the afternoon, the music scene wasn't on full blast yet, and there were way more families than Max was used to from the late night parties she'd attended at the height of her career. It also meant the afternoon sun and the humidity were merciless, and Max's shirt was sticking to her back.

"Oh, you never told me what your favorite part of New Orleans was." Jade took another sip. She was nearing the bottom if the spluttering sound the straw made as she sucked was evidence.

"Being free. We have three whole days off!" Max spun around, unable to contain her glee, Mary Tyler

Moore style. Though she hated to admit it, life on the road was a lot tougher on her in her forties than it had been a decade ago. Also, she'd never mention Moore to Jade, who'd undoubtedly give her a confused "who's that" look.

"That means a lot more of these!" Jade held the drink up in the air once more.

Maxine arched an eyebrow. "Is that why you arranged for Cindy and Rick to go on a steamboat river cruise?" The happy couple had been ecstatic, gazing at each other with moony eyes so bright Maxine didn't envy Jade's sleeping arrangement on the other bus.

"I don't know what you mean." Jade tried very hard to maintain a straight, stoic visage. "I thought it was a nice gesture for all that she's done for me."

"Sure, along with the tickets you got them for the alligator feeding excursion and the cemetery tour. If I didn't know better, I'd say you were trying to arrange things so you can get blotto without the watchful eye of Aunt Cindy on you."

"Oh, you think you know me so well, Maxine Gardner," Jade teased. "Actually, what I'm most thankful for is having a real bed to sleep in, and not whatever that thing on the bus is supposed to be."

"A luxury is what I'd call it," Max countered. "When we first started going on tour, we slept in your grandma's van." Maxine's forty-plus neck would never tolerate that kind of arrangement again.

"At least you didn't have to put up with Cindy and Rick and their crazy monkey sex."

The day's previous mint julep threatened a reappearance. "They do *not* have crazy monkey sex," Max said in a hoarse whisper, grabbing Jade's arm so she could look her straight in the face. "Do they?"

Jade shuddered. "For two old people, they do."

"Old people!" Max squealed, lightly slapping at Jade's shoulder. "Watch it. I'm closer in age to Cindy than you."

"Do I need to remind you that when you came over, Cindy was wearing mom jeans and *gingham*? Cindy's internal age is exponentially higher than yours. Hell, I'm probably older than you if we're taking maturity into account." Jade shook her grenade-drink, a frown falling into place as she realized it was empty.

"Hey!" Max couldn't help but laugh at the dig. "First, you call me old. Now, I'm immature?"

"Which do you prefer?"

"I need to think about that." Max crossed her arms, but there was no arguing because she knew Jade was right. Max had worked hard to present herself as 'forever young,' and more than a little of that image had spilled over into her personality. Not that Jade needed to be calling her out.

Jade laughed, clearly also aware that she'd scored on that point.

"Do you know what goes really well with that drink?" Max asked.

Jade gave her cup a dubious look. "I hope it's not red beans and rice, because I'm still full from lunch."

Max gave a half smile at the memory of the wonderful food. "You have to admit, though. They know how to do them here."

"That they do."

Maybe it was all the tourists surrounding them, but Max was overcome with the need to show Jade some sights. "Have you ever had a beignet from Cafe du Monde?"

"I've had one from a box with the Cafe du Monde logo on it. And once we tried to make coffee from the can you can get at the grocery store."

"Totally not the same thing. Come on." Max took Jade's hand, dragging her toward the water where the cafe stood. "I really hope the line isn't too long."

Jade trotted behind her, surprisingly steady on her feet considering the massive amount of alcohol she'd consumed. "People stand in line for a beignet?"

"It's the thing to do in New Orleans."

"I thought listening to jazz and getting drunk were the things to do."

"Okay, those are crucial parts," Max agreed, even as she made a mental note to keep a closer eye on Jade's drink orders. Not that the woman was being even half as irresponsible as Max had been at her age, but she couldn't seem to fight the wave of protectiveness she felt. That was probably Cindy's fault. "Trust me, though. You can't leave New

Orleans without having a beignet smothered in powdered sugar."

As it turned out, the line wasn't too bad. Max's heart was light as they snaked their way through the marble-topped cafe tables and black chairs to the counter to order.

Jade gaped at the scene. "I feel like I'm at Disney World."

"Because we're in a line?" Max guessed. "You did know New Orleans Square was based on a real place, right? Like, New Orleans. It's right there in the name."

"Yes, smart-ass. What I meant was, doesn't this look like a scene out of a Disney movie? There's Jackson Square across the street with that church that's just about a dead ringer for Cinderella's castle. A line of horse-drawn carriages waiting for passengers. In case you missed it, the fucking Mississippi River is right there. With a *paddle boat*. You can't get more nostalgic Americana than this." Jade stopped talking and made a face. "I guess you can but probably not for the better. Don't get me started on the Andrew Jackson statue. Point is, this doesn't feel real. It's like I'm in a dream."

"I always feel that way here. A pleasant dream, not one where I wake up screaming and all sweaty." Max tugged on her shirt. "Okay, I'm sweaty, but the humidity is insane here."

"I'm used to it," Jade said, and Max believed her. The woman certainly looked cool and collected. And gorgeous. Not that Max should be noticing that, especially now that they were free of the watchful eyes of Cindy's spies. There was no telling what kind of trouble they could get into if Max let her guard down.

Lead me not into temptation. The old Sunday school phrase popped into Max's head, a remnant of those times a neighbor had taken Max along to church with them out of a mixed sense of pity and duty, since it was no secret her dad wasn't about to do it. The prayer made as little sense to her now as it had then. Who needed to be led into temptation? Max was perfectly capable of bounding straight toward it on her own.

They reached the front of the line, and Max was grateful for the distraction, ordering a bag of beignets to share. The best way to avoid one kind of temptation was definitely to give in to another. Max was all too ready to swap out her inappropriate thoughts toward her companion with some wholesome gluttony toward fried dough and sugar. *And some coffee for my friend.* A little sobering up would hurt no one.

When the woman at the register announced the total, Jade reached for her wallet, making Max chuckle.

"What?" Jade asked.

"Nothing really. It's just you're always insisting on paying your half."

Jade shrugged one tanned shoulder. "It's how my generation does things. Splitting the bill."

"It's refreshing. Most people just take from me."

Which was probably why she didn't keep many people around for long.

"That's awful."

Max shrugged. "People can be, but then someone comes along and surprises the heck out of me and makes me believe in the good in humanity. Thanks for that."

"You're welcome, I guess." Jade continued to hold out her money, but Max waved it away. Reluctantly, Jade put the bills back into her wallet.

"Let's enjoy these by the river. There are some steps we can sit on." Max led them to the concrete stairs, finding a spot for the two of them to sit to enjoy their beignets.

"I can't believe I'm sitting here with you," Jade said dreamily after a minute had passed, "eating fried doughy goodness, staring at the Mississippi."

"Out of those things you listed, which one surprises you the most. Me, beignets, or the Mississippi?"

"How do I separate the three? You will forever be associated in my mind with these." Jade raised one of the beignets, sprinkling the ground with sugar, and then waved to the river with her other hand. "And that."

"I can live with that, I guess." Max lifted a beignet and turned it in her fingers to admire it. "There are way worse things."

"It's been an amazing day." Jade shifted slightly, bumping Max's shoulder by way of saying thanks.

The sun hung in the sky to their right. Not close to sunset, but low enough to make the beams dance along the water. A barge floated by, and off in the distance was a bridge.

"This has always been one of my favorite places," Max said, drinking in the view. "When I was a kid, I read Huck Finn, and I wanted to climb onto a raft and float down the Mississippi to get away from my father."

"I'm sorry." Jade's voice was low and full of compassion. "Mom only ever told me snippets about all that."

"I only remember snippets now." Max looked to the water, her heart growing heavy. "He's been dead a long time, and it had been years since I last saw him before that. You know, that first day when I came to NC to see Cindy, I drove to my old house without thinking. It wasn't there. Demolished. And I felt... nothing." The edge of the cement step behind cut into her lower back. "I can't remember his voice. The screaming, yes, but not him speaking normally. Maybe he never did."

As if uncertain what to say in response, Jade pointed to a piece of graffiti on the step, reading it aloud, *"Don't hate urself."*

"Good advice." *Yourself* was spelled wrong, but Max couldn't shake the feeling it was an omen or something.

"I like this one." Jade pointed to the drawing of a bee with the words: *I guess it bee like that sometimes.*

"Cute." Smiling, Max pointed to *Feel It* in black lettering in a pinkish-purple bubble.

"Oh, that's a good one." Jade ripped a piece of beignet off and handed it to Max. "Are you feeling it?"

There seemed to be a deeper meaning in the way she asked, but Max didn't know what it was or how to respond. With the closeness of Jade's body and the simple companionship of the day, Max was feeling a lot of things, but none of them were safe to mention. Besides, Jade had been the one to set expectations, right?

"I try," Max replied vaguely. "Like this tour. It's leading to good things."

"Such as?" Jade lifted an eyebrow in a suggestive way.

"I like spending time with you." Max tensed, uncertain if she should have admitted that so readily. What would Jade think she meant by it?

Jade's enigmatic smile didn't help, as easy to read as the fucking Mona Lisa's. "That's nice to hear."

"I talked to Skip this morning." Max cleared her throat, anxious to bring the conversation back to work, where they both knew where they stood. "The record label is green lighting a live album. They want to record it when we do our final show at Belmont Park in New York."

"Really?" Jade nearly slipped off the stair, and Max

lunged to grab her shoulder, envisioning her rolling all the way into the water.

Righting Jade, Max said, "That's not even the best part."

"How isn't that the best part?"

"They're loving our new sound." Max's stomach fluttered as she prepared to reveal her carefully crafted surprise. It had taken a few weeks and a lot of strings being pulled, but she'd managed it.

"The band's?" Jade scrunched her face, as if trying to figure out what was new about the nostalgic music they played.

Max geared up. "No, ours. Do you remember being pissed off with me on opening night, and changing the last two songs on the fly?"

Jade snorted, raising one eyebrow. "How could I forget?"

"The songs or being pissed?" Max joked.

"As with you and the beignets, those things are forever connected in my mind."

Max nodded in agreement. "The crowds are eating it up. Believe it or not, so are the guys at the record label. After all these years of saying no, Skip thinks they may be willing to listen to a demo of something new. Not the same old songs they've made me stick with for years."

"That's wonderful, Max."

"Here's the thing." Max set her drink down on the step, eager for the reveal. "I've arranged for us to have some time in a real recording studio. You and me."

Jade bit her lower lip, a flicker of doubt in her eyes instead of the excitement Max had expected. "No Cindy?"

Max frowned. "Well, no. Cindy's been to plenty of recording studios in her day. I thought it would be something fun for you."

Unnervingly, Jade's worry did not dissipate with this explanation. "What do we tell Cindy? She's not really over you screwing her the first time."

"Me?" Max felt a jolt of genuine shock. "I never did anything of the sort."

"The recording of "Constant Burning," Jade pressed. "The one that launched your solo career. You had Cindy and Mom cut out of it entirely."

God, that. The biggest hit of her career continued to be a ghost haunting her.

"That wasn't my doing," Max insisted, her heart pounding under the unfair accusation. It suddenly became very important to her to clear her name. "I only went solo after that because I knew Cindy and Grace were planning to bail on me. Didn't your mom or aunt ever mention that part?"

"Nooo." The way Jade said it, it was hard to tell whether she believed what Max was saying. "I think if we record together and Cindy finds out it was part of something for the record label—"

"Let's not get ahead of ourselves," Max interjected.

"I don't even know if they'll actually follow through. We don't have to share anything we do together with them. But I'd like to show you this studio. It belongs to a friend, and it's amazing. State of the art. Total legends have recorded there."

"Yeah?" It was clear Jade was tempted. "You're sure we couldn't go with Cindy?"

"It's tonight or nothing, I'm afraid," Max answered truthfully. "Cindy and Rick are on that river cruise."

Jade's eyes widened as a smile teased her lips. "We're going to the studio tonight?"

Max checked the time on her phone. "In exactly one hour. Got other plans?"

CHAPTER EIGHTEEN

T he studio was shadowy inside, the lights turned low and the flicker of the LEDs on the console standing out stark like stars. Inside the booth with Robert, the sound engineer, Jade bore witness to Max's frustration.

There'd been twenty takes of the song. A cumulation of small mistakes were turning what was supposed to be a sublime experience into a disaster.

Robert glanced at his watch before hitting the button that allowed him to speak to Max in the other room. "Do you have another song, maybe? We could try that."

Through the glass, the older woman appeared defeated, shoulders slumped and eyes blank. Jade struggled to understand what she was seeing. Every bit of the time spent with Max gave the illusion that when it came to performing, nothing rocked the rocker. In the studio, all the insecurities Jade had observed here and there came to the forefront.

There was no sugarcoating what Jade was witnessing. Max was absolutely crushed.

"I might have another song," Max said, but there was no missing the doubt that encased every word. Jade felt a tug in her chest, a desire to swoop in and fix things.

The sound engineer not-so-discretely glanced at his watch again.

"How long do we have the studio for?" Jade asked the man, worry flitting through her like moths swarming a campfire.

"The room's technically available for you the rest of the night, but…" He didn't need to add that he hadn't planned on being there that long.

"Do we need to be supervised?"

"Nah, the owner's known Max for years," Robert said. "I trust her to lock up and turn off the lights. But between you and me, she's shit when it comes to working the equipment. Without me here to do it, she'll end up with the record equivalent of taking a photo with the lens cap on."

"Is that right?" Jade couldn't help but chuckle at the mental image. "I hear she's like that with cars, too. But these *are* just demos, right? Not finished tracks?"

Through the glass, they heard Max start strumming

hard discordant chords. Angry and grating, Max's frustration manifested in sound waves.

"That's what I was told."

"Good. So, they can't totally suck, but they don't need to be perfect. Could you show me the bare minimum of what I need to get a decent demo?" Jade pointed at the board. "I've been watching, and I know which button records and some of the various boosters, but—"

He looked over, impressed. "You don't need much more of a crash course, then. That'll do for now."

"Perfect." Jade lifted her chin, determined. "I'm going to try to help her figure out what's not working. But it might take us a while. Do you want to go home?"

"I appreciate it." Robert didn't bother to appear on the fence about it, quickly grabbing his keys. "I don't know, though. I've worked with Max on albums before. This thing she's going through right now is new. Hopefully, you can help her through it."

He was out the door, calling a quick goodbye to a confused Max and practically running to the exit. Max came into the booth. "Where's he going?"

"I told him he could go home."

"I don't have a good take, though. Something's off."

Jade swiveled her stool to face Max. On the steps next to the river, Maxine had been all enthusiasm, and it was imperative Jade get Max back to that feeling. "Which is happening, why?"

They locked gazes, and the heat that smoldered there was almost too much to bear. After a month of pretending it wasn't real, that this thing between them had been a one-time thing that fizzled and died, the truth was it was like live coals waiting for a puff of oxygen to roar back to full force. They were different ages with such different life experiences and futures ahead of them. It would destroy Cindy if she ever found out. In short, there were so many reasons to snuff it out. But in this moment, Jade didn't want to. She wanted to fan the coals until the flames were hot enough to burn forever.

The silence of the studio turned the world insular. All of New Orleans was beeping and hustling around them, but soundproof walls cut it all away.

"I'm not sure what's wrong," Max admitted, her shoulders crashing downward under the weight of looming failure. "I'm not feeling the tune."

Jade hadn't been feeling it, either. It wasn't just the constant mistakes. The piece had sounded stale and lackluster, meaning Max's heart wasn't in it.

"What made you write it?"

Max went to a couch and slumped into the deep cushions, the black leather squeaking as she got comfortable. "I didn't have any other ideas, but I knew the label wants fresh stuff."

"This track has those vibes, if that's okay for me to say."

Max's face scrunched. "Yeah. It's the truth. I don't know how to get the words in the right order. It's like, in my mind, I can picture them, but by the time I try to get them out, they're jumbled and meaningless."

Jade wanted to push Max more on that, relating in so many ways, but feared Max was quickly approaching her breaking point. Jade's foot bounced. "Do you want my help?"

"What? Right now?" Max's face pinched.

"Yeah."

"You were probably right before." Max buried her face in her hands. "Maybe the world doesn't need another love song."

The words snapped back, and suddenly, Jade thought perhaps she'd been wrong. The issue wasn't love but intention. "The world always needs love." Jade's voice was soft, her tone hushed.

Max's response was raw and tortured. "What do I know about it, though?"

Jade wanted to say what Max had was an ocean of mismatched emotions. Too many conflicting feelings crashing against one another, leaving nothing but foam and chaos. "Fuck. It could be so many things. The magic of this experience, maybe? Or your dad—" She'd meant to cut it off sooner but quickly recovered. "Losing my mom for sure, and how all of this is tied into the gift she gave me."

"My family experience isn't about love. More the lack of," Maxine said.

"Which will make it powerful," Jade argued. "Sadly, I think more people can relate than say that wasn't their experience. Let's face it, our childhoods leave a lasting mark."

"*Stain* is a more fitting word. It's like when you wear a new shirt for the first time and spill coffee or something on it. No matter how much you scrub it, there's still a faint outline, reminding you it's not perfect." Max shrugged. "That's the nature of life. How do I put *that* into a song?"

"I have an idea." Jade pulled out her trusty notebook, quickly adding scribbles in thought bubbles.

Max hovered over Jade's shoulder, humming a few notes before singing the fresh words. A thrill rippled through Jade as Max's deep, gravelly voice, provided the depth of pain Jade's words alone couldn't.

They continued this way for well over an hour, Max singing, rearranging the words as she did.

Within another hour, Max was back at the mic.

The biggest difference between this song and a standard Matchstick tune, Jade realized, was the speed. Max was slowing this one way down, her voice low and mournful. The hurt oozed out of Max, the festering wound finally coming out into the light to begin the healing. The beauty of it was indescribable.

After several takes, Max came back to Jade, exhausted and defeated. "We can't use this one."

"It's really fucking good, though," Jade argued, excitement over what they'd accomplished coursing through her.

"But it's about my dad, and I just..." There were tears in Max's eyes, threatening to spill over. "This isn't what I want people to know about me."

Jade nodded, taking Max's hand. "I get it. I do. The song I was working on about my mom is like that, too. It would kill me for the fans to hear, for Cindy to know how I felt sometimes. But, Max, this song is *good*."

Max let out a tortured sigh. "I know. It's maybe the best thing I've ever done."

"Let's not give up yet." Jade checked the time, chewing her lower lip as she wrestled with a plan. "It's ten o'clock now. Let's keep going until midnight. We'll change the words together, shroud the meaning. But it's too good to let this go."

Max swallowed, lifting her drooping chin as if with renewed purpose. "Okay."

They worked nonstop for two hours, reaching into the depths of their souls to fit words to Max's music. It was so close, but not quite there. At one point, Jade grabbed the guitar. The melody she'd been humming in the bus flew from her fingertips to the strings, changing with each time through, blending Max's original melody with the reworked lyrics until they reached a seamless whole that was entirely different from what Max had created before.

Jade was breathless as Max played it through for her, joining in as they reached the chorus. "This is it."

"Let's record it," Max said, finally seeming at peace. "It may or may not work in the end, but for right now, it will help get the demons out. For both of us."

Jade went into the booth and queued up the recording. It began to run, the red light flashing for active, and she made her way back into the studio.

Max reached for her guitar, picking the first progression before singing. The resonance of her voice turned Jade's emotions into a powerful tornado inside. With a nod, Max signaled for Jade to join in, and they sang the song they'd created together.

It wasn't perfect. Jade could spot transitions she'd want to smooth over, but the instrumentals layered in her mind. She could hear the drum track she'd add, the bass line...

Then it was finished.

When Jade didn't move or speak, Max went into the booth. The red recording line flicked off. Jade could still see it behind her eyelids. The haunting hollowness, the way Max put it all on the line, showing her invisible scars, like the stain on the T-shirt. The same way she had done.

Jade crossed the studio cautiously. She crouched in front of Max and, before she understood what was happening, Jade reached up to cup Max's cheek. Max covered Jade's hand, a strong, calloused thumb brushed away tears falling from Max's eyes, and Jade couldn't tell if Max knew the source. It was like she was having an out-of-body experience, but also wanting to comfort herself.

"You should know," Max said, "that I'm pretty pissed at you right now."

A startled Jade rocketed up. "What? Why?"

"Because that was my first song that's truly me, and it's fucking golden. Because of you. I've known me for a long time, and I've never been able to plumb my soul in four decades. You've known me for a hot second and see me inside and out."

An unexpected laugh erupted from Jade. "It's my thing. Seeing people." Jade rushed to add, "Don't make a *Sixth Sense* joke. Not right now. I feel like I ran a damned marathon. So much effort. You must be even more exhausted."

"Yes and no." Max's gaze bordered on searing.

Jade returned to cupping Max's cheek. Max, in turn, kissed Jade's palm, making her breath hitch, as if that was the most erotic move.

The problem with vulnerability, with peeling apart layers she hadn't even realized were there for her and Max, was the two of them needing comfort from the other who truly understood what lay beneath. Exposure required warmth afterward, a blanket to make them safe again.

"We can't," Max whispered. "We said that one time was the only time." But her other hand found its way to Jade's thigh.

"Yes, we can." Jade sucked in a breath, then slid onto the floor, catching Max's hands before the woman could pull away. "I'm not asking for forever. We don't have to tell anyone."

She opened her legs and tugged gently. Max moved between them. Jade's thighs cradled Max, and she reached up to bury her fingers in blonde curls, lightly tugging at the strands. "You're clearly hurting," Jade said. "This is just you reeling from loss."

"But—"

"No buts." Jade leaned close and nuzzled Max's jawline. The smell of sunscreen and sweat but also the amber scent of expensive shampoo filled her nose. "If it's for the tour, only temporary, then what does it matter? I've been feeling good for the first time since Mom started really being sick. Is it so wrong that I want to keep feeling good as long as possible?"

Strong fingers clamped into her thighs above her knees before releasing, palms smoothing up toward her waist. "I don't want to fuck you over," Max whispered.

"Then *don't* fuck me over." Jade nipped at an earlobe, her pulse racing as Max groaned. "Just fuck me. Fuck me, and make music with me until this is finished."

Max moved closer, her hands slipping under the

cotton hem of Jade's tank top. "Are you sure you can be finished?"

No, but blood pulsed in Jade's ears, and she throbbed between her legs. No, she didn't think she could ever be finished with this. Jade didn't see the woman who'd been her mom's enemy becoming Jade's nemesis as well.

She saw someone who fit into her world, her music, so perfectly it ached.

Did Max feel that? No doubt she was attracted to Jade. But the woman had bigger things to focus on. Music after the tour. Her songs. Max probably didn't have time for a relationship or coddling a heartbroken young woman who didn't know what to do with her life. Break a promise and chase a dream or give in and be doomed to a career she didn't want.

"When it needs to be over, I can walk away," Jade said, willing the words to be true. She could be pragmatic. Then, because she didn't want to talk anymore, Jade kissed Max.

Their lips pressed together, soft and full. It was a slow kiss, different from their first, angry kiss. Jade took her time, tasting Max, tracing her lips with a tip of a tongue, teasing.

Max moaned, and her lips parted, allowing Jade to explore her further. Their tongues slid and wrestled. Max's arms went around Jade's waist, her head tipped back. Jade shifted on the floor.

Their fronts pressed tightly together, and Jade

locked her arms around Max's shoulders, needing to edge out any space between them. She pulled close enough she imagined she could feel the kick of Max's heart.

The kiss was as slow as it was hungry. Want built in Jade's body, her limbs growing loose and eager while her core was pulling tighter and tighter.

Max pulled her tank top off, and the chilly air licked at Jade's exposed skin. She shivered, but that could have been just as much from the fresh suck of Max's hot mouth on her neck as it was from the contrasting temperatures.

Eager to touch more of Max, Jade set about undressing the woman. Each button on her shirt was popped with care, revealing inch after tantalizing inch of skin. Sliding it off slim shoulders revealed a lacy black bra, Max's pebbled nipples visible under the flimsy fabric.

Humming in appreciation, Jade lowered her mouth and licked at one of the nipples. The lace was rough against her tongue. Max's fingers threaded through Jade's hair, pulling her closer, and Jade let herself go.

She pulled hard, sucking as much nipple and breast into her mouth as she did fabric. Her teeth closed lightly on the bud, and Max's hips jerked. Jade shifted her attention to the other breast, sucking and laving, moving back and forth until Max squirmed.

With care, Jade shifted, helping Max to stand.

Kneeling in front of the woman, Jade undid the button of Max's jeans, peeling the skin-tight denim off. The scent of her lust hit Jade, who bit back a moan.

Matching black panties were quickly discarded, and Max sat on the chair near the recording equipment.

Jade put her hands on Max's knees and pushed her legs apart. The low light of the studio still shone brightly enough to reveal the slick slit and wet curls between Max's legs.

Leaning in, Jade lightly licked at the outer lips, tasting the desire there. Max grumbled, and Jade couldn't help but smile before answering with a firm lick, tongue sliding between the folds before swirling over Max's clit.

The taste was sweet and uniquely Max.

I want her to come on my face.

Jade started to work in slow, languid strokes. The last time had been all angry desperation. She was going to savor this, to seek out all the spots that made Max's toes curl.

Max seemed to be on the same page, calling out soft requests. As she grew more impatient, Jade made sure to listen carefully. When Max's hips slid down the chair more, Jade pushed her thighs up, supporting Max and fully exposing the plump, swollen pussy.

"I want your tongue in me," Max moaned.

Happy to oblige, Jade began to thrust her tongue into Max's tight channel. Her nose was buried in the wet folds, and she used that to her advantage, keeping pressure on Max's clit.

"Fuck," Max hissed, wiggling but held in place by Jade's strong arm.

She recalled how Max had liked things vigorous, and so after another minute of fucking her with her tongue, Jade pulled back. She smirked at the pitiful mewl Max answered with.

The woman's disappointment didn't last long. Jade pushed three fingers into Max, feeling the tight stretch of the woman. Hands clung to her shoulders as she began to fuck her, pushing deep and stroking the place inside Max that sent the woman howling.

They rocked together, Jade using the undulating motion of their bodies to find Max's pace.

"Fuck," Max gasped, hips pumping, "I'm going to come."

Jade's fingers were squeezed, Max's body clenching and stiffening as she cried out, low and throaty. She slowed her stroking, letting the woman ride her hand until she sagged.

"You're so sexy when you come." Jade slid her damp fingers into her mouth, sucking clean Max's pleasure.

She moved up, kissing Max's hip bones and taut belly, licking at the undersides of her breasts. As Jade moved, she slipped her own pants off, straddling Max's thigh. The cotton of her boy shorts soaked through, the sewn seam stretched across her swollen clit.

Max put her hands on Jade's hips, thumbs tucked into the creases and stroking. Bracing herself on Max's shoulders, Jade began to grind on the thigh, the pressure exquisite. It wasn't going to take much. Getting Max off had been hot enough to bring Jade close to the edge.

She rode Max, circling her hips and bearing down until her body tightened with the promise of release.

"Come for me," Max said, using her grip to pull Jade more firmly on her thigh.

The pulse between Jade's legs flared brightly, pushing out until her body was rigid, her hips jerking and grinding hard, wringing out every last second of the orgasm that shot through her and left ripples of sensation in its wake.

Jade sank onto Max, panting in the crook of the singer's neck. A hand stroked her back in slow, soothing circles.

"You're incredible," Max murmured in her hair. Sweat slicked between them, yet Jade didn't want to pull away.

"Thank you." Her voice was hoarse. Jade pressed a kiss to the pulse point, feeling the flutter of a heartbeat against her lips. It was just as fast and jagged as her own.

It wasn't forever. She knew that. But in that moment, Jade felt whole and supported in a way that she hadn't in a long time. Like Max saw her, heard what she wanted, and instead of telling her to box it up, Max encouraged her to go for it.

For the duration of the tour, that's what Jade would do. As often as she could. She was going to live and if not love, then at least fuck like there was no tomorrow.

CHAPTER NINETEEN

The phone on the side table rang, its shrill jangle cutting through Max's unconsciousness and poking at a massive headache she would have been happy to sleep through. Her mouth was cotton. What the hell had she gotten up to the night before?

The phone was incessant. All at once, the luxuriously warm tangle of limbs surrounding her rolled away, leaving Max chilled and slowly coming to terms with wakefulness.

Oh, right. *That* was what she'd been up to the night before. The studio with Jade. And then back to her room at their quaint French Quarter inn.

Just as the pieces fell into place, the phone stopped.

"What time is it?" Max asked, addressing the question more to the time gods than to her still drowsy companion.

"I feel like we just went to sleep," Jade said with a moan, dragging a pillow over her face.

"Probably because that's accurate."

Another phone began to sound with short, insistent vibration. It wasn't the phone in the room this time, nor was it Max's cell phone. With her head still half buried, Jade slapped her hand around on her nightstand until the source of the disruption had been located.

"Hello?" she croaked. At least Jade sounded as rough as Max felt. If the woman's youth had managed to help her wake full of sunshine and energy after their long night, Max might have cried.

"What do you mean I wasn't there—I mean, here? When?" The bed shifted as Jade bolted upright, stiff. Jade mouthed the name *Cindy* to Max. "Well, that's weird. I must not have heard you knock. Maybe I was already asleep."

At the sound of Jade's tight voice, anxiety tweaked the strings in Max's chest. She shifted up onto her elbow, eyes like sandpaper as she worked her eyelids open. Jade was staring at her, eyes wide with panic. Without making a peep, Max tried to ask *Is she there now?* Jade shook her head vigorously, and Max let out a sigh of relief.

"Yeah, I did just wake up. It's what time? Eleven!" Jade was fisting the sheets hard with her free hand. "Uh, yeah. Okay. Can you give me twenty so I can shower and stuff?"

Max was fully awake now. Dread was an ice pick to her brain, hammering away behind her left eye in tandem with the headache from lack of sleep. Was Cindy putting two and two together? She pressed her ear to Jade's phone and heard Cindy saying something about sleeping the day away like a teenager.

"Don't be silly," Jade was saying, utterly lacking conviction. "I'm hungover. No, I don't know where Max is. Have you called her room?" A pause as the response came through.

Max tossed her hands in the air, wishing Jade hadn't planted the idea in her aunt's head. The last thing she needed was for Cindy to try calling again and somehow hear the ringing through Jade's phone.

"Okay, right." Jade cleared her throat, whether from nerves or to get Max's attention, it wasn't clear. "Yeah, I'll meet you in the courtyard in twenty minutes. Enjoy your coffee."

As Jade wrapped up the call, Max sprang out of bed, picking up another bit of garbled chipmunk reply chattered out of the phone's speaker. Jade released the sheet and pointed frantically to the phone and then to the clothing that had been draped—or more accurately, flung with zero regard for where they landed—on several of the hotel room's surfaces.

The warning was unnecessary. Max was well aware their watchful mother hen of a bandmate was on the move. There would be little time to spare. Max's head swam. She had to pause, getting her bearings, before moving as quickly as she could to collect Jade's clothing.

"She's having coffee downstairs in the courtyard with Uncle Rick," Jade said in a gush as soon as the call was done. "I've gotta get out of here without her seeing me."

"Ya think?"

Max's heart thudded against her ribcage. When was the last time she'd had to hurry someone from her room, like a guilty teenager breaking the rules? Max couldn't remember. Probably when she'd actually been a teenager, which was longer ago than she cared to admit. Her body, pissed at the lack of sleep, didn't want to cooperate.

Jade moved the edge of a curtain just enough to see outside. "Shit. I think every table has an unobstructed view of the walkway."

Quick. Think.

Cindy and Rick were staying in a room on the ground level, facing the inn's lushly landscaped courtyard. Max and Jade had rooms on the second floor, several doors apart, connected by a narrow walkway with an ornate wrought-iron railing. It would be a good fifty-foot dash with nowhere to hide from the second Jade was out the door.

Max went to the window, peering out. "Do you know which one they're at?"

"We'll have to open the door to check."

"I'll do it."

Jade was now hopping into one pant leg, and Max prayed the woman had been calling from the hotel phone in her room, not sitting in the courtyard watching their doors like Cerberus, ready to attack.

Max opened the door slowly, cursing that the storm door was swollen with humidity, causing her to put her weight into making it budge slightly to view the courtyard.

No sign of Cindy or Rick.

Jade stood behind Max, only half her shirt on, the arm still holding the phone poking out from the hem. Realizing she no longer needed it, Jade tossed the phone onto the bed and shoved her arm through the sleeve.

"You may need to be prepared to throw yourself down and do an army crawl," Max whispered hoarsely. She wasn't sure why she was whispering, except that the moment seemed to call for it. "Keep close to the wall."

Max lifted a finger to her lips, pantomiming the need for absolute silence, as if she had all the experience in the world in this type of situation. Talk about a terrible end to what had been an amazing night together. It didn't take a genius to read the expression on Jade's face and realize she was of the same opinion.

"Go," Max whispered.

Jade had one leg out of the door when Cindy's

voice echoed across the courtyard. "Look, Rick! There's a lizard on the fountain."

Jade pulled back into the room, eyes wide with panic.

Stomach threatening to revolt, Max tucked around the corner, keeping her eye on the space below. She caught sight of Cindy and Rick at a table beneath a wide umbrella, their view of the upstairs walkway seemingly obscured. She motioned to them, and Jade nodded that she saw them, too.

"Now," Max whispered, shoving Jade out the door while keeping her eyes glued to the back of Cindy's head. Jade dashed to the end of the walkway and disappeared through her own door in a flash. Only then did Max truly dare to take a breath.

"Okay," Max muttered to herself. "Better tidy up, just in case."

She was about to slip back inside and close the door when she realized Cindy had turned in her chair and was staring straight at her face.

"Max!" Cindy screamed, causing Max to tense like a prisoner caught in a searchlight.

Struggling to play it cool, Max stepped onto the narrow balcony. "You bellowed?"

"Why aren't you answering your phone?"

"I keep it on silent," Max yelled back. "No one ever calls me, unless it's a robocall."

"I was talking about your hotel phone."

"Oh…" Max offered an exaggerated shrug. "I didn't

even know I had one. Maybe you called the wrong room."

"Maybe." Cindy shielded her eyes, making it difficult to determine if she bought that excuse or not. "Hey, don't tell me you overslept, too."

Max's eyes darted downward, only now realizing she'd thrown on the first two items of clothing she could find, which were a tank top and boy shorts. In other words, she was standing outside in what was essentially her underwear.

Correction. The boy shorts weren't hers. She'd stolen Jade's underwear.

Fuck.

"I've been working on a song," Max rushed to explain. "Had my headphones on." Max hoped that wasn't too much, but maybe it would stop Cindy from asking any more questions about why she hadn't heard the phone.

"Okay, I'm coming upstairs in a minute to grab Jade, but I'm going to stop by your room first." The way Cindy said it, she was clearly not asking for permission.

Max lifted a hand in acknowledgement as she shut the door. As soon as she heard the latch click, she threw her back against it and let out a breath. That had not gone as well as it could have. She could only hope Jade was most of the way through her shower by now.

Speaking of showers, if Max didn't take one, Cindy wouldn't have to guess how she'd spent her night. The smell of sex that clung to her skin would be a dead giveaway. More whirlwind than human, Max showered and dressed. She was drying her hair with a spare towel when she heard the knock at the door.

And spotted Jade's phone, still in the middle of her rumpled bed.

"Max?" Cindy called out.

Max froze where she was, one hand reaching toward the phone and the other toward the door, effectively stuck in the middle and not accomplishing a goddamn thing. Real smooth.

Cindy knocked again. Abandoning any hope of hiding the phone, Max grasped the door knob and swung the door open completely. Max's bandmate was looking chic, her silk shirt draping perfectly and her hair in a fresh, blunt bob. Her eyebrow was so arched it appeared sculpted and the sort of a mother hen-ness Max remembered from the old days.

Cindy waltzed in, her eyes scanning the room with unconcealed nosiness. "Nice room. I wondered if it would be the same as the one I'm in."

What she left unsaid but heavily implied was she'd half expected Max to have demanded a mega star suite, maybe have it stocked with a bowl of only green M&Ms or a live goat or something. Max gritted her teeth, not willing to let herself fall into the trap of getting her hackles up.

More importantly, Max focused all her energy on

not turning her head to stare at Jade's phone. If she didn't look at it, maybe the evidence would disappear.

"What was it you wanted to stop by about?" Heart in throat, Max smeared a smile on her face, hoping it looked genuine.

"I want to talk to you about breaking the rules." Cindy placed a hand on her hip, fixing Max with a stare that nearly stopped her pulse.

"What rules are you referring to?" As if Max didn't know. The wrecked bed and forgotten phone might as well have been a neon sign announcing her night of debauchery with Cindy's niece.

"No partying." Cindy held up her finger, pointing it at Max's face with each word for emphasis.

"I swear on my favorite guitar I was working on a song all night." It was a hundred percent true. She and Jade had been recording until after midnight. That meant it had technically been morning when they'd started ripping each other's clothes off.

After all these years of practice, Max was nothing if not a master of technicalities.

"We'll see what my niece has to say about that." Cindy pulled out her phone. "I'd better give her a jingle and let her know to meet us down here."

"No!" Max nearly lunged at the device in Cindy's hand. If she dialed Jade's number and Max's bed started to vibrate, the jig would be up. "Er, I think I heard a door shut down the way. That's probably her."

Cindy gave Max a dubious look, but for once, the

stars aligned, and the sound she'd heard actually had been Jade leaving her room.

"Good morning!" Jade announced, entering through the door that had been left open, looking as fresh and wholesome as if she'd had a full night of uninterrupted sleep. In her bedroom. Alone.

Cindy whipped around to face Jade, still wearing her sternest expression. "I was lecturing Max about breaking the rules."

"The no partying rule," Max rushed to add so as not to make Jade go through the same heart-stopping trauma she had a moment before. The moment Cindy glanced away, Max pointed to the phone on her bed. Jade's eyes widened before she blinked away the shock.

"We weren't partying," Jade was quick to say. "We were working on a song."

"Both of you?" Cindy's brow furrowed. "Together?"

"Yes." Jade gave an eager nod. "We were at the studio until well past midnight, but I promise there was no partying going on. It was strictly work." Jade also seemed well versed in technicalities, as she'd technically sobered up considerably by the time they'd arrived at the studio.

At the mention of the studio, which Max had conveniently tried to leave out of her version, she briefly closed her eyes, wishing she had a time machine.

"I thought you were in *here* working on the song."

Cindy's puckered lips said Max had some 'splaining to do.

"I was," Max said rather lamely, all creative excuses having dried up in an instant, right when she needed them most. The only thing that provided any relief was seeing Jade inch toward the bed and grab her phone, sliding it into her pocket. At least the most damning evidence had been concealed. "After leaving the studio, around one this morning."

Cindy turned to Jade with a *butter wouldn't melt in her mouth* smile. "You know what, Kitten? I need that New Orleans guidebook I loaned you the other day. Can you get it for me?"

"Right now?" Jade pressed her lips together tightly, seeming to realize she'd made a blunder by revealing the recording studio detail.

"Yes."

"Why?" Jade squeaked.

"Because we're going to go sightseeing today." Cindy continued her innocence and light routine, but Max wasn't fooled. As soon as Jade was gone, she knew she was in for a world of hurt. "I feel so guilty about how much time your uncle Rick and I have been spending without you, I thought it would be fun to have a girl's day out on the town."

"Oh, well, uh…" Jade gulped.

"Please go get the book." Cindy blinked. "Now." Max could basically start measuring herself for her coffin if Cindy's demeanor could be trusted.

"Ooo-kay," Jade cast a glance in Max's direction as if saying sorry for leaving her alone with Cindy.

As soon as Jade was gone, Cindy rounded on Max like an angry guard dog. "Listen to me. I don't know what kind of game you're playing, but you'd better watch yourself."

"What do you mean?" Max hugged her chest, Cindy's words so sharp they'd nearly pierced her straight through. There was no doubt about it. Cindy knew about her and Jade. Max was going to die.

"Oh, come off it." Cindy let her hands fly into the air. "The worst part is she trusts you, and you're taking advantage of that. She's fifteen years younger than you! She has no idea how the world works."

Max was briefly infuriated for Jade, who was once again being relegated to the position of young child instead of late-twenties woman. "Hold on," Max spluttered. "Jade's a grown adult."

Having become intimately acquainted with some of the things Jade knew how to do, Max could vouch for her being anything but a naive little flower.

"She may be an adult, legally," Cindy countered, "but she doesn't know anything about recording contracts. She'll get eaten alive."

Wait... It suddenly occurred to Max that she and Cindy might not be on the same page. "Contracts? I'm sorry, Cindy, but you've lost me."

"Don't play coy. It's no secret Skip always wants to get his claws into the next big thing."

Max was well and truly lost. "What does Skip have to do with this?"

"I know full well if there was a recording studio being offered up, it came from him. I don't trust that man. I don't trust *you* much more. One wrong move and—" Cindy sliced a finger across her throat. "Just because I'm having a blast on this tour, doesn't mean I'm not paying attention. I am. No monkey business."

At exactly the wrong time, Max remembered Jade saying Cindy and Rick had been having crazy monkey sex, and she nearly burst into laughter. It took every shred of determination she possessed to hold herself together. "Cindy, I assure you I am not working on Skip's behalf. The studio was totally my idea, a last-minute lark. But I should have mentioned it to you, and I'm sorry."

Cindy folded her arms, sizing up Max. It was clear she wasn't fully swayed, but there was nothing more Max could do. Finally, Cindy let her arms drop to her sides.

"I haven't forgotten how you betrayed us by leaving the band and going solo." With that, Cindy was out the door.

It took a full minute for Max's heart rate to come down out of the danger zone. What the hell had all that been about? And the comment about Max leaving the band? Sometimes she wondered exactly how Grace and Cindy had deluded themselves so completely about the breakup. There was a more pressing issue, however. Max wasn't entirely sure, but Cindy suspected her of something. That much was for certain. That meant Max would have to be extra careful around Jade. While there were no shady business deals afoot, Max was pretty sure if Cindy found out Max had been fooling around with Jade, the woman would take it as every bit as big a betrayal.

CHAPTER TWENTY

In the darkness of night, Jade's head made contact with something hard and unforgiving. She rubbed her forehead, trying to get her bearings while her heart pounded. Fortunately, the realization that she was in her narrow bed in the tour bus came to her before she acted on her instinct to bolt upright and gave herself a concussion.

"It was a dream," she whispered under her breath. "Just a dream."

Jade sucked in a deep breath, zipping her eyes closed. All she could see was flashes of her mom in the hospital bed near the end, all the wires and tubes and machines around them. The antiseptic smell of the place seemed to creep into Jade's nose, erasing the fruity notes of the soap she'd used when showering at the venue in Nashville before hopping on the bus.

"Hold my hand?" Grace smiled thinly.

Jade's eyes flew open as if the words—half dream, half memory—had been whispered in her ear right there in her coffin-sized bunk.

I've gotta get out of here.

She needed space and doubted sleep would be on the menu for the rest of the night. Kicking back her covers, Jade checked her phone. The current location showed as Asheville, North Carolina, which Jade knew was about two hours from their destination of Charlotte.

The air coming through the vent smelled like home.

It was the closest they were going to get to her actual home on this tour. They'd been on the road six weeks, not to mention the week of rehearsals in LA prior, and Jade would be lying if she said she wasn't feeling it.

Maybe that explained the dream. Or perhaps it was all the sneaking around she'd been doing with Max, stealing kisses behind a pile of sound equipment back-stage when no one was looking, or sneaking off for a quickie like they had tonight in the showers. It was exhilarating, for sure, but there was always the worry about getting caught. It took a toll.

Even during their song writing sessions, Jade took caution. She tried not to look too eager whenever the opportunity arose to ride in the other bus, nor to spend so much time with Max to the exclusion of the others that it would become remarkable. Ever since

New Orleans, it seemed Cindy was watching like a hawk.

Jade swung her legs out from her bunk, doing a half roll to land soundlessly on the carpeted floor with her bare feet. She padded softly toward the front lounge, nearly jumping when she saw a shadowy figure move ahead of her.

"Jesus!" Cindy clutched her nightshirt over her heart. "You scared the crap out of me."

Yeah, same.

"Sorry," Jade said, coming up beside her in the kitchenette. "Couldn't sleep."

"Me neither." Cindy reached into the refrigerator, pulling out a sparkling water for herself and handing one to Jade. "What's keeping you up?"

"Mom." Jade twisted the cap off the bottle and took a sip, relishing the bubbles on her dry throat. "You?"

"Same, Kitten." Cindy sighed. "The closer we get to Charlotte, I almost feel like she's here with us right now."

"I keep thinking about those last nights with her. Sitting by her bedside, her hand so cool and frail as I held it. She used to have such strong hands. It's stupid, but—" A lump in Jade's throat blocked the rest.

"I know. The illness stole that from her, yellowed her skin and eyes as her liver failed." Cindy sniffed, closing her eyes as if trying to block out the memory of her sister's last days.

"All because of that stupid bat tattoo," Jade spat out. The animosity she had toward the tattoo would never diminish.

Cindy sat on one of the couches. "The one on her left hip," her aunt agreed, remembering.

Jade took a seat on the couch opposite. Her mom had been covered in tattoos. Most were gorgeous, the sharp lines and artistry of them making her body something lovely and magical. The bat, on the other hand, had been distorted, the ink muddied, almost like a child's drawing that had water spilled on it, causing the shape to blur.

"She got it after a show, you know." Cindy pursed her lips, as if delivering definitive proof the rock and roll lifestyle led directly to death and destruction. "We were low on funds, so sometimes after a show we'd just ask the crowd if someone had a floor to crash on."

"A far cry from where we are now," Jade commented, but Cindy's eyes were clouded by the past, and she didn't seem to hear.

"One of those nights we ended up at some old crust-punk's house, and his uncle had a tattoo machine. Everyone was drunk and high, and suddenly getting tattooed seemed like the best idea to Grace."

"Sounds like Mom." Even through the sadness, Jade had to chuckle. She'd heard this story before, and it was both bitter and sweet. The bold, impulsive, fun side of her mom and the consequences of that impetuousness.

"The dude didn't change needles, big surprise. It was a disaster waiting to happen, which frankly sums up most of the time we spent touring." Cindy balled a fist and dug it into the arm of the sofa. "I knew better. I should've stopped her."

"It could've happened regardless," Jade said softly. "You know how Mom was back then. She was a risk taker. You couldn't watch her every second."

"No, especially not when I had Max to babysit." Cindy gave a snort. "That one really did me in."

"I'm sure she would love to hear you say that." Jade couldn't contain a grin at the thought of a young Max raising hell and putting Cindy through her paces.

"Still, I should have been more careful with Grace." Tears swam in Cindy's eyes. "She was my responsibility, and I let her down. I sure as fuck won't do the same with you." She reached for Jade's hand, squeezing it hard. "What a high price to pay for a mistake. I need you to make me a promise, Kitten."

"Don't get any basement tattoos from weirdos?" Jade understood Cindy's sentiments but wanted to protest. She wasn't her mother. Now, though, with her aunt so vulnerable…

Cindy's answering smile was a moment of brightness, but it didn't remain. "Yes to that one, too, but you have to promise me to never do something that destroys your whole future."

"You and Mom both, I swear." Jade gave a tortured groan. "She literally made me swear it on her deathbed. But what if my future is the one thing I can't have?"

Cindy tilted her head. "What does that mean?"

"Specifically? I promised Mom not to follow in her footsteps. That was what she made me say. Don't follow in her footsteps. But what does that actually mean?"

Cindy tapped her fingertips together as she silently regarded Jade. Finally, she sighed and said. "Let me guess. You're loving being on tour?"

"Yes, and it's killing me."

Cindy turned her head, lost in thought.

Grief waved an accusing finger at Jade, as if to say "You don't care about her." Bitterness welled inside her. She hadn't forgotten her mother and the promise she'd made, but Jade also hadn't anticipated finding joy so soon after the loss. Both on the road and with Max. Not that she could admit that second part, not to Cindy.

Mostly, though, Jade was angry. A deep, seething mad at her mom for forcing her into a deathbed promise. How fucking unfair. How fucking mean, to use her death as a way to weight the scales in her favor. She had shackled Jade with that promise. Now she was gone, and Jade couldn't even tell her how angry it made her. It scalded her insides, leaving them raw.

Jade couldn't stop her mind from racing. Two desires that were like opposite ends of a tug-of-war rope. The promise to her mother that she would play it safe or the reckless joy of chasing a dream and risking failure.

Should she choose stability or satisfaction? Live long-term or in the moment?

Where did Max fit into the picture, if at all?

"WELCOME to the PNC Music Pavillion, Kitten. Our tour may have started in LA, but this is where it all began for the Matchstick Girls, back in the day." Cindy's face turned wistful. "Charlotte, I mean. I can't believe I'm back here playing after all these years."

With Cindy at her side, Jade took in the venue from a vantage point previously unknown to her. She'd been to plenty of concerts here, but she'd never been delivered to the back door. The venue's crew were all over the place, moving with efficiency and authority. She watched as two of them stepped to the bus and, with the driver's assistance, began to pull out their instruments.

"It's still so strange to see that," Cindy said, hand pressed gently as she steered Jade toward the door. "Back in your mom's day, we carted our own instruments, did our own setup."

"Do you miss that?" Jade wouldn't mind being in charge of setting up her kit, if only because it would have given her something to focus on other than the enormity of realizing her only home state show was mere hours away. They'd played so many cities already, but this one loomed large in Jade's imagination.

She'd be on stage in front of thousands of fans who not only knew the music, but in many cases had known her mom personally, watched her perform in dive bars. Jade couldn't kick the feeling that her mother would be among those in the crowd. The question was, would her mom be frowning or grinning at seeing Jade on stage?

"Sometimes I miss the old days, but Max was right about one thing. Touring like this?" She gestured to everyone and everything, as if showcasing the year's top model cars. "This is way more relaxing."

They went inside, and Jade was forced to blink several times as her eyes adjusted from the glaring sunlight to the dim lighting of the long, narrow hallway that was lined with framed posters of bands that had performed in the space over the decades. Several were signed, the gold sharpie shining through the protective glass.

As they walked, Jade counted on two hands the bands she'd have killed to watch play live. Now, she was a member of their exclusive club.

"If mom had experienced this kind of tour," Jade mused. "I wonder if she'd have wanted to stick with music even after the band broke up."

Cindy came to a stop so suddenly Jade almost

crashed into her, turning to Jade with a suddenly concerned face. "I'm an asshole for not asking this before. I was—I still am—mourning the loss of Grace, and I guess I didn't want to make you feel on the spot about something so sensitive."

The concern and vague quality of Cindy's statement set Jade on edge. "What are you talking about?"

"I know Grace was very close-lipped about our time in the band. I tried to respect that. But why, exactly, do you think she quit playing in front of audiences and didn't look for other opportunities?"

"You mean other than wanting to be a mom?" That had been the reason given for most of Jade's life, and it was, on its own, a completely acceptable reason. But acceptable hadn't always felt fully authentic, especially since her mom didn't quit with Jade's birth. It was like Jade only had half of a ripped photograph to go on.

"Right. When she was on the road, she was so *bitter* all the time."

Jade thought of every interaction she'd seen between Max and Cindy. She replayed the way their voices changed and their faces shifted whenever they spoke about Grace. Pairing that with the tidbits they'd dropped along the publicity tour like breadcrumbs, she approached what was nestled in her chest.

"I think Mom disliked people, and she hated situations she couldn't control. Even touring like this, with all the bells and whistles and perks... I haven't felt in control much. More like I'm along for the ride."

Cindy nodded in approval.

Jade bit her lip. "But then I don't understand, not really, why it was so important to her that I not follow in her footsteps? Even with not having control, not once has anything felt... unstable. She was so concerned with stability and longevity. But Max has that. Why not me?"

It felt good to ask it out loud. Jade needed to weave the varying feelings she had over her mom's extracted promise to understand why it had been necessary in the first place. "I'm not her," she added.

"No, you're not," Cindy agreed. "But you're experiencing a fairy tale version of a music career. It isn't just skipping the grind of small clubs and starving artist bullshit. Yes, we've spent a ton of time together. You and Max even more so."

Jade's skin heated at Cindy's observation, worried they'd somehow raised suspicion.

"You haven't been on the road year after year. You haven't spent that time crammed in small spaces and lacking in privacy with people you love but who know exactly how to push your buttons for longer than a few weeks."

"What if I don't go in with a band? I could be a solo artist, like Max," Jade protested. "You know drums aren't my only passion. I play guitar. I sing. Mom taught me well, considering she didn't seem to want me to use any of it."

She thought about the songs she'd written. So far,

they'd been for herself, and she had no desire to ever share them, but working with Max in the studio had unlocked a new understanding that she might really have what it took to succeed. Music and stability in one package.

"What exactly is Max telling you?" Cindy's tone was sharp. "Because whatever she's saying, you shouldn't take it at face value. I fear she's trying to work you on Skip's behalf."

"What are you talking about? Max isn't working me."

"Why else would she be spending so much time with you these past few weeks?" Cindy scoffed. She bit down on her lip, as if realizing how harshly that had come out. "No offense, Kitten. It's just you're fifteen years younger than Max, and I've never known her to be the mentoring kind before. Which leads me to believe there's something in it for her."

"Like what?" Jade was outraged, even if she could think of at least one thing that was in it for Max. But it wasn't like she could tell Cindy Max was in it for the mind-blowing orgasms.

"She's probably trying to gain your trust to get you to sign a contract." Cindy continued her rant. "Max knows how to play people. She knows you don't like disappointing people, for example. You'll put your own wants aside to make others happy."

Frowning, Jade responded, "Like promising not to chase the career I want to make my dead mother happy?" It came out ringing with petulance, but instead of sounding defiant and punk-rock, it made her sound childish.

The smirk on Cindy's face meant Jade's rebuttal didn't hit too hard. "Exactly. I've been thinking about our conversation from earlier. I'm hoping, by the time we finish, this dream will be out of your system."

People hustled up and down the hallway, forcing Cindy and Jade to shift and hug the walls.

"Cindy," Jade finally said after pressing herself flat so two men hauling an enormous amplifier could go by. It gave her the much-needed chance to change her original word choice of *fuck you* to the much more palatable, "I miss Mom."

"Me too."

"And I think you're wrong," Jade informed her, determined not to be a people pleaser any longer where her aunt was concerned, no matter how much she loved her. "You're wrong about Max."

"Maybe." Cindy visibly shook as she finished the conversation with, "We should start getting ready for sound check."

CHAPTER TWENTY-ONE

Max stepped out of the elevator and stood in place as Jade advanced to the center of her upper east side Manhattan apartment, twirling in a circle as she took it all in.

"I can't believe this." Jade's eyes swept the interior of Max's apartment, landing first on the curved staircase that went to the main bedroom on the upper floor, then to the pristine white sofas and natural wood coffee table that was the size and shape of a giant kettle drum. When she got to the set of double French doors that led to the private rooftop terrace, Jade's jaw dropped. "You actually live here?"

"Sometimes I find it hard to believe myself, even after twenty years." Max tucked her hands under her arms, relishing the pleasant chill of the air-conditioning. "It's nothing like the ramshackle place I grew up in."

"Twenty years?" Jade moved closer to the floor-to-ceiling window that offered an amazing view of the skyline. "Not a bad purchase for a twenty-two-year-old."

Pride blossomed in Max's chest. It *was* a nice home, even if she rarely got to spend time there. Now, as they neared the ending of the tour, she was glad to be able to share this part of her life with Jade.

Though as soon as they played the final show, there wouldn't be an encore.

"I used the earnings from my first big solo album. It's turned out to be one of my better investments, and I wish I could say I'd bought it because I knew the open floor plan, the skyline views, and the location near the park would add major value, but that would be a lie."

"Why did you buy it? Square footage?" Jade guessed. "Number of bathrooms?"

Rolling her eyes at her younger self, Max gestured behind her toward the door to the elevator. "I had heard somewhere that Christina Aguilera's apartment had a private elevator, and I felt I deserved the same. It was literally the only thing on my list."

Jade scanned the interior again, letting out a low whistle. "In that case, I'd say you got lucky. My God, look at the skyline. Is that the Empire State Building?"

As Jade stood in front of the window, Max slid behind her. The skyline never got old for her, but seeing it with Jade's fresh awe was making her feel more appreciative. And, possibly, a bit frisky. "Actually, it's the Chrysler building," she whispered against Jade's ear. The woman shivered, and Max felt a rush of heat between her legs.

"It is?" Jade slumped against Max's chest. "You must think I'm such a noob."

"Why?" Max inhaled deeply, filling her senses with Jade's musky scent.

"I'm standing in your apartment, sporting an *I Love New York* T-shirt, like a goofy tourist. I can't even tell the difference between two of the most famous buildings in the world."

"Architectural knowledge is overrated." Max wrapped her arms around Jade's waist and nuzzled her face into the crook of Jade's neck. "And there are many words I'd used to describe you, but *goofy* isn't one of them."

"What words would you use?" There was a hitch in Jade's breathing when Max nibbled on an earlobe.

"Sexy. Confident—"

"I'm not confident," Jade butted in.

"Interesting. You're not arguing about sexy."

"Wh—Oh. You got me there." While Max couldn't see Jade's face from her current vantage point, she could imagine the flush seeping into the woman's cheeks. Even if it was just in her head, the vision was irresistible.

There weren't going to be many more moments like this. It had been hard enough all summer to find time alone together. With the end of the tour looming, Max felt a desperate need to make every moment count.

"I've got you here, too." In one swift movement, Max hoisted the *I Love New York* shirt off of Jade, along with the sports bra she'd worn beneath.

"Someone will see." Jade whipped around, scrambling to cover her tits with crossed arms while Max laughed.

"We're on the top floor of the tallest building on this street. No one can see." Max drank her in. "Only me."

Their eyes met, the sexual tension sizzling between them. Jade's breathing grew faster, her chest rising and falling as she let her arms drop to her sides, leaving her exposed. All of New York seemed to spread out behind her, yet Jade was all Max could focus on.

"It's a shame no one can see. You're so fucking beautiful." Max ran a finger down the side of Jade's face, along her neck, tracing her collarbone.

Down the length of one arm. Up her taut belly.

Max's hand landed on Jade's ribs. The way the woman's breasts rose and fell with each shaky breath had Maxine's heart racing. "I have no idea why you don't have all the confidence in the world. Don't you hear the audience, night after night, screaming your name?"

"They scream yours, too." Jade's words came out breathy, like she was struggling to stay focused on what she was saying as Max's hands continued to explore her naked torso.

"The crowd adores you."

And they don't call for me like they do for you. Not anymore.

Max blotted that thought out by capturing Jade's lips, pressing her against the glass wall, both hungry for the other.

"Should we move to the bedroom?" Jade asked, out of breath.

Max slowly shook her head. "Let's stay here."

Jade looked over her shoulder at the floor-to-ceiling window that offered an unobstructed view of the New York city lights, her eyes growing large. "I feel like I'm going to fall."

"It's only fair," Max whispered, her heart seeming to expand inside her chest.

Jade whipped her head around to Max. "What does that mean?"

Fuck. Letting that part slip had been a mistake. Max didn't want to answer. There were so many things she'd been able to open up about with Jade, but admitting *that* was too much. "It's just... I feel the same. About the view. It's exhilarating."

Jade started to speak, but Max silenced her with another kiss. Talking was dangerous. After eight weeks on the road together in close quarters, there was no telling what might be said in the heat of passion. Words that seemed so right in the moment but had far-reaching consequences when the tour was over.

No doubt Jade would be relieved Max didn't proclaim her love. It would avoid the awkward truth. Someone as stunning as Jade with her whole future sparkling in front of her had little reason to be interested in an old rock chick like Max for long. It was simply a good time while it lasted.

It was fine. Max was used to it. That had been the story of her life since childhood. A mom who ran out. A father who would have sold Max to the highest bidder for a thirty pack of PBR.

"Just so you know"—Jade cupped Max's cheeks in her palms, holding her head so she could look into Max's eyes—"I think you're pretty amazing."

It was a bolt out of left field. Had Max said any of her thoughts aloud? Her stomach twisted. It wasn't unpleasant, but—

"I—"

It was Jade's time to cover the awkwardness with a searing kiss, but she also hefted Max's shirt over her head, tossing it on the floor near the stark white sectional.

Max needed to be close to Jade. She reached to undo the button and zipper of her jeans. Jade was of the same mind, doing her best to strip Max, all the while the two continued devouring each other's mouth.

A troubling thought clawed at the back of Max's

mind, that this was it. This was the piece that'd been missing from her life. The unquenchable desire to be with someone. For weeks the two had been stealing these moments, each time Max hoping she'd find peace. She had, briefly, but it was always coupled with wanting more. More time with Jade. When she wasn't in Max's line of sight, Max went as cold and desolate as the dark side of the moon.

How it had happened, Max wasn't sure, but Jade had become the center of her universe. They had less than a week left together. What would happen after their last show, when the tour was over and it was time to part ways?

Desertion.

Again.

Why did this keep happening to her? Her chest seized up, her throat constricting.

"Hey." Jade had cupped Max's cheeks again, her eyes penetrating through Max's soul, an unmistakable expression of concern on her face. "I'm not going anywhere."

Max could only blink in response. *Do not cry*, she ordered herself, *even if they're happy tears*. She felt the wet in her eyes, threatening to ignore her internal demands.

"I'm not going anywhere," Jade repeated, a statement and a promise wrapped into one. Maxine couldn't allow herself to believe it. Not fully.

Their bodies collided.

Tongues wrestling.

Hands exploring bare skin.

Max slipped her hand under the waistband of Jade's panties, pulling them down to the floor. She ran her fingers along Jade's slit, letting out a satisfied moan as she encountered a hot, inviting wetness. Jade was ready, and so was Max. Ready to do what she'd only imagined since the day she'd moved in and saw this window with its perfect, sexy view.

"Turn around," Max directed, withdrawing her hand to allow Jade the freedom of motion to do as she'd been told. With a questioning look, Jade complied. "Put your hands against the glass and spread your legs wide."

"Max..." Jade's words trailed off into a nervous laugh. After a moment of hesitation, she did as Max had asked. "I'm going to get handprints all over the place."

"I don't care," Max said with a slight growl. "I'll have my housekeeper take care of it."

"I knew it." For some reason, Jade seemed to find this particularly hilarious, or maybe it was her nervousness at standing naked in front of a window that overlooked one of the largest cities in the world. "I told Lottie you'd have a houseful of servants to do your bidding."

"They're hired help! I'm not sure I'd call it a houseful. It's just Emily who does the cleaning, and Pete who comes by to take care of the plants on the—" Max stopped, laughing. "Why am I talking about this right now?"

Keeping her hands on the window, Jade twisted her head to cast a glance over her shoulder. "I don't know. Do you not have anything better to do?"

"Oh, much better," Max assured her. "I've had a bit of a fantasy when it comes to this particular window. If you're up for it, I'd like your help in finally making it come true."

"You've lived here twenty years," Jade pointed out with an incredulous tone. "You're saying in all that time, you've never had anyone willing to help you with this fantasy? Exactly how twisted is it?"

"It's *not*," Max said, indignant. The truth was, she'd barely brought anyone back to her place at all over those years. It was her private space, an oasis. There were plenty of other places to fuck women you didn't particularly know or care about without inviting them into your home. "Let's just say I've been saving this for a special… time."

Or more accurately, a special person. But again, Max didn't think saying so would be wise.

"Okay," Jade said after a moment. "I'm willing to give it a try, as long as I can still say no later when I know what you actually plan to do."

"You can always say no." Max trailed her palms along Jade's back, raising goosebumps in the wake of her touch. She felt confident Jade wouldn't say no. "I'll be right back."

"What?" There was a hint of strangled panic in Jade's voice at the prospect of being left alone. "Where are you going?"

"I need something from upstairs. I'll be right back."

Max flew up to her bedroom, eager to run from the truths she was dancing too close to with Jade. The fantasy would save them both. A thrill shivered through her as she found what she was looking for and got ready.

To her absolute delight, Jade had remained in front of the glass, her palms braced on the window. The silhouette of the young woman was enough to stop Max in her tracks. She'd never seen anyone so perfect, so beautiful, in all of her life.

"I can hear you," Jade said. "Are you ready to fill me in?"

Max almost giggled at the choice of words. "Yes," she mustered. "I really, really am."

Closing the distance once more, Maxine shook her head. So many times in her career she'd been told how lucky she was. Discovered in her teens. A multi-platinum solo debut when she was scarcely in her twenties. She'd toured the world several times over, had money, women, and fame.

Yet this was the first time she could remember *feeling* lucky. Grateful for the young woman with the strong back and arms made muscular through years of intense drum sessions. For Jade, a muse and a mistake all in one.

"What do you think about this?" She held out the vibrator, its microphone shape belying the fierce humming Max knew it was capable of.

Jade swallowed. "I think that's a personal massager. What exactly were you hoping for?"

Max pressed against Jade's back, absorbing the woman's warmth and smelling her arousal. "I want to fuck you with this"—Maxine looked down at the strap-on she was wearing—"while you use this."

"Oh." Jade licked her lips. "That's not nearly as twisted as I was imagining."

"Told you."

For effect, Max pushed the button, and the wand buzzed to life. Jade shifted her legs wider in response, and Max moaned. Sliding a hand down Jade's back, Max squeezed Jade's ass before moving her hand lower, teasing at the wetness she found.

With a shaky breath, Jade took the wand from Max. Now freed, Max wrapped her other arm around Jade's torso, pulling the woman's hips out a smidge farther. Jade groaned as Max positioned herself behind and carefully entered.

As Max began to slowly pump her hips, Jade brought the humming head of the wand to her clit. The moment it struck home, her body jerked in the sexiest way. Leaning in, Max nibbled and kissed Jade's shoulder, fingers digging into Jade's hips.

"Think of everyone in this city," she whispered, luxuriating in Jade's slickness. "All of those people below us, in the buildings around us... they have no idea you're up here, pressed against my window."

"Oh God," Jade groaned. Her hips began to move, pushing back against Max.

"You're glorious." Max changed her angle and increased her speed, Jade's sounds of delight encouraging her.

They found a rhythm. Like they always seemed to. Jade gasped and moaned, her body occasionally jerking as she reconciled Max's relentless strap-on and the intensity of the wand. Max wanted to drink her in.

"I'm going to—"

Jade didn't finish before her body went taut, her howl of pleasure sending ripples of joy through Maxine. The young woman sagged, and Max was there to hold her. They slid to the floor, the squeal of flesh on glass eliciting a crazed giggle from Jade.

"I hope your fantasy didn't stop there," the other woman said as she rolled Max onto her back and straddled her, the strap-on pressed to Max's belly.

"It did, sadly," Max replied, voice husky. "Fortunately, after years in the music industry, I've gotten good at improv."

A BUZZING SOUND penetrated the fogginess in Max's brain. It took a moment for her to place it, but when she did, the pit of her belly went cold. "That's the doorman ringing."

"What?" Still basking in the afterglow of sex, Jade blinked slowly, clearly not comprehending a word Max had said, let alone the meaning.

"There's someone here, wanting to come up." Max struggled to her feet and strode to the intercom by the elevator, determined not to think about what she must look like with the strap-on still jutting out from her pelvis. She pressed the answer button. "This is Max."

"Ms. Gardner, there's a Skip Foster to see you. Says he has an appointment at eight o'clock?"

Was that tonight? Max's heart raced as she tried to conjure up a mental image of her calendar. *Shit. Shit, shit, shit.* "Uh... right. Um, what time is it now?"

"7:55, ma'am."

"Yeah, I'm gonna need those five minutes. Can you hold him off until then? Maybe a couple minutes beyond that." Now was a good time to pray that the holiday bonus she'd given the doorman last year had bought her some goodwill.

"You got it."

Max was shaking as she turned to Jade, who by now had scrambled to her feet and was gathering up scraps of clothing from the floor. "Skip's here."

"I heard." Jade's eyes went to the window, widening in horror at the handprints and smudges all over the glass. "I don't think we have time to wait for Emily to take care of this. Do you have Windex?"

"You're not cleaning my window, especially not naked." Max gestured to the stairs. "You can go up there to get dressed. I'll take care of the window and send Skip on his way as soon as I can. I am *so* sorry about this. I completely forgot about his text."

As Jade scurried up the stairs, Max surveyed the floor and tried not to panic. Jeans, a T-shirt, and a bra. But no underwear.

What a great time to be forced to go commando.

Max put on the bra in record time, followed by the T-shirt. She had one leg into the jeans when she looked down and got a shocking reminder that she had still not removed the strap-on. Recalling the complicated arrangement of straps and closures holding the apparatus in place, Max felt sick. No way would it be any easier coming off.

The elevator whirred as the machinery prepared to deliver the enclosed compartment to the ground floor. She was running out of time. Steeling her nerves, Max pulled on the other leg of her jeans, tucking the protruding silicone dildo along one leg.

"Jesus, seriously?" Max tugged at the zipper, trying to ease her jeans closed around the uncomfortable bulge. How the fuck did men put up with this shit?

With some quick adjustment, Max was fairly sure the fake penis in her pants would not be obvious to a casual observer. Which was a good thing, because another whir of a motor told her Skip was on his way up. Her eyes swept the room. Everything was in order.

Except the stupid, smudge-covered window.

In a burst of superhuman strength and agility, Max lunged for the six-foot potted palm near the entry to her kitchen and yanked it in front of the window. Problem solved.

And just in time. The elevator stopped, and the door opened.

"Skip." Max offered a smile she hoped was welcoming and not scary. "Just so you know, I'm a little under the weather tonight. I was getting ready for bed."

"Don't worry. I won't be long." Skip's eyes panned the space. "I don't suppose you've seen Jade, have you?"

"What? Here?" Max grimaced at the shrillness of her voice. "Have you tried her hotel?"

"Yes. No joy." He raked a hand through his hair. "Your assistant said you, Cindy, and Jade were getting together tonight to go over some stuff before the final concert tomorrow."

Oh. Dear. God.

Jade was upstairs in Max's bedroom, and Cindy was on her way? How the hell had Max let something so vital slip her mind? She cast a wary glance at the potted plant that was so heroically covering the evidence, knowing exactly what had caused her memory lapse.

"So... she's not quite... uh..." Max swallowed, hoping she could remember to breathe and not pass out. "What's the urgency, anyway?"

"I heard through the grapevine that three other talent firms want to sign her. I need to get to her first."

"Dude, do you even know how pervy you sound sometimes?" Max flung herself onto the couch, nearly yelping as the dildo she'd forgotten about crushed into her thigh. She yanked a throw pillow into her lap to hide the telltale bulge, blinking back the sudden sting of tears.

Yeah, sure. Skip's the perv in this situation.

Looking horrified, Skip lowered himself onto the edge of a chair, like he wasn't sure if it was okay. "My daughters are older than she is. It wouldn't even cross my mind."

The tension in Max's shoulders eased a tiny smidge. She'd known Skip long enough to know he was a lot of things—a self-centered, money-hungry bastard, for instance—but not a creep. "Sorry. I'm on edge. The end of a tour always stresses me out."

"Look, I get it. I'll get out of your hair." Though he said this, he made no move to leave, settling back into the chair. Because of course he did, when Max needed to get him up and out before Cindy arrived. "This contract thing with Jade is kind of a time sensitive matter."

"Oh yeah?" Even though Max knew she needed to herd his ass to the elevator, her pride wouldn't let her quite yet. "If you're in the mood to talk contracts, maybe you could fill me in on mine. Have you made any progress with the record label about a solo album?"

"Uh…" The hesitation on his part was answer enough. "I'm sure we'll get there. Just need a little more time."

"Come on." Max balled her fist and slammed it into the pillow on her lap. "Don't bullshit me. You haven't even brought it up with them, have you?"

"You never sent me the demo you promised," he shot back.

Which was true, because she hadn't exactly recorded one. She'd managed to lay down tracks for the song about her dad that would never see the light of day and for a duet with Jade that wasn't hers to share. After that, well, Max had found herself too distracted to keep working, in the most delicious way. A way that had put the recording studio to good use but left her with nothing she could share with Skip.

"After all this time, I didn't think I had to audition," Max spat back. "The songs are coming, okay?"

For the first time in a long while, Max felt confident this was true. The songs she'd been penning since New Orleans were rough, but they wouldn't take much polishing to come up with a hit. The way the lyrics had poured from her and Jade when they'd worked together, the way Max's spirits had morphed as she heard it come to life—Max had been floundering before, but having Jade beside her had held a mirror up, forcing her to admit how much she'd been phoning it in. It had stopped being about the music a long time ago, but she was only now realizing it.

Something was stirring in her, something promising. She'd be golden as long as she kept Jade by her side.

"Sure, sure." Skip rubbed his hands together. "Did Jade record anything? Does she write?"

Max toed the plush rug, watching the shades of cream shift as she moved her foot back and forth. She wanted to come back around to *her* career, not Jade's. But could she even differentiate anymore? "Okay, here's the deal. She did write something, and it's incredible."

Skip's eyes narrowed in accusation. "Why the fuck didn't you send it to me?"

"Because it's not mine to send." Max knew Skip could work wonders for Jade, but Cindy would murder Max on the spot if she stepped in. Besides, the more Max got to know the young woman, the clearer it became that Jade needed to set her own terms and boundaries. Skip made that difficult, hence Max's current predicament.

"Max, come on. I'm not a monster. I'm a manager." His irritation was evident in the deep scowl that etched his features.

"Is there a difference?" she joked, but he didn't laugh.

"I admit it. I'm after her for the money. That's true of all my clients. Why do you think I've stuck with you for so long? You've had a rough past decade, but I knew you were worth investing in." He smiled. "And this Matchstick Girls tour has been quite the payoff."

His words re-opened a wound she'd hoped had started to heal; her career was in jeopardy. Rock and music was all Max knew, and unlike Jade, she didn't have years of youth spread out ahead of her to figure it out. She had her guitar, her voice, and a GED she'd barely managed to complete on the road. With effort, she kept a mild smile pasted on her face.

Skip's expression softened, and she saw the moment most of his manager-mode fell away, leaving a man who was her business partner and, to some extent, a friend. "I'm sorry," he said, keeping his voice down. "I didn't mean to make it sound like—"

"Like I'm no good on my own anymore?"

He winced. "It's the business. You're at this weird age where you aren't old enough to be a classic icon, like Joan Jett or Debbie Harry, but you aren't in your twenties anymore, either."

"That's fucked up, man. It's your job to make me marketable."

Not old enough? That was fine. She didn't feel old. For the most part, she was doing the same things now that she'd been doing twenty years before. No, she wasn't in her twenties anymore. But how much did that matter?

"I don't make the rules. At least you still look hot as fuck," he offered, like he was giving her a participation trophy.

"Gee, thanks."

"Promise you'll talk to Jade for me. I want to protect her. Rock and roll's a cutthroat business. That's why I've been hounding you for this. It's in both of your interests."

Max's eyes narrowed. It didn't sound like Max was factoring in as anything more than a stepping stone. "How do you even know she wants more of it after the tour ends? Cindy says Jade's going to start with the North Carolina Symphony in the fall." Max knew better. She wasn't sure if Jade had officially turned down the offer, but in those moments of openness, it was clear that wasn't the life Jade wanted. But Skip didn't know that, and she was feeling too flummoxed to give him an inch.

"We can't let that happen!"

Max agreed, but as before, this wasn't her call to make. Besides, he was asking her to do his job for him. If she managed to get Jade on board, would Skip focus his energy on reviving Max's career? Or would he cut his losses and run?

"Can you talk her out of it?" Skip practically pressed his palms together. "Come on, Maxie. I've always been good to you. I'm asking as a friend. Help me. I'll even cut you in on a percentage, like a finder's fee. What do you say?"

Before Max could reply, a red-faced Jade appeared at the base of the stairs, wearing an inside out *I Love New York* T-shirt, her feet bare, and her mussed hair flying in every direction. She looked like a vengeful goddess set on destruction. Before Jade could even open her mouth to speak, Max feared she was the woman's first target.

CHAPTER TWENTY-TWO

A nger burned every fiber of Jade's being. Had she heard Skip right? He was here to get her to sign a contract, and Max was going to get a percentage. Just like Aunt Cindy had said.

Un-fucking-believable.

Was that all this had been to Max the whole time? No, she refused to believe it was true. But even as she tried to chase the doubt away, she could hear her aunt saying Jade was too young for Max, that she was being used. It traveled through her like the venom from a snake bite, getting ever closer to her heart.

She had to face facts. There was no reason a legend like Max would be interested in a newbie like Jade once the tour was over. All Jade meant to Max was a bit of fun while it lasted and maybe some cash to line her pockets in the end. Thinking otherwise would simply lead to heartbreak.

Hadn't the stories from her mom and Cindy been enough of a warning?

Max was staring up at her from the couch, eyes wide with something like shock or maybe fear.

Fear was good. Jade could work with fear. With all the world treating her like a child, it was good to remind at least one person she was an adult who was capable of making things miserable.

On the verge of hot, angry tears, Jade closed her eyes and steadied her breathing before speaking. "Why is everyone intent on planning my life without bothering to ask me, or even *think* about, what *I* want?"

"That's not what I'm doing." Max quickly raised her eyes to Jade's. "We were just—"

"I heard the whole thing," Jade interrupted. "Or enough of it to realize Aunt Cindy was right. I shouldn't have trusted you."

Skip frowned, seeming unable to process Jade's presence. "That elevator must be really quiet. I didn't hear you come in."

"Maybe you were too busy conspiring with Max to notice anything else." Jade stared daggers at the manager.

"Now, hold on a minute." Skip held up his hands, palms out, and gave them a slight wave. "You won't be talking like that when you see the contract I've brought with me." God, he truly had one thing on his mind.

"That you brought with you to show Max, not me!

Don't deny it. You didn't know I was here. God, it's like a matchmaker showing up to discuss how many goats I'm worth for a dowry. Might as well sell me off to the highest bidder."

"That's completely uncalled for." There was ice in Max's tone, telling Jade she'd gone too far. Even so, Jade found herself able to push a little more.

"Is it, though? Because there was a lot of chatter about me, my music, and my future a few minutes ago, but you know what's funny?" Jade clenched a fist, opened it, and clenched it again. "I wasn't in the room. I get it when Cindy does it. She'll always think of me as a kid. But I thought it would be different with you. I thought we were—"

Jade stopped dead, not sure what word she'd intended to use to finish that sentence. Partners, perhaps. They had, after all, been writing songs together. But the word alluded to the other thing between them, the thing they couldn't talk about in front of Skip. If she dared utter the word out loud, would Max think it was because she wanted more?

Did she want more?

"Jade, I understand you're upset." Max's tone was calm, with more warmth than before. If she'd filled in the blank on what Jade had been on the verge of saying, she gave no indication, but at least she wasn't visibly freaking out. "I promise. When I told Skip I'd meet with him, I thought the business he was coming here to discuss was about my own contract." Her face fell. "I guess I should've known better. As a woman at forty-two, I might as well have one foot in the grave."

As this sank in, Jade's anger for herself faded, roaring into indignation on Max's behalf. She turned to Skip with the full force of her ire, aiming it at him with the intensity of a hurricane. "What the fuck have you been telling her? That she should enjoy the final embers of her career before riding off into the sunset? Hell no."

"The Rolling Stones and Aerosmith will probably still be touring when they're in their nineties," Max muttered, her eyes twinkling with something approaching amusement—or maybe pride—as Jade railed on.

"The idea that a woman in her early forties is past her sell-by date is more of the same patriarchal bull-shit that Max and the Matchstick Girls have been fighting against since day one. If you honestly think she doesn't have a long career ahead of her, you're even more of an idiot than I thought." Jade's shoulders heaved up and down as she paused to catch her breath. How had her mom, Cindy, and Max done it all those years ago? Raging against the establishment was fucking exhausting. She turned to Max. "You should give him the song you recorded in New Orleans. The one about your dad." Because it was amazing, and if this manager didn't know a good thing when he had her right beside him, he'd sure as hell realize it when he heard that song.

"You told me you didn't record one." Skip sounded hurt.

Max shook her head, eyes widening. "That's because it wasn't—"

"She did," Jade interjected. If Maxine was going to conduct meetings on Jade's behalf, then Jade was happy to do the reverse. "And it's brilliant. A whole new side of her and the type of stuff she should have been doing this whole time. You would have known that if any of you had used your brains instead of your penises to make business decisions."

Max covered her mouth, and though she was trying to be subtle, it was obvious to Jade she was hiding a laugh. "I think you should go, Skip. Cindy's supposed to be arriving soon, and there will be hell to pay if she sees you here. Leave the contract if you want, but as I was going to tell you a few minutes ago, whether Jade wants to look at it is totally up to her. I refuse to influence her on this."

Jade's heart fluttered. "You were going to say that?"

"I was trying to tell you," Max said softly as she rose to see Skip to the door. Jade followed close behind. The manager shuffled like a wounded puppy, but Jade refused to feel remorse. "You were too busy trying to bite my head off."

"I'm sorry." They were simple words but heartfelt, and Jade hoped they would suffice for not having given Max the benefit of the doubt. There'd be time for more thorough apologies later.

"It was almost worth it to get to watch you come to my rescue." With Skip walking in front and unable to see, Max gave Jade a wink.

Skip pressed the call button for the elevator, and the machinery roared to life as Jade counted the seconds before she and Max were alone again. With the contract to consider and renewed belief that Max had her best interests at heart, there were questions about the future Jade wanted to discuss.

As the door opened, Aunt Cindy stepped into the apartment. Jade froze. For a moment, her aunt looked around in awe of the impressive space, but then her brow furrowed as her eyes fell first on Skip, and then Max and Jade.

"What's going on? Are you meeting behind my back?" Cindy snapped her fingers, motioning for Jade to get behind her, as if she might need a physical shield from whatever Skip and Max had planned. "I knew I couldn't trust you two with Jade."

Jade's blood reached the boiling point again, this time thanks to Cindy, who prodded with another finger snap when Jade failed to respond.

"Stop doing that!" Jade had to restrain a foot stomp. "I'm not a dog who will come when you call."

Cindy turned on Max, incensed. "This is your doing. I should have known you'd be tearing my family apart by your selfishness once again. Breaking up the band wasn't enough for you?"

"What do you mean by that? You and Grace left me

to fend for myself." Max folded her arms across her chest like she was clutching a security blanket.

"Keep telling yourself that, Max," Cindy jeered. "I know what really happened."

"I don't. Anyone care to explain?" Jade motioned for someone, anyone, to fill her in. But unsurprisingly, Jade had become invisible once more. This was going to have to stop, because the time of making other people happy at her own expense was over.

"Cindy, babe. You've got this all wrong." Skip's attempt to placate her was about as successful as the Hindenburg landing. Jade could all but see the burning, explosive landing all of them were hurtling toward. Was there nothing she could do to stop it?

Cindy was one step away from hysterical. With fire in her eyes, she spat out, "You're the last person I want to be in a room with!"

Skip stepped back, clearly wounded.

"I will not let you get your claws into Jade. She's not having this life. Not with either of you in it. I can't believe as soon as my back's turned, you convinced my niece to come over here to meet with Skip."

"That's not how it happened," Jade insisted, unwilling to allow this injustice to stand. "Skip showed up out of the blue. This wasn't Max's doing."

"Why were you here so early, anyway?" Cindy asked. Her eyes became slits as she took in Jade's disheveled appearance. "Is that what you wore to dinner with your friend?"

"What friend?" Max looked confused.

"Uh," Jade's eyes dropped to her bare feet, simultaneously registering that her T-shirt was on backward, the tag sticking out of the top.

"Your shirt's inside out," her aunt pointed out, ever so helpfully. "Admit it. You didn't have dinner plans at all."

Jade's heart stuck in her throat. There was no way Cindy wouldn't be able to put two and two together and come up with sex.

"You came over here to sign a contract with Skip because Max talked you into it." As Cindy's wild eyes flashed, Jade nearly laughed. Apparently, Cindy wasn't as good at math as Jade had given her credit for. But her determination to demonize Maxine was bordering on insane. "This is unacceptable. That's it. We're done."

"What do you mean by that?" Panic clawed at Jade's chest. Exactly how broadly was her aunt talking when she said they were done?

"I mean pack your things, Kitten. We're going home." Cindy's jaw muscles tensed. "Tonight."

So many emotions exploded in Jade, making it difficult to grasp onto just one. Panic, anxiety, guilt... and rage. That last one was burning magma hot, and Cindy had unintentionally placed herself in the line of fire.

"The hell we are," Jade shouted. "Our last show is tomorrow night. We can't quit the tour before the final concert."

"She's right," Skip chimed in. Up until then he'd kept his mouth shut, but now it seemed his manager instincts had gotten the better of him. "The show's sold out. We'd lose a ton."

"*You* would lose a ton, Skip." Cindy pointed her finger at him, and if she'd had the ability, Jade didn't doubt her aunt would've shot laser beams out of the tip straight into his chest. "Or don't you think I know how to read the fine print of a contract after all these years? No, you know I can. That's why you wanted to keep me away from this meeting. I expect that from you, but for a while there, I almost thought Max was my friend."

"Cindy," Max said, "I swear to you—"

"I don't want to hear it," Cindy screamed, her voice echoing from the high ceilings. "You have gone too far this time. I am taking Jade back to North Carolina, and neither one of us will ever speak to you again!"

"Aunt Cindy, stop!" Jade commanded, unwilling to let this go any further. Her aunt was way out of bounds. "I'm telling you for the last time, I am not skipping the final concert. I am not going home with you. I am *not* a child anymore."

Instead of speaking to Jade, Cindy turned to Max, enraged. "You betrayed me, and you betrayed Grace. I don't know how you can live with yourself."

At the mention of Grace, Max blanched. The sight of tears forming in Max's eyes over this unfair accusation made something inside Jade snap. *My mother is not a weapon.*

"Max hasn't betrayed anyone. This isn't her fault." Jade's breathing was quick and shallow, and her head spun from both emotion and lack of oxygen. "I didn't come over here to meet with Skip about a contract. I was here to be with Max."

Only when she'd stopped yelling did Jade truly hear what she'd said. With mounting fear, she watched Cindy put the clues together in her mind as she took in Jade's inside out shirt and bare feet with renewed understanding. Once again, she whirled on Max.

"Oh my God, you're having sex with my niece?"

"No!" Max's denial came out as a strangled, high-pitched screech. It reminded Jade of the sound a wounded animal would make. Only belatedly did it start to sift in that she'd outed Max. The situation was escalating out of control.

"I mean, I've heard of some crazy midlife crisis bullshit," Cindy continued, her hands flying as she spoke, "but you seriously decided to carry out your experimentation with a... a—"

"If you call me a child right now," Jade said in a trembling voice, "I swear I will never speak to you again." Her body hummed with indignant anger at her aunt but also the mounting fear that she'd hurt Max. Badly.

Meanwhile, Max had not said a word. Or moved.

Or possibly breathed. She appeared to be as still and pale as a marble statue while Cindy laid into her.

"Wait. You two..." Skip looked on the verge of passing out. Despite being on the edge of a break-down, Jade almost laughed. How had the man not at least entertained the idea the moment Jade walked into the room looking like she'd just rolled out of bed?

Skip wheeled about to Max. "Is this true? Because the *is she, isn't she* routine is one thing, but if you confirm this, you can kiss any semblance of a career renaissance goodbye."

Max looked like he'd blasted her with a sawed-off shotgun. Hell, that might've hurt the woman less. What in the hell was wrong with everyone?

Jade balled her fists. "What if she doesn't want to continue playing games with her life, Skip? Have you ever considered that? This isn't a chess game, where you get to move pieces around for world domination. Tell him, Max. Tell him the truth."

Max continued to say nothing. Like she always did. Like she had her entire life. Yes, Jade had done some-thing wrong, but come *on*. She was standing up to her aunt, for Christ's sake! Max should be able to be truthful to them about this, at least.

"You can't keep hiding like this. You have to say something." Anger flared in Jade's breast, but it quickly cooled to panic. She pointed at Max, hand trembling. "If you can't be honest about your life, you are going to end up alone."

If it came out sounding like a threat or an ultimatum, it didn't matter. It was too late for Jade to take any of it back, and some part of her didn't want to. She and Max were so *good* together. Perhaps there'd been a modicum of hope that after the tour, they'd still fight to be with each other.

"Listen here," Skip scolded. "I'm the only one who's looked out for Max's interest her entire life. Not her dad. Not her bandmates. I've been there for her, through thick and thin." He even sounded like he meant it. Max's lower lip trembled.

"Can we get back to the issue at hand?" Cindy demanded. "We had rules for this tour. Neither of you followed them."

Jade was done. "I am so sick and tired of your rules. Mom's rules. Everyone wants to tell me how to live my life, and even when I tell you what I want, you don't listen. No one cares what the fuck I want. No one!" Tears were streaming down Jade's cheeks as she jabbed a finger at Cindy. "I'm sick of this. You know what? I'm done!" Jade pushed the elevator call button, grateful when the doors opened instantly. "I'm done with people speaking for me, and I'm done with people who can't speak up for themselves."

She ducked inside and slammed her palm into the button for the lobby. The doors shut. As she rode downward, all Jade could see was the silent devastation in Max's face, like her entire world had been destroyed.

Correction. Like Jade had destroyed her world.

All Jade wanted to do was race back upstairs, but she knew in that instant that Max would never allow it. Max would never want to speak with her again after this. She'd ruined it all. Whether Jade wanted Max out didn't matter. It wasn't her call.

For all her anger that others were hoisting their choices on her, she'd up and done the same thing to Max but about something so personal.

She whimpered, the smooth mirror of the elevator reflecting someone terribly distraught.

Clutching her phone, Jade dialed the only person she could think of who could make things better.

"Lottie?" she said when her friend answered. "I need you to come to New York. Right now. I've really fucked up."

CHAPTER TWENTY-THREE

Max sat on the terrace, warm August air causing a sheen of sweat as she pressed her knees to her chest, rocking back and forth in the darkness.

Cindy knew.

Skip knew.

Soon the whole world would probably know.

Max wasn't sure what to think about that. It'd been her secret all her life. Okay, not the best kept one, but still, she'd never confirmed or denied, making her feel more in control.

Jade had forced that secret out of the closet. In Max's mind, the knowledge of her queerness was like one of those weird dancing skeletons from the old black and white cartoon, cha-chaing its way into the world and refusing any attempt to return to the darkness.

Max should shove it back in, force the door closed, but damn, the more she thought about it, the more that skeleton wanted to be alive and free. Who could blame it? Maybe Max could let it be. What harm would it really do if people knew now? The world had changed a lot since the 1990s. Marriage equality was a thing, even. Max had never thought she'd see that happen.

Yet, while more people were accepting, there was still backlash. Still haters. Still the threat of violence. Lost gigs. Lost revenue. Her second chance she'd worked so hard for flushed down the toilet before she'd even had the opportunity to try.

Her heart raced.

Jade had been wrong to blurt it out. It wasn't her secret to spill. Max thought that had been clear. She would *never* have done something like this to Jade. Not that there would have been a need. Jade was out and proud.

But she was from a different generation. How much could Maxine hold Jade's fierce determination against her?

Max ran a finger over the scar she'd gotten from the frozen milk carton that had been chucked at her back in the day. That had been the punishment for the simple crime of being a girl in a man's world. What would the punishment have been if everyone had known Max was *into* girls, too? The possibilities were too terrible to contemplate, filling her with dread.

The still, humid air pressed down on Max.

Below, the streets teemed with cars, yellow cabs, and people. No one knew she was up here, all alone, scared. Her home, her oasis, was now a reminder of how isolated she'd allowed herself to become.

She should call someone and talk it through with them.

Who would I call?

Max had plenty of fans but no close friends. No exes to speak of, either, just women she'd had sex with when the opportunity arose and she could be discreet. No one ever lasted very long in her world. Maybe that was the problem with hiding a major part of your life. It meant you never let anyone see all of you, making it impossible to have a real friend, a confidant, the type of relationship where they would hold you while you cried on their shoulder.

In a city of millions, Max had never felt so alone.

When she was onstage, thousands of fans screamed her name and connected with her, even if it was all an illusion. No one knew the real Maxine Gardner. How could they? She'd done everything to prevent that from happening as a way of protecting herself.

Not just emotionally, either.

When she was a teen and had first experienced attraction toward other girls, Max had known her father would hate her queerness. Hate it with every fiber of his being. What he hated, he'd tried to destroy. Hell, he hadn't liked her all that much when he'd assumed she was screwing guys. That had earned words like *slut* and *tramp* being hurled at her. When she'd dressed up a little, put on some eyeliner, or did her hair in a way that he hadn't liked, he'd threatened her with his belt. Sometimes he'd carried through on the threat, the leather strap stinging the backs of her thighs, leaving red welts for days.

You'll put on a longer skirt to cover that now, won't ya? he would jeer. He knew how to get his way because she did, every time.

It twisted her insides to realize how much she'd let that bastard infect every nook and cranny of her life, controlling her. Terrified and ashamed. For forty-two long years. After so long, hiding became her knee-jerk reaction. Chameleon mode, if anyone even hinted she might not be the perfect daddy's girl. The need to avoid pain was so deeply tattooed in her she didn't know if there was a way to undo its awful message.

Nonconforming, my ass. I've been conforming since I could walk.

Max scrunched her fingers into her hair, tugging hard, wanting to pull the pain out by its roots like weeds in a garden. If she thought it'd do any good, she would let out a primal scream for all of New York to hear.

Actually, what was stopping her?

Max got to her feet, placing her hands on the railing, and let out a scream to end all screams. She belted it out with her diaphragm, strengthened by years of singing, projecting all the way to New Jersey. She continued until she couldn't get any sound out. She stared into the blackness of the night, realizing no one heard her. The pain of crushing loneliness knocked her legs out from under her, and she crumpled into a bawling mess on a rattan lounge chair.

What had been the point of hiding who she was? To earn the respect of a man whom she despised? Who hated her despite her pretending to be something she wasn't?

Pathetic.

All those wasted years of being terrified that the tiniest slip would wreck the illusion. When you lived that way, you stopped yourself from sharing even mundane aspects of your life, because slipping up was that easy. A simple question like how was your weekend came loaded with landmines. Mention you spent it with someone, the questions rolled in like sniper fire. So, it was best to stay with grunts and shrugs, joking innuendo, and misdirection.

Max rested her head against the bricks of the terrace wall, still radiating the heat from the sun like an oven. As she stared up toward the heavens, she raised a clenched fist. "You fucking bastard! I hate you!"

Another scream ripped through her.

It wasn't enough.

How had she lived this way for so long?

She needed to get the shit buried so deep inside

out, or she wouldn't survive. But how, if she couldn't talk to anyone? The only person she'd been able to bounce ideas off of was Jade, when they collaborated on songs. No one got Max like Jade. Max was pretty certain Jade had no use for a coward.

If only Max could explain to Jade. The fear. Embarrassment. The brutality of sadness. How it tore you up, piece by piece, until you were a shell of yourself. How many nights had Max woken at three in the morning, crying because she was alone and knowing without a doubt there wasn't another soul on the planet who loved her for her. Everyone in her life had wanted something from her. No one saw her. No one got her. No one cared for her. Max hadn't let anyone have the chance.

Until Jade.

She'd known how stifled the younger woman had felt, but seeing her roar at Skip and Cindy like a goddamned lioness had been exhilarating. Torn between petrified and in awe, Max had been rooted to the spot as accusations and demands were flung at her. Jade, though, had decided it was enough.

And Cindy still blamed me.

Max leaned back, staring up at the sky. The vitriol Cindy had for her had felt unwarranted. Oh, she'd known there'd been harsh feelings. But the way Cindy's face had flamed red as she hurled accusations...

There was so much more to the story. Max wasn't

going to get answers by sitting back and letting others make the decisions for her. Hiding wouldn't get her out of trouble. There was a friendship to repair, a show to put on, and fuck, if she was even a smidge lucky, a girl to win back.

The answers weren't going to happen on the phone or at a meeting, though. Max wasn't the *let's talk things out* type of person. No, she communicated through music. Already, a melody was stirring in her head. She could hear it as clear as if it were coming from the radio. Her finger twitched with the need to pluck her guitar strings. Words formed themselves into verses and a refrain.

Max wasn't the talking type, but she sure as hell could pour her thoughts and emotions into a song. Even if no one would ever hear it. Even if Jade would never speak to her again. Max had to get the song out, if only to keep the darkness at bay.

CHAPTER TWENTY-FOUR

Bleary-eyed from a sleepless night, Jade had to blink her eyes into focus before she could make out the words on her phone. Twenty unread text messages from Cindy. Nothing from Max. Ignoring the stab to the gut that accompanied that discovery, along with the low battery warning that flashed as she unlocked the screen, Jade flipped to the airline app to retrieve Lottie's updated flight information.

Landed. Finally.

Nothing about the so-called Mexican cantina where she'd been waiting near LaGuardia Airport's baggage claim for the past four hours made it the type of place anyone in their right mind would want to spend their time. The decor was as bland as the food, the seating nothing more than a line of bar stools facing a mostly white wall. The shelves of liquor bottles might've held some appeal if Jade trusted herself to drink, but since she didn't, they mostly gave off a depressing and slightly desperate vibe.

Not unlike Jade herself.

"You're here." Jade fell into Lottie's open arms the moment her friend arrived, wheeling a carry-on bag behind her. "I was beginning to think I'd imagined the part where you agreed to hop on the next flight." The last time Jade had needed a hug this badly had been when Grace had passed. Lottie had been there for her then, too.

She was truly the very best friend, even if her advice had been the catalyst for this disaster.

"I'm sorry about the delays. Typical airline bull-shit." Lottie held on tightly. "But, of course, I'm here. Why wouldn't I drop everything and come running when you needed me?"

"Because everyone hates me." Jade sniffed loudly. It was as if, once in Lottie's presence, she could allow herself to hit the maximum level of pitiful. "You haven't gotten the memo yet."

"Sit." Lottie steered Jade back to her barstool, plopping down on the one next to hers. "Okay, good. Now tell me what the heck is going on. But first, should we order something?"

"Based on what I've seen while I've been waiting, I'm not sure I can recommend it. This is nothing like the place we went to in LA."

"How about nachos?" Lottie waved to the server behind the counter. "No one can mess up nachos."

"Still a gamble. Given how the past twenty-four hours have gone, I've learned I have a particular talent for messing up just about anything." Jade reached for the condiments, aligning them in order by color.

"Oh, honey, it must be bad if you're trying to clean this dump." Lottie squeezed Jade's shoulder. "As for the nachos, you aren't the one making the dish."

Her joke hit home, and Jade managed a chuckle. Lottie nodded approvingly before asking, "Are you finally going to tell me what happened?"

Jade swallowed, tears stinging her eyes. "Where do I even begin?"

"Maybe with the *everyone hating you* part," Lottie said gently. "That can't be true, but why do you think that?"

"I did a bad thing. So bad." Jade wrung her fingers while Lottie ordered two margaritas, which Jade was almost certain would taste nothing like they were supposed to and would almost certainly make her tipsy. She didn't care.

"What's the bad thing you've done?"

"I went to Max's place—"

"Did you two—?" With eyes full of excitement, Lottie finished by mouthing the word *fuck*, ensuring no one could make out what she was saying.

"Yes," Jade said quickly, waving her hands dismissively. "But that's not the worst of it."

"Oh no." Lottie's happiness drained away, replaced by a glum pout. "Was it bad?"

"It was—"

"Wait, were you bad?" With a horrified look, Lottie clamped a hand to her mouth. "Too starstruck? I could see that happening to me. One time I had a date with the lead singer of this band that was playing a club in Laguna Niguel, and I—"

"Lottie." Jade grabbed her friend by both shoulders, fighting off the urge to laugh and cry in frustration. "Stop!"

"I can't ask how it was?" Lottie pouted again. "Because I've daydreamed about it for, gosh, how long now? I feel like I need to know some details here."

Despite the fact her world was ending, Jade managed a small chuckle. "I know focusing isn't your thing, but I need you to try." Jade drew a deep breath, waiting until Lottie was looking her in the eyes with undivided attention. "I outed Max."

"Outed like, out? Ha! I knew it. I knew she was." Lottie reached for her phone. "Where are they reporting it? I don't see an alert."

Jade shook her head. "Not online."

"Oh." It seemed to take Lottie a moment or two to process the possibility of something happening to a celebrity that wasn't available for the world. "It's not trending, then?"

"I really hope not." The server brought the margaritas, and Jade grabbed hers to take an enthusiastic sip.

It tasted like vaguely lime-flavored battery acid, and she did not care. "I doubt either Skip or Cindy would do anything like that, even if Skip is an opportunistic devil and Cindy's beyond vindictive when she's angry."

Lottie's perfectly plump lips formed a circle. "I don't think I'm following. What exactly happened?"

"I outed Max to her manager, Skip. And to Cindy. At her apartment, while wearing my clothing inside out in that special way that screams: *I just had sex!*"

"Hold up, sugar." Lottie reached for her drink, taking a sip and making a face like her taste buds were threatening to go on strike. "Oh wow, this is like... oven cleaner, maybe?"

"I've never tasted oven cleaner but maybe." *Maybe it could scour away how shitty I am.*

Despite looking like she wanted to throw up, Lottie took another long swig. "Are you telling me that Cindy didn't know Max is into women?"

"Correct."

"It's not like a new thing? She's always been gay?"

"That was my impression, yes." Jade tapped her fingernail on her glass. "She sure didn't seem to be inexperienced."

"Aha! So the sex *was* good. You had me worried." Lottie grinned broadly before attempting to be serious again. "I might be able to see your aunt being clueless. I mean they were young, and it was the 90s. Plus they'd been out of touch for years. But her manager? I

339

know for a fact he's been in the picture since the beginning."

"So?"

"So, he knew. He just didn't want to admit it. Hell, everyone under the rainbow has known it for the longest time, if they were paying any attention." Lottie shrugged. "We've been waiting for her to confirm."

"Yeah, well. She didn't have the opportunity to. I did it for her." Jade slumped forward, burying her head in her hands. She could still see Max's shocked, frozen expression as the elevator doors closed. How could anything ever make that right?

"It's not the ideal way, no."

"She's never going to talk to me again. NEVER. In all caps." Even the appearance of the nachos did little to brighten Jade's outlook, in part because the chips were burnt on the edges and yet somehow the cheese did not appear to have melted in spots.

"How did they do this?" Lottie made a face as she took a chip and popped it into her mouth. Despite her obvious disgust, she continued to nibble, though Jade was too distraught to join her. "Max might be mad, but come on. Is she the type to burn things to the ground for a mistake? It was a mistake, right?"

"Of course, it was a mistake," Jade assured her. "I was actually coming to her rescue, because Cindy was accusing her of plotting something with Skip to take advantage of my innocence when it came to contracts."

"You figured being gay is way better than being a cheat?"

Jade snorted at her friend's succinct summary. "I guess so. I don't think I had really thought it through."

"I could see that," Lottie said with the authority of someone who had done many things without thinking before.

"As for burning things to the ground, that's exactly Max's MO. She has a scorched earth policy and doesn't look back. She takes the 'matchstick' in Matchstick Girls seriously."

"She can't avoid you. You're in a band together."

"For one more night," Jade muttered, her stomach tightening so quickly she was thankful she hadn't risked the nachos.

"She has to be professional enough to be on stage with you. Then you can explain. Apologize. Beg."

Jade's heart raced as her breathing became shallow, indicating the start of a panic attack on the horizon. She'd thought they were a thing of the past. It was as if a steamroller were beginning to move over her chest, flattening her lungs. "I don't think I can go tonight."

Lottie stared in a dazed way. "You have to."

Pain popped in starbursts in Jade's airways. "I can't... breathe."

"Woah." Lottie sprang into action, stroking Jade's back. "Let's breathe. Come on. Breathe in. One, two, three, four, five. Now out. You've got this."

Jade focused on the feel of Lottie's hand. Jade

followed it in her mind as it made large, soothing circles on her back. With effort, she connected to the touch, matching her breathing to the up and down of her friend's palm.

After a few minutes, Jade's breathing was back in control, though she was shaking from head to toe. "God, Lottie. That hasn't happened since right after my mom got her diagnosis. What am I going to do?"

"I know you don't want to, but honey, you have to show up for the gig. You were born to be a rocker. Your mom—"

"Made me promise not to follow in her footsteps." Jade breathed in deeply to ward off another descent into panic.

"Because she was scared you'd end up like her, but that's never going to happen. You're too responsible." Lottie tilted her head to one side. "Remember when we were in high school and someone thought you were the substitute teacher?"

Jade let out a weak laugh. "It was picture day. For some reason, I decided I wanted to wear a suit."

"Because you're like that. Responsible." Lottie's tone suggested Jade was an alien creature, but one she clearly loved. "If your mom had been able to see you perform the way you are now, she would have been your biggest cheerleader. She always was mine, and I'm not even her kid."

"She would've adopted you in a heartbeat," Jade said with affection and a hint of melancholy as the familiar ache of loss tugged at her. "She wanted me to have steady work. A 401K. All the things the symphony has to offer. The last thing she envisioned was the rock 'n roll lifestyle, being on tour. I sure as hell know she didn't picture I'd be sleeping with someone like Max."

"Your mom never got to see you on tour. You've been amazing, and I have to admit, it's been difficult not to hate you. Do you know how many musicians would kill to be in your shoes? You're living the dream." Lottie was warming to her pep talk, her volume ramping up with each new assertion. "You've been on tour all summer. You're killing it. Meanwhile, I've been in a band at Disneyland, paying my dues to have even half your chance."

"You're earning it. Me? I blew it. Kaboom!" Jade lifted her hands to simulate the shape of a mushroom cloud. "You should have seen the look in Max's eyes. It wasn't just anger. She was so devastated. She hates me."

"I kind of doubt that."

"Maybe it doesn't matter if she hates me or not. The dream was over, anyway. Cindy doesn't want to continue with Matchstick Girls. She was having a blast, but she's been clear this tour was a one and done."

"What about you and Max continuing the band? Assuming she doesn't actually hate you," Lottie added. "Which, she doesn't. No way."

"Max doesn't want to be in a nostalgia band. She shouldn't." Jade struck the countertop with her palm for emphasis. "She's amazingly talented but hasn't been given the chance to break free of the Matchstick Girls box. She needs to be playing her own music."

"Right." Lottie frowned. "Where does that leave you?"

"Nowhere." Jade propped her head up with a palm. "Going the symphony route after this summer sounds like death warmed over. I don't think I'm cut out for that work. I don't have a band anymore. I'm fucked. *This* is probably what my mom wanted to spare me from. The drama and heartache. Don't knock your Disney gig. At least it's steady work."

"Yeah," Lottie gave a snort. "Living the dream."

"You know what you want, and you're going after it." Jade made a half laughing, half groaning sound. "You're a step ahead of me."

Lottie swung her legs around on the barstool to get a closer look at Jade's face while asking, "What part of the tour did you enjoy the most? Was it life on the road? Being in a band? Or being with Max?"

Jade didn't answer.

After several awkward moments of staring and not speaking, Lottie started bouncing on the stool. "I knew it! Your eyes lit up when I said being with Max. Ding, ding, ding! We have a winner!"

"You're conveniently overlooking the part where she hates me. I might be able to join another band, but when Max and I worked on songs, we jived in a way that's hard to put into words. Not only did I mess up our relationship, but I totally fucked up being able to work with her." A yawning chasm of despair loomed ahead, and Jade shut her eyes, as if somehow that could keep her from falling in.

Lottie took on the demeanor of a general giving a rousing pep talk before battle. "Do you know what you need to do?"

Jade shrank back. "What?"

"Finish your drink. You have a concert to get to."

Jade shook her head, tempted to grab the barstool so Lottie couldn't drag her from it. "I can't face her."

"You will, and you must. I wouldn't be your best friend if I let you play the coward card now. Not after everything you've done. I've never known someone so strong. Day and night, you sat by your mom as she was dying, and you didn't break. You were there for her when she needed you the most. If you can do that, you can face Maxine Gardner and say sorry." As Lottie downed her drink, shaking off the burn of the alcohol, Jade could almost hear rousing patriotic music swelling to a crescendo. "Come on. We're catching a cab."

"It's fifteen miles to the venue, and sound check starts in"—Jade checked the time—"fifteen minutes."

"Perfect," Lottie, the California driver, declared. "Text Max to let her know you're coming, and leave the rest to me."

Jade tried to open her phone again but got a blank screen. Her battery had given up the ghost. Fitting. "I can't. It's dead."

"Give me Max's number," Lottie said, pulling out her phone.

"It's not 1995, Lottie. I don't know anyone's number."

Her friend gave an exasperated huff. "It's fine. I have Cindy's. I'll text her as soon as we have an ETA." Jade wasn't sure Cindy would be there, either. At this point, though, Lottie was in full general mode, and there was no stopping her. The only thing to do was to salute, say, "Yes, ma'am," and hope you ended up where you were supposed to be.

Outside, Lottie flagged down a yellow cab. "We need to get to Belmont Park. I'll give you an extra hundred if you can do it in fifteen minutes."

"Belmont?" The man craned his head over his shoulder. "Lady, you're nuts. The way traffic's backed up right now, it'll be an hour if you're lucky."

Jade gasped. "I'll miss sound check completely."

"Drive," Lottie said to the cabbie, her optimism untouchable. "If there's one thing I've learned in life, it's better late than never."

CHAPTER TWENTY-FIVE

Max paced the floor in the backstage greenroom, her mind a jumble of worries. There hadn't been a single word from Jade since she'd left Max's apartment the night before. Now it was time for the sound check, and Jade still hadn't arrived, nor was she answering her phone.

"It isn't like her to be late." Glancing at Cindy, who had just slunk into the room without a word, Max pressed her lips together, pondering whether it was worth breaking the uneasy silence between them. For Jade, she decided to risk it. "Have you heard from her?"

Cindy shook her head, not making eye contact. After the emotional turmoil Max had been through over the past twenty-four hours, this was the final straw. Besides, she needed somewhere to focus her wild anxiety.

"You know, I always expected that if the secret about my sexuality came out, some people would turn their backs on me," Max said. "I didn't expect you to be one of them."

"You think my problem with you is *that*?" Cindy's eyes grew wide, her expression the very definition of sarcastic. "I couldn't care less that you're gay, Max. I'm not even that surprised! How could you think that? My problem is that you were having sex with my niece."

"That seems hypocritical," Max replied, crossing her arms. "It's okay for her to have sex with women but not me."

Cindy's face bordered on apoplectic. "Don't be ridiculous. First of all, if anyone gets to act a little hurt, I think it should be me. You kept this vital piece of information about you under lock and key all these years. How could you not confide in me, or in Grace? That hurts, a lot. But bottom line, you can sleep with anyone you want. Except Jade." Cindy wagged a scolding finger at Max. "This is all your fault!"

"How is this my fault?" Max already regretted speaking to Cindy, but now that she'd done it, she couldn't easily go back to silence without coming across like a petulant child.

"You broke the rules." Cindy stomped her foot, demonstrating that Max did not have a monopoly on childish behavior.

"Which rule would that be? The no sex rule?" There was no hiding the bitterness in Max's heart.

Cindy had known Max most of her life. She was one of the few people who knew about her troubled childhood and the shit she'd had to struggle through. Yet, after Jade had basically pried Max out of the closet with a crowbar, Cindy was being a jerk about it. Some friend. "Get off your high horse. You and Rick have been breaking that rule daily since the tour began."

"That's different." The way Cindy shifted uncomfortably in her chair suggested she was playing back what she'd said and realizing she wouldn't be able to defend it if pressed. Good. It had been a ridiculous rule in the first place. *None* of them was a child.

"Anyway," Max said, "this isn't about your stupid rules. This is about Jade."

"Yeah, you better believe it's about Jade." Cindy planted her hands on her hips. "How could you do this to her?"

Max's hands flew into the air. "What, exactly, have I done?"

"You took advantage of her," Cindy nearly shouted, lowering her voice as she received some looks from the stage crew. "My rules were there for a reason."

"Yeah," Max shot back. "To make you look ridiculous. Besides, rules can only go so far. It's like when you're a kid, and you want to eat chocolate cake every day for breakfast, but your dad says no. You swear when you're an adult, you're going to eat chocolate cake every morning, but do you? Of course not.

Because you're an adult, and you know it would make you sick. That's what being an adult is."

"Leave it to you to pat yourself on the back because you don't eat cake for breakfast," Cindy scoffed. "You've never grown up. You take what you want, do what you want, and to hell with the rest of us. All I know is if Grace had followed the rules, she'd still be alive. I took my eyes off her for a second, and now she's dead."

There was a moment Max's heart threatened to stop. How had they gotten here?

"What the fuck are you talking about?" Max stared at Cindy, trying to fathom how her brain worked. Did she really harbor that much guilt? "How did you go from chocolate cake to death?"

Cindy's eyes were wet. "It doesn't matter. What matters is Grace was a wild child, and it was my job to protect her. I was the older sister." The painful warble in Cindy's voice was impossible to miss, and it was clear the guilt Max had sensed was only the tip of the iceberg. Max thought back to those early years.

How Cindy had never fully joined them in the fun. Ever the vigilant third, making sure the other two didn't get into too much trouble.

How much had Cindy assumed they were her responsibility?

"Don't beat yourself up." Empathy softened Max's demeanor. "There wasn't a force in nature that could control that little sister of yours. You know it as well as I do. It's what made Grace amazing. And terrifying. She was like a thunderstorm. Beautiful when the lightning strikes but also dangerous and destructive. Mostly to herself. We were kids."

"So is Jade," Cindy insisted, her voice threatening to crack.

"That's the thing, though. Jade *isn't* a kid. She hasn't been for a long time. You have to start recognizing that. She's older than you were when you and Rick got married. She's more responsible than I am."

She still hadn't arrived, and the opening band was taking the stage. That could only mean one of two things. Either Jade was in trouble, or she'd been so mad at Max that she'd decided to quit. Which ultimately meant Cindy was right. This was all Max's fault.

"When Rick and I got married, we thought we'd have a family of our own. But it didn't work out that way, so Jade became the kid I never had." Cindy rubbed her head, unable to disguise the stress she was feeling. "She always will be, no matter her age. I swore to Grace I'd watch over her. Always."

Max was growing more agitated by the second. "Then stop arguing with me, and help me figure out where she is. She's not answering her phone. Jade was in a bad mental state. We need to find her."

Cindy gave Max an inscrutable look. "You really care about her, don't you?"

"Of course, I do." Max's head was reeling. "I love her, dammit."

"I don't know what to say." Cindy's gaze remained focused on Max. "Does Jade know this? Have you told her?"

"She must know. But… No." Max's head drooped, the enormity of the issue penetrating her brain. "Shit."

Cindy raised an eyebrow. "It didn't occur to you that she should be the first to find out you're in love with her?"

"Add it to the list of things I'm not good at, okay?" Max snapped. If something happened to Jade, she'd never forgive herself. Sure, Jade was an adult, but she was a beautiful woman roaming a city with a lot of bad people. Anything could happen.

Or maybe she was halfway back to North Carolina, never to speak to Max again. If that was the case, Max couldn't blame her. Over the past weeks, Max had done nothing to let Jade know the depth of the emotions. Each time things had skimmed closer than Max was comfortable with, she had made sure to back away quickly. Skip coming over had looked bad. There was no denying that. Then there was the way she'd frozen up when Jade announced they'd been sleeping together. Denying it as if ashamed.

Why would anyone—but especially a modern woman like Jade who was used to embracing who she was—be willing to put up with Max's closeted bullshit? How many times had she scoffed, reminding Max "times were different?"

No wonder Jade was gone. She'd rallied to speak up for Max, and Max had stayed silent.

The sense of abandonment washed over Max, icy and familiar at the same time. Jade was just another person in a long line of people who had left Max behind. She should've been used to it by now. Even so, Max could feel hot tears rolling down her cheeks.

"Hey, hey. It's okay." Cindy's eyes started to water, too. "Don't cry. She'll be okay."

"I know I should be the one saying that to you," Max said through sniffles. "But I can't lose her, Cindy. I can't. The way I've been hiding our relationship... it wasn't just because of your rules. I've been hiding my whole life."

"You're going to have to be willing to be honest with her, and with everybody, if you even want a chance of having it work."

"Do you know why I stayed in the closet so long? My dad. He wouldn't have accepted me. Never. Even with him gone, it's like I'm still scared he'll find out."

"No offense, Max, but your dad was a special kind of asshole."

Max gave a snotty chuckle. "Yeah, yet I didn't want to let that fucker down. For the longest time I assumed no one would accept me if my own father wouldn't. I followed my dad's rule. It didn't do me any good, and it made me resent the shit out of that man."

Cindy's shoulder's fell, and Max could see the final dregs of fight drain out of the woman. "I think our scars from the past have fucked us both up, my friend." Cindy grew solemn. "It's why we do what we do. But I'm starting to see how I have to let my niece be her own woman, or she'll end up hating me."

"I don't think she could hate you." For all the resentment, Jade had been nothing but caring and forgiving for the entirety of the time Max had known her.

Cindy jumped when her phone vibrated. She frowned as she looked at the screen. "It's a text from Lottie."

"You mean Jade's friend from LA?" Max gripped her elbows, hugging her waist. "Why is she texting you? Oh God. Has something really bad happened?"

Cindy waved her hand as if to get Max to be quiet. "She's with Jade. Jade's phone battery died. They're in a cab, stuck in traffic."

"In LA?" Max's heart threatened to pound out of her chest. They were supposed to be on stage in a few minutes.

"No, Lottie's here in New York. She says they're close to the venue, but she doesn't know how long it will take."

Out on the stage, Max heard the opening band playing their final song. Minutes stretched out in silence. Still no Jade. Inside Max's chest, her heart scratched like a rabbit in a cage.

Max looked to Cindy, nerves on edge. "Think we can get the opening act to go back out there and stall for us?"

"A stadium full of New Yorkers?" Cindy jerked a thumb to the crowd, the grumbling becoming palpable. "What if we go out there and start the show as planned? We can put Roxie on drums." It was a reasonable idea, but Max couldn't stomach the thought.

Max shook her head. "It doesn't feel right, starting our last show without Jade."

"Do you have a better idea?"

Only one possibility came to mind, but one was all she needed. Max grabbed her acoustic guitar. "Yeah. You stay here. I'm going out there."

"What are you going to play?" Cindy demanded.

Max shrugged, her casual stance hiding the spike of adrenaline coursing through her. "Something for Jade."

Max stepped out on stage. The crowd quieted, a hum of expectation in the air, as if everyone was whispering, *What's Max going to do with that guitar?*

That was the wrong question, not that the crowd knew what was in store for them. If she put too much more thought into the plan, she'd flee. *Stick with the steps, Maxie.*

There was a stool off to the side, one she tended to use for some of the slower songs. Max took it to the middle of the stage and sat down, guitar plugged in and in place. "Hey, everybody. We're sorry for the wait. Fuckin' New York traffic, right?"

The crowd ate that up, responding with hearty laughter and jeers. Max's tension eased. These were her fans. They had loved her for years, even when nobody else did. Even if nothing in her life was going right, she could count on them to be there for her. Right now, she was going to be there for them, entertaining them. Quiet confidence overtaking her, Max strummed the guitar, the music already transporting her to the place she needed to be.

"We're down by one band member right now as we wait for her cab to weave its way through the mess. In the meantime, I thought I'd play you guys a few songs." The melody her fingers had been picking out as she spoke made its way to her ears, making it impossible for her to stop now. The show must go on. "So, listen. This is something new. I haven't played this in concert before. Actually, I haven't played it for anyone." She waited a beat, building the moment. "Well, just one person."

The lights were a shield, isolating her on the stage. The energy from the crowd was quiet and expectant, pulsing with curiosity.

Closing her eyes, Max strummed the guitar, playing through the song but holding back the words. In her mind, she was back in the studio in New Orleans, Jade beside her, pouring all the hurt and anger at her father —all the disappointment of her youth, and the feeling of never being enough—into every word and every note.

"It has words, too." Max smiled as the crowd laughed at her joke. "When I wrote it, I wasn't planning on anyone, you know, listening to it."

More laughter. These were her friends, her family. All those lonely years after the band had broken up, when she was out there touring by herself and hadn't had anyone to lean on or trust, the audience had always been there, lifting her up. The more she warmed up with them right now, the more she felt the urge to unburden herself.

"I didn't have a great childhood," Max confessed, talking to the eighteen-thousand people in front of her like they were friends sitting in her living room. "My dad, he was... It doesn't really matter what he was. Anyway, when I played this for my friend, I told her that childhood is like wearing a white T-shirt, brand new out of the package. It's like our parents spill something down the front. Tea. Coffee. I don't know, maybe red wine. Cheap beer in my old man's case. No matter how hard we scrub, it never quite comes out. Anyway, I call this song 'Stain.'"

Max closed her eyes once more and started singing, lost in the words and the memories. But this time as she sang, it wasn't the bad memories of her childhood she was reliving, but the night in the studio in New Orleans. Writing songs on the bus with Jade as they passed through small towns with no names and long stretches of empty road. When the song ended, the audience was silent for a moment before erupting into a thundering ovation that transported Max to a space of emotional safety she wasn't sure she'd ever experienced before.

A lump formed in her throat, and she swallowed hard.

"Thank you." Max rocked back and forth on the stool, energy coursing through her, along with an overwhelming need not to hide anymore. The applause continued to be thunderous, and she waited, years of understanding the audience guided her timing. Finally, it quieted a bit, with only a few *I love you*s and *you rock*s being screamed out.

The vibe was perfect. The moment felt like hers to command. As if, by singing the song, she hadn't gotten the stain out of the T-shirt, but she'd been able to fold it up and tuck it away. She had new clothes to wear. "Earlier, I said I had played that song for a friend. That's only part true. She's a lot more than a friend." A questioning murmur swept through the crowd, but instead of being afraid, Max embraced the moment. "Yes, I do mean that exactly the way it sounds." The noise in the crowd grew, punctuated by a smattering of applause. "Wow. I guess I just came out of the closet, live on stage, although I'm not sure I was very hidden in there. Even *I* heard the rumors about me, and I'm always the last to know anything."

Max laughed along with the audience. It was over

and done, and she hadn't combusted into flames or heard the snap of a leather belt. Only peace.

"I've got another song. It's one I just wrote, so excuse me if it's a little rough. But, remember that woman I mentioned?" Max chuckled as the joke got the desired response. "Yeah, I guess you do. Anyway, I wrote it for her. She hasn't actually heard it yet, so I'm probably committing a major relationship faux pas."

"Who is she?" a voice called out as Max strummed the guitar.

Max shook her head. "Nope. Still gonna keep a few secrets."

She thought she heard someone else ask if it was Jade, but it might have been her imagination. Regardless, she concentrated on singing, which was needed considering the song was less than twenty-four hours old. She hadn't been lying. It was more than a little rough. But as she neared the end, the audience let out a massive cheer.

"Gosh, thank you," Max said but then turned her head and caught the real reason people were going wild. While she was lost in her song, Jade had stepped onto the stage. "Oh. You're here."

"Yeah. Nice song."

Max's heart beat wildly as she tried to read the expression on Jade's face but failed completely. Happy? Sad? Mad? Max had no idea. "It's, uh… new." Max was still speaking into her mic but the audience had disappeared, eclipsed by Jade.

She was standing there with red-rimmed eyes, her high-waisted jeans and oversized tank top fitting her perfectly. Maxine had been so afraid she'd never see those brown curls piled high again. Jade's face remained an aggravating neutral. "I heard. I've been backstage a few minutes now."

"How… many minutes?"

"Oh, a few." Which meant she'd heard every word Max had said. If there any doubt about it, that melted away as a flicker of something moved in Jade's eyes. All at once, Max knew what it was. It was love. It was also at this point that Max realized Jade had brought her guitar. She played a few chords of the song they had worked on together in New Orleans, lifting an eyebrow as if asking for permission to continue.

Max, throat clogging with emotion, nodded.

Jade waved to the crowd, a huge smile brightening her face. "Hello, everyone! I'm sorry for running late. To say thanks for your patience, we're going to play another new song. It's one Max and I worked on together while we were on the road. It may be a departure from our usual Matchstick Girl fare, but tonight seems like the perfect night to show you what she's been holding back from all of you."

"Not anymore," Max spoke into the mic. "I'm not holding anything back anymore."

Especially not from you.

"Is that right?" It was almost as if Jade had heard

the unspoken words, and her response was a challenge, one Max was finally up for.

"It is." Max played a few notes, slowly, pausing to speak again. She was addressing the crowd but looking directly at Jade. Like everything they did, they were in sync, working the music and the crowd yet staying true to each other. "Remember when we were working on this, and my heart wasn't in it? You asked what was wrong, and I said the last thing the world needed was another stupid love song."

The audience lost it, laughing and cheering. Maxine couldn't help but grin like an idiot.

"I remember." Though Jade maintained her composure, her tone was thick with emotion. The crowd settled immediately, responsive to them. Eager for this. If only they knew how much more desperate Max was for it. And how fucking thankful she was that she'd finally found what she'd been looking for. "I told you the world could always use more love."

"That you did." Drawing a breath, Max began playing again. A look passed between them, and they started singing together, the words and music they'd created.

It was a flawless performance.

As the stadium reverberated with thunderous applause when it ended, Max leaned close to Jade so she could hear. "I didn't believe you back then, about love."

"Do you now?"

"I definitely do. I love you."

To prove she was telling the truth, Max put her hand behind Jade's head and drew her closer until their lips met. Then she kissed her, right there on stage, in front of eighteen thousand witnesses.

CHAPTER TWENTY-SIX

Gripping Max's hand on one side and Cindy's on the other, Jade took one more bow. She'd taken so many her sides were beginning to ache.

"Thank you, New York!" Jade hollered, thankful this was the final show. Her voice would be hoarse come morning. The pounding applause beat at her back as they finally turned to go. There'd been two encores, and they didn't have anything left to give.

"I'm not going anywhere," Max said with a laugh as they exited the stage. "You can ease up on the grip of death."

"No way." Jade tightened her grip even more. "Not after yesterday. I thought I'd lost you."

"Need I remind you"—Max wiggled her fingers as if trying to increase blood flow—"you're the one who didn't show up to sound check. I was sure you'd left for home and were never coming back."

"I would never have done that," Jade assured her, giving a final squeeze before letting go, although she regretted it instantly. It was pandemonium backstage, even more so than usual.

"Maybe," Max said, "I had to think I'd lost you in order to find myself."

"Oooh, that's deep." With a teasing grin, Jade leaned in for a kiss, stopping short of Max's lips. "Can I?"

"Anytime you want." Max craned her neck to capture Jade's lips. They kissed long and deep as the world scurried around them. When they finally parted, Max said, "Not sure you noticed, but not only have I officially come out tonight, but I also declared my love for you in front of thousands of people."

"Eighteen thousand," Jade said with a laugh. She still couldn't believe what she'd witnessed. "I did happen to catch that, yes."

"I sure hope so because as grand gestures go, I think I nailed it." Max put her hand up for a high five. When Jade didn't give her one, Max high-fived herself then patted herself on the back for good measure.

Jade rolled her eyes. "How did I miss this part of your personality?"

"My awesomeness?" Max guessed.

"Sure," Jade deadpanned. "We'll call it that."

"Jade!" As they entered the VIP waiting area, Lottie

rushed across the space, slamming into Jade with enough force to nearly knock her off her feet. "That was the best concert I've ever seen!" Jade wrapped her arms tightly around her friend.

"Thanks for getting me here. Not just tonight but over the years. As a thank you, let me introduce you to Max." Jade turned to her girlfriend. Could she call Max that now? "Max, this is my best friend, Lottie. The super fan I've been telling you about."

"Warning, more likely." Lottie giggled as she shook Max's hand, shaking it up and down like a broken water pump that she was still desperately trying to squeeze some liquid out of. For all her practice in LA, Lottie was looking completely starstruck now. "I can't believe I'm meeting you. Wow, what a show."

"It's really great to meet you," Max said with a level of sincerity appropriate to meeting your significant other's best friend. Jade wondered how Max would feel knowing she'd been the number one guest in Lottie's "spank bank" for years.

"I have to get something off of my chest." Lottie suddenly went from gushing fangirl to deadly serious. Like, mafia-level intensity. Even Jade took a half-step back. "If you ever do anything to hurt Jade, I will make sure you regret the day you were born." Lottie paused a beat before topping her threat off with a maniacal laugh that raised hackles. "Kidding, of course. But, also, not really."

Jade stepped closer, looping her arm protectively around Max's elbow. "I wouldn't push Lottie on this."

"I'll try really hard not to," Max promised, a look of genuine fear on her face. Jade could imagine her making a note to call Skip and ask for bodyguards.

"Okay, now that the death threats are out of the way, shall we head to the after-party?" As the reality hit her that the tour was over, Jade felt happy and sad at the same time, not to mention overwhelmed by everything. She held Max's arm a little tighter. "I need a drink. I want *all* the drinks."

"Should I be worried when she says something like that?" Max asked in a stage whisper to Lottie.

"We should keep an eye on her," Lottie whispered back, "to avoid another sprinkler incident."

Jade shot Lottie a death stare.

Max's eyebrows shot up. "A what?"

Jade stepped in front of Lottie, clapping a hand over her mouth. "It's nothing. Nothing at all."

Max mouthed *we'll talk later* to Lottie, which earned a snicker in reply.

Jade gave an exaggerated sigh. "It might have been a huge mistake introducing the two of you."

The private party was being hosted in the rooftop ballroom of a hotel overlooking Manhattan. It was a beautiful view, though nothing beat the one afforded by Max's apartment window. Especially under certain circumstances. Jade giggled to herself.

"What's so funny?" Max asked.

"Oh, nothing," Jade said slyly. "Just thinking about city views." Her body throbbed in turn with the memory.

"Is that right?" There was a twinkle in Max's eye. "Any view in particular you'd like to see?"

Jade was about to answer when she spotted Roxie talking with several members of the crew. Jade went up and gave hugs all around. Was it really possible she wouldn't be seeing these folks again? They'd shared cramped living quarters and rehearsals. It reminded Jade of camp and how devastating returning home after the summer had always felt.

"Twenty-eight shows later," Roxie said, "and I think I can finally manage that guitar part. Thanks for never making me do it before a live audience."

"You would have been fine," Max assured her, though Jade knew she shared Roxie's sentiment.

The woman shook her head, her smile stretched wide.

"I've learned a lot from you—both of you. I've never been so proud of a tour. Thank you for the amazing opportunity." Roxie hugged them both and then ran for cover with some of the dancers.

"It's amazing to me that someone so talented can also be deathly shy," Jade remarked when Roxie was out of earshot. "I wonder what it takes for her to go on stage night after night."

"That's what we do, no matter the fear, because not performing is much worse."

"What do you mean?" Jade asked, but at the same moment, Skip arrived, waving for both Max and her to join him. Jade sighed. After all the things he'd said about Max's age, the man wasn't forgiven in her book. "I wonder what he wants now." Jade knew, though.

"Everything okay?" Max asked Skip, looking like a kid about to be scolded.

"Where's Cindy?" Skip attempted a reassuring tone, though he wasn't very good at it. "This involves her as well." At least he'd learned that lesson fast.

"You're making me nervous, Skip." Jade scouted for her aunt, spying her with Rick by the bar and beckoning her to join them.

"You guys don't have drinks. Everyone needs drinks." From the sound of things, Cindy had already followed her own directive at least once or perhaps even twice. She was about to head back to the bar, but Skip yanked on the hem of her shirt to make her stay.

"Drinks can wait," he said.

"Since when do you turn down drinks?" Cindy joked, but after getting a load of his grim expression, she quieted.

"There's no easy way to say this," Skip began, instantly sparking an ulcer in Jade's stomach. "The other night at Max's—something both of you said, or didn't say, really—it's been weighing on me."

"What are you talking about?" There was an underlying panic to Cindy's words, and Jade couldn't blame her. She wasn't sure she'd ever seen the manager so serious, which led her to wonder if there was a contract issue he'd unearthed. Or worse, that Max's fears about being out were about to become real. *Did he not hear the same audience I did?*

"Yes, what is it?" Jade echoed.

"Well, Cindy said Max left the group to chase a solo career."

Jade frowned. That was the first story she'd ever heard about this band she'd come to love so much. The rift that had broken her mother's heart. "She did."

"Yes. The career part," Skip agreed. "But she wasn't the one who left the group."

"Look, Skip," Cindy warned. "I've only just begun to tolerate you again after all these years. Don't ruin it by lying to us now."

"I'm not." Skip held up his hands in a defensive posture, as if fearful Cindy might slap him. "Here's what I need to know. Why did you say it that way when you know you and Grace were already leaving the band?"

Cindy's jaw dropped. "What the hell are you talking about? We had no intention of leaving the band."

"Hold on," Max interjected. "Skip told me that was the plan. He said you and Grace told him so."

"Then he lied to you," Cindy barked, adding a snarl for good measure.

Jade flinched, caught in the middle of an unexpected skirmish.

"Listen here," Skip commanded, his voice growing in volume. It had the desired effect, with both Max and Cindy going quiet. "I didn't say I'd heard it from Grace and Cindy. I said I heard it from the Weathers family."

Cindy gave Skip a sardonic look. "There's a difference?"

"In this case, yes. It was Mrs. Weathers who came to me and said that her girls were quitting the band. She said it just like that. *My girls are quitting the band, Skip.* I was totally shocked because you guys were about to make it big."

"My mother did that? No way!" Cindy shook a menacing finger in Skip's face. "She didn't say that! It wasn't true. Why would she do that?"

Max reached for Cindy's arm, her demeanor almost childlike. "Are you saying you two didn't leave? Because that's what I was told. You two were quitting, abandoning me, and I was going to have to fend for myself."

Jade began to see connections that made her ache as she understood.

"No, that's not how it happened. Skip has to be lying," Cindy spoke through gritted teeth. "My mother wouldn't have done that. She wouldn't have gone behind our backs. Mom knew how much it mattered to us."

"Whoa, whoa. I think you two need to go back into your corners." Jade's head was spinning, and she felt like a referee at a boxing match. "Aunt Cindy, think about it. Why would Skip, or Max, lie about it now? The tour is over."

"Because I can't imagine your grandmother doing such a thing," Cindy replied, tears in her eyes.

"Can't you?" Jade conjured a mental image of her late grandmother, a woman who had been equal parts loving and strict. Formidable was perhaps the best word to describe her. "Grandpa's health was starting to fail, the band was on tour all the time, and she was stuck with a five-year-old who wanted her mommy."

Cindy pulled back like Jade's words had given her a physical shock. "It was our band. Grace and I formed it. It was ours. She had no right."

"You really weren't planning to quit?" Max could barely get the words out. "You weren't abandoning me?" Jade reached out and took her hand, knowing how badly Max must be reeling.

"Absolutely not," Cindy said. "Grace and I didn't plan on quitting. Not until our vocals were taken off 'Constant Burning,' which was a shitty move."

"That's on me." Skip placed a hand over his heart, more earnest than Jade had ever seen him. "Cindy, when your mom told me you two were quitting, that the Matchstick Girls' days were numbered, I wanted to protect Max. Help her go solo. So, I had the song remixed. I thought I was doing the right thing, honest to God. Max didn't have anyone else looking after her."

"You did that for me?" Max's eyes teared up.

"I still don't understand why my mother would do that." From the way Cindy said it, however, Jade could tell she was coming around to believing Skip was telling the truth.

"It sucks, doesn't it?" Jade couldn't keep herself from commenting. "A family member stepping in and dictating what to do with your life. It's like a Weathers family trait."

"Oh, don't even." Cindy huffed, crossing her arms. "This is different."

Jade mirrored the action. "How so?"

"I'm doing it to protect you."

"I'm sure Grandma said the same thing to herself," Jade pointed out.

"B-but," Cindy sputtered, not adding anything else to her defense.

"Maybe this is the right time to tell you," Jade said to her aunt, "that when you and Uncle Rick head back to North Carolina tomorrow, I'm not coming with you." Courage was taking a new welcome flight within her.

"What will you do?" Cindy sounded frightened, but Jade took it as a good sign that her aunt hadn't outright tried to put a stop to it.

"I'll be staying with Max in New York for a few days." Jade looked to Max, who still seemed stunned by Skip's revelation. "If that's okay with you?"

"Of course." Max flashed a smile, but Jade sensed it would take quite a bit more time before she was able to work this new information into her existing world-view. What does a woman who is used to being abandoned do when she finds out people loved her after all?

"After that, I know the record label wants a meeting next week with Max in LA. I thought I might go along." Jade looked to Skip, whose face lit up like a thousand-watt bulb.

"What about the symphony?" Cindy asked.

"That was Mom's dream, not mine. I think this family is done making decisions for others, don't you? Enough damage has been done."

Cindy rolled her neck, letting out an anguished sigh, "Are you sure about this, Kitten?"

Jade paused, a sense of calm washing over her. "I've never been more certain about something."

"Your mom would be proud." Cindy's tone was wistful, filled with resignation if not total acceptance. Jade would take it as a good first step. She hoped, in her heart, the words were true.

"You know," Jade added, "I haven't even decided what I'm going to do yet."

"It doesn't matter. Your mom would be proud no matter what. I am, too." Cindy sniffled. "I can't believe all of this, but I know one thing, it's time to let the past stay there. All of this distrust and shit, it's making me look old, and we all know, I am *not* old!"

"Not a day over thirty-nine," Max offered. "Maybe

you should start being the little sister, instead of the mother hen."

"Come here." Cindy wrapped Max into a hug.

Jade joined.

Skip stood awkwardly to the side before Max motioned for him to join the circle.

Then, much to Jade's shock, Cindy offered to buy Skip a drink.

"It's an open bar," Max butted in.

Cindy jabbed her with an elbow. "Just because the truth is out in the open about a lot of things doesn't mean you have to be honest about every little detail."

Max tipped her head back, laughing.

When it was just the two of them, Jade said, "You really thought my mom and aunt were leaving the band?" She could only imagine how that must have felt. How much harder it must have been for Max to come ask them for the reunion tour in spite of it.

"I did. It hurt like hell. First, my mom left me, and then they bailed." Max swallowed hard, pain etching her face. "I won't lie. It did a number on me."

"I'm sorry, Max. So sorry."

"It's not your fault."

Jade bit her lower lip. "It might be. I used to ask my grandmother when my mom was coming home. Like, all the time. I think maybe she did it for me."

Max nodded slowly. "I can see that. I wish it was handled differently. I was only a teen, and still pretty raw and insecure, but I might have understood."

"I'm not sure I ever will," Jade admitted. "What is it about the women in my family that they all seem so set on controlling everything?"

"Asks the woman who is such a neat freak she tried to clean my window naked." Max laughed as Jade gave her arm a playful punch. "I'm just saying if that's as far as you take it, I can probably get used to living with that."

"I imagine Emily will appreciate it." Jade raised an eyebrow as the rest of what Max had said started to sink in. "What do you mean exactly by you'll learn to live with it? That sounds awfully permanent."

"I guess it could be." Max shifted on her feet, her cheeks turning pink. "I mean, after all these weeks on tour, I've grown accustomed to having you around. I'm not sure I want to adjust to that not being the, uh... case."

"Oh, I see." Jade sucked in her cheeks to hold back a grin. "You want to keep me around because you don't like change. Very romantic of you."

"Well, now, I think before we go too far in settling things, there's some vital information I need to know." A sly expression crossed Max's features. "What was this sprinkler incident I heard about?"

Jade covered her face with her hands. "I'm going to kill Lottie."

"Come on. How bad can it be?" Max tilted her head to one side. "Like, so bad I would decide I didn't want you to move in with me even though I'm madly in love with you?"

"It's really embarrassing." Jade frowned, her brain playing catch up. "Wait, you considered not living with me?"

"I'm not answering that, or budging from this spot, until you tell me in great detail."

Jade tried pulling Max's arms, but her feet stayed put. "This isn't how grown-ups handle situations."

"I never claimed to be a grown-up."

"I want it on the record I'm doing this under duress."

"Noted."

"Fine." Jade stuck out her tongue at Max, although her heart was soaring too high after Max's declaration to truly be bothered by it. "Back in college, I got really drunk and somehow ended up on a golf course. I woke up to a weird sound, and the next second, I was in a deluge of water. I started screaming I was going to drown. Turns out, I had passed out next to a sprinkler."

"That's epic!" Max started to tap her leg, humming a snippet of melody. "I think there's a song in there somewhere."

"Don't you dare!"

"If you want me to stop," Max teased, "you're going to have to get creative."

Creative, huh? Jade could do that.

She pulled Max to her, claiming her mouth and

kissing her until all Max could manage when she stopped was a blink. "You were saying?"

"Was I?" Max blinked a few more times before starting to hum again. "That was a good start, but I think it might take more than that to make me forget. This is bound to be a Top 40 hit."

"Oh, I'll make you forget," Jade promised. "I already have a plan."

"You do?" Max's eyes lit up. "Care to share?"

"I'd rather keep it a surprise," Jade teased, tracing Max's cheek with her fingertip. "That reminds me, though. We might need to stop at the store on the way home tonight. We're going to need some Windex."

CHAPTER TWENTY-SEVEN

"**O**kay, ladies." Standing outside the headquarters of the record label Max had been with since she was a teenager, Skip rubbed his hands together like a pitcher preparing to throw a perfect game. "You two let me do the talking in there, all right?"

Max chuckled to herself at Skip's usual pregame antics, but Jade tensed, immediately suspicious. "Why?"

"This is what you pay me for, sweetheart." Since they'd arrived in LA, it had not escaped Max's notice that the number of sweethearts, babes, and other vaguely condescending nicknames Skip used in conversation had increased exponentially. As had Jade's propensity to bristle every time he spoke. "My job is to dance with the big dogs."

Oh boy. Jade was *not* going to like that one.

Jade started to speak, but Max tugged on the back of Jade's shirt in warning. She needed to calm down. Skip was a big talker, but he wasn't a complete asshole. Sure, he could teeter on that tightrope, but now more than ever, Max knew he was one of the few people in her life who had truly been looking out for her since she was a kid. Which was what was going to make this meeting particularly hard.

"You can go in now," said a receptionist in the lobby, wearing a headset and looking like a recording artist herself. Or a model. Possibly both. This was LA, after all, where you hustled your butt off until you made it or died.

There were two men waiting in the conference room, their outfits expensive and their hair immaculate. Max had been told their names but had forgotten, and frankly, she wasn't sure it mattered. There was a good likelihood they'd been issued from a movie studio's central casting to play the roles of Record Executive Number One and Record Executive Number Two. It was also possible they were robots, sophisticated animatronics perfectly formed out of lightly bronzed plastic. If that was the case, they were fairly convincing.

As soon as they'd entered the room, the one wearing a dress shirt and tie but no jacket—Max decided to call him Number One—jumped to his feet, offering a surprisingly lifelike hand to shake. His teeth were blindingly white, another piece of evidence in support of her robot theory. "I can't tell you how excited we are about this meeting. We know we'll be able to do great things together. So great."

"So great," parroted the second, slightly older but just as plastic executive who would henceforth be known as Number Two.

Max had met these types before. They were the ones who blew smoke so far up your ass you couldn't sit down for weeks. Imagining them as hulking lumps of sophisticated artificial intelligence made her smile.

"Didn't I tell you their tour would be a smash hit?" Skip pulled chairs out for Max and Jade, positioning himself between them.

Bold move, Max thought, imagining she could hear a faint growl coming from Jade's throat, like an overprotective bulldog.

Max almost expected Jade to shove him out of the way, but fortunately this was still Jade they were talking about, the one who had more maturity in her little finger than Max had in her whole body. The shoving thing was Max's style. Jade responded with more subtlety, biting down on her bottom lip and staring with an intensity that produced an unexpected but pleasing reaction between Max's thighs. The sooner this meeting ended, the sooner they could get back to their amazing hotel room with its private hot tub and room service.

Being a rock star did come with some perks.

"Your live recording in New York City—that's the

most amazing thing we've heard in a long time." Number One threaded his fingers together, resting them on the table. "We know there's been some legal wrangling over some songs from that night. The impromptu ones that weren't part of the set list we signed contracts for. But, I want to state right now, we want those." He pressed a finger onto the tabletop, whitening the tip completely. "Without them, the record is good, but not blow-your-mind fantastic."

"They've been clear. They don't want them to be part of the recording." Skip offered his no-bullshit smile, and Max was reminded why she'd wanted him there. To do her dirty work. "Our lawyers say they own the rights to them." He held up his hands as if to say, *Sorry, what can you do?*

"Come on, ladies. Can't we negotiate? What we have in mind is a three-record deal. Three." Number Two held that many digits in the air, whether to help emphasize the label's generosity or because he wasn't convinced female musicians could count that high without assistance was anyone's guess.

Skip looked to Jade and then to Max, practically salivating, but Max shook her head. Bless the man, but her mind, and heart, were made up. Placing a hand on Skip's arm, Max leaned over the table.

"This past week, Jade and I have been thinking."

"That can be dangerous," Number Two joked, increasing the odds his early display of fingers had been intended for their mathematical benefit.

Fuck him.

"I know, right?" Max joked back, eagerly awaiting the look on his plasticine face when he realized there would be no cajoling her into seeing things his way. "At first, we were set to sign a deal with you, but then we came to our senses."

Number Two's smile slowly ebbed from his face. Number One wore an identically grim expression.

Definitely robots.

This felt better than it had any right to feel. "Before the tour," Max said, "I was convinced my career was dying, if not dead. However, after the response on the road and working on new music, I—we, actually"—Max cast an affectionate glance toward Jade, who was sitting on her hands, most likely to avoid wringing anyone's neck—"realized we want more control."

"We can work with that," Number One was quick to offer.

"I think Max misspoke," Jade interjected, so calm and collected Max suppressed a shiver. Damn, her girlfriend was hot. "What she meant to say was, we want *all* the control."

Skip flinched but didn't try to argue. Max wished she could check his vital signs, make sure the blood pressure was good and his poor ticker wasn't set to explode with this latest turn of events. Ever the professional and once again proving he was in her court, though, Skip said nothing, letting her pave the way.

"What are you going to do? Crowdfunding?" Both

men on the other side of the table laughed as if that was the most insane thing they'd heard. Another strike against them.

Max simply raised an eyebrow and shrugged. "It's one option."

"It'll ruin you," Number Two promised. "Look how people reacted when the singer Amanda Palmer tried it." Number One joined him in what could only be described as meanspirited laughter.

"There is that," Max said, remembering the backlash. "However, when the writer Brandon Sanderson recently did almost the exact same thing, he was hailed as a genius."

"Yeah. It's funny." Jade tapped a finger on the table. "I wonder why that is. Put both of them side by side and what's the difference between the two?"

"One's a singer, and one's a writer?" Number One guessed.

"One's a woman, and one's a man," Max replied in the same singsong tone the young man had used. "Let's face it; when a woman does something, it riles the public. When a man does it, well, he's considered brilliant."

"All the more reason for you to stick with us," said Number Two, a shit-eating grin making its way back onto his face.

"I'm done being controlled." The steel in Jade's tone told Max she was right on the edge of losing that temper she'd been doing such a good job of holding in.

Max was going to need to hurry this up. She hoped the hotel tub came with bubble bath and some massage oil. Jade, who hadn't built up a tolerance to record industry bullshit like Max had, was going to need it after this.

Though, she mused, she wished Cindy could witness this. Where Jade was concerned, there was no need to worry about the music world railroading her.

Apparently, pretending that the best way to deal with temperamental artists was to decide they didn't exist, Number Two turned to Max, oozing charm out of every pore as if he hadn't just insulted her a few minutes before. "Max. *Maxine*. You know how this business works."

"I do." Max scratched the back of her head, more as a way to keep her hand out of sight so they didn't see it tremble. This was it. The moment of truth. "Which is why I think we can do it on our own."

"I think you're making a big mistake. Huge." Number Two's face hardened. It seemed like he was holding back some choice words, and it was killing him. Either that or his robotic circuits were over-heating and causing a glitch.

"It's possible." Max pressed her lips together, bobbing her head. "But, it's our decision to make."

Number One folded his hands in supplication. "Skip—"

Skip, who must've known Max well enough at this point to know when she was serious and couldn't be manipulated, got to his feet. "I'm sorry, gentlemen, but I support Max and Jade one-hundred percent. You've got the live record, and it'll do very well for you. But the new songs and three-record deal are off the table. Have a good day."

It wasn't until they'd reached the elevator that Skip managed to say in a whispering croak, "I hope you two know what you're doing."

Max chuckled. "Thanks for not saying that in there."

"I wish I'd known the plan when we went in."

"You adjusted well," Jade said, placing her hand on Skip's shoulder.

"I don't understand, Max." Skip transformed from the cocky manager she'd always known into someone who seemed uncertain. Even a little fragile. If Max had aged more than twenty years since they'd started working together, so had Skip. For the first time, Max could see it in his eyes. "I don't know what my role is anymore. It seems like you don't need me."

"We should talk about that because I know how much you've been there for me all these years. You've been like the dad I never had, watching out for me and helping me grow." Max's heart clenched, threatening her resolve. But she and Jade had talked about this. Their future was bright, if only Max had the courage to do what needed to be done. She couldn't allow affection or pity to get in the way. "I also know it's time for me to leave the nest for both of our sakes."

"You two are the next big thing." Skip's eyes grew wide, almost desperate. "I want to stay with you guys."

"There's always another new, fresh act around the corner," Jade said gently, coming to Max's rescue when tears thickened her throat and threatened to keep the words from coming out. "From what Max has told me, that's where your real nugget is, finding and polishing for the big show. With us, you'd be skipping vital steps."

"Besides," Max quickly added, "we may be determined, but that doesn't mean we'll be successful. It's a risk I'm willing to take, but not one I can ask you to take with me."

"I'm too young to retire." Skip's lips trembled, and it took everything Max had not to give the man a hug. She would eventually, but right now, she needed to keep it professional, if only to get through this intact.

"I don't expect you'll ever retire," Max said, hoping he knew how grateful she was.

Skip's shoulders slumped, accepting defeat. She was truly, weirdly going to miss him. "What do I do now?"

"Hey." In lieu of a hug, Max gave him a gentle punch to the shoulder. "Just because Jade and I are going solo doesn't mean I would ever leave you high and dry. I happen to have a line on the next big thing—"

"Excuse me," Jade interrupted, trying to look stern

but not pulling it off completely. "I think I should get credit for this part."

"She's right." Max offered Jade an apologetic nod. "This part was Jade's idea, but I'm totally on board with it. I think you two will really hit it off."

His eyes lit up. "Who is it?"

"You'll see." Max felt a giggle rising in her chest. She loved the anticipation, and it made her feel better to see Skip engaged and excited instead of heartbroken. "Picture a woman with southern charm, a total wizard on the keyboard, with a sultry voice that will make people swoon."

"I like it." Skip wore his hungry look, an excellent sign. "When can I meet her?"

"Well..." Max stroked her chin, pretending to think. "How do you feel about a little trip to Disneyland this evening?"

"Disneyland?" Skip's forehead crumpled in obvious consternation. "Is this because your dad never took you? Or is this what happens to old managers, like when you send an old dog to a farm upstate?"

"I wouldn't do that to you, Skip. Not after everything we've been through," Max assured him. "Although if you want to buy me a stuffed Mickey and a churro while we're there, I won't say no."

CHAPTER TWENTY-EIGHT

J ade leaned a shoulder against the cold, hard surface of the hotel room door, her feet crying out for mercy as she fished the keycard from her pocket. "I had no idea how much walking we would do today."

"Have you never been to an amusement park before?" Max teased.

"Not as an adult. When I suggested going there so Skip could hear Lottie perform, it didn't occur to me that you'd want to go on every ride and stay until closing." They'd at least used some rock star leverage to skip to the front of most of the lines. Jade was too tired to feel remotely guilty about it. If anything, it had given her a thrill to be recognized as readily as her more famous companion, a total first for Jade. But it had been an exhausting day, and as the door swung open, she was already kicking off her shoes. "Oh, sweet relief."

"Don't tell me I've worn you out too much. I still have some plans for us for tonight." Though Max's tone was sultry and suggestive, Jade couldn't hold back a giggle. Max's brow lifted. "What?"

Jade pointed to the rainbow mouse ears on Max's head. "Are you planning to wear those to bed?"

"What's wrong with them?" Max touched her souvenir hat with obvious pride.

It had been a strange delight to discover the woman's deep love for all things Disney. Max had even been able to recite a scene from *The Little Mermaid* with the "Ariel" they stumbled across, complete with belting "Poor Unfortunate Souls" in her trademark husky voice. When kids had lined up for her autograph, they had no idea what they were really asking. The parents shyly requesting selfies, however, did.

"Nothing's wrong at all. They're adorable." Jade giggled again. It was possible she was venturing into the realm of delirium. "I'm not opposed to dress-up and role-playing, but I have to be honest. A mouse with a squeaky voice doesn't rank high on the hot fantasy list."

"Fine." Max swept the ears off her head but held onto them, turning them slowly in her hand as a pensive expression stole across her face.

Sensing a shift in Max's mood, Jade sat down on the sofa and stretched her legs in front of her, rotating her ankles as she patted the cushion beside her. "Sit. Talk."

"Why do you think I need to talk?" Even as she asked, Max sank onto the sofa.

"Because I know you. After eight weeks on the road, I can nearly read your mind."

Max made a playful spooky gesture before asking in a faux-mystical tone, "Does that mean you already know all my naughty plans for tonight?"

"That doesn't take mind reading," Jade said with a laugh before shifting to a more serious tone. "Tell me what you're thinking about. Ever since the meeting with Skip, you've been full steam ahead. Are you worried about something?"

"Worried? No." Max looked at the mouse ears in her hand again. "It's just, growing up, I always wanted my dad to be the type who would take me to amusement parks and buy me junk food. But mine wasn't like that. I don't think he even liked me."

"I'm sure that had nothing to do with you," Jade said softly, resting her hand on Max's knee, her throat constricting at the painful admission.

"The only reason he tolerated me at all was that after my mom left, Dad could barely function. But he always made me feel worthless, even when I was taking care of him. He cut me down every chance he got, and I learned early on that people will use you for whatever they can get. My dad. Skip..."

"Skip did buy you those mouse ears," Jade pointed

out. "And a churro." Skip had been downright generous with his affection after meeting Lottie. He'd even walked with Lottie as she turned in her two-week notice, regaling her the entire time with promises that in another month Lottie would be a star. He might say that to all the musicians he was trying to sign, but in Lottie's case, Jade believed it.

"Yeah, he did." Max let out a soft laugh. "I was being honest earlier today when I said Skip was more like a parent to me than anyone else in my life. Sure, he wanted to make money off me, but he did his best to watch out for me, too. I could've had it much worse."

"Skip's not as bad as I thought he'd be," Jade admitted. She remembered her first impression, which had been heavily colored by Cindy's dislike. But Max hadn't been the only one to prove to be far better than expected. "I'm glad you had someone looking out for you."

"I had a lot of people, more than I knew. I'm glad I finally let down my guard long enough to see it." Max paused as her voice trembled. "If I hadn't met you, I think I would've spent the rest of my life with that niggling fear that I really was worth as little as my father thought."

Jade stifled a pained gasp. "Please tell me you don't still think that way."

"Not anymore. Even though I didn't have a great

start in life, look at me now. I have a fantastic girl-friend. I love my career, and I'm finally taking a risk I've wanted to take for so long now, but I never knew I had the courage deep down to do it. Not until you." Max kissed the top of Jade's head. "Thank you for believing in me."

Jade took Max's hand and gave it a squeeze. "Without you, I would've spent my life taking the safe route to avoid catastrophe." In the end, Jade was certain that without Max's bold encouragement, she'd have been too afraid to disappoint Cindy and her mother's memory.

"The symphony?" Max guessed.

Jade nodded, shuddering a little at the thought of what might have been. "Was it safe? Absolutely. Would it have made me miserable? No doubt. But I was too afraid of falling to ever risk seeing how high I could go. Until you came along. I never would have told Tweedle Dumb and Tweedle Dumber back at the record label this morning to take a hike if it wasn't for you. Why do you think chasing dreams is so terrifying?"

"Are you scared?" Max looked deep into Jade's eyes, coaxing the truth from her.

Jade swallowed. "Absofuckinglutely."

"Good. If you weren't, I'd think you were insane."

Jade's stomach tightened. Their plan had been hashed out in the midnight hours while tangled up in sheets and each other. It had been easy enough to believe they didn't need a record contract if they started their own record label. If they owned their own label, there'd be no one pressuring them to push out soulless "hits." Max helped her feel confident, but what if they were being delusional? "Is it too big a risk to go it alone instead of letting the record label do the heavy lifting?"

"Not at all," Max assured her. "Together, we're stronger. I have no doubt that the record we're going to make will be successful. We already have two standout songs for it."

They'd uploaded the live recording of one on a streaming service, and it was tracking higher than anticipated. "We know the fans love them," Jade said through a yawn that she swiftly attempted to stifle. Judging by Max's face, Jade had fooled no one.

"I should put you to bed." Max rose from the couch, holding out a hand to help Jade up.

"Yes to bed," Jade said, using Max's hand to raise herself to her feet. "But not to sleep. I believe you mentioned some other plans first."

"Really?" Max's eyes sparkled with teasing. "Oh right. I did say I had a few things up my sleeves for tonight."

"I was hoping sleeves wouldn't be involved." As Max headed toward the hotel suite's luxurious bath-room, Jade followed, still clutching Max's hand. "What did you have in mind?"

"I'll give you a hint. Bubble bath and massage oil."

Jade went giddy at the images forming in her mind. "How did you guess that was what I needed?" Her muscles were already aching with anticipation of the massage oil. Between her legs promised to be as wet and slippery as the bubble bath.

"Eight weeks on the road together, remember? If you can read my mind, I can do the same for you. You seemed stressed in the meeting earlier today, so I had the hotel send up an assortment of products from their spa."

Jade was going to be able to adapt to this rock star life quickly. "Did you hire someone to do the massage?" There was a chance, she supposed, that Max needed the same treatment.

Max scoffed. "No. I think I've seen enough movies to figure out a massage."

Jade couldn't hold back a snicker. "What kind of movies have you been watching? The ones where you pay per view?"

"A girl's got to have some secrets." Max offered a saucy smile, the type Jade could feel all the way to her toes. "But you're welcome to try to find out."

"Oh, I intend to." Jade pulled Max close, tangling her fingers through strands of Max's blonde hair. She used her grip to position Max's head just so before slanting her mouth across hers, the first of many kisses for the night. "I'll figure out all your secrets, even if it takes me a lifetime to do it."

"A lifetime? I like the sound of that." Before Jade could respond, Max deepened the kiss, all the world's distractions fading until it was only the two of them, the future stretching out with endless possibilities.

EPILOGUE

S topping her black SUV in the driveway beside the perfectly manicured lawn, Max pressed the middle button on the garage door opener and waited for the door to rise. She wasn't sure which felt more surreal, that she was now the type of person who owned a garage door opener, or that the sight of this cookie-cutter suburban house with its seasonal wreath on the front door immediately flooded her with a deep sense of happiness over coming home.

Walking up to the front door felt different, too. Her chest remained tight but out of eager anticipation rather than dread. Then there were the house keys jangling in her hand. It turned out she didn't need those, however.

Jade opened the door with a look of wide-eyed surprise. "I thought you weren't getting in until tonight."

Leaving her rolling suitcase in the entryway, Max pulled Jade to her, kissing her cheek. "I caught an early flight. I missed you."

"You were in New York less than a week." Jade leaned in for a proper hello kiss, the type that still sent sparks flying the moment her lips met Max's mouth.

"I didn't think I was going to survive," Max admitted. "I never would have guessed a year ago that I'd be so desperate to see the Raleigh airport."

"I missed you, too." Jade rested her forehead against Max's. They snuggled close for a moment before Jade shifted gears. "Oh, guess what I heard on the radio this morning when I was making coffee?"

"Was it Lottie's song?" Max asked in a teasing tone. She didn't have to guess, but Jade's delight was worth playing into. "You get more excited to hear Lottie's songs on the airwaves than ours!"

As Max stepped into the living room, she couldn't help marveling at how different the house looked from the first night she'd seen it nearly a year ago. Every stick of beige furniture had been replaced with vibrant jewel-tones, and covering one full wall was a hand-painted mural of a vintage Matchstick Girls concert poster. It had only been a rough sketch when Max left for New York, but the artist had made tremendous progress while she'd been away.

"What do you think?" Jade pointed to the mural, unable to contain her excitement as her entire body wriggled like a puppy.

Max couldn't drag her eyes from it. She, Grace, and Cindy had been perfectly rendered with loving brushstrokes in colors that cut to the quick. But Jade deserved an answer, as many of the changes had been her idea, and she'd stayed in North Carolina to make them happen. "Fucking fantastic. The whole feel of the place is punk rock."

"Yeah, I love it, too." A pensive look overtook Jade's expression. "I think this is the way Mom would've wanted it, if she hadn't always been so scared the other moms wouldn't let their kids come over to play if she didn't conform. She gave up so much—"

Max put a reassuring hand on Jade's shoulder. "Don't think that way," Max urged. "She loved you and would do anything for you. Including suffer the indignity of a house that looked like it had been coated with oatmeal."

"At least we had the basement." Jade's face lit up, and her body vibrated with excitement. "Oh my God! You haven't seen it yet. The guys finished a week early."

"Finished?" Max's eyebrows shot up to her hairline. "You mean the recording studio is finally done?"

"I couldn't believe it either when they told me. Like, when does any construction project ever finish early?" Jade grabbed Max's hand and pulled her toward the basement door. "I can't wait to show you."

"I can't wait to see it." They were a few steps from the door when Max's phone buzzed.

Jade stopped. "Need to get that?"

After checking the caller ID, Max shook her head. "Nope. Just a confirmation. I never knew how much hustle Skip did for me. My phone seems to ring off the hook. It's never-ending texts, calls, messages on social media, and emails." Sometimes the amount of notifications on her phone would make her dizzy with wonder.

Jade gave Max a knowing look. "For all the complaining, you don't seem too upset by it."

Max stepped closer to Jade, lowering her voice. "Can I tell you a secret?"

"Always and let's just get this out there, on the off chance you didn't know this. I want to know everything."

"Noted."

"What's the big revelation?"

"I never thought I was cut out for business, especially since I never went to college, but I kinda like it. I'm good at it. I can't remember a time when I've been busier, and I fucking love every second."

From her father's constant pessimism regarding her potential to Skip's repeated assurances that she shouldn't have to worry about details, Max had never experienced being in full control. Ownership did come with heaps of responsibility, but it also made her feel good about herself in a way she hadn't understood she needed.

The corner of Jade's mouth quirked. "Even though I roped you into organizing the Womyn's Festival this summer?"

The festival had been an ambitious proposal, an event for indie singers that showcased a lot of new talent that had been floundering in the strict confines of traditional recording contracts. Though her task list was monstrous, Max was thriving on it.

"It was a brilliant idea. And that call I just got? I'm pretty sure that was Skip's assistant confirming Lottie's on board to perform." They'd been working back and forth for a few weeks, and it had been all but certain.

Jade's face lit up. "That's fantastic!"

"I know it's mostly for indie singers, but what's the point of running a festival if I don't bend the rules? Especially if it means my girlfriend now owes me a few favors." Max waggled her eyebrows.

Jade let out a snort. "You'll do anything for sex."

"Correction. I'll do anything for sex with you." Max snaked an arm around Jade's waist. "Speaking of which, I've been gone for a whole week."

"Six days. Don't you want to see the new recording studio first? Come on." Jade slipped from Max's grasp, beckoning her with a crooked finger. "Work first, then play."

"You're no fun," Max said with a pout. "It's a good thing you're not the boss."

"Who said I'm not?" Jade arched an eyebrow, and it was all Max could do not to groan. When Jade looked at her that way, the physical effect was instantaneous. The truth was, Max would do anything the woman asked her to do, which made Jade the very definition of her boss, even if unofficially.

There was nothing left to do but obey.

Max's jaw dropped the moment she reached the bottom of the stairs. "Oh wow! This is amazing."

The basement had been divided, the area with the instruments not quite as spacious as before, but what was behind a glass window made the sacrifice worthwhile.

"No more renting studios," Jade announced with glee. "We can now record our future hits right here where Mom taught me everything I know."

The new recording equipment was state of the art, and Max marveled at all the blinking lights for a full minute, afraid to touch anything. She'd finally gotten used to the controls on her car, but this looked way more complex.

"Did they show you how it works?" she asked hopefully.

"They did," Jade assured her. "Here. Check this out."

Jade pressed a few buttons, and Cindy's voice boomed from the speakers. "This is Cindy Weathers, but you might know me better as a member of the Matchstick Girls."

"Yikes!" Jade flipped a dial, turning the volume down. "Sorry about that. I'm still getting used to everything."

"Is that the new commercial for the music school?" Max chuckled to herself. "I still can't believe she's using the band as a hook after she avoided being connected with it for so fucking long."

"It's working, too. I had dinner with her last night, and she said she had to hire two more instructors. So many little girls want to grow up and be in their own band." Jade flipped a switch, and the console went dark. "I even caught Aunt Cindy wearing one of our tour T-shirts out in public the other day. She's finally embracing her inner rock star. It's a huge improvement over the sparkly tops and mom jeans."

"I never thought I'd see the day, considering how things were when the band broke up. Talk about a one-eighty." Max loved hearing it, though. Having Cindy back in her life had come with ups and downs, but sometimes friendships were like that. Cindy was most definitely a friend.

Family, really.

Jade was still recounting her dinner. "The tour last summer has given Aunt Cindy a new lease on life. She's fitter now than I've ever seen her. And, not that I particularly wanted her to confide in me about it, but she and Uncle Rick are still acting like they're on their second honeymoon."

"Who knew sex on a bus could work such magic?" This earned Max a massive eye roll.

"At least I don't have to hear it anymore."

"Oh, come on." Max gave Jade's shoulder a playful nudge. "I think we owe a fair bit of gratitude to tour bus magic ourselves."

"I don't know." Jade ran the tip of her tongue along her lower lip. Max watched every centimeter of the pink tip's travels. "Do you remember that night in New Orleans in your friend's studio?"

"How could I ever forget something like that?"

"Tour bus sex isn't bad, but recording studio sex is next level." Jade shot a meaningful look at the brand-new recording studio that filled half their basement.

"Oh. You mean…" Max's cheeks burned as she realized what Jade wanted.

"We just so happen to have our very own, right here, waiting." Jade ran a finger down one of Max's flaming hot cheeks. "Unless you're too tired from your flight."

"Never. You get me that hot at the drop of a hat."

"Good to know. I like having this effect on you." Jade wrapped her arms around Max's neck, planting a sensual kiss. "I love knowing you better than anyone on this planet."

Max's heart pounded, heavy and sure, each beat

rich with love and adoration. But before they could get sidetracked…

"Remember upstairs you said you didn't want me to keep a secret?"

"Yeeesssss," Jade dragged out the word, leaning back in caution.

"It's nothing bad. At least I hope not, because it's not easily undone."

The caution did not, in fact, lesson with the assurance. Jade's face shuttered. "Now you have me worried."

"Let me show you, and you can decide." Max started to undo her jeans.

"Is this another of your pathetic attempts to finagle sex?" Jade teased, though her expression retained its wariness.

"Isn't that why you brought me down here?"

"Oh, right. I did." Jade giggled. "Carry on."

Max slowly lowered her jeans, the freshly inked skin still tender.

Sitting over her right hip bone was an American Traditional style heart, complete with heavy black outline and pure red coloring. Instead of a Cupid's Arrow punching through, however, the tattoo artist had drawn a drumstick. The woodgrain had been particularly painful, the fine lines taking time. Maxine had many tattoos, but sitting for that one had been special.

"Oh, Max. I absolutely love it." Jade reached out to

trace it, only to stop just shy of the still-healing skin. Max watched the woman's eyes glisten with tears as they took in the drumstick.

"I'm not big on getting my girl's name tattooed on me, but this is even more personal."

"I friggin' love you." Jade kissed Max.

"I friggin' love you more."

Jade's fingers found their way into Max's hair, pulling lightly so the roots hummed happily. "You know," Jade said, low and sultry. "I think I have the title of a new song."

Maxine was already becoming foggy with lust, but she managed, "What?"

"We Make Beautiful Music Together."

Max couldn't help her scrunched nose. "That's awful. The sentiment is true, but the title gets a firm veto from me."

Jade laughed heartily, and heat reached every inch of Max's body. "We can work on the title then. We've got all the time we need."

A HUGE THANK YOU!

Miranda here. First, thanks so much for reading *Another Stupid Love Song*. When Em approached me with the idea to cowrite this book with her, I was thrilled. You see, Em has been with me on my writing journey from the very beginning. She was my editor for some of my first books, including *Telling Lies Online*, and has played a developmental role in many subsequent novels.

One of the things I've always enjoyed when working with Em is the way she can hone in on weak spots in a manuscript and intuit exactly what is needed to push a sentence or scene to the next level. The best part this time was that, unlike with my own projects where I have to interpret her notes and decide how to make a fix, I could hand it over to Em to work her magic. The result was a finished book that my other longtime coauthor, TB Markinson, called "beautiful to read and hotter than heck." We sure hope you agree!

If you enjoyed this story, Em and I would really appreciate a review on Amazon, BookBub, Goodreads, or whatever platform you like to go to for reading recommendations. Even brief reviews help immensely, as do mentions on social media. Every little bit helps!

I also hope you'll take a moment to sign up for my newsletter. Subscribers will receive my debut novel, *Telling Lies Online*, for free. Also, I run lots of giveaways, including paperbacks, ebooks, and audio, each month. For cat fans, I like to share adorable photos of my two cats, The Sisters of Chaos, who tag team to destroy everything in my house. I also give regular updates on my gardening triumphs and tragedies, sneak peeks into my works in progress, and lots more.

Here's the link to join: https://mirandamacleod.com/list

You're also invited to sign up for Em's newsletter for a free copy of her debut novel, Critical Hit, along with periodic newsletters about writing, trivia, and more.

Here's the link to join: http://eepurl.com/hKLhYv

Thanks again for reading *Another Stupid Love Song*. It's because of you that both Em and I are able to continue living our dreams of being writers. Your readership is a wonderful gift, and one we appreciate immensely.

Miranda & Em

ABOUT THE AUTHORS

Miranda MacLeod lives in New England and writes heartfelt romances and romantic comedies featuring witty and charmingly flawed women who love women. Before becoming a writer, she spent way too many years in graduate school, made costumes for professional theater and film, and held temp jobs in just about every office building in downtown Boston.

In addition to writing, Miranda is co-owner of I Heart SapphFic, a website dedicated to promoting and celebrating sapphic fiction. Her novel *The AM Show*, cowritten with TB Markinson, won a Golden Crown Literary Award in 2022.

To find out about her upcoming releases and receive her debut novel, *Telling Lies Online*, as a special gift, be sure to sign up for her mailing list at mirandamacleod.com.

Em Stevens is a best-selling author of queer fiction. She currently lives just outside of Raleigh, NC with her people and her animals.

Raleigh is so close to her heart she often uses it as a setting in her novels. (Y'all means all!) While she hasn't been a writer all of her life, she has always been a storyteller. Tall tales from a young age morphed into hyperbole-fueled anecdotes in her early adulthood.

Now she puts stories into novels and is quite thankful for beta readers and editors.

When she isn't writing or editing she reads voraciously, steeps herself in horror movies, and tries to get outside every now and again.

To find out about Em's upcoming releases, be sure to sign up for her mailing list at http://eepurl. com/hKLhYv.

Printed in Great Britain
by Amazon